SICK BOYS

SICK BOYS

CLARISSA WILD

Dedication

All my little sicko sluts who want to be spit-roasted ...
This is for you.

Prologue

PENELOPE

"You belong to us."

His voice is heady, dark.

Just like his soul.

Pure depravity seeping into my veins, consuming me whole.

He stares into my eyes, the obsessive greed flowing through me unrecognizable. I want this man more than I need oxygen to breathe.

But I wasn't prepared for wanting *them* as well.

Dylan Caruso and Alistair King, friends of Felix Rivera ... the guy whose fingers are coiled around my neck right now.

His thumb pushes my lips apart, and he slides his fingers inside, across my tongue, swiveling back and forth as his two friends double-team my holes until my eyes roll into the back of my head.

Moans fill the room, a mixture of all four of us.

Coiled. Twisted.

Nasty.

Delicious.

I can't get enough, even when it stings and hurts like hell.

Felix leans in, his fingers still deep inside my mouth. "Now say it," Felix whispers. "Say you're our whore."

Not even a second passes before I speak the words I thought I'd never say out loud. "I'm your whore."

Felix's sinister laugh fills this grimy bathroom.

At first I hated it, but now? Now I want to laugh with him.

I didn't believe him when he said he would taint me.

I was wrong.

So wrong.

I never begged anyone to take me before. Until I met them.

These dangerous boys of the Skull & Serpent Society slithered into my life, injecting their toxic venom straight into my blood.

And I let them. Willingly.

Knowing I would spiral.

Until nothing was left but corruption.

I

PENELOPE

In their eyes, I see death.

The famous boys of the Skull & Serpent Society sit on a makeshift throne of chopped wood stacked high in front of the bonfire in the middle of the woods.

Dylan Caruso, the one in all black with silvery-white hair and black roots, rings and tattoos all over his hands, seductive hooded eyes covered in kohl, and a killer smile, flicks a lighter on and off.

Alistair King sits next to him in his black netted outfit covered in thick jewelry, his curly, light-brown hair softly swishing in the wind, and a devilish smirk on his pale face as he looks down at the girls.

But worst of all is Felix Rivera ... a brown-haired guy with a face so sharply cut and intense sanpaku hazel eyes so deeply sunken in that it does honor to his society's name.

Not a pretty boy, but a chilling boy.

And definitely not one you'd want to cross paths with.

Around those boys, several other students and society members hang on their lips, listening to their wicked stories of blood and mayhem.

It could be lies. Or it could all be the truth.

No one will ever know.

They make sure of that.

Or so I've been told by my sister.

The mossy ground contains alcohol and drugs scattered everywhere. People smoke pot and cigarettes, and mix different kinds of alcohol, while some go crazy on the music, dancing like they're summoning an old God.

Beyond the main area, some people huddle close to the trees, smooching. I spot a hint of skin, and moans erupt from the area. Clearly, people are fucking around, and I'm not about to find out.

I walk through the party searching for my sister, keeping my head down, but I can't find her. Panic begins to build. "Eve, are you here?"

I yell out her name again and again.

No response.

All I hear is the crispy fire and the loud music blasting into my ears from the speakers atop the wooden tables. The distraction is too much, but I won't give up. I know she's here somewhere.

I check my phone again, reading her text for the fiftieth time.

I can't do it anymore, sis. Please don't be mad at me. I've done everything I could and more. It's never going to be enough. And I refuse to go through life ... broken. Split in half by a decision that wasn't mine to make.

So I will stop it now.

This bonfire near The Edge will be the last night spent at this godforsaken university for me.

I love you, sis.

And whatever you do, don't ever get involved with those boys of the Skull & Serpent Society.

xoxo

Eve

The Edge. A set of gloomy rocky cliffs just beyond Priory Forest with a huge, beautiful waterfall cascading into the deep.

Or so I've been told.

I've never been here until today, but the scene matches my sister's description.

Before her texts turned eerily dark.

What happened to her? Before she came to the university, she was the prime example of a happy student. And now ... these texts she's been sending me lately are riddled with pessimism and hopelessness.

God, I hope she's okay.

Laughter erupts from the bonfire area, and I tuck my phone back into my pocket.

The guys of that Skull & Serpent Society chug a whole flask of liquor with ease, sharing it among one another.

One girl lunges at Dylan and hugs him tightly around the neck, throwing her boobs into his face while also twirling her fingers through his platinum-blond hair like he's a plaything. Another girl tickles Alistair's bulky arm, making him look at her while he's trying to tell the rest of his story.

But the worst of all is Felix and the girl on his lap, playfully toying with his short hair while he looks like he wants to kill her.

I'm not sure he'd pass up the opportunity if given the chance.

I push through the sea of trees, moving farther and farther away from the party. The more distance that's created, the quieter it gets, until nothing but the sound of the waves softly hitting the cliffs is heard. Beyond the horizon, there's only water and a moon shining brightly above.

I pass the last line of trees and come to an abrupt halt, grabbing one of the trunks as my breath falters.

There, on the edge, my sister stands with her arms wide open.

Her eyes turn to me, the glossiness in them heart-shattering.

A single tear trickles down her cheeks.

And then she jumps.

2

PENELOPE

Weeks later

"Are you sure about this?" my mother asks as my father sets my bags on my bed.

"Definitely," I reply.

Mom throws me a concerned look. "But you know the history of this university..."

I know what she's getting at. But she won't say it out loud.

This was my sister's university. The place she once called home.

And now it'll be my home too for the time being.

Mom suddenly gives me a big hug. "I just want you to be okay."

"I know," I reply.

"It's not too late to change your mind," she adds.

"I'm not gonna change my mind," I reply, glancing at my dad, who's been awfully quiet.

She used to let me leave so easily, but now? It's like she's sticking on me like tape.

Finally, she pulls away, allowing me to breathe again.

"And if you need us, call, okay?" Mom adds, grabbing my shoulders.

"Yeah," I reply. "I'm fine. I'm fine. I just need to get used to this place, that's all. Piece of cake."

She sighs out loud and kisses me on the cheek.

"C'mon," my dad says, and he tugs at her arm to get her to move. "Let's go so she can get settled in."

"If anything happens, text me," Mom reiterates. "Immediately."

She must be panicking that I might do the same as my sister, and I get that. "Don't worry, I will."

I nod as Dad physically drags her out of the room and shuts the door. "Good luck, Penelope," he yells. "You know I'm just one call away."

I grin and shake my head. Obviously, my mother's been having a difficult time knowing I wanted to go to Spine Ridge. After what my sister went through, this should have been the last university on my list.

But I'm not here just to study.

I'm here for revenge.

I grab my sister's diary and open it up, sifting through the pages, picking apart all the names, the images, the text she wrote alongside their faces. I've imprinted everything in my brain to remember everyone who ever harmed her.

I will fucking find them. And when I do, there's gonna be hell to pay.

Noise across the street distracts me, and I walk up to the window. A bunch of guys throw beer at each other outside a dorm. One of them stumbles over the puddle and falls on his ass, and they all pour their beer over his face, then laugh.

What a ridiculous ritual. Obviously only something a fraternity could come up with.

I roll my eyes and turn to unpack instead.

Suddenly, my door swings open, and a girl walks in, dragging her suitcases behind her. Her curly black hair whips over her shoulders, sweat dripping down her forehead as she plops the bags down onto the second bed in the room.

"Hi!" she says. "Sorry for the rude entry. Jesus, this building has one too many staircases." An awkward laugh ensues.

I grin and offer her a hand. "You're my new roommate. Name's Penelope."

"Penelope ... nice!" She shakes my hand. "I'm Kayla Pearce. So this is your first semester here at Spine Ridge U, too, right?" she asks. "I didn't see you at the orientation."

I make a face. "Yeah. I transferred late, so I missed it."

Her face pops. "Oh really? Before even starting at the other university? I didn't even know that was possible."

I shrug. "This university has ... more opportunities." I clear my throat before I say too much.

"Well, it was a good decision because now you're my roomie." She winks. "And I already know you and I are gonna be besties."

I smile at her. "You sure about that? I can get mad weird."

She laughs. "Even better." She empties her suitcase, and all the dresses and pants tumble out in one big pile. "Wow, I really brought too many clothes."

"Never too many clothes, right?" I wink.

She smirks. "See, you get it. Crystal always tells me my suitcase might explode, but I know how to fucking pack."

"Crystal?" I muse. "Another roomie, or...?"

"My best friend at this university," she replies as I tug at the zipper of my suitcase. "We met a few weeks ago at the bonfire."

Bonfire—

I rip open the zipper so wildly it breaks off.

Kayla comes to stand beside me. "Oh, well, I've got a small repair kit. Maybe we can fix that."

"It's fine," I lie, quickly chucking it in the trash. "It was about to give out anyway." I grab some clothes and hang them in the closet to try to get my mind off the word she said. "So best friend, huh? I'd love to meet her."

"Maybe we have some of the same classes." Her eyes glimmer as she grabs her schedule. "Wanna compare?" She gasps and grabs her phone. "Before I forget, can I have your number? I mean, since we're roomies and all, we might as well hang out."

"Sure." I grab my phone and give it to her. "Go ahead."

She enters her number into mine while I enter mine into hers.

"There," she says, handing it back to me.

I give her phone back too and grab my schedule. We place them both on the table next to each other. Her courses are similar but not the same. Only a few overlap later in the week.

And then I check today.

My eyes almost bulge out of my skull. I have a class in about ten minutes. How did I not know this?

"Oh my God." I quickly grab what I need and shove it into my backpack.

"Late?" Kayla asks.

I nod. "I'll talk to you later!"

"Was nice meeting you. Good luck on your first class!" she yells as I rush out the door.

Of course I'm late again. Typical. I already missed the orientation because I was too late applying to the university. I can't fucking miss my first class too.

I guess that's what you get for switching universities at the last minute.

Though it's nice that I've already made a new friend.

I don't make those very easily.

On my way out of the building, several students wave at me and say hi, so I quickly say hi back and hurry. I'll stop and chat later because I don't have enough time right now.

Class is almost starting, and I have to run all the way to the other side of campus.

I should really get a bike.

I dash across the pavement, ignoring the noise coming from the fraternity across the street, and head straight for the big buildings.

A lot of students sit outside in the grass, eating a quick breakfast, talking with each other, and playing games and football. And then there's me, running around like a chicken with its head cut off, trying to find the entrance.

When I finally make it, I pause to catch my breath with my hands on my knees, sweat dripping down my back. It takes me a few seconds before I can finally look around. It's as gorgeous inside as it looked outside, with wooden panels and large paintings all around, old oak doors leading into classrooms, big, wooden, circular staircases, and giant glass panes to show off the garden view.

Lots of money flows into this university—that much is clear.

But it's also easy to tell, judging from the Prada, Gucci, and Louboutin that some of the students around me are wearing.

I feel wholly out of place in my Diesel jeans here.

Throwing my bag over my shoulder, I make my way to the classroom, checking my notes again and again to make sure I'm going the right way. I've managed to keep the panic at bay for a while now, but it's slowly creeping up on me now that I'm running late. Because if there's anything I *don't* do, it's being late.

I got that trait from my father, who's punctual to the littlest of details.

Hurrying through the hallways, I pass people so quickly I almost bump into them, and I apologize profusely as I run to the room I'm supposed to be in.

However, the hallway is blocked off right where I need to be.

I peer over the students gathered around.

One guy throws books at another guy while that one simply laughs and shrugs. But the first one doesn't quit and suddenly lunges at the guy. The whole crowd erupts into gasps and laughter, egging them on as they begin to throw punches at each other, gripping hair and tearing clothing into shreds.

Suddenly, behind the ruckus, a familiar bunch emerges.

The three boys who put my nerves on edge.

Dylan, Alistair ... and Felix.

An air of darkness follows them wherever they go, like a cloud of rain in the dusk.

As they walk down the hall, Dylan casually throws a lighter into the air and continuously catches it while Alistair throws his backpack over his shoulder. But Felix keeps his hands tightly secured in his pockets, his white shirt barely able to cover his bulging pecs and biceps.

They're headed straight toward the fight with no intention of stopping anytime soon.

And even though half the crowd begins to disperse as they come closer and closer, the fighting doesn't seem to stop ... nor do the boys.

As Felix passes the two fighting, one of them bumps into him, and he punches him sideways so hard into the wall he slumps down to the ground, groaning loudly.

Felix doesn't even break out into a sweat and tucks his hands right back into his pocket.

Everyone in the hallway has gone quiet as if collective terror is infecting everyone while they all step aside to make room for the boys walking in our direction.

Except me.

I stand still in the middle of the hallway until Felix is right in front of me.

Still, I don't move.

He tilts his head at me, the muscles in his neck straining as his nose twitches. Up close, his features, like his square jaw and pronounced cheekbones, become really defined, but that chilling stare gets me the most. Half-mast eyes, white underneath his pupils, like nothing could ever fucking bother him ... until now.

"Move."

In his gruff voice, that one word could make anyone's skin erupt into goose bumps.

But not me.

I tilt my head the same way he did.

His eye begins to twitch.

Seconds tick by like minutes while I can practically feel people's gazes boring holes into my back. But I don't care. I've lived with stares and laughter my whole life, so I'm not afraid of bullies anymore. No one can hurt me if I don't let them.

And especially not guys like them.

Dylan frowns at me and smirks. "Might wanna listen to him."

I ignore him and keep my gaze on Felix, who refuses to look away, just like me.

He's much taller than I am, and he physically has to bend over to get on my level. Too close for comfort as he leans in to stare at me.

"I said move."

No wonder my sister wrote about him in her diary.

I lick my lips and say, "Make me."

His nostrils flare. He leans in even closer until he's beside my face and breathing into my neck, and he whispers, "Don't tempt me to twist your fucking nipples because I will do it in front of everyone here... *Penelope.*"

My eyes widen as his flicking fingers inch upward, close enough to push through on his threat.

But that's not what frightens me the most.

My feet instinctively step away to create distance between us as my veins run icy cold.

His fingers are still in the correct position. The left side of his lip creeps up momentarily, only to sink right back into that deadly, emotionless expression he wears.

His hands lower, and he shoves me farther out of the way, with his buddies following suit as they saunter down the hallway like they own the place.

And all I can do is stare at these killer boys because ...

How does he know my name?

3

FELIX

Penelope, Penelope ...

That name has such a nice ring to it.

Nice enough to taint.

Nice enough to corrupt.

My nostrils flare. If she hadn't stepped aside, I would've latched onto those perky nipples peaking through that small black top and twisted them in front of everyone until she screamed my name.

A filthy smirk forms on my lips, but it quickly vanishes when I remember who she is.

She's not supposed to be here.

Pen.

My fingers clutch around the one I'm holding, almost snapping it in two. Not much is worse than having to sit through an economics class, listening to a teacher blab on about stuff I don't fucking care about.

With the exception of one thing.

That girl sitting there in the row below me.

How many classes do we share?

One is already too many.

Her eyes fixate on the man in front of the screen, and I have to admit, she's putting up an amazing front by pretending she doesn't care. But I know she can feel my eyes penetrate her skull.

If I could, I'd pick apart her brain right this very second and expose all the secrets she's keeping.

But that would take the fun out of things, wouldn't it?

And I live for the fucking fun because nothing in this fucking university ever is.

You have to make it, and that's what we've been doing for the past year.

But she ... she could spoil it all.

And I'm not about to let her.

Dylan shoves me in the side with his elbow, and I look his way, low-key tempted to shove this pen between his ribs. "Stop staring at her. What if people notice?"

"Do I look like I care?" I retort, flicking the pen up and down.

He raises a brow. "What happened to keeping a low profile?"

"Since when do you listen to your father?" I scoff.

His face darkens as he casually leans back on his chair. "You know why."

I roll my eyes and look away. "You do whatever the fuck you want."

He snorts, shaking his head. "You really wanna go down this route again?"

"So what if I do?" I quip, staring at him.

He tilts his head until his white pretty-boy hair falls over his face like he's testing me, but I don't fucking care.

I've never cared about any consequences—not today, not yesterday, and certainly not tomorrow.

"Whatever," he scoffs, running his fingers through his hair. "You know what you're getting yourself into, and it isn't even worth it."

"Yeah ... I do know, and it's fucking worth every second of my time," I say. I raise a brow in return. "Do you know why?"

His lips twitch. "What? Just because some girl stood in your way, you wanna make her your next toy?"

"She's not *some* girl," I retort, holding up the pen. "Guess her name."

He narrows his eyes, glaring at me like I've lost my mind.

I eye the pen.

"What? Pen ..." Suddenly, his eyes widen. "Penelope?"

His voice is so loud it echoes through the room, far enough to reach the rows down below where she sits.

Penelope turns around, gazing at me with hawk-like eyes, just like she did when she stood in my way. Close enough to hear us speak, yet far enough to stop me from grasping her purple hair and tilting her head to whisper filthy shit into her ear.

Her gaze never breaks, and ours doesn't either.

I know she heard.

I hope she fucking did.

Because she fucking smiled at me.

Smiled.

When all I could think of was ripping her little black top and checkered miniskirt to shreds.

My eye twitches. The pen in my hand snaps in half under her gaze.

Pen ... I will fucking break you.

***

PENELOPE

Weeks ago

My eyes burst open as I sit up straight in the bed, breathing heavily. My heart is going a million miles an hour as I recount everything that happened that night. The forest, the music, the moon, my sister jumping to her death, and those boys listening to my endless screams as I ran to the edge to try to save her.

Too late.

I saw her body disappear into the water deeper and deeper until nothing was left but the silence in my heart.

Tears form in my eyes, but I push them away and shove my blanket off my body to start my day.

Trying.

That's the only thing I've done these past few days.

But my legs feel like they weigh a ton.

Especially today.

This day when my mom has not stopped weeping since yesterday.

This day when my dad has taken phone call after phone call just to take his mind off what's happening.

I go through the motions without really thinking about it, putting on black pantyhose, a long black dress, and a beautiful brooch. One my sister gifted me on my birthday. A reminder of the day she left to go to Spine Ridge University for the first time.

My fingers instinctively touched the brooch.

I look at myself in the mirror, wondering if she can see me right now.

If she's trying to tell me it's all going to be okay.

But it won't because she's gone.

And I know it's thanks to them.

Those fucking boys.

My fingers tighten around the brooch, and I struggle not to rip it off.

Instead, I bite my lip and head for the door.

Downstairs, my mother's still crying her eyes out, sniffing into tissue after tissue. The empty boxes are stacked on the table.

When she sees me, she swiftly wipes away her tears and snot, pretending she's not crying, but I can clearly see the marks on her cheeks.

"Penelope, are you ready?" my father asks after he tucks his phone back into his pocket.

I nod. I don't want to say the words out loud because I know I'll burst into tears like my mother, and if she sees my tears, it would break her even more. As her only daughter left, I need to be strong.

My father helps my mother off the couch, and we all walk outside toward the car waiting for us.

Every step slowly feels more and more like a blur. Like I'm not really here.

My mind is still at the party on that cliff, with her glossy eyes staring right back at mine wondering why I didn't come sooner to save her.

I get into the car, and it drives for what feels like hours and hours until we finally arrive at our destination.

The room where the service is held is boring, white, too pristine, and clean, with only some bundled flowers left and right of the casket to provide some happiness to the otherwise dull affair.

Eve would have hated it.

She was always so happy and shined like the sun, radiant and full of color.

She was the complete opposite of me, but it's also why I loved her so much ... and why I miss her more than anything.

The dark wood of the casket burns into my retina as I stare at the place her corpse rests.

So peaceful and mundane, unlike her death.

My heart aches.

My mother cries beside me, and I try not to let it get to me, but it's hard knowing what she's lost.

It's almost impossible to cry with all these people around me. I feel like they're all staring at my back, wondering if I'm going to say anything after my father speaks about her in front of the pulpit.

But I wouldn't know what to say to these people except fuck you for driving my sister insane.

Because I know her peers are here watching us.

Pretending to mourn with us.

They are the cause of her misery.

I know because she tucked a book underneath my door the night she died. In it, she wrote about all her wishes, dreams, secrets, and truths.

All the shit she'd been through.

And all the people responsible for it.

I keep it close to my heart.

As the service finishes, everyone breathes a sigh of relief.

Some sad music plays, and one by one, people come forward to pay their respects to both the casket as well as us.

Then the casket is moved outside, and we all follow the hearse to the cemetery.

While everyone has gathered around a hole in the ground, my sister is slowly lowered inside like a deathtrap.

Horrifying.

I hate it.

I hate that I have to stand here and watch Eve be buried without even a semblance of justice.

What can I do?

Nothing. It's too late.

Too late to save her.

I close my eyes and blink away the tears as well as the invading memories.

This guilt will eat me alive one day.

My mother hands me a rose. When it's my turn, I throw it on top of the casket, a last goodbye to the sister I didn't want to lose and who was too young to die.

I glance over my shoulder so no one in front of me will see me cry.

But the tears refuse to come when I see three boys standing behind one of the large trees in the cemetery.

The same three guys I saw at the bonfire the night she died.

Felix, Dylan, and Alistair.

Guys who wouldn't give a care in the world about anyone dying.

Yet they're here, unafraid.

It's a message.

The wind blows through my purple hair, and I tuck a strand behind my ear, never breaking eye contact.

I want them to know I saw them.

And I want them to know I will *never* give up.

I will never stop finding the reason for her death.

And if they're here, it only means one thing.

They know something I don't.

And I'll find out what exactly it is.

Even if it costs me my fucking soul.

4

PENELOPE

Present

After my classes for the day are over, I make my way to the gardens outside. Kayla asked me in a message to meet her there. I can already see her sitting on a plaid blanket in the grass with a bunch of other students, casually sipping their drinks and eating their food.

When I get close enough, Kayla waves. "Hey, Pen, you finally made it." She pats the plaid blanket next to her. "Come sit."

I sit down beside her and introduce myself to the rest of the group. "Hi, I'm Penelope. You can call me Pen."

"Hey, Pen," the girl next to Kayla says. "I'm Crystal. Nice to meet you too. You must be her new roommate, right?"

The boys opposite of me give me a hand. "Hey, I'm Jeremy."

"And my name is Calvin."

I eagerly shake their hands.

"This is our little group," Kayla says. "We eat lunch here together almost every day." She takes a bite of her sandwich. "Did you bring something?"

"Yeah," I reply, and I pull out my own sandwich that I made in a hurry this morning at my parents' house before I arrived here. A peanut butter and jelly sandwich, all smooshed up. I should really check out the cafeteria here.

"So Kayla told me you switched schools," Jeremy says.

"Yeah, this university was actually my preferred university," I explain even though it's a lie I made up on the spot. "So I made a last-minute switch."

"Awesome," Calvin says. "So what are you studying?"

"Economics. I want to take over my dad's business one day." I add a smile.

"Obviously," Jeremy says, "I mean, we're all studying business at a business university."

Crystal laughs. "I only want to be rich."

Kayla and Crystal bump their drinks against each other.

"Same, girl, same," Kayla jokes.

I take another bite of my sandwich. "So you're Kayla's best friend, right?"

Crystal blushes and grabs Kayla's hand. "We've only known each other for like a few weeks now, but it feels like it's been ages."

I take another bite of my sandwich. Swallowing it is hard, though.

Because across from me, a few yards away, leaning against a stone fencing, are none other than Felix, Dylan, and Alistair. They're smoking what appears to be marijuana right here on the university's grounds without even a single care in the world even though I know that isn't allowed here, let alone in this state.

But rules don't apply to boys like them.

"Don't look." Kayla nudges me, pulling me from my thoughts.

"What?" I mutter.

"If you stare, they'll see," she murmurs, leaning in to whisper. "You do know who they are, right? Those guys belong to the Skull & Serpent Society."

"No, I don't know them," I lie.

I technically don't *know* them, but I have definitely heard of them.

"That society is like the worst of all the fraternities near this university combined. No one ever gets in except when they've got the right connections, and with that, I mean the criminal ones." Kayla lowers her eyes at me. "They practically run this place."

So they're the leaders? Interesting. That only makes me want to look harder.

"You really don't want to mess with those guys. Even a simple look can trigger them to come after you," Kayla explains.

"How do you know?" I ask.

"Because they targeted her brother a few months ago," Crystal explains, injecting herself into the conversation.

Kayla cringes. "Only because he dared to try to apply to their society. Gave him a rough initiation and then told him he didn't make it."

"What did they do?" I ask.

"Well, it involved piss," Calvin fills in. "I only know that because of what one of my friends told me. I wasn't there myself."

Crystal gags and nearly vomits right there and then, but she covers her mouth. "Excuse me."

"Okay, I get the picture," I say.

"Point is, you don't ever want them to point their arrows at you," Kayla says. "I know they do a lot of bad shit, but if you stay out of their way, they won't cause you trouble."

"They're sick," Crystal adds.

"Right," I mutter, but I'm way too distracted by the fact that Felix's eyes have already homed in on me.

And no matter how hard I try, I can't look away.

He's been staring at me in class too, even mentioning my name to his friend Dylan.

And I didn't give it to him, so there's only one way he could know.

My sister.

***

DYLAN

Felix can't stop staring at her.

In a way, I've only ever seen him look at the people he either wants to fuck into oblivion or kill.

And now that I know who she is, neither can I.

I wonder why she transferred here, out of all places. It can't be a coincidence.

I take another hit and burn away whatever remains of my restraint.

A smirk forms on my lips. Looking at her now, maybe I should go up to her and just ... ask.

Some girl suddenly bumps into me and slaps her arms around my neck. Cathy, Sadie, Kiera ... I don't know, I don't remember, and I don't care.

"Hey, Dylan. You up for some fun later this evening? Carry on where we left off at the bonfire?"

The mere mention of that fucking party puts me on edge.

I throw her arms off me. "No, I have other plans."

She eyes Alistair. "Is he taking up all your time again? You two planning something?" She licks her lips. "A surprise?"

I tilt my head. "If we were, it's now ruined."

"Aw, Dylan," she muses, pecking me on the cheek. "You're sweet."

"Well, it's not for you."

Her smile fades as quickly as the autumn leaves, and it's fucking magnificent. "Oh, I thought you had something planned for my birthday."

Is it?

"Yeah, well, my schedule is full, so see you next week, okay?" I wink and turn toward the guys so she can't butt in again.

"Yeah, I'm keeping my boy busy." Alistair throws his arm over my shoulders to pull me into our group.

The girl tries for a moment but gives up after a few attempts at squeezing underneath my arm. Deflated, she walks off, her heels *click-clacking* across the pavement, a snooty look directed at me thrown over her shoulders.

What was her name again?

All I can think about is that girl sitting there in the grass and how much she reminds me of someone else ... someone I used to know.

I take a final whiff and chuck the smoke away.

A tasty afternoon snack.

Just like her.

My phone suddenly buzzes and pulls me from my thoughts.

"What's that?" Alistair asks.

"Fuck," I say under my breath.

"Oh, that fucker?"

I ignore Alistair and head straight for the biggest building on the campus. The place I abhor and rarely enter unless necessary for classes ... or to visit my goddamn father.

The thought of having to visit him makes me want to fucking punch a hole in the wall. But if I damage even a single inch of his property, there will be hell to pay.

I clutch the banister and head up the old wooden stairs to floor three, where the rooms are inaccessible to the rest of the students and even me when not summoned.

Grinding my teeth, I knock on the third door.

"Come in."

I open the door and stare at him while leaning against the wall. "You called?"

"Texted," he replies, only glaring up at me briefly before returning to the mountain of papers on his desk.

"It's a metaphor," I reply, folding my arms.

"I don't have time for duplicity. Sit." He points at the chair in front of his desk.

"Can you at least ask?" I retort, raising a brow.

"No."

He can't even look at me.

My nostrils twitch, but I still bite my tongue and march over to the chair, scooting it back loudly before plopping my ass down. For good measure, I throw my boots on his desk.

"Don't do that," he says.

"Why not? It's comfy," I reply.

His eyes lift from his work again and finally connect with mine.

"Do you like the boots you wear?" he asks.

"Yeah."

"The food you eat?"

I narrow my eyes. Where is this going?

"The frat house you live in?"

"What about it?"

"Who do you think pays for all that?"

I roll my eyes. Here we go again.

"Oh, don't tell me ..." I put my finger in front of my mouth. "You."

"Exactly," he replies. "Now are you going to be respectful, or do I have to force it out of you?"

The way he looks at me makes me grind my teeth, but eventually, I put my feet down.

"Good boy."

"Don't," I growl.

If he speaks to me again like I'm a dog, I'm going to bite like one.

"You'd better be grateful," he retorts.

"Oh, like you?" I quip.

"I am grateful." He looks me dead in the eye. "For this job."

Not for his son.

"And I'm not about to lose it thanks to you."

I shrug. "You literally run the campus. Who's going to fire you?"

"Did you forget about the board?"

Grinding my teeth, I look away, annoyed. "Felix can talk with his dad."

"Felix and you need to shut the hell up, sit down, and do your fucking work," he growls.

Now he's got my attention.

That kind of aggression ... it flows through my veins too.

He slams a stamp onto a paper and pushes it into his folder. "Do you understand?"

"Is that why you brought me up here? To lecture me?"

He licks his finger and grabs the next paper. "It took me fucking days to solve all the mess you boys left this summer. I'm not about to let you fuck it all up again." He points at me. "Behave."

"Or else?"

He tilts his head, and he grabs the box cutter, clutching it too tightly. "Don't test me, Dylan."

"Whatever," I say, sighing. "I can't stop being me." I get up.

"No, you're too much like your father," he growls back, still sifting through his papers without even looking at me. "Now go and fucking study like an actual college student."

He waves me off without even looking at me, so I saunter off with my hands tucked in my pocket and kick open the door.

The moment I cross the threshold, a peculiar set of eyes stares back at me from below the staircase. They widen in shock and immediately turn away, hiding behind the pillar next to the stairs.

But I know she's there.

Her footsteps as she bolts bring a grin to my face.

I'll never resist a chase.

I rush down the stairs and see her run through the hallway, heading straight for the emergency staircase in the back instead of the one below mine. But I know this place like the back of my hand, so there's no way she can outrun me.

And I'm not letting her get away after catching her snooping on me.

Halfway across the hall, Felix comes up the staircase behind me, and yells, "Dylan, what the fuck? You here too?"

"Dad's interrogating us. Doesn't matter," I say, shaking off my annoyance. "It's her, the girl, she eavesdropped."

His eyes turn murderous as I point at the emergency staircase, and he nods and runs right back down the stairs.

I open the door leading to the emergency staircase and head inside. "Oh, Penelope ... where are you?" I murmur, looking up and down the stairwell. It's quiet. Too quiet. "I know you're in here ... there's no point in hiding." I lick my lips. "I *will* find you, and when I do, you'd better pray for mercy."

5

PENELOPE

Did Dylan just ... tell me to pray for mercy?

Fuck, Kayla and Crystal were right.

These boys are sick.

I shudder in the corner of the staircase, sweating profusely.

Every step I take, he can hear. How do I escape? I could head up or down and try to find a door. But he'll definitely hear, and when he does, he'll come after me.

I swallow down the nerves, trying not to make a sound as I slip closer toward the edge of the railing to see where Dylan is. But once I do, I see him looking right at me through the banister one level above mine, clutching the metal with a devious grin on his face. And he actually leans in and licks the fucking railing.

He gloats. "I see you ..."

Not a second do I wait.

I bolt off, stumbling over two of the stairs as I run down.

I can hear his footsteps coming after me, rushing down the same stairs, and my heart trembles in my body from the mere sound.

Fuck, why didn't I take better precautions when I tried to snoop in on his conversations with his father? I should have at least tried to hide better. But I was so invested in what they were saying, trying to decipher what it meant when his father talked about the mess those boys left this summer that I completely forgot I could be caught.

"Better run as fast as you can, Pen, because if I catch you, there's going to be hell to pay!"

Fuck, fuck, fuck!

I have to get out of here and fast.

I skid across the floor and rush down the next set of stairs with Dylan right behind me, practically jumping down the stairs.

I'm almost down, almost where the rest of the students are, where he can't get to me without exposing himself as a terror to the rest of the campus.

I jump down the last set of stairs and bolt to the door. But the second I grasp the big handle, it opens from the other side.

And none other than Felix fucking Rivera stands in my way.

"Where are you going, Pen?"

His hazel eyes bore into mine, a hint of insanity hiding behind them. A promise of what's to come if I don't escape now.

My heart throbs in my chest.

I step back, but all it does is lock us both in as he walks closer, the door closing behind him.

Behind me, Dylan continues to race down the stairs.

All my exits are blocked.

What do I do?

I contemplate my options, grasping my bag to find the one pair of scissors I have with me. But Felix swiftly grabs my bag.

"Motherfucker, let go!" I yell as he rips it out of my hands.

"Fuck no," he retorts.

Without a second thought, I storm at him, trying to punch him for stealing my shit, but I don't get far. With one hand, he's able to hold me back ... by my head.

My fucking head.

One hand.

Fuck him.

"Fuck you!" I growl.

"So much spice for something so small and fragile," he says, smirking like a crazy bastard. His fingers coil around my hair, and he pulls at it, lifting me by my head alone. "Easy to break."

"Get your hands off me!" I flail around, trying to kick him, but he keeps me at bay with ease.

Dylan's footsteps close in behind me. "There you are, little rat."

"Rat?" I gasp. "Fuck you! I didn't do shit."

"No? You sure were happy to snoop in on my conversation with my father," Dylan quips as he walks toward me from the back. My eyes turn sideways as far as possible, but I can only see half his face as Felix keeps me in place just by my hair.

"Did you follow me?" he asks.

Maybe I did, but I'm not going to tell them that.

If I did, I might not make it out of this alive.

"Answer him," Felix growls.

"Or else what?" I quip. I look around, trying to find the cameras so someone will see me in trouble, but there are none. This must be one of the few places on campus without security. Just my luck.

"Let go of me, you asshole!" I kick and tug until my feet finally touch the floor again.

But Felix refuses to release me, his grip on my hair so tight my eyes begin to water.

"You want me to let go?" Felix raises his brow as he pulls me even closer until my back hits his firm, muscular body. He rasps into my ear, "Earn the right."

"You were listening in on my conversations," Dylan says. "What did you hear?"

"Nothing," I reply.

"Yes, you did," he says, and he steps onto my toes, pushing down until it makes me grind my teeth from the pain. "Now tell me ... *what did you hear?*"

"Just some stuff about the summer," I say.

"Hmm ..." He nods, narrowing his eyes. "A messy summer indeed." His fingers rise to meet my face, and he grabs a strand of my purple hair.

I bite in his direction, making him pull back.

"Nasty girl."

"You should see how nasty I can get if you don't let me go right now."

Dylan laughs in my face.

Felix chucks my bag at Dylan. "Check it. See if there's anything of use."

Use?

For what?

Dylan rips it open, chucking all the contents on the concrete ground before throwing the bag aside. Then he goes to his knees and picks apart all of my things. A water bottle, my phone, my books and pens ... and my sister's diary.

"Sure, destroy my stuff. You just want to humiliate me, don't you?" I growl.

"No, Pen ..." Felix whispers into my ear. "If we did, we'd make you get on your knees and lick our cum off the floor."

My eyes widen.

Holy shit.

"Give me back my stuff," I growl.

"Come and get it," he taunts, but when I try, Felix's grip on my hair reminds me of the fact that I'd have to rip out my hair to get away from him.

Fuck.

What do I do?

Dylan bends over and searches through the rest of the pile that came out of my bag until he finds the one thing I had hoped they wouldn't find.

As his smile disappears, he holds up my diary with two fingers.

The one my sister gave me.

The one filled with all the information I need to find the one who made her jump.

"What's in here?" Dylan muses.

I can't let them take it.

No fucking way.

Right when the pages flip to the mention of their names, I twist around, Felix's grip tightening on my hair as I grasp the pen tucked deep in my pockets and shove it into his arm.

***

FELIX

Yowling, I let go of the girl, immediately going for the pen lodged into my flesh.

She fucking stabbed me.

With a pen.

She storms at Dylan and snatches the diary from his hands while he's distracted by my pain.

"You little rat, give it back!" Dylan snarls as she runs toward me.

The pain is sharp, but I ignore it as I lunge at her.

She jumps away like the little rat she is, kicking me in the balls.

I groan in pain while she opens the door and shoves it into my face, avoiding my quick grasp for her top.

Then she runs off, through the hallway, toward the mass of people, out of our reach.

But every once in a while, she still glances over her shoulder, nervously checking if we follow her.

Oh yes.

It's game on now.

"She knifed you," Dylan says as I rip the pen from my arm.

The wound bleeds into my shirt, but the pain doesn't faze me anymore.

All I can do is fucking smile at the girl running away from us right this very second while I bring the pen to my lips and lick my own goddamn blood.

One of these days, I'm going to lick hers.

6

PENELOPE

I speed-walk through the hallways of the big building, past all the students going about their day, and pretend I'm fine. I clutch my diary close to my chest, fiercely protective of the only thing my sister left me that gives even a hint of what might've happened to her.

Something involving those guys. Something they don't want me to know.

I hope Dylan didn't see his own face on the pages because if he did, I'm fairly sure they'll be coming for this diary next.

I look behind me again to see if they're still there, watching me. But when I peer through the tiny window in the emergency door, there's nothing left to see.

They're gone.

Vanished, as if they were never there, chasing me, scaring me until my heart almost jumped out of my chest.

I run into the nearest bathroom and lock myself inside a stall, breathing a few times to catch my bearings.

I feel queasy.

Nauseous.

I just stabbed a guy.

And not just any guy ... Felix fucking Rivera.

One of the leaders of the Skull & Serpent Society, the most notorious frat house on campus, known for their devilish initiations and rules.

Will he come for me now?

Panic floods my veins, but I shake it off and flush the toilet.

I'm not going to let a bloody pen ruin what I came here to do.

He won't report this.

After all, I could pin them for harassment.

But he surely won't forget.

I swallow and gather my nerves before opening the stall.

Get your shit together, Pen.

It's all a part of their game. They're trying to intimidate you because you're getting too close. Which means you're on the right track.

I walk out and look at myself in the mirror, then check my hair. A few strands are definitely missing. The fucker actually ripped out some of my hair trying to hold me down.

A smirk forms on my face. Well, he didn't fucking win, that's for sure. And if I had to lose a few hairs to make a point, then so fucking be it.

I turn on the faucet and splash my face, but when I look up, someone's staring back at me through the mirror.

I shriek before realizing it's Kayla.

"Chill, it's me," she says.

"Oh my God," I say, pressing my palm to my chest to calm down my heart.

"Sorry. My pen spilled all over my goddamn shirt." She turns on the faucet next to me so she can tuck her shirt under it. "Middle of class, too." When she looks up at me, she frowns. "Shit, what happened to you?"

"What?" I ask perplexed.

She points at my black lace top. "There's blood."

I look down and see the stain.

How did I not notice that in the mirror?

"Oh ..."

Kayla glares at me.

"I had a nosebleed," I lie, and I quickly grab a tissue and shove it up my nostril. "Happens to me sometimes."

She looks over my shoulder. "Where's your bag?"

I shrug. "Lost it."

"What? How? You still had it when you said you needed to go to the toilet."

Oh, that's right. I told her and her friends I had to take an emergency toilet break to follow Dylan, but I completely forgot about it.

"Oh, I must've put it down somewhere outside while running to the toilet." I laugh it off because I really have no answer to that.

She narrows her eyes at me. "Are you sure you're okay?"

Why do I get the feeling she's not telling me everything she knows?

"Yeah, I'm fine," I lie.

"Because Crystal told me she saw you run out of the emergency exit," she adds.

Oh fuck.

I shake it off. "It's nothing."

When I attempt to leave, she grabs my arm and says, "Wait. I just ... want you to feel comfortable enough to tell me the truth. I want to be a friend."

I nod, smiling. "Of course."

She looks me dead in the eyes, her fingers still gripping my arm. "Was it those boys?"

My pupils dilate, and I jerk my arm away.

How does she know?

"I know you've been looking at them," she says. "Are you involved with them? Is that why you transferred here? Because of those guys of the Skull & Serpent Society?"

I pull away and quickly open the bathroom door to get out. "It's none of your business."

"Please, Pen," she says. "I'm sorry, I don't want to scare you away."

She follows me all the way outside the building, and I don't know how to get rid of her without being mean to her face. She's the first friend I've made since I came here, and I don't want to ruin things. But I can't tell her everything either. If I did, it would put her in jeopardy.

"They're after you, aren't they?"

Her words make me stop in my tracks midway across the campus.

I turn around on the gravel road and look at her. "Thank you for giving me a warm welcome. I really appreciate it. I just ... can't."

I sigh and shake it off. I'm already involved now. But I won't let her go down this dangerous hole with me.

Serpents are hiding there, waiting to swallow people whole.

***

Lying down on my bed, I sift through the pages one by one, gazing at all the things my sister wrote about her peers. About a girl she had a fight with, Sadie, a boy named Peter she despised because he bullied her, Nathan, and some of her other classmates too. Tiny snippets of all the things she did with them, parties, random outings, movies, games, even just studying. She laid it all out in this little diary like a collection of memories. A peek into the world she once belonged to.

A world I've now infiltrated.

The page turns, and two familiar faces pop up again.

Dylan and Alistair.

Both take up an entire page in her little diary.

Their names are circled, their devious grins unsettling. Haunting.

A piece of the page has been torn off that has Dylan's last name on it.

And I know it was there before.

My heart begins to pulsate with fear.

What if Dylan ripped it out?

Fuck!

I slam the book shut for a second, groaning with anger. I should've paid more attention when I snatched it back from him, but I was in too much of a hurry to get away after stabbing Felix.

Grumbling, I open the diary again. Even though a part is missing, these pages still hold the secret to my sister's untimely death, and I can't turn away from it, even when I'm pissed off a part of it got stolen.

The page next to Dylan and Alistair is what captures me the most. Felix Rivera. His picture stands out among all others, larger than the ones of all her friends. It takes up almost an entire page. And his face is circled, adorned with hearts and skulls and snakes. But the text beneath it is what strikes the most fear into my heart.

Don't stop.

Don't look back.

Don't fall.

Run.

303.

The words and numbers are repeated over and over again like a mantra splurged onto the pages, ink splotches everywhere. A mantra she kept saying to herself. But why?

And why does it remind me of the day she jumped?

The image of her falling to her death off the cliff as I rush to grab her hand suddenly overtakes my mind, and I push back the diary and lean up, swallowing back the bile.

These words ...

Someone's responsible for her death. I just know someone pushed her to do it.

I just have to figure out who and why.

Suddenly, the door opens, and Kayla walks in without saying a word, casually throwing her bag onto her bed. I swiftly grab the diary and hold it close to my heart, worried she might see what's inside.

She sits behind her mirror and starts rubbing the makeup off her face with cotton pads. The black skin underneath is pristine and flawless, unlike mine.

She reminds me of my sister.

Friendly. Sincere. Gorgeous in every way.

And it stings in my heart that I don't know how to engage with that anymore.

"I'm sorry," I say. "About today."

She glances at me through the mirror.

"I didn't mean to be an asshole."

"No one does," she replies, smiling. "Sometimes we just are."

I nod and look away, feeling like I just can't connect with people anymore. Not since ...

"Hey." Her voice makes me look up. "It's okay." She approaches me and sits down beside me on my bed. "You're going through something, aren't you?"

Oh God.

The waterworks begin, but I still push most of the tears back, allowing only a single one to roll down my cheek. Kayla doesn't have to see this, and my sister definitely deserves more than just some tears.

"Oh no," she murmurs as she pulls me close so I can lean on her shoulder. "Cry if you need to."

"I've already cried enough tears," I say, feeling the rage coil and twist its way into my heart.

"If you wanna talk about it, I'm here," she replies. "I'll be here waiting until you're ready."

I lean up and look at her. "Why are you so nice to me?"

She shrugs. "Everyone deserves kindness. Tell you what, how about we go get some takeout?" She puts her arm around me and shakes me a little. "Get your mind off things."

My stomach growls just in time, making us both laugh. "I'd love that." I put the diary underneath my pillow.

"C'mon," she says with a smile while she hooks her arm through mine. "I know the perfect place around the corner."

7

ALISTAIR

I wrap the bandages around his arm and tie them in a knot.

"Jesus, can you hurry up?" Felix barks.

I stare up at him. "You can go to the nurse's office. Or do it yourself if you want to."

His nostrils flare, and he looks out the window at the lavish gardens. The Skull & Serpent Society house provides the best view of the well-kept grounds of Spine Ridge University. That's what you get when your parents donate tons of money.

"Whatever," Felix says after a while. "I'm just antsy."

"Because of that girl you mentioned?" I look up at him while putting on the tape.

"You weren't there. You should've seen the fucking look on her face after she stabbed me," Felix says.

"What ... did it remind you of the view in the mirror?" Dylan casually spouts while leaning against the doorpost with his arms folded.

Felix throws him a glare. "You think this is funny?"

He snorts. "No, but you getting stabbed ... that's new."

"So she's a feisty one," I reply. "I know you've got a thing for that."

"Oh, she's more than that." Dylan walks toward one of the big red seats in the middle of the Society game room and flops down. "She's Eve's sister."

My eyes widen.

Fuck.

I knew I recognized her from somewhere. She was that girl at Eve's funeral.

"Why do you think I lost my shit when I found her snooping on my conversation with my father?" Dylan leans forward to poke the flames in the fireplace with a poker. "It can't be random that she's here."

"No," Felix snarls, clutching the seat's armrest. "She's here with a purpose."

I get up and put away the box, then focus on him. "Stop using your muscles, it needs to heal."

"I'll do whatever the fuck I want," he growls back.

I shrug. "Okay, fine, then tear through the wound I just stitched for you."

"Not again, please." Dylan sighs. "We've got enough on our plate as it is."

Felix gets up and paces around the room. "Penelope ..."

"That's her name?" I grin. "Nice."

Felix grinds his teeth. "No. Not *nice*. We need her gone before she starts poking her nose in places it doesn't belong."

Dylan leans back in his seat, twirling the fire poker. "Okay, what's your plan?"

Felix punches his fist into his own hand. "Take care of it."

I shake my head. "Another body? That'll go over well with our pops."

"You got any better ideas?" Felix quips, glaring at me from across the room.

I shrug. "Why not just leave her be? What's she gonna do?"

"Stab me," Felix retorts.

"You cornered her," I say.

"She snooped on him." Felix points at Dylan. "She deserves punishment."

"Sounds like that went well," I reply.

His eyes twitch in that way they always do when he's about to throw hands. He storms right at me, but Dylan puts the fire poker between us. "Remember the first rule. No fucking fighting in the Society house.

Take it outside if you guys wanna have a brawl." He rubs the leather seat. "This thing's way too expensive to get a scratch."

"Don't fucking tell me the rules," Felix snarls. "I *made* them."

"Weren't you also the one who said they count for everyone?" I raise a brow.

He's boiling with rage now, but I don't care.

He isn't mad at me, but he sure as hell would love to take it out on me.

"Guys. Let's focus on the real issue here. The girl." Dylan eyes both of us until Felix eventually heads to the fridge. He takes out two canisters of beer, chugs them down with ease, then stomps on them.

"I've got something you might like," Dylan says. With a smug smile on his face, he pulls a piece of paper from his pocket. "Tore this out of that fucking diary of hers."

Felix marches toward him and snatches it from his hand. "That's your fucking name." He looks up, incensed. "She's been writing about us."

"Interesting," I mutter.

I wonder if she already wrote about me even though we haven't yet spoken.

She must've seen me around.

Felix throws the paper back at Dylan. "I want to know what else that fucking diary says."

"Wait ... are you thinking what I'm thinking?" Dylan mutters.

Felix's eyes fill with violence. "We're going to have some fun."

Dylan jumps up from his seat, the excitement on his face getting me hard and ready to go. "Oh yes, now you're talking."

***

PENELOPE

I definitely needed this warm teriyaki chicken sandwich. Oh my God, Kayla knows the best places. This stuff is so good it actually makes me groan. Delicious.

"Good, huh?" She laughs and takes a bite out of her own grilled sandwich. "This is Crystal's favorite."

"I can definitely see why," I reply, chuckling, and I take another bite.

I used to love getting takeout with my sister, but ever since she died, I haven't gotten any. But I will eat this with a smile. She would've wanted me to.

We walk around the campus borders, where the gates are overgrown with thorny roses, a flower that perfectly matches the university's name. Outside is an amazing overlook view of the sprawling Crescent Vale City below the mountain, and to the right is Priory Forest, where I made the most awful memory in my lifetime.

I take another bite and quickly look away while we slowly make our way back to the sorority house. With the dimmed lights at night, this campus looks cozy, unlike its name.

"So what's with that diary you hid under your pillow?" Kayla asks.

I swallow down my sandwich, surprised by the sudden question. "Ahh... it's just a diary." I add an awkward smile, but I don't know if she'll believe me.

"Oh, Crystal keeps one too," she replies. "Sometimes I steal it and put crazy shit inside just for her to find." She sniggers.

"Yeah, I don't share mine with anyone," I say as we walk back to the Alpha Psi building.

She pauses. "That's cool. I mean, I wasn't going to steal yours." She places a hand on my arm. "Your secrets are safe."

Phew.

I really don't want any of my new friends snooping through all the shit Eve wrote about their college mates. Even though Eve would've been a sophomore now, I'm sure Kayla and Crystal hang with some of Eve's past classmates.

"Hold up, lemme take a pic." Kayla pulls out her phone and leans in. "Smile."

I grin as hard as I can, trying my best to put up a front. When it's snapped, she pops it on Instagram.

Suddenly, she comes to an abrupt halt in front of the sorority hall. "Hey, isn't that our window?"

I gaze up at where she's looking. The window is clearly open, the curtains blowing in the soft night wind.

It was closed when we left.

"Could one of the girls have opened it?" Kayla mutters.

I don't wait another second before I rush inside, putting my sandwich on the cabinet before I bolt up the stairs and through the hallways, all the way to the end where our room is. But when I open it up, I stand frozen in the doorway, completely in shock.

The whole place is in ruins.

The bookshelf is turned over, books and other stuff are riddled across the ground. Tables and chairs flipped over, all cabinets ripped apart, contents shredded, spilled all over, all our pillows and blankets thrown onto the floor ... and my diary is gone.

Oh God.

"What happened?" a girl across the hall asks as she peers over my shoulder.

"Oh my God," another says. "Come see this!"

More girls come out of their rooms to look at the destruction in our room.

Destruction we did not cause.

Kayla rushes up the stairs behind me and pushes through the crowd until she bumps into me. Peering over my shoulder, she gasps.

"Pen, what happened?" She goes inside to collect some of the books while I pick up what's left of my bed.

I search beneath the pillow and the bedding, but the diary is nowhere to be found.

It's not just gone.

It's stolen.

My jaw tightens, my nostrils flaring as I stand.

"It was them," I say, gazing at Kayla over my shoulder while the other girls in the sorority watch us with keen interest.

Kayla frowns, confused. "You mean the—"

"Skull & Serpent Society."

The other girls all gasp collectively.

"So I was right ..." Kayla mutters, clutching the books that survived. "They are after you."

My fist balls. "Yeah, well they chose the wrong target."

They brought the violence to my safe space and stole something of mine that no one is allowed to see.

They think this is a fucking game?

They can have one.

8

FELIX

I sift through the diary, pages hanging loosely by the glue. It's barely kept together after we raided that fucking room, but at least we got what we came for.

"Man, that Alpha Psi sorority smelled so bad." Alistair waves his hand in front of his face. "The perfume was practically gassing people."

"No wonder we never go to their parties," Dylan jokes as he slouches down in his seat.

I put a finger in front of my mouth, shushing them both. They don't like it, but I don't care. We've got more pressing matters than parties at a dumb sorority.

I hold up the page that shows my face along with all the hearts and skulls that embellish it, the sight of which makes me want to pluck my own eyes out.

"Wow," Alistair says, laughing. "She's obsessed with you. She even drew hearts."

No fucking way.

I flip the pages back to where two pages are completely dedicated to them.

"Us," I say.

"Oh ..." Alistair says.

She drew hearts around their faces too, so it's not only me she has an obvious crush on.

Or had. Before she fucking stabbed me.

"So who cares?" Dylan shrugs. "Lots of girls are obsessed with us. Comes with the territory of being the rich playboy."

They don't get how important this is.

I lean forward in my chair. "It matters because she's the fucking sister." I flip through all the pages in front of them. "And she made a hate book."

"Hate? Where?" Dylan scoffs.

I point at one of the pictures that includes all three of us. Our faces are scratched out. "There are more accusations all over the book."

Dylan leans forward, suddenly engaged. "Shit. You mean like ... implying something?"

"What else do you think I fucking mean, Dylan?" I growl.

"Holy shit," Alistair says.

"Exactly," I reply, throwing the book on the table in front of them. "We need to keep an eye out on her."

"We need to know what exactly she knows," Dylan says.

Alistair picks up the diary and sifts through it. "Did her sister tell her all those things?"

"Do I look like I know?" I bark back.

"Okay, chill, I mean, it could be worse, right?" Alistair says.

My fingers dig into the seat. "How?"

"She hasn't gone to the police," Dylan says.

"Yet," Alistair adds.

"She won't," I growl, rubbing my chin. "I won't fucking let her." I make a fist and pound it onto the seat. "I don't care what it takes. She can't fucking tell anyone whatever the fuck she knows." My eyes fixate on Dylan's. "Nothing leaves this room. Nothing."

He nods. "I know the rules."

"If push comes to shove ..." I mutter.

"It won't," Alistair says.

"You sure about that, Ali?" I grumble, glancing at my wound, flexing my muscles. "Because this one seems even more violent than the other."

Suddenly, the door to our private study bursts open, and I'm about to lose my shit. "What the fuck, Jason? I told you to knock before—"

"There's a girl at the fucking front door," he says.

"So?" Dylan frowns. "It's not Freaky Friday yet, tell her to come back later."

"She said you guys were waiting for her. Her name's Penelope."

My eyes widen, and I almost crack the wood of the seat's armrest.

So ... she's finally seen her room.

I'd hoped she was there when we came through the window so we could force her to give it up, but this ... this is even better.

Now she'll have to beg.

"Let her in," I say through gritted teeth.

Jason nods and closes the door again.

"Are you sure this is a good idea?" Dylan whisper-yells.

"Yeah, if this is what I think it is, she's coming for the book," Alistair adds.

Tilting my head, I reply, "Good. I wanna see how mad she can get." I lick my teeth and wait until Jason returns with the girl.

Penelope, Penelope ... what have you gotten yourself into?

You're about to find out how much worse things can get.

There's a knock on the door, and Alistair quickly grabs the book and stuffs it under his shirt.

"Come in," I say, biting my lip when the door slowly opens and behind it a girl dressed in a little black top and a checkered skirt appears. She's still wearing the same outfit from earlier today when she chose to pierce my skin with a pen.

Dark. Tempting. Edgy.

Easily destroyed.

Just like her fucking face will be when I'm done with her.

9

PENELOPE

There they are.

The three perfectly fucked-up boys of the Serpent & Skull Society.

The boys who run this place.

And they're sitting on their luxurious, red velvet seats, staring at me with disdain like they're the fucking gods of this earth.

Felix lights a cigarette and blows out the smoke in my direction, then hands his cigarette to Dylan, who also takes a long drag.

"So ... Penelope ... you think we're waiting for you?" Felix asks, spreading his muscular legs because they barely fit in the seat.

The door behind me closes, and I'm eerily aware of the sound it makes.

Especially when it's locked.

Fuck.

I knew it would be dangerous to come here, but I didn't expect that fucker Jason to actually lock the door on me.

No turning back now.

"I know you broke into my room," I say.

Better throw it all out on the table right away.

"Do you now?" With a devious grin, Dylan leans back, looking me up and down. "Where's your proof?"

"Give me the fucking diary," I say through gritted teeth.

"What diary?" Alistair mutters, sitting awkwardly in his seat like he's hiding something.

I know they have it. I know it was them. They know it. But the fact that they deny it to my face pisses me off.

"I'm not here to play games," I say.

"I am," Felix says, and he takes the cigarette back from Dylan and takes another deep drag, blowing it all out in one go until the room practically fills with smoke.

I push away the need to cough.

"I know you fucking stole it," I say, stepping closer to show them I'm not afraid.

Felix looks up at me from his seat, his eyes still at half mast, still as cold as ice. "What if we did? What will you do?"

His gaze darkens, and so does mine, while my hand tightens around the knife in my pocket.

I didn't come here without something to ensure my safety.

Especially after our last encounter.

"Why did you take it?" I ask as I come closer and closer.

But there's no answer. All they do is smirk and glare at me.

This book ... means everything to me. I *need* it back. And I am done fucking waiting until one of them admits the truth.

I pull my knife from my pocket and point it at Felix. "Give it to me. Now."

For the first time since I've seen him, an actual smile forms on his lips before it fades into oblivion as though it never even existed. Brief, but a smile nonetheless.

"What are you going to do? Slice me? Stab me like you did in that hallway?" He leans in, closer and closer, until his face is mere inches away from the point of my blade. "Do it then. I dare you."

Is this fucker insane?

The knife is lodged firmly in the palm of my hand, but I don't move, not even an inch, because I know the scars I can cause will be permanent. And it would definitely make it harder to escape from here.

"Go on ... just the tip," he muses, leaning in until the tip pierces through the slit of his mouth, and it opens up, his tongue slipping out to curl around the blade like only a snake would.

I retract the knife.

Stabbing him wouldn't get me what I wanted.

The other two boys laugh.

"Shame," Felix mumbles and leans back in his seat again.

He's taunting me, but I won't fall for this trick.

"No, you're the shameful ones for stealing what belongs to me," I say.

"Sounds like it's important to you," Dylan says, taking another drag of Felix's smoke.

"What's inside?" Alistair asks. "Secrets?"

"None of your fucking business," I snarl.

"But it is." Felix's fingers curl, and his nails dig into the leather. "You came here into our fucking house just to get it back." He throws me an arrogant look. "I want to know why."

"Like I'd ever tell you," I retort.

"You will if you want it back."

Got him. "So you admit you took it?"

His brows rise. "Depends."

"On what?"

"Your answers."

My nostrils flare.

"Did you write it?" Alistair suddenly asks.

When I merely stare at him, Felix says, "Answer him."

He's testing me. But I can play this game. "No."

Dylan's eyes narrow. "Then who did?"

"My sister."

Felix's fingers twitch. "Say her name."

"Eve." I tilt my head. "But you already knew that, didn't you?" I lean on my knees to look him in the eyes. "Because she told you my name."

A filthy smirk forms on his lips again, but it disappears as quickly as it came.

"I already like her," Dylan muses.

"Don't," Felix barks, and the other two immediately look away.

So he really is the one in charge.

"Like? Chasing after someone in a stairwell is not something I'd do to someone I 'like,'" I rebuke.

"We do," Dylan replies, licking his lips.

A chill runs up and down my spine.

"Tell me why you three were at her funeral." It's a long shot, but I have to try.

"Why should we have to explain ourselves to you?" Dylan answers.

"All her friends were there," Alistair adds.

"Friends, yes," I say.

Felix's eyes narrow. "Are you implying something?"

Yes, I am. But I won't say it out loud. Not while I still need something from them.

"Just give me the fucking diary. It's no use to you," I say through gritted teeth.

"So it's important to you," Felix muses. "How important?"

"She was *my* sister. She didn't want anyone to read it. Except for me," I say, still clutching that knife firmly in my hand.

His brow rises. "How do you know?"

"I just do," I say, tired of these games. "Now give me the diary."

He tilts his head. "Show me what you're willing to do, then."

I frown. "What? Why? It's mine."

With a dead-serious look, he says, "Get on your knees."

Is he for real?

My fingers tighten around the knife. "No. No fucking way."

Why would he think I'd do that willingly? I don't fucking know what he's planning, and I sure as hell know what these boys are capable of. It can't be anything good.

"Well then, I guess the diary is gone forever," Dylan muses from his seat, pushing out his cigarette in the ashtray.

"I need it," I growl back. "This isn't a joke."

"I'm not joking either," Felix replies, eyeing my knife. "The question is ... what are you willing to do to get it back?"

I grind my teeth in frustration, contemplating whether I should stab him again. But it's three against one, and they would not let me walk out of here without an equally painful scratch.

"Twirl around for me," Felix taunts. "Let me see what's underneath that skirt."

"Perverts," I mutter under my breath.

Dylan laughs. "Thanks for the compliment."

Of course they'd see it as a compliment.

There's a glimmer in his eyes. "You haven't even seen us at our worst yet."

"Now twirl, or you'll never see that fucking diary again," Felix says, gawking at me with those eyes that scream dominance.

He wants to overpower me.

Make me submit.

And if I want that diary back, I don't have any fucking choice in the matter.

Fuck.

Sighing out loud, I slowly twirl around so the skirt doesn't rise too much, but I can still catch a glimpse of their mischievous and victorious looks, and they piss me off.

Felix suddenly stands up, and his hand coils around my wrist the moment I reach the end of my spin. His grip is firm, painful even, and I struggle to jerk free.

He's face-to-face with me, and it makes it hard to breathe.

"Let go of me," I growl, trying to keep my bearings.

Violence flickers in his eyes. "No, I don't think I will."

He shakes my wrist so hard I lose my grip on the knife, and it drops … right into his other hand.

Before I can even react, he's already thrown it to Dylan, who easily catches it. He twirls it around in his hand, showing off the fact that I'm no longer in control.

They are.

My body floods with panic, but I swallow down the nerves.

Felix's free hand latches onto my shoulder. "In fact, I think it's about time you go down on your fucking knees." Gripping my wrist, he forces me down until I collapse onto the floor from his overpowering strength. With his darkening gaze on me, I struggle to even react. His half-mast killer eyes alone could pin anyone to the floor.

He releases my wrist, only to grab my face, pushing my cheeks together. "That pretty face deserves to be destroyed." His fingers slide down to my chin, and he pushes it down, forcing a thumb inside. "You want your fucking diary back?"

When I try to speak, he shushes me. "Just nod."

Fuck. I hate him so much. But I still nod because I can't even say a word without gargling from his fingers slowly pushing farther down my tongue.

"Then be a good little fucking slut and gag for me," he growls, stuffing his fingers all the way inside until his knuckles hit my teeth.

Tears well up in my eyes, and I cough out loud, trying to resist the urge to vomit.

"That's it. That's the little slut-face I'm looking for," Felix murmurs, leaning in to spit on my face.

Dylan and Alistair laugh. "Get her."

When Felix pulls his fingers from my throat, I gag and mutter, "Fuck you."

"Gladly," Felix replies. He slowly tugs down his zipper. "But first, you're going to show me just how much that throat of yours can take."

My eyes widen. He's really going to make me do this, isn't he?

Fuck.

I want to scream, but it wouldn't do a thing.

I'm in their lair, and no one here would help me.

And if I don't do what he wants, I'll never see that diary again.

I have no choice.

Making a face, I stare him down as he tilts my chin down so my eyes follow. His abs tighten through his shirt as he pulls his cock right through the hole of the zipper. It's hard. Curved. And huge. Much bigger than any of my previous lovers.

But that's not the thing that makes me gasp.

It's the number of piercings.

Four of them, at least, an ampallang through the glans and a ring below in the frenum, one barbell through the shaft, and a ring through the pubic. Jesus.

"Like my jewelry?" He pushes my chin down until my lips part. "You'll like it even more when they slide across your tongue."

"You're fucked up," I say.

"You don't even know how badly," he retorts. "Now part those pretty fucking lips for me, Pen, and let's see how fucked up you can get too."

Before I can even say another word, he's already slipped his hard-on into my mouth. The cold sting of his barbells hit my palate, almost making me gag, but he keeps going, ignoring all the coughs and heaves I'm doing as he goes deeper and deeper.

"That's it. Show me how much of a fucking slut you can become," he groans. "Now suck my cock like a good slut would."

I wrap my tongue around his shaft.

Then I bite down.

He growls but doesn't pull back.

Even when the metallic taste of blood sits on my tongue.

"You think a little blood will make me stop?"

SLAP!

My cheeks sting with heat from the palm of his hand.

"She bit you?" Dylan asks, and he flicks his finger. "Ali. Put it in the fire."

Alistair jumps up from his seat, the diary tumbling from his shirt.

My eyes widen as he rushes for the fireplace in the back and holds it in front of the flames.

No!

Felix grabs my chin and forces me to look at him. "Now, are you going to behave?" he growls.

I nod, but it's a reluctant nod, one of fierce rebellion.

Alistair slowly pulls away, even though he's still close enough to the fire to chuck it in if I don't do exactly what I'm told.

Fuck.

I've really gotten myself deep into trouble.

Felix's fingers push into my cheeks as he forces my lips around his shaft. "Your tongue belongs to me now. And I will fuck it how I see fit."

He thrusts inside without warning. I struggle to even breathe.

He holds my face in place, making it impossible to move, let alone speak as he ravages my mouth over and over. His barbells cling against my teeth and scrape my throat raw.

Tears well up in my eyes—not from the rage but from the way he plunges inside and makes me gag.

But the worst part of it all is how I can feel my panties slowly growing wet.

Fuck. This should not be happening.

I ignore the desire building in my body and focus on the moment, trying to get through it without losing my sanity.

But it's hard, so hard, with those twisted half-mast eyes coldly glaring deep into my soul with heartless cruelty.

He pulls out, only to thrust back inside all the way to the base.

Brutal.

"Take it like a good fucking slut, Pen," he groans.

His length bobs up and down against my throat, making me intensely aware of every passing second.

Because I can't. Fucking. Breathe.

When he pulls out again, I suck in the oxygen, worried I might not have any the next time he does it.

"Stick out your tongue," he says.

I wish I could say no.

But this diary ... it's more important to me than my own body.

When I do, he plunges back in with no remorse, fucking my face as he holds it in place.

"I'm going to fucking coat your tongue with cum, and you're going to swallow it all," he groans.

When I shake my head, he grabs a fistful of my hair and buries himself to the hilt. "You don't get to say no to me, Pen. This is the deal. You want your diary? You'll eat my fucking cum to get it. Now lick."

I struggle to even stick out my tongue without gagging, but I persist.

And from the vicious look in his eyes, he's not amused.

"You can take it deep. You've done this before. I can feel it." He slaps my cheek again. "You like it rough, don't you?"

I'm not going to answer his taunts.

He knows why I'm here.

He's trying to mess with my head.

"Then fucking choke on it," he says, and he thrusts in so fast I still gag.

Grunting, he buries himself until all his barbells and rings are inside my mouth, and an explosion of cum fills me up.

Oh God.

It's warm and salty, and I can't keep it all inside.

As he pulls out, I drop on hands and knees and heave it all out onto the hardwood floor.

But I can still taste him.

And I can still feel my pussy throb.

Fuck.

"Bad Penelope." Felix grabs me by the hair and shoves me down onto the floor. "I told you to eat my fucking cum. Now lick." He drags my face through until my tongue dips out, and I taste him all over again.

Fucking hell.

This is the most insane, debasing thing I've ever done.

And those boys up there, watching him, they're viciously smiling like they're enjoying the show.

Fuck them and fuck their fucking faces.

"Clean it," he growls. "These floors are expensive as fuck."

"You got what you wanted," Alistair suddenly says. "Let's finish this up?"

"I decide when it's done!" Felix barks at him, making him clutch the diary tighter.

Then Felix shoves his boot on my back, forcing me to lie on the floor. "And I'm not nearly fucking done with this girl who made me bleed."

"I'll make you bleed even more for doing this to me," I spit out.

His eye twitches, and he leans in, grabbing my hair to make me look at him. "I'd like to see you try, rat."

"Don't fucking call me that," I seethe.

"Oh, how about whore, then?" He pushes me down in the puddle of cum and puts his dick back into his pants. "I'm done. Let this whore out."

What? Not without my diary. Not after what he just made me do to get it back in the first place.

"Aw ... and I was so looking forward to my turn," Dylan muses and waves the knife around like it's a plaything.

Like he meant to use it on me.

I shiver.

Alistair holds out my sister's diary to Felix. "What about her book? A promise is a promise."

Felix grumbles. "Fine."

He snatches it from Alistair's hands and chucks it at my face, the pages rolling through the same cum that was just deposited deep inside my throat.

I quickly snatch it off the floor as I get up on my knees, but some of the book's pages are completely soaked. God-fucking-dammit.

"Have fun with your sister's fucking diary," Dylan says.

As I come to a stand, clutching the diary tightly against my chest, my sticky hair clings to my shirt, and half my face is covered in semen.

And they start to fucking snigger.

"You'll pay for this," I growl at Felix.

He doesn't seem fazed at all. Cold. Uncaring. Except for that one glimmer in his eyes. "You know where to find me if you want to make good on that fucking statement."

I turn and rush out the door, ignoring all the looks and catcalls from the other guys living in this house whose eyes almost bulge out of their skulls from the sheer amount of filth on my face.

But I'll hold my head high.

Even though I know I can't escape these boys ...

These boys who will ruin me.

"I can't fucking wait to see you again ..." Felix calls after me. "Next time, I'll make you beg."

10

FELIX

I snap my fingers at one of the maids my father hired who's dusting the hallways. "Clean that up," I tell her, pointing at the puddle.

She nods and hurries into the cleaning room to collect a mop and a bucket filled with soap water. Then she sinks to her knees on the floor in our study and wipes away the leftover cum and spit.

"That was over surprisingly quickly," Dylan says while toying with his metallic white hair. "I would've loved to have a turn too, but no one asked."

"She stabbed me," I growl.

"Yeah, yeah, I know," he says, rolling his eyes. "You earned her first."

"Earned?" Alistair scoffs.

"Don't," I growl at him.

He makes a face. "What if she goes to the police?"

"She won't," I say. "Too much is at stake. She has that diary for a reason. She's trying to find out what happened to Eve."

Dylan's brows rise. "So you're saying there might be a chance ...? Not that it really matters." He gawks at Alistair.

A smile tugs at the edge of my lips, but I stop it from growing. "She'll come back."

"Do you think we went too far?" Alistair asks.

"Fuck no." I stare at the fire, watching the flames dance. "It was only a small taste. And I can't fucking wait to take a bite."

"Sounds like you had some fun." Dylan gets up from his seat. "Now I'm going to have to take a shower to cool off."

"Phew, mind if I join you?" Alistair asks, raising a brow.

"I don't like sharing the heat," Dylan replies. "Yo, Felix, get some fucking rest, man. You look like you came straight from hell. We've got early tests tomorrow morning."

"I'll get some nerd to finish my homework for me," I reply, glancing his way as he walks out the door. "And if your father gives you shit again, tell him I'll ask my father what he thinks about his position there."

***

DYLAN

Fuck, that was way too hot and too fucked up not to arouse me.

The oak stairs creak under my feet as I make my way to my room. I have a private shower all for myself, just like Alistair and Felix. The others who share this house with us have to make do with shared bathrooms.

Perks of being a part of the rich kid club who own this place.

Well, not literally ... but everyone here knows who pays for this Society, and that alone makes us in charge.

No one dares to defy us for fear of having to face our fathers' wrath.

But they don't even know our fathers aren't the dangerous ones.

I turn on the shower and pull off my clothes. I'm still hard and throbbing from watching that scene unfold.

A part of me revels in the fantasy that I was the one who thrusted into her throat instead of Felix.

But if this girl is as relentless as Felix says she is, I might get my chance soon enough.

I step under the shower, close my eyes, and let the warm water rush down onto my face. My hand slides down my chest, my abs, all the way to my cock, which is still rock hard from the mere memory imprinted on my brain.

So ... the sister, huh?

I never imagined there could be anyone as interesting as Eve.

Until I laid eyes on Penelope.

A spicy little girl, that's for sure. I never expected her to actually come and get that diary back ... and get on her knees for it.

My hands instinctively move to my dick, sliding up and down the shaft. I'm too hot and bothered by the image of her sucking cock and licking the cum off the floor.

Good God, when was the last time someone went that down and dirty for us? Too long.

Just like it's been too long since I last gushed all over this bathroom wall.

But fuck me, do I wish it was her throat right now.

My fingers roll across the tip, stroking faster and faster, and my other hand moves to my nipple as I moan with excitement. I'm bursting at the seam, my balls tightening with a desire for release. So I flick the head and thrust into my own hand until an explosion of cum spurts out and onto the walls of my shower.

But when I open my eyes again, Alistair is there in the door opening, looking at me. "Enjoying yourself?"

I stop and turn away. "Sorry."

He shrugs. "I don't mind."

"What are you doing here?"

"I wanted to see if you still had shower gel. Mine's empty."

"Sure, it's over there," I say, and I point at a shelf.

He quickly grabs it and smiles as he walks back to the door. "Thanks." He doesn't leave, though. "The girl got to you too, huh?"

I turn off the shower and look down at the droplets of cum swirling into the drain.

Alistair sighs. "Hate to be the one left out."

A filthy grin spreads on my lips. "She's a freaky one ... and she's looking for something only we can help her with." He folds his arms while listening intently. "So let's give her what she needs."

***

PENELOPE

I run home fast, ignoring every stare I get as I enter the Alpha Psi sorority.

"Oh my God, what happened, Pen?" Crystal asks as she sees me storm down the hallways.

"Not now," I reply as I head into my room.

"Pen?" Kayla drops her book when she sees me, but I quickly hide in the bathroom and shut the door.

"Penelope?" Crystal's voice sounds clearer than before, and I can hear her footsteps barge into the room. "Kayla, do you know what happened to her?"

"No, she just ran in looking pale as a ghost."

"Didn't you see how wet her hair looked? Almost ... sticky."

Fuck. I hate to hear people talk behind my back. It's exactly what happened in high school, and even then, nothing I did could ever stop it. It always made me hide in the bathrooms, trying to escape the shame.

I promised myself I'd stand up for myself this time.

I promised myself I wouldn't take shit anymore.

And look at me now, covered in Felix Rivera's cum.

I barely recognize the girl in the mirror staring back at me.

I swiftly grab my toothbrush and scrape off my teeth minute after minute, spitting out the gunk, only to apply more toothpaste to my brush and re-doing it all over. But no matter how many times I keep brushing, I can still taste him in my mouth.

Suddenly, someone knocks on the door.

"Pen? Are you okay in there?" Kayla asks.

"I ..." I don't even know what to say. Instead, I turn on the faucet and splash my face with water. The sludge slowly drips down my cheeks, and I wipe it off with some tissues, chucking them into the trash with rage.

That guy meant to degrade me.

It wasn't just for fun ... it was a warning.

And that means I'm getting closer.

"Pen? Do you need help?" Kayla asks.

I stare at myself in the mirror, clutching the sink. This girl doesn't need help. She needs to toughen up. Because there's no way in hell I'm going to let these boys and their sexual debauchery get in my way of finding out the truth.

For Eve.

"Don't worry about me," I say. "I'm fine."

It's a lie, but it's a lie I tell well. And I knew going in that I needed to face these boys alone. Especially now that I know what they're capable of.

I take in a deep breath and clean myself off with a few tissues before I turn on the shower for a much-needed deep rinse.

However, no amount of soap lathered all over my body can rid me of the stain on my memories. And every time I close my eyes, he's there, fucking my skull.

My pussy throbs, and I open my eyes, squeezing my legs together.

Why does this keep happening?

Even now, my body still reacts to the way Felix used me.

And the water that rushes down my skin creates goose bumps everywhere. Or maybe it's the mere memory of feeling him thrust inside my mouth.

I swallow, and I can still feel the scratches his piercings left deep inside, but instead of it reminding me of how much I hated it, all it does is make my clit thump harder.

What is going on? I've never had this with any of my previous fucks.

Then again, this wasn't a fuck in any sense of the word.

Nor was it something I ever thought I could do.

And for some reason, the thought still brings my hand down my belly and between my legs to try to quench that fire raging inside me.

I start to circle my clit, ignoring the voices in my head that tell me it's wrong.

I'm completely soaked even though I'm in the shower, and all my senses are on overload.

It feels so damn wrong, but I keep going, desperate to stop those desires brewing inside me.

I need this, even when I tell myself I don't.

I need the release.

So I keep going, flicking my fingers back and forth across my sensitive area until I finally find the release I was hoping for. With my mouth shut tight, I try not to let any sounds escape, but it's so damn hard.

Especially when the last image that flashes through my mind was all three of those boys watching me while I licked up the cum from the floor.

Jesus.

Since when am I so fucked up?

I turn off the shower and rub myself dry.

I really need to get my mind off this.

I grab my clothes and throw them into the dirty clothes basket, taking out the diary stuck between my skirt and top. It's still drenched and filthy from what they did. But the images and text inside appear undamaged.

I breathe a sigh of relief as I take more tissues and clean it up as best as I can. Then I take my pill as I do every day, but I'll keep a watchful eye from now on in case they attempt more fucked-up shit.

Those boys probably thought they could deter me from trying to find out more with their kinky games.

Wrong.

The only thing that matters is finding out why my sister wrote that fucking note to me. The rest is all noise.

Now that I have the diary back, I'm going to make those fucking boys talk about Eve, or I will tell the fucking world they were responsible.

And I don't care if that's a lie or not.

I can pin them down with ease, knowing what's inside this diary.

They played with fire when they stole it from me.

Now they're going to burn.

11

ALISTAIR

Days later

I take some bags of chips and a bunch of Cokes from the shelves and tuck them into my pocket when no one's looking. The cameras in the corner won't catch me in this spot because I checked beforehand what way they're pointing.

Still, there's the cashier to bypass.

I pull out my phone and check my texts while leisurely strolling through the aisles. How to avoid detection? Pretend you're just like the others shopping here.

Only I don't tend to pay for any of it.

There's no reason.

I don't *need* any of this fucking stuff.

But I want to feel the rush.

With a big smile on my face, I approach the front section of the shop.

The moment I spot a familiar face near the ice cream aisle, close to the exit, I come to a halt.

My eyes widen when she turns her head and looks straight at me.

Penelope.

What the hell is she doing here?

I turn another corner, headed straight for the chips aisle, but when

I glance over my shoulder, there she is again, clutching a tub of vanilla ice cream in her arms.

I stop right in front of the milk section and turn around to face her. "Are you following me?"

"Maybe, maybe not." She raises a brow. "Where are Felix and Dylan?"

I'm surprised she found me here. She must've been tracking my movements, which means she's been keeping tabs on Dylan and Felix as well.

"They outside waiting for you?" she asks.

I shrug and ignore her, but she keeps hammering down on me.

She eyes me up and down the same way she did when Felix demanded she get on her knees. And fuck me, the mere memory makes my cock twitch.

"What are you doing?"

"Nothing," I reply, adjusting my nuts through my pockets.

She glances at my pockets. "Got something in there?"

She's smarter than I thought she'd be.

"You trying to steal shit?" she asks.

Nosy girl.

"Why do you care?"

She folds her arms. "You're rich, yet you can't pass up the opportunity to steal it anyway. Why?"

"Call me an adrenaline junkie," I answer, tilting my head. "I love the thrill." I lean in to whisper, "But most of all ... I love to watch."

With a dead-serious face, she says, "You know I won't let you and your fucking buddies walk all over me, right?"

Adrenaline courses through my body at the thought of running as fast as I can.

I normally manage to walk out of any shop with ease with all the goods I could ever want, but this girl ... this girl is going to make it hard on me, I just know it.

Those fiery eyes of hers tempt me to respond. "Do you think threats work on us?"

"I don't care." She closes in on me.

"Go home and eat that tub of ice cream," I reply.

She ignores what I say. "Do you think I'll let you walk after what you did to me?"

I tilt my head, smirking. "I didn't do shit."

She suddenly shoves me against the fridge, and some of the milk containers tumble to the floor, dirtying my new Balenciagas. Fuck.

I don't get pissed off easily, but that'll do it.

"That won't be all I'll destroy," she says through gritted teeth.

She really is a spicy one, just as Felix said.

I like it.

"Was that why you fuckers stole my diary? To fuck with me?" she sneers. "Which one of you stole it?"

A smirk forms on my face.

"It was you, wasn't it?" she asks.

I won't deny that stealing is my forte. "Doesn't matter what the answer is, it won't change the fact that you've now become Felix's whore ..." I lean in, my blood curdling with desire when I smell her woody perfume. "And if you don't stop digging, Dylan and I will have a turn as well."

She twitches, visibly shaken by my comment, her eyes slowly focusing on mine as though she's having trouble even looking at me.

"In your fucking dreams," she growls.

I tap her forehead. "Watch me make those fucking dreams a reality."

I pass by her and head for the exit, but she quickly trails me. "You think I'm going to let you fucking walk away?"

"Watch me," I reply stoically.

She follows me around the store with her bucket of ice cream. "I'll get you to talk."

"There's nothing to talk about," I reply, heading straight for the front door before things go south.

"Fine," she retorts and immediately heads for the cashier.

My eyes widen when I see her point at me and say the words, "That guy is trying to steal your stuff."

Fuck.

Of course she'd try to get me arrested.

I bolt off as fast as I can toward the parking lot while the sirens inside the store go off. Several guards chase after me, along with the store's cashier.

"Alistair!" Dylan yells from his car as he watches me run up to them with lightning speed. "What the fuck happened in there?!"

"Talk later, just fucking drive!" I yell as I jump into the passenger's seat and slam the door shut behind me.

Dylan hits the gas and laughs like a maniac as he veers off the road and makes a screeching U-turn. "That's one way to get the adrenaline going. WOO!"

Felix suddenly chucks a knife into the dashboard. A clear warning.

I turn to look at him.

"You'd better fucking explain, or I swear to God—"

"It was the girl. Penelope," I explain. "She was there. She snitched on me."

His brows twitch. "So she's following us."

I nod. "Seems like it. It's too much of a coincidence. And I've seen her hanging around the building too often."

"Of course she is," Dylan muses. "She's obsessed now that she's gotten the D!" He licks his teeth. "And I can't fucking wait to try out that dirty mouth for myself."

Felix chucks his other knife at the seat Dylan is in, and it lodges into the side, missing him by a hair. But Felix only misses on purpose, never by accident.

"Watch it."

Is he defensive over her?

Dylan throws him a deadly look through the mirror. "You're not the only one allowed to have fun."

Why are they so obsessed with her?

All I see is a bunch of fucking trouble.

"I wasn't having fun," Felix replies, tapping his fingers onto his knees. "I was teaching her a lesson."

Dylan smirks. "Then the next lesson is mine."

12

FELIX

This class is the most boring one of all.

Finances.

Dylan and I failed this dull class last year. So now we have to retake it because our fathers won't allow us to fail. Obviously, it would look bad on the family name.

Not that I fucking care.

There is one thing I fucking care about, though, which also might happen to be the least boring thing in this class.

Eve's fucking sister, Penelope.

She's sitting in the front of the auditorium near the professor.

Her little black dress barely covers her legs, clad in fishnet stocking, and about five or six chains adorn her neck, maybe to make her look tough even though I know she isn't. Her purple hair stands out among the other girls. But the funny thing is, she doesn't want to be noticed.

Too late.

I pull out my phone and hold it up to take a quick picture.

That'll be a nice addition to my spank bank.

Someone bumps into her with their elbow, a friend, probably. She turns and stares at me. It's the first time our eyes connect since I filled up her pretty little fucking mouth.

My lip twitches. Her cheeks flush.

Her brows draw together, and she swiftly turns around again.

Mad I made her think about licking my cum off the floor.

I might make her do it again.

When the professor finally finishes blabbing on about shit I don't care about, he ends class. Everyone gets up, so I wink at Dylan, who quickly rushes down the steps to the only exit, just as we'd discussed before we came to this class.

There's no way I'm going to go at Penelope with all our classmates and a fucking professor watching. I'm not that stupid. People here adore us. In fact, half the girls are fawning at Dylan while they walk past him out the door, blowing kisses on their way, some even trying to give him their numbers.

He's the flirty one of us three, and he does it so well, it makes me want to hurl.

He knows how to use his good looks to his advantage.

But I know that smooth smile hides a killer in plain sight.

I lick my lips as I watch Penelope pack her new bag and wait until she looks up. Finally, she spots Dylan at the front door saying bye to everyone, and her body grows rigid.

She turns to glare at me, and I simply tilt my head, a smirk tugging at my lips.

I tap my fingers onto the desk, her eyes widening.

You'd better run now, little Pen ... before it's too late.

Before you become our next prey.

***

DYLAN

Penelope hastily turns around again and throws everything into her bag. But as she closes her bag, a part of the zipper comes loose, and almost all of her books come tumbling out again. As if it was meant to be.

The professor is the last one to pick up his books and hurriedly stuffs everything into a bag, which he slings over his shoulder while munching on a sandwich.

"See you later, boys," he tells me and waves at Felix as he leaves the auditorium.

Penelope swiftly grabs all the books strewn across the floor and tucks everything into her broken bag, holding it close to her body as she runs down the chairs, but the teacher just left the room, so I shut the door right before she gets there.

I can hear her suck in a breath behind me, the mere sound awakening all my senses.

And fuck me, I can't wait to hear those breathy moans she gave Felix when he stuffed her to the brim.

With my back turned to her, I smile and push the key into the lock, then glance at her over my shoulder.

Her eyes widen. Panicked, she steps backward. But the only other exit is at the top of the stairs, and Felix stands there, waiting for her to choose.

Me or him.

It's going down either way.

"Penelope ..." Felix calls from the back as he continuously taps the small desk in front of him. "I don't think you know what you've gotten yourself into."

Her face turns as white as snow, and she quickly looks my way, seething. "Open the door."

I fold my arms. "How about no?"

From the back door, Alistair emerges, and he shuts that door too, tucking the key into his pocket.

"How the fuck did you both get keys?" she mutters.

I smirk. "Perks of being the dean's son."

She glances sideways at Alistair, who casually strolls down the stairs and throws Felix the key over his shoulder.

She clutches her bag tightly, skittishly looking around like a mouse caught in a trap.

Good.

I love seeing the fear building in her eyes. It gets me fucking fired up like nothing else. And the more of a fighter she is, the better it'll feel to break her.

"What do you want?" she asks.

"You're the one who cornered me in the store," Alistair says as he approaches. "So I think it's about time you started talking."

"You're the ones who need to explain yourselves after you stole my sister's diary," she growls back. "After you ..." Her cheeks stain red.

"After what, Penelope?" Felix muses as he slowly walks down the steps too, the menacing look on his face making even my hairs stand up. "After I dragged your face through my cum?"

She swallows, visibly shaken by the mere memory alone.

"So you have thought of it," Felix boasts, sticking his hands into his pockets as he closes in on her.

Even with him in her face, she still manages to speak up. "You violated—"

"You liked it," he interrupts, a hint of a smirk tugging at his lips. And he leans in to softly whisper, "And you'll beg me to do it again soon."

Goddamn psycho. I love it.

"What? No, I didn't," she retorts, clenching her teeth like she's upset he'd even suggest. "I did it to get the diary back." She eyes my pocket. "Give me the fucking key, Dylan."

I pull out the key and twirl it around. "Oh, you mean this key?"

She lunges at me and tries to snatch it from my hand, but I quickly retract my arm, lifting it high up in the air where she can't reach, not even on her toes. And it brings me lots of joy watching her struggle as she rubs up against my chest.

Suddenly, Felix grabs her from behind, his arms snaking around her waist.

"Hey! Let go of me!" she squeals.

She punches at him, but he locks her arms underneath his grip. Felix's firm hold is not something anyone can escape easily. Within seconds, he's pushed both her arms behind her back and pinned them there with one hand.

"You motherfuc—"

He puts his other hand over her mouth. "Don't yell, little slut." Her eyes widen and sparkle with rage, and it makes me snort. "Don't want to alert the other students, do we?"

She's killing me with her eyes. I've never seen so much anger come from one girl before. It's vexing. And exhilarating.

My bulge grows harder and harder as I get closer and dangle the key in front of her. Right before she attempts to free herself, I pluck it away and tuck it back into my pocket.

"You should've stayed out of our way," I tell her. "But you couldn't stop yourself from tailing Alistair, could you?"

Her brow furrows, but whatever she tries to say is blocked by Felix's hand.

Alistair leans down on a chair. "To be fair, we did provoke her."

"She provoked us first," I rebuke. "By flaunting that fucking diary in our face."

Her whole body quakes as Felix shoves her onto the table and forces her to sit down while he keeps her arms pinned down.

I tilt her chin and make her look at me. "What's it for? Is it a hate book? Why did your sister have pictures of everyone in there?"

She clenches her jaw, and Felix whispers into her ear, "If you yell, I will silence you with my dick in your mouth again." He slowly lowers his hand to her neck, keeping a firm grip on her throat and wrists. "Now answer him."

She doesn't say a word.

A filthy smile forms on my lips.

Guess I'll have to convince her.

I get up close and personal, tilting my head to take in her short-length black dress, taking my time to swoop over her fishnet stockings and those thick boots underneath. With that purple eyeliner matching her hair, she reminds me of those girls who wear kitty headphones.

I wonder if she can purr.

I grab her cheek and caress it softly. "Talk ... or I'll make your pussy speak."

She shudders in place but keeps her mouth shut.

So I slide my hand from her cheek all the way to where the seam of her dress begins and slowly lower it, sliding my fingers inside. She hisses when I grip her tit and pinch her nipple.

"You still want to stay silent?" I ask.

I toy with her nipple, circling it, tugging at it until I spot her taking a gasp.

So I lean in and whisper, "You're going to make noise ... whether it's words or a moan, I will hear you."

My other hand slides down her body until I reach her fishnet stockings.

RIP!

It comes undone at the seams easily, and I tear it all away until there's one big gaping hole. And a pair of panties begging me to take them off.

She attempts to cross her legs, but I push them apart and stand between them. My hand dives in, and I press one finger onto her clit.

Just like that, she sucks in another breath.

"Not so strong now, are you?" I muse, slowly circling her slit until she begins to writhe in Felix's arms. "So sensitive. So ... needy."

"Shut up," she sneers out of nowhere.

My brow rises. "Oh, the little slut can talk?"

She immediately slams her lips shut again and attempts to wriggle loose from Felix's grasp, but he's much stronger than she is. But we all know that, including her. She just wants to pretend.

Pretend to be strong.

Pretend to want to escape.

But secretly, she wants nothing more than to submit.

I flick my fingers along her sensitive parts through the fabric of her panties until I find a wet spot. I slide my finger through, and her whole body tenses up. "Already wet for my finger now? Tsk. So easy." I lean away and lick my lips. "I wonder how hot you can get."

I fish my lighter from my pocket and turn on the flame.

Her eyes flicker in the light, pupils dilating quickly.

I bring the flame closer and closer to her little pussy, right underneath that pretty little fucking black dress of hers that I'm dying to burn away so I can see what's underneath.

"NO!" she shrieks, fighting off Felix to no avail. "What do you want?"

"Tell us why the fuck your sister had pictures of the whole school in her diary," Felix rasps into her ear. "I want to know all her fucking secrets and yours."

"I don't know why. I never asked her," she says through gritted teeth.

"How did you get your hands on that diary, then?"

"She left it for me after her death," she says, swallowing. "Why the fuck are you asking me any of this? I don't fucking know why she did what she did, okay?"

I tilt my head, pulling away the lighter just a little. The flame was enough to motivate her to talk, but her answers won't help us at all.

"How the fuck do you even know my sister? You weren't even in the same class," she says, incensed. "Did you bully her too?"

I burst out into laughter. "Bully?"

"Yeah, you three are fucking bullies, and you know it," she says, staring me down. "It was you boys, wasn't it? She killed herself because of you."

My whole body grows frigid. "Because of us?"

"You were there that night of the bonfire!" she yells.

"We didn't make her fucking jump."

"She left me a fucking note calling you out."

What?

A note?

There's more than that diary?

Felix shakes his head and momentarily releases her from his grip to rub his face.

Suddenly, she whips out a knife and cuts his arm. He yelps and loses his grip entirely.

I lunge forward to grab her, but she kicks me in the nuts.

Fuck.

That hurts.

I bend over, heaving, trying to keep the pain from making me vomit.

She runs up the steps to the back of the auditorium.

"Get back here," Felix growls, chasing after her.

I can't fucking move, but Alistair is in pursuit too. "Fuck, you let her go!"

"She fucking cut me again," Felix snarls back.

I groan from the pain, trying to move, but it's impossible. God, her kicks hurt like hell. She must've trained them.

But there's no way she can escape, not without the keys.

She kicks the doors so hard that a dent appears, and I'm impressed. "Don't let her escape," I call out.

She looks around as Felix and Alistair approach from behind.

"Give up, Pen," Felix snarls. "You're not going anywhere until we finish with you."

"I'm not letting you put one finger on me," she growls back, and she runs for the emergency case on the wall against the left wall, knocking in the window with the back of her knife. Without a second thought, she pulls the fire alarm.

My eyes widen. Fuck. We didn't take it into account ...

The fire alarm begins to fill the hallways.

The doors click.

Our eyes connect.

And she immediately dashes for the door.

Alistair runs up the final steps, but she grabs a chair and chucks it at him.

He ducks away, caught between two chairs and a desk.

And as Felix runs up behind her, she throws open the door and bolts out.

Seconds later, the sprinklers go off, immediately dousing the flame in my lighter and all our clothes.

Felix roars with rage and grabs the seat Alistair is stuck in and throws it at the wall. Then he helps him get up, and they both peer out the door while I finally manage to make my way up the stairs with soaked clothes.

But no one is left because hundreds of students are all rushing for the exits, thinking it's a lockdown of the school because of an actual fire.

"We lost her again," Alistair mutters. "What if she talks?"

"She won't," Felix says, clenching his teeth. "She wants the same thing we do."

Alistair narrows his eyes at me. "Answers?"

A smirk forms on my lips. "Revenge."

13

DYLAN

"So you're telling me you didn't pull that fire alarm?" my father asks as he taps his fingers on the desk.

"No, I told you already," I reply, leaning back in my seat.

"Get that smugness off your face," he barks. "You three were the only ones visible on the cameras."

"I told you, there was a girl," I say.

He slams his hand down onto the desk. "I warned you to fucking stop with those girls." He points at me. "Those girls will be the end of your education. Your job. This legacy that I've built from the ground up." His gaze lowers. "Your fucking life."

I make a face. "Gee, Dad, thanks for the threat."

"You think I'm joking, but this is fucking serious. You should be happy I'm still allowing you to step foot on this campus after what you and your friends did."

Now he's going too far.

My fingers claw at the seat. "We didn't do shit."

"A girl died. And you were involved," he growls.

I keep my mouth shut, but I'm boiling with rage.

"I don't care what your reasoning behind all this bullshit is. But this needs to stop." He grinds his teeth. "Today."

I get up and march to the window to stare outside. I can't stand to look at him one second longer. I'm getting blamed for something

I didn't even fucking do. It's always the same shit with my father. He always thinks I'm the bad guy.

"Sit your ass down. I wasn't finished yet," he says.

"I am."

I hear his chair scoot back, but I'm not afraid. Not anymore.

No amount of pain he ever dished out comes close to what I've already endured.

He stands behind me, staring out the window with me.

But all I can focus on is Penelope, sitting there in the grass with her friends, watching the firefighters check if there really is a fire they need to put out. Like a perfect angel.

Innocent.

Liar.

He places a firm hand on my shoulder. "Is that her?"

I nod.

"And you think one simple girl is worth risking everything I've given you?"

I sigh out loud. "It's Eve's sister."

I can feel him freeze up, and his fingers dig into my skin. "Stay. Away."

***

PENELOPE

The whole school was in an uproar over who pulled the fire alarm, but obviously, I'm not going to tell anyone it was me.

Especially not now that the three boys have been called into the dean's office. One day, that's all it took for the officials to find the "culprits."

I'm lucky the cameras only pointed at the doors, or everyone would've seen Dylan put his hands on my body. I still can't get it off my mind, even now, a day later. It's as if his fingers left a mark on my skin, despite the fact that he didn't even ... touch me.

All he did was fondle me through the fabric of my panties, but it was enough to make me soaking wet.

Fuck.

I hate how easily my body gives in to physical touch.

I sigh and try to focus on my homework, but it's hard when that devilish face keeps popping up into my memories, that devious smile, and those fingers rolling through his metallic blond hair.

No wonder girls fawn all over them.

Something about those guys is magnetic.

Something ... unforgettable, that's for sure.

I roll my eyes. Look at me, all ridiculous and shit.

They're fucking bullies. That's what they are, plain and simple.

He tried to fucking set fire to my fishnets. Who does that? Like you have to be insane to think that's okay. Or hot.

I swallow down the lump in my throat and open a new browser window. I have to find out more about these boys. They knew Eve, I'm sure of it now. I just don't know how. Maybe she fell for them, and they laughed in her face. Perhaps they hurt her in a way that made her want to end things.

My fingers dig into the palm of my hand, but I push my feelings aside and search until I find some information. There's not much to find about Alistair, but I can find the name Caruso all over. And it makes my jaw drop.

Because Dylan's father's picture pops up, and he's posing right in front of this fucking school with an award in his hands and a smile on his face. Spine Ridge University dean.

That's him.

That's the man Dylan spoke to when I listened to their conversation.

Oh my God, no wonder they're allowed to get away with so much bullying and violence. They punched a dude into the wall, literally trapped me on school grounds several times, and not to mention the bonfire, which is close to school grounds ...

Dylan's father must've been giving them a pass.

Fuck.

I slam my fist onto the table.

I click to the next website search I was doing and find Felix's father as well. Mr. Rivera, billionaire with several companies under his belt, including a very famous private club called RIVERA that's all over the world, a major retailer selling clothes, and of course Spine Ridge University board member.

My fingers squeeze the mouse so hard I almost break it.

Goddammit.

This explains so much.

Suddenly, something is slid under my door.

I check and frown, confused. "Kayla?"

She told me she was going out to a restaurant with Crystal, but maybe they came back early.

Still, there's no response, so I get up from my seat and pick up the package. It's badly packed in recycled paper with only a wire keeping it all together. I pull apart the wire and the paper comes apart.

I shriek and drop it all to the floor.

Inside is a note covered in blood.

I know you're Eve's sister. I've seen you around campus. Watch yourself. Or you might end up facing the same fate.

I immediately open the door and run out. "Who was that?"

In the back of the hallway, a girl runs away, and I immediately go for the chase. Without shoes and in my pajamas, I bolt through the hall, ignoring the many faces peeking out the doors to see what all the ruckus is about.

I rush down the stairs while the girl is already ahead, running through the common living room. I follow her all the way to the kitchen and out the back door into the dark of the night.

I finally catch up with her a few steps away from the sorority and jump on top of her.

We fall into the grass, and I fight her for control while she shrieks like a banshee. When I've finally pinned her to the ground, I see who it is.

Sadie.

The girl my sister once fought with.

I grasp her by the hair and growl, "Did you put that note under my door?"

She whimpers. "Please don't hurt me. Please!"

"Was it you? Did you make her jump?" I seethe in her ear.

She cries out, "What? Who?"

"Eve!"

I pull her hair again. "No! Jesus. Why would you even—"

"Then why did you leave that note?" I interrupt.

"I was told to do it!" she screams.

"Bullshit!" I slam her face into the mud.

"No, it's the truth. Please, you gotta believe me!" She's crying real tears now, but I don't know if they're sincere or if it's because she got caught.

"Some guy told me to put that under your door. I didn't know what was inside," she adds.

"What's his name?" I grit.

"Nathan," she replies. "I don't know his last name. He's one of my classmates at Business and Hospitality."

Nathan? Where have I heard that name before?

Maybe it's in the diary. I should check it out and see if it's legit.

Maybe he's the one responsible for my sister's death.

My nostrils flare, and after a final push, I get off the girl.

She spins around and crawls backward away from me. "Jesus Christ. You literally attacked me."

I flick my hands, shaking off the mud as I stare into her eyes. "The fucking package he made you shove underneath my door contains blood."

Her whole face turns white, and she looks like she's about to vomit.

The door behind me slams open again, but I pay no attention to the girls swarming out of the sorority.

"Girls!" The sorority leader, Tilda, steps forward. "Did you forget about rule number one? No fighting."

I gaze at Sadie, threatening her with a look.

She's got the wrong one if she thinks she can mess with me.

"It's fine," Sadie suddenly mutters to Tilda. "We were ... fighting over a boy."

Tilda frowns and then bursts out into laughter. "Girls... boys are never, ever worth it. Trust me."

Two people approach from the side of the road, Kayla and Crystal. When they see us, they immediately come running toward me. "What happened here?" Crystal asks, eyeing the girl behind me.

Sadie gets off the ground after two girls from the sorority help her. "I'm okay," she says, patting down her clothes. "It's only a little mud. No worries."

She's trying to play it off.

Good.

Because if she gets me fucking kicked out of this sorority, she'll be in far deeper shit than she already is.

"It won't happen again. I promise," I say.

"Well, you've broken a rule now, so I have to punish you both," Tilda says, rubbing her lips together. "But we'll talk tomorrow. Get some rest first. And no more fighting, or it'll turn into an actual suspension. Understood?"

I quickly reply, "Yes."

Sadie nods.

I don't want to get kicked out over trying to find out what happened to my sister, so I'll have to do things more secretly from now on. Keep my cool. No more losing my temper.

Although, I now finally have an actual lead.

Sadie walks around me, avoiding getting too close for fear of a punch. I'd probably do the same if I was her.

Kayla approaches and grabs my arm. "Did you two fight?"

I nod. "She shoved a note underneath my door."

She frowns. "Oh ... okay. Well, that doesn't seem like a big deal."

I sigh out loud and wait until the rest of the sorority girls have gone back inside before I pull her to the side. "Look, I can't explain it, but something evil is going on at this university."

Kayla listens intently while Crystal looks confused.

I sigh again and rub my forehead. Guess I'm going to have to tell them. "This summer, my sister killed herself."

"Oh, I'm so sorry for your loss," Kayla says, her face softening. "No wonder you were crying."

I avert my gaze. "She was bullied, and I feel like someone's responsible for her death."

Kayla gasps. "Oh shit."

"Are you sure?" Crystal asks.

"She left me a diary, and I'm pretty sure the people she mentioned were part of her choice."

"Wow," Crystal says, flabbergasted by my story.

Kayla frowns. "So this fight with Sadie ..."

"She pushed a bloody note under my door with a threat on it."

"Oh Jesus. Bloody?" Crystal slaps her hand in front of her forehead. "This is way above my comfort level."

"Calm down, Crystal. We don't know anything yet," Kayla says.

"What if it's the Mafia?" Crystal says.

I shush her. "Not so loud."

She blushes. "Sorry."

"Point is ... I'm going to find out whoever was responsible for the fact that my sister felt she needed to end it all. And that note is all the proof I need."

"Are you going to go to the police?"

I mull it over for a second.

Any normal student would under normal conditions. But nothing about this university or my sister's death is normal, and if I did go to the police, I'll definitely become their next target.

Whoever's behind this wants me to stop looking, wants me to stop putting the spotlight on them. So I'll have to take things from a different route. Be inconspicuous and under the radar.

But I won't be able to do it on my own.

"I'll think about it," I answer.

Crystal parts her lips. "But if it's a threat, you have to—"

"I don't want to cause any more problems," I interject. "I have enough as is."

"Oh, right," Crystal says.

"You do what you feel is best," Kayla says, and she rubs my arm. "But I have to say, you're racking up a lot of enemies for a freshman."

I laugh. "Well, I'm ready to knock them out if they try me."

Crystal snorts. "Yeah, we saw that." She eyes the sorority's front door.

"Oh, Sadie will be fine," Kayla replies. "It's not like she's so fucking nice to begin with."

I almost choke on laughter now.

"Wow, you guys have some enemies too, huh?" I say as we go back inside.

Kayla rolls her eyes. "Don't even mention her fucking name. I'm glad you tore some hair out."

Crystal leans in and whispers, "That girl once tried to rip Kayla's hair out of her scalp because she thought Kayla had kissed her crush."

"She deserved this, just saying," Kayla says as we walk up the stairs. "Well, anyway, let's go to bed. Sleep on it," she tells me.

I nod and yawn, but I'm not sure I'll be able to sleep tonight.

Someone's made me a target now.

And I'm not gonna let this rest.

I will find that fucking Nathan guy, and when I do, he'd better pray for mercy ...

Because I'll stop at nothing to avenge my sister.

14

PENELOPE

Months ago

"Oh my God, it hurts!" I squeak, trying not to look, but it's hard when the needle keeps puncturing my skin. God, it makes me want to pull my hand back.

"It's almost done," Eve says. "You can do it."

"Did yours hurt this much too?" I ask.

"Yup, but it's worth it," she says.

"Fuck," I growl, and even the tattoo artist laughs.

Finally, it stops, and he wipes off the excess ink. "All done."

I breathe out a sigh of relief as I sit up straight, feeling a little woozy in the head. "Phew."

"Look at it," Eve says.

I hold up my arm and admire the beautiful calligraphy. "Eve."

"Now we finally match!" she squeals, and she hugs me tight.

Her arm was tattooed in the same calligraphy font with my name, and we push our arms together to admire them in the mirror at the back of RINGO's shop.

"Satisfied?" the tattoo artist asks.

"It's perfect," Eve says. "Right, Pen?"

I nod, and I hug her tight. "Thank you, I love it."

"Well, you gave this to me last year, so I figured I'd repay the favor," she says, laughing.

"I deserve it," I jest back, winking.

"Now let's go eat some fucking cake. We've got a birthday to celebrate."

She pinches my ass and then walks off to pay at the cash register before we both walk out of the shop.

"Man, it stings so much," I say as we make our way down the street.

"It'll calm down. Keep the clear tape on, though," she says.

"Did your other one hurt that much too?"

"What? This one?" She points at a small circular line on her hand. "Not really. It's too tiny."

I smirk at her self-assuredness. She's so much like me it almost hurts because it's like watching myself in a mirror. "What does it mean anyway?"

Her eyes briefly widen before she averts them and laughs it off. "Oh, it's nothing. I was testing if I could do a real tattoo, so it needed to be something tiny and ... insignificant."

"Oh," I reply. I thought it'd be more important. Oh well.

A shiny new ring draws my attention, and I gasp as I grab her hand. "That's gorgeous! Where'd you get it?"

She blushes. "Oh, I got it from one of my besties at university."

"For your birthday?"

She pauses and looks at me for a moment. "Uh, yeah. Of course."

It's almost as if she forgot.

At least she'll never forget us both getting each other tattoos as a gift. Her name on my skin and my name on hers, a forever reminder of our bond.

And I can't wait to show Mom and Dad.

Suddenly, she whips out a card. "Look what I have."

I take the card and look at it. "Eve Richards. Age ... twenty-one?"

I look up at her beaming smile. "Awesome, right?" She snatches it right back out of my hand. "Had them made a couple of days ago."

I frown. "Them?"

She rummages in her pocket and holds out another one. "Tada! Happy birthday, Pen."

I take the fake ID from her, staring at my photo on the card. "Oh my God ..."

"Awesome, right?" She wraps her arm around me as a smile forms on my lips.

We're not old enough to go out drinking yet but we are old enough to get tattoos. But this ... this is definitely a game changer.

Eve winks at me. "Now, who's ready to go on our first-ever real party tonight?"

Suddenly, her stomach rumbles, and we both look at each other before we burst out into laughter. "Okay, but first ... let's get that freaking cake."

***

FELIX

Present

Music calms my violent soul.

Loud bass, low voice, just the type of sound I need to stop the surge of adrenaline flowing through my veins.

I grab the straw off the table and snort up some of the cocaine, getting high as fuck in front of everyone, even the servers.

Here in one of my father's clubs downtown, RIVERA, I can do whatever the fuck I want without repercussions because the manager knows better than to get in the way of his boss's son.

Besides, everyone who gets into the VIP room is rich as fuck, and rich fuckers don't fucking care about any rules. And neither do I.

I lean back and enjoy the show. On the stage in front of us, a bunch of girls are dancing around a pole. One of them slowly takes her top off, flaunting it in the air before chucking it at Dylan.

He puts his fingers in his mouth and whistles at her, then puts them in front of his lips and sticks his tongue through, pretending to lick her pussy.

I roll my eyes. Always the fucking flirt, even with girls he doesn't want.

"What?" Dylan retorts when he sees my face.

"You make me sick sometimes," I reply.

"I'm just having fun," he says. "You should try it sometime. You're beginning to look like a corpse. Maybe it would bring your black heart back from the dead."

"Too late. I'm already in hell."

I look away, but all I see is pussy on dick everywhere.

This club doesn't shy away from private dances. It's the full monty, including lip service, and I don't mean the agreeable kind. But I don't want to watch some random dude getting a BJ in the club.

All it does is remind me of those sweet fucking lips of that dirty little slut named Penelope wrapped around my shaft.

I close my eyes and sigh, taking in the music and letting myself slowly sink away into oblivion. Because all of that is better than having to think about the one girl I should not be thinking about.

Again and again, she creeps into the forefront of my mind with that fucking diary of hers.

Why did she want it back so desperately she was willing to get on her knees for me?

Is there information in there about Eve's death?

"Jesus, you look like you're about to kill someone. Lighten up," Dylan tells me. "You normally love this. What's changed?"

"Penelope."

"She's messing with your head," Alistair says, taking a sip of his drink.

"Better stay away for now," Dylan says. "I don't want to get on Dad's bad side again."

"Scared?" Alistair jokes, raising his brow at Dylan.

"Some girl isn't worth losing my entire life for," he retorts, chugging down his drink too.

"It is for me," I say stoically.

"Don't let her get under your skin," Alistair says.

"Too late."

I sit up straight and stare at the stage, ignoring the girls who make their way toward us.

"Oh, look," Alistair says. "Boobs."

"Like you ever cared about those," Dylan jests, and he winks at Alistair.

"Hey, I don't discriminate." Alistair sticks out his long tongue that could make any fucking girl spread her legs.

The girl dances her way toward Dylan, and he tucks a wad of cash under her thin string. She starts dancing in front of him, sweeping her thick boobs along his face while bobbing her ass up and down, and he slaps it when she makes a turn. She puts his hands on her ass and starts twerking like crazy, and Dylan gets all fired up, grinning like the horny motherfucker he is.

Alistair keeps staring at him like he's jealous the girl chose him.

But I couldn't care less.

And when the girl on stage stops twirling the pole and makes her way to me, probably thinking she could get some quick cash, I turn my head. But she still tries to sit down on my lap.

I throw her off, and she falls to the ground. Audible gasps erupt in the VIP room. The girl throws me a snooty look and scoffs. "Fuck your money, scrawny bastard."

I grab her by the throat and lean in. "The name's Felix Rivera."

Her eyes widen. "Bu-bu... that's this club's ... name."

"Exactly." I throw her back to the floor, and she crawls away slowly, then scrambles to her feet and rushes to the back of the VIP section, disappearing into the dressing room.

"Jesus, relax a little," Dylan tells me.

"I'm not here to touch some titty," I say.

"The only tits he's interested in are Penelope's," Alistair jokes. "But those are the only titties he's never going to get."

I pull my gun out of my pocket and point it right at his forehead.

Everyone's suddenly screaming, and they all run out of the VIP section, including Dylan's private dancer, but I don't fucking care.

"Penelope. Is. Mine."

Alistair stares me down but then sighs out loud. "Fine. I don't fucking care." He looks away and folds his arms.

I slowly lower my gun and tuck it back where it belongs. We're all alone in the VIP section now.

"Now I lost my fucking tiddies too," Dylan scoffs. "Goddammit, Felix. Really?"

"Got the whole damn university throwing themselves at your feet, and you want to stick your dick up some whore you have to buy?"

"Because she doesn't know me. It's more fun when they don't want me," Dylan retorts, sighing out loud as he leans back in his seat. "I think you can relate."

My eyes twitch, and I look away again, back at the pole, even though no one is dancing. But I don't need some random girl dancing around the pole to get excited. Because in my mind, I see a girl twirling right in front of me, slowly peeling off her clothes while having eyes only for me, her purple hair sweeping from left to right across her shoulders as she tilts that pretty fucking head just the way I like it.

"You know, I think it's about time we kicked up some dust at the university. Have a filthy fucking party right on campus grounds," Dylan muses.

"Oh, it's Halloween soon," Alistair adds. "Perfect for a disgustingly rich fuck fest."

"Oh yeah, I love it already," Dylan says, licking his lips.

"Knew you would," Alistair says, snorting. "Of course, only you can come up with this, even when your dad already hates our guts."

"Eh, fuck him. He doesn't care about a party at the frat house. He's too busy running that boring university."

Dylan grabs the paper and takes a big sniff of the coke, getting high as a kite.

But even though I took some, I don't ever get addicted to drugs, or to alcohol, and not even to life.

There is only one thing I can ever get addicted to.

Vicious little whorish girls I can bend and degrade.

And I know a girl like that will definitely show up at a Halloween party, ready to kill.

15

PENELOPE

I make my way through the hallways of the university on a mission to find that fucking Nathan guy, wherever he is. All I have to go off is the picture my sister put in her diary, but I've got it imprinted in my retina. I'll find the fucker someday. He can't hide forever after sending me that fucking note.

My sister never mentioned Nathan to me, and his spot in the diary is tiny. Why wouldn't she talk more about him if he was the bully who made her jump?

"What course did we have again?" I ask Crystal to stop myself from overthinking things.

Crystal checks her schedule. "We're both going to Financial Risk Management. It's just around the corner."

Crystal and I share this class and one other with Kayla, so she sees this as a prime opportunity to get to know all about me. But I'm not the kind of girl to simply dish out everything there is to know about me. Because people always have ulterior motives, and anything I say can and will be used against me.

I come to an abrupt halt in the middle of the hallway, where Alistair tacks a piece of paper onto a bulletin board hanging from the wall. He glances over at us.

Fuck.

I hide behind a pillar and pull Crystal with me.

"Whoa, Pen, what's going on?" she asks. "Who did you see?"

"Alistair."

Her eyes widen. "Those Society boys?"

I put my finger in front of my mouth.

When I lean sideways to gaze at Alistair, he smirks and casually saunters off, pinning more of the papers as he goes.

Goddammit, he saw us.

No point in hiding.

"He's gone now," I say, turning around the corner of the pillar.

I head straight for the bulletin board and snatch the paper off. It's an invitation to a Halloween party.

My heart begins to thrum.

"Oh wow, no, absolutely not. God no." Crystal laughs while I stare at the note. "Wait, you're not actually thinking of going there, are you?"

This is perfect.

"Pen, please tell me you're not going to that party," Crystal says.

"He put this here for me to find," I say.

She grabs my shoulders. "Pen, listen to me. All those boys have the money and power to make anyone disappear. If you get in their way, if they think you're a threat, they'll destroy you."

My nostrils flare. "They can fucking try."

I need to be there. If I can't find that Nathan guy here on campus, I'll definitely find him at a party hosted by the three richest fuckers in this university. And it's a Halloween party too, with mandatory Halloween outfits.

A smirk forms on my face.

I guess it's time to go back to that serpent's den.

***

I pull up the bustier of this bright red and black costume that looks more like some erotic underwear for pleasure. The only reason I'm wearing this is because I know they won't let me into the building if I don't. One of the stipulations on the note I snatched off the bulletin board. *Dress sexy*.

Well, if they want sexy, they can get fucking over-the-top sexy ... my way.

I pop my lips and apply some thick red lipstick and a black lip liner to create an ombre look, then put on my eyelashes. And finally, I draw on some blood droplets. When I'm done, I lean back and look at myself in the mirror. With this cape and these bloody marks around my mouth, I look like a certified vampire on the way to her next victim.

Perfect.

I grab my purse and check if I have everything like my phone and my trusted knife that I've used several times before when I needed protection. A gift I once received from my father who didn't know what to get his girl for her birthday. It turns out, it was the best idea ever.

With a smirk on my face, I march out of the bathroom and head straight for the door.

"Whoa, where're you going looking like that?" Kayla asks as she pauses the show she was watching on her laptop.

"A party," I reply.

"You don't mean the one at the Skull & Serpent Society frat house, right?" She throws some popcorn into her mouth.

"That's the one."

She almost chokes on some kernels. "What? No, you've got to be joking. They're the worst. Do you even know what you're getting yourself into? Like their parties are legit known as the place where people go to get fucked up and possibly even die."

"I'm going to try to find this Nathan guy there. It's a party. It can't be that bad."

She laughs. "They've literally hazed people to death."

"This isn't a hazing," I reply, putting on my sky-high black heels.

"So? People die. It's a thing there. Not even to mention all the drugs and alcohol involved." She rolls her eyes. "I mean, I've been to a few parties, but those guys?" She makes a funny face. "They're really into some fucked-up, lewd shit."

"I'll be in and out. That's it," I say, opening the door.

She sighs. "You sure you don't need me to come with you?" She crawls off the bed in her pajamas and nightcap. "Because I will. I just have to put on some shoes."

I chuckle. "No, it's fine. Go watch your show. Don't worry about me. I'll be fine."

"Okay, if you say so," she replies as I close the door. "But call me if something happens, and I'll come out with my tits swinging!"

I snort. "Thanks, Kayla! See you later."

I run down the hallway, ignoring the many looks I get as I pass open doors, and I rush down the steps and out the door. The air is chilly outside for an October night, and I definitely didn't dress for the weather. I dressed to impress.

I dress to lure in boys like Nathan, who do bad things and think they can get away with it.

And when I finally get close enough ... I'll bite his fucking head off.

***

DYLAN

Chilling on the couch with two girls in my arms and amazing music playing over the speakers is just the way I like to spend a night. This Halloween party couldn't have been better planned. All the food, booze and drugs you could ever want at our fingertips, casually scattered across the house on several tables, along with cups and snorting strips. I've got people covered together with Alistair, who bought most of it. He stole a few bottles here and there. Not because we can't afford it but because it gets him off like nothing else.

We're all a little crazy in this fucked-up house.

In fact, it's a fucking requirement for anyone who wants to join.

The Skull & Serpent Society only accepts people willing to go beyond depravity. They get a hazing filled with obscenity, filth, and body fluids. Just like any of our gatherings.

The cost is steep.

But the price?

Immeasurable.

This Society is the home of all future CEO's, world leaders, and generations of the ultra rich.

Everyone wants to be here, even the fucking girls, who can't ever get in since it's a boys-only club. The only exception is for a party like now.

Everyone ... except one fucking girl.

I take a drag of the pot the girl on one of my knees offers me, and she giggles when I blow the smoke out in her face. The other girl starts rubbing my chest, wriggling her fingers underneath my expensive smoking so she can twirl my red tie around her finger.

"Hey," the other girl says, and she grabs my coat too, shoving the other girl's hand away. "I was first."

I laugh and put my hands on both their asses, my dick already growing hard as a rock just from their display of jealousy. "Girls. Girls. There's plenty to share."

"There's always more room here," Alistair comments from the couch across from me, patting the red leather on his left side. To his right, a girl gently caresses his chest, while sometimes trying to peel away the mask, which he immediately blocks.

"Always ready to steal, huh?" I reply.

A smug grin follows. "It's what I do best."

He licks his lips and eyes down the girls as one of them begins to touch my hard-on, and he bites his lip.

He whispers something into the ear of the girl sitting next to him. She promptly glances my way before she begins to touch his thighs, creeping closer and closer to his crotch.

I smirk.

I enjoy a challenge.

Felix suddenly appears behind Alistair, and he puts his hands on both ends of the couch. "What do you two think you're doing?"

Ali's girl quickly crawls off him and runs off to dance with some-one else.

"Enjoying the fucking party," Alistair responds, "which you now ruined. Thanks."

Felix pulls out a knife from underneath his hoodie and holds it over his neck.

"You think I'm threatened by a knife?" Alistair says, and he literally leans into the blade until he begins to bleed. "I live with you for fun."

Felix pauses and then retracts the knife. "Wouldn't expect anything else from a fucker like you."

Then he turns his gaze to me. "Stop jerking off. We've got work to do."

The two girls slowly drape away from me.

I frown, annoyed. "Work? What the fuck?"

I was just about to enjoy a very public jerk-off session, and now all I'm left with are blue balls. He'd better have a good explanation.

"I'm about to combust here, Felix." I get up from the couch to follow him. "Can't you give us a break?"

"You think two girls touching you is ecstasy?" he asks as we walk through the sea of people and into the giant hallway. "Save your fucking jizz. I've got something better."

"Like what?" Alistair chimes in. He's followed us unseen. I'm always surprised when he manages to do that. It still makes me jumpy.

Felix takes us aside in a secluded corner of the Society, near the library. "Penelope. I saw it on the cameras. She's here. And I'm going to fucking find her."

16

PENELOPE

A guy at the front door of the Skull & Serpent Society checks me out with narrowed eyes, then waves me through, allowing me in. I don't wait a second before I slither past, afraid he might double-check and deny me access. Luckily, he's too busy talking to three girls with blond wigs and Barbie costumes who were waiting behind me.

I go inside and gaze around at all the decorations, letting the booming music guide my way. It's bustling with people, chitchat filling every damn area of the building. Even the staircases are taken, with only a narrow path available to get upstairs. Someone is in every corner, whether they're smoking pot, drinking heavy booze, or hooking up.

And I don't mean just kissing ... I mean full-on body gripping, panty-ripping, tit-squeezing, dick-grinding action. Against the concrete support beams, on the expensive leather seat sprawled around the hallway, in the closet behind the staircase, and even on the fucking floor.

My eyes instinctively slide up to the cameras hanging all around the premises. Someone must be watching all of this action going down with their hands down their pants.

I hope they don't spot me.

I swallow and push ahead, keeping my eyes focused on the target, no matter how hot it gets.

I've been to Halloween parties before, but never ones this explicitly horny.

In front of me is a big party room that's jam-packed with people, the scent of sweat, smoke, and sex filling my nostrils. That must be where the main part of the party is taking place.

I wonder if Nathan's there.

"Drink?"

I almost jolt up and down from the sudden voice in my ear.

Someone's right behind me with three cups. "Damn, they've got servers here?"

The guy laughs. "No, I'm a pledge. We help out with parties."

I grab one of his cups, wondering what's inside. "Ah, so this is part of the hazing?"

He nods. "The nicer side."

What does that even mean? "Nicer?"

"Yeah, the bad shit comes later."

"What kind of bad shit?" I ask.

He shrugs. "Oh, they make you drink some laced stuff. There's some nude runs, beer throwing, lots of chugging, a pissing contest, some more drinking. Anyway, that's what I've heard. I've yet to go through it. This is my second day."

I've seen the beer-throwing thing. Not something I'd want someone to do to me. But I doubt that's the worst they can do.

"Well, good luck with that. Thanks for the drink," I reply, and I walk off.

"You're welcome! If you need more, you know where to find me," the guy yells after me.

But I pour his drink into the first potted plant I can find. No way am I touching any of these because next thing I know, I'll be stumbling through the streets, blacked out from it being laced.

No thanks.

I head into the main room, overwhelmed by how many people are here. People dance and bump into each other, grinding away to the music. Booze is flung around and lands on someone's dress, but no one seems to care. They all cheer, and some guy even starts licking it off her skin.

I turn the other way and head into the room on the left. A kitchen that's barely recognizable as the entire counter is covered with bottles of liquor. Two girls are making out on the sink, and I don't want to barge in on their fun, even though the place is filled with people.

I head back into the main room and look around, trying to focus.

That's when I spot that face I saw in my sister's diary.

Nathan.

He's going upstairs.

My eyes home in on him wearing that clear red hoodie that stands out among all the other people here, and I immediately go for the pursuit.

But there's a whole bunch of people in my way. I struggle to cram between the bumping bodies. The sweaty and hot place makes it hard to breathe as I push my way through the crowd.

By the time I get to the stairs, he's long disappeared. But he can't have gone outside, which means he must be in one of the rooms, and I'm going to find him.

I rush up the stairs, barely avoiding some beer spills on the steps. I step aside and pass by a couple making out on the banister. I go into the first room I find, but it's just some trashed student chamber filled with dancing people.

The next one is a random student's room, and someone crashed on the bed, vomit dripping down onto the carpet. Gross.

I head farther down the hallway and open the next door, but there's literally two boys on the bed having sex. Jeremy and Calvin. And I just busted in on them going ham on each other. Fuck.

"Sorry!" I say, blocking my eyes with my hand. "Wrong room."

"No worries, babe," Jeremy calls, laughing. "Just close the door, will you? Thanks."

"Of course," I reply, embarrassed.

I quickly run off to the last few doors in the hallway, but when I push the door handle, it's jammed. Locked. Fuck.

"Sorry, taken!"

Must be a bathroom.

I don't want to lose the opportunity to find Nathan, and there's a bunch of rooms up here that I haven't checked yet, so I move on. And the next door I open is the first one that isn't filled with people dancing or fucking around.

The room is huge, much larger than the other ones I've seen, and there's a lot of expensive-looking furniture. The closet is open, and I can spot the Armani from here. Jesus. Kayla and Crystal weren't lying when they said the Society guys were rich as fuck.

However, what surprises me more is the number of skulls in the room. Paintings, penholders, wallpaper, carpet—literally everything is decorated with skeletons. Like a literal reminder of death.

I walk farther into the dark room, ignoring the chill in my heart, and look around. I gently call out, "Hello? Anyone here?"

But there's no response.

There's another door in the back and a light is on. A private bathroom maybe?

I walk toward it, wondering if Nathan might be showering or taking a piss in there. I don't fucking care if his ass is hanging out or he's butt naked, I'm going to confront him about that fucking note, and I'm going to find out if he bullied my sister to death.

I grip the door and open it up.

There's no one inside.

What the fuck?

Suddenly, the door behind me closes.

The lock is turned.

In shock, I spin on my heels.

But the person standing in the door opening doesn't look anything like Nathan.

In fact, he isn't even wearing that red hoodie.

It's someone in a long black hoodie and a green Purge LED mask that turns the eyes into crosses with a terrifying smile that's sewed up.

In the dark, it's almost as if the face comes alive.

"Hello, Penelope."

Oh God.

That voice. I'd recognize it in a second.

Felix Rivera.

I knew there was a chance I'd bump into him during my search, but this is too much of a coincidence.

"How did you know I was here?" I say through gritted teeth.

He laughs, tilting his head, which makes the mask look super creepy. "I saw you looking into the cameras."

Shit. I'd forgotten about them.

Of course, he'd be looking through the footage.

"So you creep on your own guests?" I ask.

He steps forward, so I take one back. "I take every precaution ..."

Against unwanted guests? What a joke.

"Your buddy Alistair hung those invitations all around school. Not my fault I checked it out."

"You don't think that was intentional?"

He laughs again, and it's a visceral laugh that I can only describe as mania.

Just as chilling as the mask he's wearing on that stoic face of his.

"Oh, Penelope ... you have so much to learn." He puts his hand over his face, his fingers squeezing the mask, like he's holding himself back from tearing into me. "But I will fucking teach you."

A shiver runs up and down my spine.

He walks even closer, and I shudder in place, wondering if I should pull the knife on him. But if I do, things will go south very quickly. I have to time it right.

My eyes flick to the door. There's a keyhole. He must have the key in his pocket somewhere, and there's no way I'm going to unlock it without it.

"What are you doing here, Penelope?" he asks.

I suck in a breath. "Why do you care?"

"Because this is my room."

His room? Whoa. That only makes this skeleton room a whole lot scarier.

"And you're trespassing," he adds.

"I'm looking for someone," I say.

"Who and why?"

"Some guy called Nathan. And none of your business."

"Lesson number one ..."

His voice is dark. Heavy. Too heavy.

And I don't like the tone.

"Everything that happens in this house is my business."

Fine. I'll play along.

"Someone in your fucked-up Society bullied my sister," I spit. "And I'm going to find out who. Because they're responsible for her death."

His body tenses. "You accusing people of murder?"

I tilt my head, defiantly standing my ground. "Maybe I am."

He walks closer. Too close to my liking.

I clutch my bag tightly, but freeze when he gets up close and in my face until I can see his eyes behind that mask. His cologne penetrates my nostrils, reminding me of that time I was on my knees with him deep in my throat.

The mere memory sparks another flicker of pleasure, which I quickly tuck away, never to be spoken of out loud.

But in his eyes is that same glimmer, the same kind of wicked need I saw before.

And it makes my whole body erupt into goose bumps.

His hand suddenly anchors around my throat in a heartbeat.

I gasp, but the air refuses to escape.

Panic floods my veins, and he leans in to whisper into my ear, "Do you think I killed her?"

I don't know how to answer. I don't know the truth.

But I want to know. Desperately.

His grip slowly tightens around my neck. "Say it."

"Yes," I say.

He lets out a small snort. "I like it when you squeak."

His hand slowly moves toward my chin, and he grips it so tightly I can't escape. I've never feared for my life, but I do now.

What if he's the one who chased my sister off the cliff?

What if Nathan was just a ruse, a mailboy sent by Felix?

"Good girls don't get what they want," he groans, pushing down on my chin until my lips part. "Bad girls get what they deserve."

He sticks two fingers into my mouth, slowly sliding them across my tongue. I'm overtaken by confusion and the sudden surge of lust coursing through my body that I don't know how to even respond, let alone act.

With his fingers alone, he manages to subdue me. "Perfect," he groans. "Just needs a little training ..." He goes in so deep that I gag. "But you want to be a good little slut for me, don't you?"

Fuck. I can't let him do this again.

In a moment of clarity, I bite down.

He pulls out his fingers, grating against my teeth.

His blood drips down onto my tongue, and I spit it out.

"Such a fucking spitter ... it's about time someone taught you how to swallow," he growls.

"Fuck you," I say. And I rip open my bag and take out my knife, stepping away so he can't touch me. "Don't you fucking try."

He snorts. "You think I'm scared of a little cut?"

The fear coiling its way through my body turns me into a vicious girl. "I'll fucking slice off your balls."

"I'd love to see you try."

Suddenly, he lunges at me, and I jump aside, rushing to the window. I pick up a wooden chair and chuck it at the window, but it does nothing. Fuck.

"You think you can escape me?" Felix taunts. "Oh no, the fun is only just getting started."

"I'm not playing games with you," I say, and I run to a different window in the bathroom, where I stick my knife into the lock and crack it open by force.

The mechanism budges, and I slide it up, then jump out right as his hand wraps around my cape, hanging me.

Choking, I cough and heave, frantically tugging at the wire around my neck. Finally, it comes loose, and I fall down onto the emergency escape stairs. Above me, Felix clutches my cape tightly, roaring out loud.

"You're not getting away, Pen. Not this time."

I run down the shoddy metal staircase as fast as possible while Felix's head disappears from the window.

But I know it won't be the last time I see him.

Adrenaline races through my body as I rush down the last few steps and jump off into the garden beyond the house. But the back door slams open loudly. And it isn't only Felix casting a shadow in the bright lights behind him. Two others, one dressed in an all-black robe kept together by a rope with an eerie skull mask on, and another one wearing a black suit with a red tie and an Anubis wolf half-mask, the filthy grin underneath definitely belonging to Dylan.

It's them.

"You'd better run fast," Felix growls.

I don't hesitate before I run like hell.

17

PENELOPE

Within seconds, I hear their footsteps behind me.

My breath picks up as I race down the pavement and squeeze through a narrow crack in the university walls, heading straight for Priory Forest far beyond the school grounds.

"There's no place to hide from us!" Dylan yells, laughing like a crazed man on drugs.

He's right. I'm not safe anywhere. Not in my room. Not in the university. Not anywhere.

My mind guides me toward the trees, hoping and praying I might get away.

I went looking for Nathan and found three serpents lurking in their den, waiting for some prey to enter their domain. And I did it, willingly, knowing I could cross their path and be swallowed whole.

Fuck.

I should've stayed away.

Too late.

They're right behind me, chasing after me with grins on their faces.

This is a fucking nightmare come to life.

"Fuck yeah, run little whore, run as fast as you can!" Dylan roars, his Anubis wolf mask barely staying on.

I can't believe this is happening. They're fucking insane.

I have to get away, fast.

Past thick trees I bolt, jumping over stones and loose rubble lying in my way. No time for missteps, no time to glance over my shoulder.

But when I take one glimpse to my left, there's a wolf in a mask with a glint in his smile chasing me.

"I'm gonna fucking catch you!" he roars, closing in on me.

I veer to the right, but Alistair is right there, bolting through the woods, his skull mask glowing in the moonlight. Every tree a mere flicker of darkness as they both corner me.

I've never felt fear like I'm feeling it tonight.

Suddenly, a hand wraps around my arm and pulls me down on my side, my ass bumping onto a rock. I shriek as Felix knocks me farther down and crawls on top of me. I claw at his chest and punch him, but he quickly grasps my wrists and pins them in the mud.

The look on Felix's face is savage. "*Mine.*"

"What do you want?" I yell in his face. Even though he's wearing that creepy LED mask, I know he can see me. "Let me go!"

Dylan and Alistair lean over me, their masks even more terrifying from down below.

"I told you we'd catch you," Dylan says, tilting his head down to gaze at me.

"Nice outfit, Pen," Alistair says, staring at me with black-painted eyes. "Makes me wonder who you're going to suck this time."

"Fuck off!" I spit, fighting off Felix, but he's much stronger than I am. I reach into my bag, searching for the knife.

"Hold her down," Felix barks at his friends.

Alistair snatches my bag from my hand and throws it away. "You won't need this."

Then he and Dylan step on my arms until I howl with pain.

It hurts so bad, tears stain my eyes.

Felix roughly grabs my chin and forces me to look at him. "Let me see those tears, Pen." He leans in and his tongue dips out to lick the salty drops off my cheeks. "You look so fucking pretty when you cry."

"You're sick," I hiss, pulling my head away.

His fingers only clench harder, digging into my cheeks. "Yet you're the one who came to us."

"I told you I was looking for Nathan."

"Because he's in the diary?" he asks.

Of course they'd read through all of it. Fuck them.

"Because he left a fucking note under my door, and I need to know who's responsible for my sister's death!" I rasp. "And if it's one of you ..."

Dylan laughs. "If it was, what would you do? Kill us?"

Alistair bursts out into laughter.

"I'd sure as hell fucking try," I growl back.

They all laugh now.

"You're the first one to even dare to say it out loud," Dylan says. "I like it."

"Nathan didn't do it, did he? You're using him. You made her jump, and you're trying to cover it up," I say through gritted teeth.

Felix's eyes home in on mine, his body tensing against me. "You'd do anything for your sister, wouldn't you?"

I nod.

He tilts my face until our mouths are nearly aligned, and he leans in to lick the seam of my lips, only to lean back and whisper, "Then show me how far you're willing to go to find out the truth."

I gulp, ignoring the thrumming in my core.

Fuck these boys. They're only trying to use me.

When Felix pulls back, I spit on their boots. "Fuck you."

They smash their feet into my arms harder until the pain makes me groan out loud.

"Gladly," Felix replies. "When we're finished with you, you'll be creaming from all your fucking holes."

"Like I'd ever let you," I say.

"I think you will ..." The creepy LED mask on his face almost makes it look like he's smiling. "Because we're the only ones who can give you what you want."

"Just admit you made her jump," I snarl. "That's why you keep chasing me, isn't it?"

The boys laugh. "Don't you get it?"

Felix grabs me by the hair and lifts my head. "It wasn't us."

"What?" I gasp, confused as fuck. "You expect me to believe that?"

"We didn't make her jump," Alistair adds. "She was—"

"A friend," Dylan interjects.

A friend?

No. Fuck that. That can't be true.

Can it?

The three boys look at each other.

Felix drops my head on the ground. "You won't ever find out what happened to her on your own."

"Then help me!" I yell.

It's a last-ditch effort, but what else can I do?

He pauses and looks at his buddies, exchanging looks like they can talk without saying a single word.

Suddenly, he pulls a giant knife from his pocket and holds it underneath my chin. "Help you?" He tilts his head. "And what makes you think we want to?"

I shudder in place. Fuck, what do I say?

"You said she was a friend. Friends want to know why friends killed themselves."

I don't know what else to say. Even though I don't believe a word he said, maybe I can still convince them to help me instead of attempting to kill me.

Felix doesn't say a word.

"You want help?" he mutters after a while. The knife slowly drags down my neck, and I hold my breath. "Our help comes at a price." I swallow as the blade reaches the bust of my outfit. "So I'm going to ask you again ... what are you willing to do?"

"Anything."

POP!

The knife popped one of the buttons off the bust. My breasts are barely kept together by only two buttons now.

He slides the knife under the next one. "You want us to find the people responsible for your sister's death and destroy them?"

I nod.

POP!

The second one flies off, leaving only my nipples unexposed to the cold air ... and their hungry gazes.

"Then you will do everything we say," he growls.

"What does that even mean?" I ask.

"Anything and *everything* we want," Dylan adds, adding pressure to my arm until I squeak. "Our. Personal. Whore."

Fuck.

I knew they'd ask this, but hearing them say it out loud still brings chills to my body.

Felix pushes the blade underneath the final button. "Now what's it gonna be, Pen?"

I suck in a breath. "How long?"

"For as long as it takes to find the fuckers," Dylan says, running his fingers through his bleached hair. A filthy smirk forms on his face. "But by the time we finish with you ... you'll be begging for our cocks."

"I doubt that," I retort.

Felix pushes the tip of the knife into my skin, making me viscerally aware of my bad predicament. And that there might not be another option for me to get out of this alive.

Unscathed? Impossible.

I take another big gulp.

"Your body will belong to us," Felix adds. "Do we have a deal?"

Sweat drops roll down my forehead.

Not because of the answer.

But because of what they're going to do when I open my mouth.

"Yes."

It rolls off my lips so easily. As though I didn't just give my own life away.

But that word signifies the end of my conscience.

The end of my own damn sanity.

POP!

The bust gives way, and Felix immediately pushes aside the fabric to reveal my nipples to all of them. Dylan licks his lips at the sight, and Alistair even removes his mask for a moment.

"Damn, what I wouldn't give to suck those," Dylan mutters.

"Horny bastard," Alistair jests.

"But you know what? I fucking can because you're mine too now." Dylan removes his boot from my arm, only to bend over, grab my breast, and cover my nipple with his mouth.

And for a moment, I almost moan out loud—until he bites.

I try to punch him, but Felix thrusts the knife underneath my throat.

"Anything and everything, remember?" He leans in so close I can feel his breath on my skin, and his tongue dips out to drag a line across my cheek. "Little whore."

"Don't call me that," I say under my breath.

Felix covers my mouth with his hand. "I'll call you whatever the fuck I want. Because you're mine now, and I will do whatever the fuck I want with what's mine." He grips my other tit. "Now scream, little whore, scream." He twists it so hard I can't stop the yelp from coming out. "That's it. Give me all your pain and all your fucking tears."

"You're fucked up," I say.

"Oh, you haven't seen the worst yet," he retorts.

And he grips my face instead and slams his lips onto mine.

The kiss is overpowering, devouring, as if he wants to consume my very soul and take me to hell with him. With a forceful tongue, he pushes my lips open and claims my mouth, then bites my lip so hard I bleed.

He groans and licks up the blood, then gathers spit in his mouth.

"Open your fucking mouth," he says.

When I do, he dribbles it inside, and I can feel the warm juices roll down my tongue and into my throat.

"Attagirl," he says, and he pushes my mouth shut. "Now swallow."

It's disgusting. Heinous. Yet I still feel the urge to clamp my legs shut when he sits down on top of me with his hard-on poking my belly.

"You don't know what you've done, Penelope," Dylan says, sucking on my nipple like he can't get enough. "Oh, how many times I've dreamed of sucking these tits until you screamed my name."

"Hey, save me a slice too." Alistair removes his boot and walks all the way to my feet. He tilts his head sideways and says, "I can see your fucking panties from here. Did you dress for the occasion?"

"She's a vampire, can't you tell?" Dylan jokes.

Felix twists my nipple even harder until I can barely take it anymore. "She got ready to suck."

Suddenly, there's a hand near my panties, and I freeze completely. "Wait, that's—"

Felix plants a hand over my mouth. "Ours. And no one stands between us and the pussy we want."

A finger slides across my slit, feeling me up, toying with me straight through the fabric. And when I turn my head sideways, I can see the skull mask and its blackened eyes staring right back at me, like he enjoys getting caught.

"I wonder how wet she can get from us using her," Alistair murmurs.

His thumb circles my most sensitive spot, pressing harder and harder with each turn until it becomes hard to breathe.

When I said yes, I knew what it would entail.

What I'd sacrifice in order to know the truth.

But I wasn't prepared for how many sensations I'd feel all over my body.

And how badly I want to pretend I'm not getting wet.

"That's it ... getting all wet already just from a little tugging and toying," Alistair says.

"Oh, so you like getting used?" Dylan quips, licking his bottom lip.

"Knew you were a filthy one," Felix adds, and he pushes open my mouth. "Now open up. Vamps suck, don't they? Show me."

When my lips part, he shoves two fingers inside again and pushes all the way until I gag.

"Good. Lemme see those tears," he says.

He's a vicious bastard getting off on my tears.

Because I can feel him grow bigger against my skin. And from the corner of my eye, I can definitely see it too, straining against his pants.

"She's checking you out, Felix," Alistair says, still toying with me, making it insanely hard for me to concentrate on what's happening, instead of the growing desire building in my body.

"Oh, interested in the D already?" Dylan says. He releases my nipple and stands up. "Maybe it's about time we give her some, then."

My eyes widen when he pulls down his zipper.

Oh God, it's really happening.

"Lesson number two, Pen," Felix whispers into my ear. "Regret your choice? Too late. There's no taking it back."

18

PENELOPE

Felix gets up and walks to my feet, changing places with Alistair while Dylan casually pulls his long cock out of his pants. My eyes almost bulge out of my skull from the size of it.

"Finally ... my fucking turn," Dylan says, his voice laced with hunger.

I try to look away, but it's impossible when Dylan perches himself right on top of my chest, a hard-on and pointing right at my face. One single ring dangles from the tip.

When I try to push up, Alistair grabs my hands and pins them above my head.

"Oh no, not this time, little slut." Dylan grabs my face. He pulls a lighter from his pocket and flicks it on, the dancing flames drawing my attention when they hover closer and closer to my face. "Have you ever seen something burn so brightly that it set your fucking soul on fire?"

I shake my head. I don't know what he means.

He leans in, the flame dangerously close to the tip of my nose. "Burn for me."

I whimper as the fire heats up my skin, and my sweat builds. It's a kind of pain that could make a person beg. But that's exactly what he wants, and I'd rather swallow my words than please them.

"You're a fiery one, that's for sure," Dylan says as he lets the flames lick my cheek and neck. "Afraid of a little fire?"

I shake my head vehemently, denying my own fears.

I won't give them even a hint.

He leans in to whisper, "I can see you sweat, Penelope."

He pronounces my name like it's a piece of candy he just licked.

Alistair looks down at me too, licking his lips as though he's hungry just to watch me be used.

But what I'm most surprised by is the sudden hand on my pussy.

My eyes shoot up and between Dylan's thighs. Felix is bent through the knees, casually toying with me.

Oh God.

Dylan grins like a crazy motherfucker as his fingers pull down my lips until they part. "Now open those pretty fucking lips for me and show me what you can do with that tongue."

He pushes inside slowly but doesn't stop until he's completely inside to the hilt. I gag and choke on his length as pre-cum begins to lather my throat.

"Oh God," Dylan groans, and he pulls out briefly. "You weren't kidding, Felix."

"Use her," Felix growls back.

The pressure he applies to my clit is insane. I've never felt anything like this before. It's as if he knows exactly where to touch me to instantly make me want to clench my legs and scream.

But I won't, I refuse.

Dylan plunges back in without warning, his eyes rolling back into his head when he's in to the base.

"Fuck me, this is amazing," he groans. "Wrap your tongue around my cock and suck."

The onslaught of sensations makes it hard to concentrate.

"C'mon, slut, do what he says," Felix rasps, and he spanks my pussy so hard I squeal.

My opened mouth allows Dylan to sink in even deeper. "Good little slut," Dylan groans as my eyes water. "This throat is mine."

"God, you're going in deep," Alistair says, biting his lip when he looks down at my lips. "And here I was thinking she was just a fucking nosy potty-mouth. But that mouth is perfect to store some cum."

What? Oh God.

Panic floods my veins, but Alistair's hands hold me down. "Remember what Felix said. You're ours now. No take-backs."

"Exactly." Dylan thrusts in so deep I see stars. "Now let me own this fucking throat just like Felix did."

In an instant, the memory of him dragging my face through his cum floods my mind, mixing with the desire building in my body as Felix circles my clit. The confusion is too much, especially when Felix pulls aside my panties and shoves his fingers inside me.

"Wet already, little whore?" He thrusts inside like a madman. "All this just for some foreplay."

My eyes widen.

Foreplay? *This* is foreplay?

"Fuck, I'm getting hard just watching this," Alistair groans, slowly releasing my arms. "You gonna play nice, Pen?"

I can't even say a word with this shaft stuck in my mouth, but I still nod.

I don't know why. It's insane. I've lost my mind. But what else can I do at this moment while being ravaged by three sick boys? When they've offered me the only real chance at revenge I could ever get?

I need it. I want it. So I'll fucking take it, no matter the cost.

Even if it means shutting myself off.

So I let them use me, degrade me, fuck me like some fuck doll.

And I'll be their puppet for as long as it takes, as bad as it gets.

For her.

***

DYLAN

"Make that sound again, Pen," I say as I thrust in so deep she can barely heave.

Good. I like the sound. It turns me on like nothing else.

"Moan for me," I groan.

"I'll make her," Felix says, and he starts to flick her clit with his bare fingers.

She writhes around underneath me, then moans out loud while I'm inside her mouth, unable to keep the sounds at bay.

A filthy smile forms on my lips, my mask barely able to cover the depth of my depravity. "Oh yes, that's the one."

I push in and out slowly, coating her tongue with my pre-cum, and Alistair keeps looking at it. He rubs his own hard-on through his pants, not even looking at Penelope anymore with that freaky skull mask, but at me instead. Our eyes connect while I claim Penelope's throat.

I grin.

I know he likes to watch.

"Fuck her face, Dylan," Alistair encourages me. "Slow. Deep. Thrusts."

I bite my lip while fucking her mouth like it's a toy.

God, if I'd known it'd feel like this, I would've stuffed my cock into her mouth sooner.

She squirms underneath me, but Alistair keeps her nice and still while Felix destroys her fucking pussy like he owns it.

"You love this, Pen," Felix groans as he toys with her most sensitive bits. "Admit it. You love getting your little mouth fucked."

She can't even see him, but his voice alone is enough to make her whimper. That, or my giant cock.

"You're a little slut waiting for us to come and put you where you belong. On the fucking ground with our cocks in your mouth."

Fuck. I love it when Felix gets all raunchy. He knows just how to get these sluts turned on to the point where they just start to beg.

I thrust in and out, faster and faster. Her saliva coats my hard-on, wetter and wetter. It's too much.

I look over my shoulder at Felix rubbing his hand all over her pussy.

"Soak through those panties, whore," he says, laughing like a maniac. "You're gonna come with his dick down your throat."

Suddenly, she starts to wriggle underneath me, so I turn my head back and look. Her eyes are big, and she shakes her head.

I pull out for a second, and she gasps for air. "Breathe, bitch. Don't want you dying on me when we haven't even started the fun yet."

She gargles, "I can't."

"What, breathe?" I retort.

Felix amps up the pressure so much she squeals, "Come!"

"Yes, you can," Felix growls, and he plunges right back into her. "And you're going to fucking swallow his entire load while you do."

"But I—"

I thrust back inside, tired of her denial.

She knew what she was in for when she made this deal.

Now she'll learn what it means to be owned by the Skull & Serpent boys.

She struggles to cope with my size, her eyes turning red whenever I bury myself to the base. I can feel her swallow against my piercing. And fuck me, it's the best feeling in the world.

A girl like this, with a mouth like this ... She's a rare find.

Alistair laughs and smears some of her saliva all over her face. "That's the face of a fucking whore."

She grumbles with rage, but when Felix starts to thrust into her with two fingers, her eyes almost roll into the back of her head while her tongue wraps around my length.

"Oh yeah, that's it. Suck me off," I groan, and I pinch her nose, stopping her from breathing. "Take it deep."

Right then, Felix takes it up a notch. Her legs begin to quake, and her whole body tenses. And I can hear the orgasm from her goddamn mouth, the sound like fucking music to my ears. Gurgled moans burst right through the onslaught of my thrusts.

And it's so fucking sexy to hear her come that I lose myself in the moment.

I roar out loud, my head tilting up toward the sky while I come deep inside her mouth, coating her throat with my juices.

"Don't spit," Alistair says, and he gathers some in his mouth and spits on her face. "That's my fucking job." He rubs it all over her face while I'm still inside her, depositing everything I have inside her.

And goddamn, it's a bucketload.

When I'm finally satiated, I pull out, my dick still half hard. She takes in a deep, raspy breath, heaving, choking on cum. And all I can do is fucking smile like a frenzied sicko.

Oh yeah. We're going to have a great fucking time with this girl.

19

PENELOPE

Dylan laughs. "Attagirl." He slaps my cheek, pulling me out of the waves of ecstasy that took over my body. "Knew you could do it."

"Did she come?" Alistair asks, looking up at Felix.

I'm still trying to wrap my head around what just happened.

What my body just did while he was still inside my mouth.

"Feel for yourself," he retorts, swiping his finger down my slit.

And oh my God, I wish it didn't make my pussy thump.

Fuck. I can't believe I actually came.

It was like my body wasn't mine. Like it belonged to them and only them.

And that orgasm was too intense for words.

Dylan's still on top of me, keeping me from moving, when Alistair walks over to my thighs and blatantly sticks his fingers inside.

Fuck.

"Oh yeah, that pussy is still throbbing."

"Told you, she's a dirty one," Felix says.

"You got what you wanted," I say in a moment of courage. "Now get off me."

Dylan laughs. "Oh, we're not nearly done with you."

"Pick her up," Felix growls.

Suddenly, Dylan gets off, his half-hard dick still dangling out of his pants, and he grabs me by the arm while Alistair lifts my legs.

"Hey, what are you doing?!" I squeal.

But they're already dragging me across the grass, only stopping in front of a tree. They hoist me up, and Alistair unties the rope from around his robe while Felix keeps me restrained. And within a few seconds, Alistair has tied me to the tree.

"Let me go," I hiss, still coughing from the cum stuck in my throat. "This wasn't a part of the deal."

Dylan steps away and folds his arms. "Oh, yes it was. We help you, and we do whatever we want with you."

Felix steps in front of my face. "Did you put on all this makeup for us?" He grips my cheeks together, my lipstick staining his fingers. "Pretty ... but prettier with cum smeared all over."

He wipes my own spit over my face and then steps away, only to pull at his zipper.

His cock comes out completely erect, glistening at the tip, the metal rings still making me gulp. Alistair does the same, but his girth impresses me the most. The thickness of it is unmatched, and I'd hate to discover how it would feel inside me.

God, why am I even thinking this?

"You want it, don't you?" Felix mutters as he rubs his shaft. "Greedy little whore."

"No," I say.

"Lies," Dylan says, and he pulls the lighter from his pocket again, stepping closer to hold it in front of my face. "Now tell us the truth. You like this, don't you?"

I shudder against the cold tree, my body quaking with both fear and desire, while the flame hovers dangerously close to my cheeks. "Beg for it, then. Beg for their cum."

The fire stings against my skin.

"Give me your cum," I say.

I hiss when the flames lick my neck. "I said beg," Dylan whispers into my ear, like a gentle threat.

"Please," I add.

"Good girl."

Goose bumps scatter across my skin.

But I don't know if it's from the fire, or from his lips humming near my ears, moaning softly, breathing into my hair, his half-hard dick still swinging against my thighs.

"She looks good with her mouth stuffed full of your jizz," Alistair says.

I hate how they talk about me. "Shut up."

Dylan snorts. "Still got some spunk left, huh?"

"Don't worry," Felix says, thrusting into his own hand. "We'll fuck it out of her."

I swallow. "I'd love to see you try."

There. His own words thrown right back in his face.

"Oh, I will," Felix retorts, and he steps closer until the tip touches my thigh. "But first, I'll let you simmer in our juices for the night."

What? What does he mean?

He rubs his hands up and down his shaft with fervor, staring at me through his mask as if he wants to watch me break. And Alistair has to use two hands to pleasure himself. That's how big he is.

I can't keep my eyes off them both. But there isn't anywhere else to look either while stuck against this tree.

"You like to watch, don't you?" Felix asks, rubbing himself against my body. "You like to be used. Degraded. Owned."

"You wish," I retort.

Dylan holds the flame underneath my chin, forcing me to lift my head. "Keep it up, little slut. It only gets me hard again."

Fuck. I don't want this to go on forever, so I shut my mouth and wait until they finish. But I wish I could stop the throbbing between my legs.

Dylan suddenly slides his hand down my thigh, getting closer and closer to that spot Felix just completely destroyed with his fingers.

"It's about time you started moaning for them too," Dylan says.

His fingers find their way to my panties, and he tears them apart just like that.

I gasp, but the gasp is immediately cut short by his fingers dipping into my wetness.

"Fuck ... Felix was right. You're soaking wet."

Felix and Alistair pick up the pace.

"Make her come again," Alistair says. "I want to see her shiver from your fingers."

I shake my head, but it's too late. Dylan's already flicking his fingers back and forth across my naked pussy.

And I struggle to even stand.

"Moan like the slut you are, Pen," Felix says, rubbing himself against me. "And maybe I'll give you my fucking cum."

In the cold night, my body heats up like fireworks from Dylan's fingers expertly swiveling back and forth, and I'm having trouble separating my own pleasure from theirs.

Dylan's and Alistair's eyes connect, and Alistair picks up the pace.

"Fuck, I can't hold it," Alistair groans, and the spurts of cum jet out of him, again and again.

I've never seen someone come that much, but apparently, it's possible to shoot a whole glass full. But instead of filling a glass, he coats my body with it.

"Fuckkk," Felix groans.

He's right up against me as he coats my legs and shoes with it, then swipes the remainder off the tip and wipes it over my face.

But I don't even care as I'm consumed by the approaching orgasm creeping up from deep inside.

"That's it, come all over my fingers," Dylan moans into my ear.

My entire body begins to shake against the tree, and I fall apart, covered in gunk.

Dylan retracts his fingers halfway through, letting me languish in half arousal when I wish he would've finished it.

Fuck.

These assholes are already messing with my head.

Alistair and Dylan laugh. "Look at her, all spent just from a little bit of fun."

Little?

Felix tucks his length into his pants, staring me in the eyes while Dylan and Alistair walk away slowly.

"Third lesson, Pen," he says, taking a deep, raspy breath. "You belong to us now."

He smears through the cum splatters and rubs my pussy, then slides it all up my body and pushes down my lips forcefully, thrusting inside again until I gag. "Understood?"

I nod, and he takes his fingers out again, then turns around and marches off with his buddies. Dylan picks up my bag and takes out my phone, turning to look at me with a smug smile on his face. For some reason, he manages to unlock it.

How? Did they see me enter it in class? Shit.

He does something, I don't know what, but after a few seconds, he chucks my bag onto the ground and throws my phone with it, just out of reach.

Then they all turn around and saunter back to the Society house.

"Hey!" I yell, still spluttering spit and cum. "You can't just leave!"

"Watch us," Felix retorts.

Alistair looks back but still decides to turn around and walk off, and it pisses me off.

"Alistair! You fucking tied me up, and you're just going to leave me hanging to a tree?"

The harder I scream, the more they smile, and when they turn around for the final time and walk all the way back to the house, it dawns on me that I'm in real deep shit.

Because no one, and I mean no one, knew we were here.

And now I'm by myself. Tied to a tree. In the middle of the night.

God better fucking help me.

And them ... because when I get out of here, I will make them fucking pay.

20

FELIX

I dangle the rat above the cage and wait until Nessie sees it. She slithers out of her hole and snatches it from the hook with ease. Her mouth opens wide, and she swallows the dead rat whole.

Such a shame I never see the chase. The fight. The struggle as the rat clings on for life.

The handlers call it more humane to feed them dead animals.

But if you ask me, the snake is being deprived of something too.

Its natural instinct to kill.

I lower myself to look through the glass and watch her finish her dinner with a rotten smile on my face.

"I'll get you something nice to eat soon."

"You talking to that fucking snake again?"

I turn my head. Dylan saunters into my room and chucks his mask somewhere in the corner.

"Weren't you busy sexing up those bitches downstairs?" I sneer.

He shrugs and jumps on my bed, lying on it like he owns it. "It's fucking boring when you've already spilled all your juices."

"*You* ..." I murmur. "You say it like that's the case for all of us."

"Well, aren't you spent?" he says, yawning as he makes himself at home on my pillow.

I fish my knife from my pocket and chuck it right at him, missing his ear by only an inch. "I will *never* fucking have enough."

"Okay," he says, raising his hands. "No need to get violent on me."

"You're in my fucking bed."

"But your pillow is so nice." He rubs it against him, and it makes me want to rip his face off. "Some boys had sex in mine."

"So?" I raise a brow. "Clean it."

"Disgusting," Dylan rebukes. "I'm not touching someone else's cum."

"Interesting." I turn back to the snake but watch Dylan through the glass. "You didn't have any problem with it when it came to—"

"You know that's different," he says.

"You keep telling yourself that."

"We gonna talk about me or about her?" he rebukes.

I pick up another dead rat with the hook and dangle it above Nessie's cage. "What about her?"

"When are we gonna free her?"

I lower the hook and wait until she shows her fangs. "We don't."

"Wait, what?" Dylan sits up on the bed and grabs my mask to look at it. "You've gotta be kidding me. You wanna let her hang there forever?"

"You were there. You didn't care then, so why do you care now?" I ask.

Nessie strikes, fangs embedded in the rat.

"I thought we were just messing with her. Not that we'd leave her there permanently."

Nessie rips the rat from my hook. "Oh, don't worry ... she'll get untied."

"What if she goes on to tell people? What if someone finds her there? They'll know it was us."

I shrug as Nessie slowly starts to swallow the rat. "People know not to get in our way."

I turn to look at him. "I don't just want to mess with her." Dylan lights up a joint, but I steal it from his hands right before he takes a drag and take it for myself. "I want to get in her fucking head. Invade her fucking mind. Break her from the inside out."

"Whoa," he mutters, and I throw the joint back at him. He catches it with his mouth, grinning like a bastard before taking a drag. "She's not gonna let you in that easily."

I smirk and lean against Nessie's cage. "I know. But I like a fucking challenge."

Dylan's eyes narrow. "She really does behave just like her, doesn't she?" He takes another big drag and fills my room with smoke. "This is going to be so much fucking fun. Much more fun than these kind of fucking parties ever will be."

The door suddenly creaks open. Alistair sticks his skull head in and rips off his mask. "Back."

My heart picks up the pace. "You got it?"

He nods. "Was tough as hell getting into that sorority again. They really upped security after I broke in the first time. Luckily, half the girls are at our party downstairs, so there was no one to stand in my way." He holds up the diary again. "This was all she had. No other notebooks."

I frown and sigh. "We've seen that already."

"I know," he says, and he steps inside and shuts the door. "But not this." He opens it on a specific page where there's multiple cutouts of her and her sister slapped onto each other, and he peels away a corner of the photo to reveal some text.

My eyes widen, and I march toward him to snatch the diary from his hands. "She pasted these on top?"

He nods. "Read it."

I've done everything that's been asked and more. It's never going to be enough. And I refuse to go through life ... broken. Split in half by a decision that wasn't mine to make.

So I will stop it now.

This bonfire near The Edge will be the last night spent at this godforsaken university—

The rest is unreadable.

But I can tell from the handwriting it's hers.

Eve.

My hands tighten around the diary, my blood turning to ice.

It takes everything in me not to rip this to shreds.

Dylan stands behind me and checks the text over my shoulder. "Shit."

"This is the note Penelope was talking about," Alistair says.

"Are you sure?" Dylan asks.

He nods. "Positive. But we're missing some of it."

"Doesn't matter," I say. "This is all the proof we need to know she made a conscious choice." My fist balls. "And someone's to blame."

"Penelope's convinced it was us, though," Dylan says. "No wonder she tried to stab you twice."

He snorts like it's funny or something.

"I'll fucking make her pay for that, don't worry," I growl.

"I thought we were well underway with that," Dylan says, winking.

I peer at the photos hastily pasted over the text, Penelope's face drawing me in. "Oh, I haven't even gotten started."

I slam the diary shut and throw it on my nightstand.

"We need the rest, though," Alistair says.

I push past him but pause and turn. "Scan everything in that fucking diary. I want all of it digital, enlarged. Ready to print."

"What? Now?" Dylan scoffs. "But the party is still going."

"I don't care," I reply, opening the door. "And get a fucking burner phone too."

"Fine," Dylan says. "But I need to know why."

"Are you gonna do what I think you're gonna do?" Alistair asks. "You know we already agreed to help her, right?"

I'm one foot outside the door. "We never specified how." My nostrils flare as I clutch the door so tightly the wood almost cracks. "I don't fucking help. I break things. And if I need to fucking find someone, I will do it my way. By breaking everyone in my fucking path ... including her."

21

PENELOPE

"Help!" I scream. "Can someone please help me?"

There's no response, and the party is still well underway.

Fuck me. Am I going to be left hanging here until the fucking week ends?

I'm so far away from any actual populated area, I don't know if anyone could ever find me.

Only those fucked-up boys.

I've been hanging here for hours now, and there's no sign of life anywhere. I thought those boys would be back by now.

But what if they never come back?

A chill runs up and down my spine.

Surely, they don't intend to just leave me here, right?

Fuckers.

Grinding my teeth, I rub my hands together where the rope is, hoping to loosen the strings, but it fucking hurts.

"Anyone there? I need help!" I call out in a desperate attempt.

But no one replies. Again.

With every passing minute, my panic rises more and more until I can feel the cold sting of my own tears roll down my cheeks.

Goddammit, I promised myself I wouldn't let those fuckers make me cry.

Good thing they aren't here now to see me slowly fall apart. Felix would have a field day.

Grumbling to myself, I wriggle my legs back and forth against the tree in an effort to free myself, but all it does is create more chafing. Especially with all this sticky gunk on my body.

Fuck, I can still taste them in my mouth. All the jizz they squirted definitely got on my lips. And I hate how I can taste the difference in all three. One is thick and salty, and I remember it from the first time Felix filled me up. The other mildly fruity, and another one just watery salt with a hint of bitter. The latter one definitely Dylan's as I can still feel it coat my throat. And that makes it hard to focus on anything other than being completely covered in their spunk, freezing to death against a tree with half my outfit missing.

God, if anyone finds me now, have mercy on my soul.

Grumbling, I try to reach for the knot with my head, hoping I can bite through it. There's a piece that seems loose, and I barely manage to grab ahold of it with my teeth.

Grinding my teeth, I chew at it, but goddamn, the rope hurts my gums.

The pain makes me lose my grip.

The rope lowers a little ... and now it's out of reach.

"God-fucking-dammit!" I scream.

Something rustles beyond the trees.

My eyes widen. "Who's there?"

I can hear someone giggle.

Someone's finally here, oh my God.

I don't know who it is, but any help is more than welcome right now.

More rustling ensues. My heart thumps in my throat.

Suddenly, two guys fall out of a bush a few feet away from me, tumbling on top of each other, giggling with delight as they kiss each other senseless.

Until they see me.

Jeremy and Calvin.

Their pupils dilate when they spot me.

Calvin quickly jumps off Jeremy, who's half naked. Apparently, they decided to bring their sexual encounter to the woods.

Lucky me, because I would've never been rescued otherwise.

"Oh my God," Calvin mutters, and he quickly gets up.

A blush spreads on my cheeks. "Hi."

"Penelope? Is that you?" Jeremy asks, adjusting his glasses. "I barely recognize you with all that ... spunk on you. Oh my God."

If one could die from embarrassment, I'd be a corpse now.

"What happened to you?" Calvin asks as he steps closer, inspecting me.

"Calvin, don't stare." Jeremy quickly slaps his hands in front of Calvin's eyes. "She's half naked."

"Some boys tied me up and ... well, you can probably tell what they did," I say, adding an awkward laugh.

Calvin whacks Jeremy's hand away. "So it's really jizz?"

"Um ..." I look away. "No comment."

Calvin gasps. "Wow, and here I was thinking you'd just hung your titties out for no reason."

He snorts and almost chokes on it when Jeremy throws him a glare.

"Can you help me down?" I ask. I'm really not in the mood for any more antics.

"Oh, of course," Jeremy says, and he immediately walks toward me.

He picks at the ropes while trying not to touch any of the jizz those boys left on me, obviously grossed out by it.

"I'm sorry, it's hard," he says.

"This might help," Calvin says, and he pulls out a small pocket knife. "Never comes in handy until it does."

He cuts through the ropes, and I rip off the final ones, tearing away from the tree. Everything smells musky, and I feel dank. God, I'm going to need to shower for days.

"That's a lot of spunk, girl ..." Calvin says.

"I know. There were three of them," I reply.

"Are you okay?" Calvin asks.

I shrug, and quickly pull up my outfit so at least my boobs are covered. I have nothing to keep it together, though.

"Oh, here." Calvin pulls a tie from his hair and wraps it around the two top ends of my outfit, pushing it together until my boobs no longer threaten to fall out.

"Thanks," I say.

At least now I can walk home with a tiny bit of dignity instead of none.

"Did they force you to do this?" Jeremy suddenly asks.

I blink a couple of times, not knowing how to respond. "Well, it wasn't, but ..."

He places a hand on my shoulder. "Do you want us to call the police?"

The police? If they get involved, those boys will definitely make my life hell. If they end up behind bars, I'm sure their fathers will eventually find out it was me and tear me and my family to shreds. I can't let it happen.

"No, no, it's okay," I say, shaking off his hand. "I'll be fine."

"Are you sure?" Jeremy asks, following me into the grass beyond Priory Forest where my bag and phone are, which I quickly snatch off the ground. "It sounds like they—"

"No," I interject. "Nothing happened. But thank you for helping me down."

I'm shivering from the cold.

"Let me give you a ride home then," Calvin says, offering his hand.

I shake my head. "No, I'd rather walk right now."

When I turn around again, Jeremy says, "It was them, wasn't it? Felix, Dylan, and Alistair."

I pause, staring at my own hands, which are covered in their jizz.

"They've done it before, you know," Jeremy points out.

Of course, they've done it before. This is what they do. This is their shtick. How they destroy anyone who tries to meddle in their business.

But I won't go down easily.

"It's true. They're notorious," Calvin says. "Well, they don't do shit to us, of course. They mostly focus on girls. Well, except ... you know ..." He winks.

Mostly? I don't know what he's talking about. "Okay."

I continue walking, but then Jeremy says, "Wait. I don't want to be an asshole, but I need to warn you. Please, stay away from them. For your own good. This is already bad enough," he adds.

"Thanks," I say, making a fist.

I can't even bear to look at them right now.

Jeremy sighs. "I'm just trying to look out for you. I don't want you to get hurt any further."

I take in a deep breath and close my eyes only to rid myself of any and all emotions.

Discard it, just like that.

Thrown into the wind, just as my sanity.

"Thanks for the advice," I reply. "And for the help. But I won't stop. Not until I have what I want."

"You know they won't either," Jeremy says. "So unless you have a death wish ..."

"If I have to die, then so be it."

And I walk off without a care in the world, feeling their stares penetrate my back.

But I know I already sold my soul to the devil.

Time to fucking claim the bargain I made.

22

PENELOPE

Even after the extensive shower I just took, I still don't feel clean.

It's as if their sickness stained my fucking soul.

I can't rub off their scent. The mark left on my brain.

All I can think about is those masks as they cornered me in the woods and took what they wanted from me. My mouth, my body, even my pussy—all of it as if I was made just for them.

I shake off the jitters and jump in my bed.

I'll need the sleep to handle what's coming because now that they've touched me, I'm sure they'll come back for more. Maybe they'll even return to that tree, wondering where I am after they left me there to hang dry.

Fucking monsters.

Kayla lets out a loud snore, and I almost jolt up and down in bed.

I usually never get scared.

But after tonight ... no fucking wonder.

I turn around in bed, but it's hard to fall asleep with all these thoughts raging through my head. These stupid boys even invaded my safe space as the memories of them ravaging me keep floating to the forefront of my mind. And for some reason, it makes my pussy thump.

Goddammit, stop, Penelope.

They're fucked up.

Groaning, I flip around again and force myself to lie in a position I hate so I don't have to feel my body going crazy.

I've never had anything like this happen to me before.

Though I doubt many people have.

Who in their right mind would make a deal with not just one but three devils?

Me, that's who.

But I have a reason. A mission. Someone I wasn't there to protect needs me to bring her justice, so I fucking will. Even if I have to let those sick boys corrupt me.

***

I shoot up in bed to the sound of my alarm.

Did I actually sleep?

I hadn't even noticed I'd finally fallen asleep.

I rub aside the hair stuck to my face and look at the clock.

Oh my God, it's the final alarm. I've missed two of them already. Shit!

I've got a rendezvous with my parents today.

I throw off my blanket and jump out of bed, then scramble to find clean clothes. I should really take some to the dryer and get my shit together.

Kayla comes out of the bathroom, yawning. "Morning. Sleep well?" she asks while I jump around to try to get my ripped black jeans to fit.

I nod. "You?"

"Amazing," she says, snorting. "You came home late last night, didn't you?"

"Did I wake you up?" I ask. "Sorry."

"But was it a good party?" she asks, winking. "Did you hook up with anyone?" She bumps into me with her hips.

"No," I lie, quickly grabbing some cereal and milk.

"I can see the blush on your face," she jests, watching me gobble it down.

"Well, sorta," I muse. "If you can call it that."

I slurp down my breakfast while also putting on some makeup to make myself look decent after last night's onslaught.

"What's his name?" Kayla asks as she throws herself down on her bed. "Or her."

I do one last check of my room, but I can't find the diary anywhere.

"Oh, uhh ..." It's so damn hard to lie. "F... Fred."

Fuck. Where is it?

"Fred?" Kayla cringes. "Nah, you wouldn't hang out with a white piece of bread like that."

"Okay, fine. I don't remember, okay?"

Where the fuck did I put that diary? I swear to God, I left it underneath my pillow as always.

She laughs. "So you kissed some dude while drunk? Nice." She raises her brows and puts her hands underneath her chin. "Or was it more than just kissing? C'mon, I need all the deets."

"It was literally a Halloween party," I reply in a hurry.

I rummage through all my books, but the diary is nowhere to be found.

What if ... someone broke into the room again and stole it?

Someone like Alistair King.

My blood begins to boil.

"Oooh, so they had masks." Her face starts to glow.

"They tied me to a fucking tree," I rebuke, annoyed the diary is missing again.

She eyes me down. "*They?*"

Oh, fuck me. There goes the nice lie.

Now I'm really blushing.

She sits up straight. "Wait, don't tell me it's those Skull & Serpent Society boys? F as in Felix?"

I check my phone.

Fuck. No more time.

"I gotta go," I say, and I run for the door.

"Wait, you can't just drop a bombshell on me like that and then leave!" Kayla says.

But I'm already out the door. I'll explain later. I need to get out of here fast before I say things that will make her want to get involved. I've already endangered my own life. No need to endanger hers too.

***

I head straight for the coffee shop where I agreed to meet my parents down in Crescent Vale City, the one called Fi's Cups and Cakes along the road that leads up the mountain to Spine Ridge.

Mom: Penelope, are you almost here? You're late. And your dad's getting antsy.

Penelope: Coming! Five minutes max.

Mom sends me a picture of Dad holding a cup of tea and a macaron, making me grin. It's so out of character for him to pose like that, especially considering he's more of a coffee person. But he'll do anything for my mom.

I walk down the streets, completely out of breath by the time I finally reach the shop.

When I open the door, Mom turns in her seat. "There you are. I was wondering if you'd even make it."

Panting, I approach them and give her a kiss. "Hi, Mom."

"You look like you ran a marathon. Did you walk all the way here from the university?" she asks.

"No, of course not. Took a bus. But had to run from the stop," I explain, and I kiss my dad on the cheeks too. "Sorry, I'm late. Had a rough night."

"Up to no good?" He raises a brow.

I sit down on the only seat left. "You know me."

My dad grins and takes a sip of his tea. "The tea is not strong enough."

I snort. I can never tell whether he's just trying to play it cool or means it for real.

"Server!" Dad calls, raising his hand. "Another cup, please. And add an espresso as well."

"So how's school?" Mom asks. "Tell us all about it."

"It's okay," I reply. "I'm trying to catch up on everything I missed in the first month. But I'm hanging in there."

"And what about friends?" she asks, taking a sip of her tea. "Meet anyone new? Interesting?" She pauses. "Someone to keep an eye on?"

I glance at Dad. "Well, I've made some friends but also some enemies."

"Enemies?" Mom raises a brow. "Already?"

"You know how she is, Emilia," Dad says, grabbing my hand. "Just like us."

Mom laughs. "True." And she takes another sip. "Well, just do your best. We're proud of you, regardless. And if things don't work out, you can always call it quits."

"No," I say. "Not a chance. I'm gonna see this through until the end."

Dad squeezes my hand.

The server comes to bring us the drinks, interrupting our conversation. "There you go! The espresso was for you, sir, right?"

Dad nods at her. "The tea is for my daughter, thank you."

"You're welcome," the server says, and she walks off again.

I grab a macaron from the plate in front and stuff it in my mouth, the taste almost making me want to moan. Mom always knows how to find the best shops in town.

"Are you sure you're all right at that university?" Mom asks.

I take a sip of the hot tea. Spicy, just the way I like it. "It's okay. I can handle myself."

"But you know what happened to your sister, and I know what kind of people go there, and I—"

Dad grabs Mom's hand now and interrupts her. "Emilia, she wanted this. Let her do this."

Mom sighs. "I know, I'm just worried." A gentle smile forms on her lips. "I don't want to lose another one of my babies."

I lean in for a hug. "I'll be fine. Don't worry about me. I know how to protect myself."

"Do you still have the knife your dad gave you?" she asks.

I nod.

Our foreheads collide. "Don't hesitate to use it."

I glance at my dad, who studies us both. "I'm probably going to need a couple more."

He grins. "That's my girl."

23

PENELOPE

Monday

I run down the stairs and throw my bag over my shoulders before I head outside. The school grounds are bustling with people, but I'm the only one running like a chicken with its head cut off, trying to be on time.

God, I should really get a better sound for my alarm clock because this one obviously isn't loud enough to wake me.

When I finally get to the building, I'm out of breath and clutching my knees, panting like crazy.

"Had a good run?"

A familiar voice makes me look over my shoulder.

Crystal smiles at me. "Hey, Pen. Everything okay?"

"Yeah, I'm fine. You?"

"Late?" she asks.

I check my phone again. "One minute."

"Yikes," she says, but then she gasps. "Oh, you've got a gnarly-looking gash there."

I follow her eyes all the way down to my chest, where an obvious burn mark is visible above my crop top. Either from the rope or from Dylan waving his lighter in front of me.

Fuck. I can't even walk around in my normal clothes without people noticing something happened. I must've been lucky with the clothes I wore to the coffee shop that my parents didn't even notice.

"Here." Crystal pulls the scarf off her neck and wraps it around mine. "That'll cover it up."

"Thanks," I say.

"Keep it." She smiles again. "It looks good on you."

I like that she doesn't ask me what happened. Just tries to help me.

"I'll see you later," she says.

I wave as I walk to the classroom, barely making it on time before the teacher closes the door.

But I forgot that this is the class in the auditorium ... and Dylan and Felix are right there in the same spot as before, staring me down.

Without masks, it's hard to imagine these are the same boys who literally sprayed me with cum while I was tied to a tree.

I gulp and walk past all the chairs to the only spot left, feeling their eyes bore a hole into my back.

I hate that we share this class.

But what I hate even more is how I can't even look at them without being reminded of how they tied me up and had their way with me. And I know they fucking know they have this effect on me because every time I turn to gaze at them, they throw me an insufferable smirk.

Assholes.

I sit down and put my books in front of me, but it's hard to concentrate on the teacher's lecture when I'm torn by questions that I still don't have any answers to.

Suddenly, my phone buzzes.

I grab it from my pocket and check.

There's a fucking message from Felix.

What the fuck? How did they get my number?

Felix: Don't forget. I call, you come.

Furious, I text back.

Penelope: How the fuck did you get this number?

Some typing ensues, and the wait makes me bite my inner cheek.

Felix: Dylan swiped it.

Oh fuck me, so that's what he was doing with my phone last night.

I scroll through my numbers, and of course, he put Felix, Alistair, and his own number in there ... his own under the name of Sex_God.

I roll my eyes and start a conversation with him.

Penelope: Hey sex god, no one asked you to put your number in my phone.

Sex_God: You don't have to ask, it's a service, free of charge.

Penelope: You're ridic. This name too.

Sex_God: Ask me what I put down in my phone for your number...

My fingers dig into the metal of the phone.

Penelope: You know I can just block you all, right?

Sex_God: Try us, little whore. See how it works out for you.

Fuck.

Of course, it had to be something completely off the rails.

Penelope: It can't be any worse than what you've already done.

Sex_God: Got a few tricks up our sleeves. Don't worry, little whore.

Do I even want to know?

I just know this will get out of hand. I have to remind them about the bargain we made. I refuse to be anyone's plaything for free.

I go back to the conversation with Felix.

Penelope: I did what you asked. Now you do your fucking part.

Felix: Ask nicely.

My nostrils flare with rage.

Penelope: PLEASE.

Felix: Good girl.

I clench my legs together.

I could hear him say those words out loud in my head.

What the hell?

Felix: I'll see you after class. Library first floor. Historical biographies section.

I glance at him over my shoulder. He doesn't even throw me a single look even though I know he can see me looking. Asshole.

I text Alistair instead.

Penelope: You made a deal with me. You need to come through.

Alistair: You asking me to come? Again?

Fuck them. Can't they think about anything other than sex?

Penelope: I mean it. I let you do what you wanted, so now it's your turn to do what I want.

Alistair: And what is it you desire, feisty queen?

Well, I guess that's a better nickname than the others even though I know it's all meant as a big fucking joke to make me feel inferior.

Penelope: My diary is missing. Did you steal it again?

Alistair: Maybe.

I sigh out loud.

Penelope: It's mine. Give. It. Back.

Alistair: It's not up to me, and we can't.

Penelope: Why?

Alistair: Felix needs it for something.

They'd better not damage it, or I swear to God, there will be blood on my hands.

Alistair: Don't worry, it's safe.

Penelope: I doubt it.

Alistair: So what was this thing about some guy called Nathan?

I'm surprised he remembers that.

Penelope: Are you going to help me?

Alistair: Depends on your answer.

I take the note from my bag and take a picture of it, then send it to him.

Penelope: He shoved this note under my door.

Alistair: Interesting.

There's a long pause.

Penelope: So you're not going to say anything?

Alistair: I'll have a talk with the guys.

Okay.

Sighing, I put down my phone and peer over my shoulder, but they're not even looking at me anymore. Meanwhile, I'm tense as fuck as my eyes fixate on the clock, waiting for the time to pass until this class is over.

Because the first thing I'll be doing is heading straight for the library to confront them.

***

FELIX

Twenty minutes later

When the library door closes behind me, I can feel the electricity practically zing off my body. She's in here. I can fucking smell it. Her perfume lingers in the air, drawing me in like a lure. And I'm definitely coming for the bait.

I walk up the stairs and head for the most secluded part of the library. The part no one ever visits for fun, let alone to study. Who in their right fucking mind is ever interested in some old drab from some old fucker's life who lived five hundred years ago?

No one ... except me. Because I'm not here to read, and neither is she.

When I spot her behind a bookcase, my heartbeat picks up, the adrenaline flooding my body.

The ripped black jeans she's wearing barely cover her ass, and the sight makes my mouth water.

I've already felt her wetness on my fingers. Maybe it's about time I tasted it too.

"Penelope," I whisper.

She gasps. "Who's there?" She turns around and checks each case. "Felix?"

But I can easily outpace her.

From behind a bookcase, I watch her. Her face scrunches up in a pretty way when she's annoyed. Pretty enough to make me want to bend her over the desk behind her.

"I can see you ..." I mutter through a hole in the bookcase.

In shock, she turns around, our eyes connecting for a brief second before I disappear again behind another bookshelf.

But I can hear her breathe heavier and heavier with every passing second. The sound is like a drug to me.

God, I'm a sucker for a chase.

When she's with her back to me, I slide past two narrow bookcases and slowly snake my hands around her waist.

She shrieks, so I swiftly cover her mouth.

"Shh ... We don't want people to come looking now, do we?" I whisper into her ear. Her naked belly underneath that crop top pushes in and out with quick, ragged breaths, her panicky eyes finding mine when she turns her head. "I'll remove my hand if you promise not to scream."

24

FELIX

She nods after a moment, so I lower my hand to her neck and grip her throat instead.

"Good girl."

I can feel the goose bumps erupt on her skin, and it makes me grin like a motherfucker.

"You like doing as you're told," I muse, my tongue dipping out to lick the rim of her ear. "Don't you, Penelope?"

"Fuck you," she hisses back. "I only came here because I need answers."

"Oh, so that's why you whimper so loudly," I muse.

She blushes and spits back, "That's not—"

Suddenly, she kicks back and hits me right in the nut sack.

Fuck.

I groan in pain and release her from my grip, barely able to stay upright.

Still so fucking fiery ...

But I'll fuck the fire right out of her.

"You deserved that," she growls.

"For what?" I grip my package and ignore the pain, tilting my head at her. "Giving you the best orgasm you've ever had in your entire fucking life?"

She grinds her teeth, but her anger can't hide the flush on her cheeks. "Stop."

"Why?" I step closer. "Does it make you feel bad to know you got off while being degraded?"

"I didn't do shit," she rebukes.

"No, your body did the talking for you," I retort.

"The only reason I let you do that is so you would help me. When are you going to hold up your end of this deal we made?"

"When it suits me," I reply.

"That's convenient," she spits back.

She moves behind the table, but it won't be enough to stop me. "Are you afraid of me?"

"You're literally danger personified," she says. "This is self-preservation."

I grumble. "Danger personified ... corny nickname."

"I didn't come here to joke around," she says.

"Then why did you?"

"You fucking left me hanging from a tree." Her voice is laced with the kind of rage that gets me going.

I clutch the table from the other end. "You freed yourself."

"You should be happy someone actually fucking found me."

A smirk forms on my face. "Someone?"

She sucks in a breath. "Don't even try."

"But you did get away," I point out.

"No thanks to you." She folds her arms and leans back against the bookcase behind her. "How long were you going to leave me there? Hours? Days?"

I lick my lips and release the table. "As long as I deemed necessary."

She stays put while I continue to walk toward her.

"For what?"

Even when I'm right in front of her, she doesn't flinch. "To get it through your skull ..." I lean over her, planting my hand against the shelf, and tap her forehead. "That your body is mine to do with what I fucking what, whenever I want."

She swallows. "What about the others?"

"They follow my lead," I say.

"So you're in charge." She tilts her head. "Then you can tell Alistair to give me my fucking diary back."

So. He told her.

"No," I retort.

"That diary wasn't a part of the deal we made."

I grab her chin and make her look at me. "Anything you own is now mine."

Her eyes twitch. "You'd better give me a good reason not to stab you right here, right now."

Fuck. There it is. That's the fucking fighter I'm looking for.

The one I want to force on her knees, bend over and fuck until she screams my name.

"So many knives for such a small girl," I say. "I'd almost think you have a knife kink."

"Have you looked in the mirror recently?" she retorts, her eyes briefly skimming over the patch still on my arm. "You love pain, don't you?"

"You have no idea." My thumb touches her lip, and I slowly drag it down to see them part. "Especially when I dish it out."

I tip up her chin until she finally looks at me.

"You're fucked up," she lisps.

"Thanks for the compliment."

"You're welcome." So fucking snarky too. "Now are you going to keep up your end of the deal and help me?"

"I never said I wouldn't," I reply. "But I also never specified when."

"When?"

I clutch her face with one hand. "When you're done satisfying me."

Her face contorts, and she spits in my face.

Fuck.

Raunchy.

Just the way I like it.

I wipe it off slowly, making sure I get everything before I pinch her cheeks so hard she can't stop her lips from parting. And I push my fingers inside. "I told you I would make you swallow that next time." I push until I reach the end of her throat, and she gurgles. "Take it like a good fucking slut."

When her eyes begin to water, I retract my fingers, and she heaves. "Fuck you."

I brush her lips with my thumb. "Maybe I fucking will."

"I'd rather be fucked by a dead guy," she replies.

"I can arrange that."

Her face goes as white as snow. "Wha—"

"I kept all the masks from Halloween. So a mask kink too?" I grab her and pull her away from the books, then shove her against the table, pushing her face-down onto the desk. "I knew I'd found the right girl."

"Get off me," she hisses.

I hold her wrists tightly against her back while I lean over her. "You're mine, remember? And I will do with your fucking body what-ever I damn well please."

I don't back out of a deal, and it's about time she learned what that means.

I rip through what's left of her jeans, making one big hole in the back.

"What the f—we're in a library!"

I hold a finger in front of my mouth. "Quiet." With that same finger, I push aside her panties and circle her clit. She jolts up and down on the table, her eyes widening when she turns to look at me. "Unless you want them to hear you moan."

I flick her clit with one hand and hold her down with the other, watching her face slowly unravel before me. And fuck me, is it the best sight in the world.

I knew she looked good while being toyed with, but Dylan blocked most of my view on Halloween night. Now I get the full show, and it is fucking marvelous to watch her writhe on this table while I play with her.

I haven't had this much fun in ages.

Leaning over, I bury my face between her thighs.

She turns her head. "Oh my God, are you actually—"

Her voice is cut off as I thrust my tongue inside her.

Wet fucking pussy, just for me.

I normally wouldn't give two shits because I could get pussy any-time. But this one right here ... It's forbidden. Off-limits.

And that makes me want it more than anything.

I lick her little swollen nub, spreading her own wetness all over. She tastes like chocolate, rich, mouth-watering, the kind that makes me want to sink in deep. So I bury my tongue inside her crevice while keeping her down with a flat hand on her back.

"Why are you doing this?" she gasps.

I circle her clit until I can hear her breathing pick up. "Because I want to fucking lick this pussy raw until you beg for mercy."

"Fuck you," she grits.

"Keep pretending you don't like being used," I growl back, and I roll my tongue around her sensitive spots until she begins to squirm on the table. "It only makes me that much harder."

My bulge strains against the fabric of my pants, desperate to get out and plow through this whore of mine. But first, I'll bring her to the edge of insanity.

I flick my tongue across her little nub until she practically starts to moan out loud. "Oh God, you gotta stop."

"Give me one good reason."

"I can't hold it," she lisps.

"Then don't." I keep circling her sensitive spot until her whole body starts to quake. "Give me all you've got, Pen. Every last fucking drop."

A strangled moan escapes her mouth, and her pussy explodes with juices. I lap it all up and stick my tongue inside to feel her contract, and fuck me, I could get used to this.

"Again," I say.

She gasps. "What? No, I can't—"

I slap her ass.

"Don't fucking deny me what's mine, slut," I growl, and I bury my face between her thighs again. "I want to eat my fucking pussy. Now give it to me."

"Oh my God," she murmurs, but her voice is laced with lust.

Hate me, love me, I don't fucking care, I'm getting what's mine.

"Call me by my name, Pen."

"I wasn't calling you," she growls back.

"Don't pray to God when you're being licked by the devil himself."

Her legs tighten around me, but I push them apart and dig my nails into her skin so she complies. And I lap her up like there's no tomorrow, sucking on her until she falls apart again right on top of that fucking library table.

A soft moan escapes her mouth. "F-Fuck ..."

She looks spent, like a whore doped out on crack.

Exactly the way I like it.

SLAP!

"Ow!" she growls as I throw a flat hand on her pussy. "What the fuck?"

"Bad pussies need a spanking," I say.

And she definitely needs a wake-up call.

"Bad pussy?" she parrots.

"You thought I'd let you get away with stabbing me?" I raise a brow. "Not a chance."

"You just fucking licked m—"

"I took what I wanted from this pussy. And now I want it punished. Easy."

I spank her ass next, and it has her bumping up against the edge of the table. "Jiggle that ass more, Pen, and I will fucking claim that ass like it belongs to me."

"What?" she gasps. "You don't intend to—"

I stick two fingers inside her, and she practically mewls with delight. She swallows her moan back down, but half of it still leaves her mouth like a strangled mess, and it makes my killer heart throb.

"I'll take your asshole if I want to, whenever I want to," I say, slowly pushing farther and farther inside until I'm knuckle deep. "Every hole— every orifice—is mine to use and fuck."

***

PENELOPE

"You really are a sick fucker," I quip, gasping when he suddenly pulls out in one go.

Fuck.

How did I find myself in this position again? Bent over a table, used by a sicko like I'm some kind of fuck doll.

He holds up his fingers in front of my face. Both his fingers are coated with my juices. "Yet you're wet as can be."

I'm mortified.

Because I know he's fucking right. I'm still throbbing from him touching me. And the stone-dead look on his face is aggravating to say the least.

It's like he doesn't even care about what he's doing.

Like all of this is just a game to him.

A game ... to see how easily he can break me.

He thrusts in again, stopping my train of thought. All I can focus on is those fingers deep inside me, curling up until he hits the spot that almost makes me want to gyrate against the table.

Fuck. What's happening to me?

"You're so fucking wet for me. You really want to be fucked that badly by me, whore?"

I keep my mouth shut. I won't give him any more reasons to be crueler than he already is.

A hint of a smile tugs at the corner of his mouth, but it quickly fades.

His dark, soulless eyes home in on mine as he pulls out. "Maybe it's about time I did."

He's not actually thinking of—

His zipper goes down.

"I want to be the first to fuck this pussy raw." His hand swipes along my slit, rubbing my wetness over my ass. "Or maybe this fucking ass."

"Pussy," I quickly respond, begging in my head he won't pick the other one.

"That desperate, whore?" He slaps my pussy again, and I bite through the pain.

God, he's such a fucking sadist.

Suddenly, I feel that same piercing against my opening. "Beg."

"Fuck you," I hiss.

He grabs a fist full of my hair and pulls my head back. "Beg and I'll take your pussy. Now, or I'll fill up your ass instead."

There isn't even any lube. He wouldn't, right?

Fuck. He's definitely the kind of guy who would.

"Please," I say through gritted teeth.

His sunken-in eyes sparkle with desire. "Good girl."

He thrusts in without warning, without any restraint.

I gasp in shock, almost choking on the moan that follows as I try to keep it in.

He's huge.

I've never felt anything so deep inside me.

Let alone the fact that I can feel all of his piercings, flicking against my insides, and the worst one of them all pushes up against my clit.

On purpose, of course.

He thrusts in and out, and the piercing tickles my most sensitive part again and again. Slowly, at first, but once he picks up the pace, it's so hard to keep the moans at bay.

He's fucking me in the library, and I'm literally lying face-down on a table, letting him.

Fuck. What is wrong with me?

I've never been this fucking aroused.

"That's the face. Give me your best, Penelope. I won't take any less," he growls, thrusting in and out with fervor.

He fucking knows how to get me going, and I hate it.

I fucking hate how he already seems to know my body better than I do.

"I'm going to fucking fill you up," he groans. "And you're going to lay there and take it like a good fucking slut. Got it?"

When I look over my shoulder at him, I notice something from the corner of my eye. A pair of jeans that don't belong to either of us.

My breathing falters. "Someone's here. They can see us," I say.

Mortified, I try to get away, but he pins me to the table.

"So? Let them fucking watch," he growls back. "I'll give them a fucking show they'll remember."

What? He actually wants to continue with someone looking right at us?

He's insane. What if they go to the dean?

The jeans suddenly disappear, and I can hear footsteps running down the long hall.

Fuck, they're definitely going to tell someone.

Out of nowhere, he buries himself inside me to the hilt, making my mouth form an o-shape. And he leans over me to grab my face by my mouth, pushing his fingers behind my teeth like a goddamn leash.

"You thought I cared about giving a little peepshow?" he says through gritted teeth. "Nothing can stop me from using you until I've satiated every wicked, fucked-up desire in my head."

"You're fucking sick in the head," I quip.

"Tell me something I don't know," he murmurs, and he rams into me so hard I feel like I'm about to break the table.

I can feel every ridge pushing against my walls, making my clit thump with greed. Fuck, I don't think I can stop another tsunami rolling over me.

"No, no, no," I mutter.

Too late.

It's already happening, and I know he feels it because he begins to throb.

A low, rumbling laugh emanates from deep within his chest. "That's it, slut, break for me."

And he pounds into me. Three. Two. One.

An explosion of warmth fills me up, and by the time he's finished, it literally drips out onto the floor.

Fuck, I feel so fucking dirty. Who even does this in the library?

Him, apparently ... but now I do too.

He slaps my ass again, making me jolt up and down.

"You really thought you could resist," he says. "Not so feisty now, are you, slut?"

He tucks in his cock and steps away.

I get up from the table, defeated, my body still trembling from the onslaught of orgasms. My hand moves between my legs, feeling the wetness he created ... as well as the cum drooping down. Fuck. I'll have to take care of that.

"The least you can do is hand me a wipe," I say, flipping over so I can actually sit up straight.

"Fuck no." He invades my space again, only to push my panties right back where they were before, and he rubs it too, reminding me of how aroused I still am. "Keep my fucking cum right there, where it belongs, for the rest of the fucking day." He leans in to whisper into my ear. "Whenever you sit down, you'll be reminded of the fact that I fucking own you now."

I swallow away the lump in my throat. "You gonna physically stop me from wiping it away?"

A hint of a smile tugs at his lips. "I can't stop you ... but I *will* punish you if I find out you even so much as try."

I suck in a breath.

He adds, "So fuck around ... and find out."

Then he turns around and saunters off, aloof as fuck, leaving me completely shaken.

And out of my mind enraged.

25

ALISTAIR

I'm in the middle of gathering all the copies of the diary printed in one big stack when my phone rings.

"What's up?"

"Ali, is that how you say hi to your fucking father?"

Oh fuck. I should've checked the name on the screen.

I sigh. "Hi, Pops."

"Can you sound any more uninterested?"

"Sorry, I'm kinda busy," I reply.

"Busier than me?" He bursts out into laughter. "I doubt it. With all these cases I've been handling lately. Especially the one about the dude with black curly hair stealing some shit at a local shop."

Oh boy.

"You got anything to do with that by any chance?"

"No, so what did you want?" I ask.

"Sure." He clears his throat. "Anyhow, is there any chance you can speak with that Caruso kid for me?"

"What did he do?" I ask.

"Nothing, I only need him for a ... side job."

Oh fuck me. He's trying to enlist me in his off-the-books schemes again, and I don't like it one bit.

"Caruso gave part of his business dealings to his wife, so I made a deal with that woman, that Jeon ... Jan ... Jon ..."

I roll my eyes. "Jeong-Suk."

"Yeah, that's the one. I can't ever fucking remember her name." He laughs like it's no big deal.

"It's Korean."

"Of course," he adds, like he knew all along, and it makes me want to stab myself in the ear because it's so annoying to listen to. "Anyhow, I've been trying to reach her, but I can't seem to get in touch, so if you could just tell your boy to call his mom and tell her to contact me, that'd be amazing, kiddo."

"Okay, but I'm not your fucking errand boy. You know that, right?"

"You're my son, Ali," he spits back. "You think I'd ask just anyone? You'd better start showing a little respect for the hustle, Ali."

"I respect your job as chief of police. Not the other part."

"Says the guy who steals to have fun."

He knows me too well.

"I got that part from you, you know," I reply.

"I know. So what's it going to be, then?"

I roll my eyes and sigh out loud. "Fine, I'll do it."

I don't want to deal with this, but my dad always makes his business my business.

"That's my boy. Tell her I've got the goods, and I just need a drop-off point and date. That's it."

Goods. Nice euphemism for drugs and guns. Very inconspicuous.

"I can't guarantee anything, but I'll try," I say.

"Good boy," he says.

Ugh. I hate that.

"I'm gonna go back to studying now. See ya."

"Of course, son. Good luck."

I hang up the phone before he can ask me anything else and immediately call Felix.

"Hey. I've got it all copied like you asked."

"Good. You know what to do with them."

I grind my teeth. "Are you sure this is the right move? She's gonna hate us even more."

"Do it," he retorts. "I'll deal with her after."

"Okay," I say. "You'd better be sure about this because there's no way back when I'm done."

"I don't do regrets," he replies. "Just get it done."

He hangs up the phone.

Fine.

I grab the stack of papers and ring Dylan. "Yo. Hey, two questions. One, my dad called, and he wants your mom to call him. I don't know why."

"Oh, Dad's been wanting to push some of the more illicit stuff to my mom so he doesn't get caught up in another scandal with the university. She's using her maiden name."

"Right." I don't really care. "Second question: Wanna help me spread these fucking pages around today?"

"Ugh, do I have to? There's a party at the Nu Sigma Delta sorority all fucking day, and I don't wanna miss a minute."

Him and his parties.

"It'll only take an hour," I say.

"Fine, fine, I'll do it." Dylan sighs. "But you owe me."

I already know what he wants. "I'll hook you up with my dad's guys."

"That's what I'm talking about. All right, bro, see you later."

"Thanks for the help." I hang up the phone.

Everything I do, everything I need … it's all an exchange.

Whether it's money, goods, or merely their time, nothing is free.

Not in this world.

And if we want to make it, it's best to learn early on not to give a fuck.

Even when your fucking heart bleeds.

This stack of papers stares at me, but instead of getting to work right away, I sit by the window and grab my pen and paper, then start to draw.

On the grass outside, the girl with the purple hair sits with her friends, pretending to be blissfully unaware of the dangers that lurk around every corner.

But we both know that's a lie.

Underneath her unabashed veneer hides a scared little girl, looking for something to hold on to.

Safety.

I notice it all.

I don't need to feel her anger when she catches me stealing to know she's afraid.

Afraid of what she might discover if she digs any deeper.

I draw her wavy hair drifting in the wind, her pink cheeks, her brazen lip color. Painstakingly, I make a portrait of a girl who's captured my imagination as well as those of my friends.

Everything about her is ours.

Shared.

Consumed.

But this drawing ... it's mine and mine alone.

***

PENELOPE

I try my best to focus on my group of friends. I really needed a calm-down period after getting so wound up in the library.

But my mind constantly veers off track to what happened in the library. Those fucking boys. I can't ever get away from them, can I?

I made a deal with them, but something tells me they're not gonna keep their end of our bargain.

Fuckers.

I should've known better than to trust them to help me find the one responsible for my sister's misery. I should just go and find Nathan myself.

In fact, they're probably hiding him somewhere in that goddamn frat house themselves, just so they can use me for a few days longer. I mean, I haven't seen a sign of Nathan's face anywhere, not since that note was shoved under my door, so where the fuck else could he be?

Unless he's part of a different frat house than the Skull & Serpent Society.

"Pen? What do you think?" Kayla asks, pulling me from my thoughts.

"Huh, what?" I mutter, confused.

She frowns. "Do you prefer Italian or Chinese?"

"Uh, Italian?" I reply. "Sorry, what's this about?"

"We were discussing where we were going out to dinner tonight. You know. A little get-together."

Oh man, I really missed a lot of the conversation.

"Are you okay?" Crystal asks. "You seem a little distracted."

Calvin rolls his eyes and rubs his lips together. "I know what she's thinking about."

Jeremy quickly jabs him in the side with his elbow.

"Is it those boys again?" Kayla asks, side-eyeing Calvin and Jeremy. "I swear to God, if y'all are hiding something—"

"Don't make us the bad guys," Jeremy quips, adjusting his glasses.

"I'm fine, guys, honestly," I say.

"Are you sure?" Kayla asks. "You ran off so quickly after you told me about that 'thing' that happened in the woods." She makes air quotes with her fingers. "But I never got the chance to ask you all about it."

"It was my choice ..." I rub my lips together. "I don't do regrets."

She frowns. "Well, they'd better not hurt you. I've seen them with girls. They don't treat anyone right, but especially girls."

"Yeah, like goddamn throwaway fuck dolls," Calvin says.

"I don't care what they do to me," I say. "I know what I want from them, and I'm not going to stop until I get it."

Crystal looks at me intently, trying to decipher what the words really mean. But I don't want them to get too close to the danger ... too close to me.

Suddenly, someone walks past us carrying a piece of paper, and from the corner of my eyes, I spot a picture I recognize.

I immediately stand and run toward the person, snatching the paper from their hands.

"Hey!"

But I'm not paying attention to her.

All I can look at is Nathan's photo enlarged across the paper, the one that was also in my sister's diary ... Along with a note.

Chills run up and down my spine.

"I was trying to read that," the girl in front of me says, annoyed.

"Sorry, I just need to see," I say, quickly scanning the rest.

There's a request for contact at the bottom, along with a phone number.

Fuck.

"Where'd you get this?" I ask.

She points at the biggest building in the university. "They're all over the bulletin boards. So can I have mine back now?" She snatches the sheet from my hands. "Thanks."

She walks off, but my eyes are already set on the building up ahead.

"Pen? What happened?" Kayla asks, but I'm far too focused to even stop walking.

Everywhere I look, people are walking around with these posters, but not all of them show Nathan's face. But they are all pictures I recognize ... pictures taken from my sister's private diary.

The worst of them all is a poster with my sister's face on it with a radiant smile. A smile I miss so very much today.

And now it's right here in front of me, being degraded, used, disgraced.

I pull the picture off the first bulletin board I find, staring at it with tears staining my eyes. There's a note underneath her face. The note my sister wrote the night she died.

Fuck.

Why? Why would they do this?

Every step I take inside the building feels like I'm sinking deeper into the fires of hell.

People walk past me and even look at me when I pass them.

That's when I spot a poster with my actual fucking face on it.

I rip it off the wall.

There's a note on it too.

Innocent? Or fucked-up whore? You decide.

The note crumples in my hand, a fire blazing inside me that won't be easy to quench.

My eyes search the area, and I stop by every fucking bulletin board I find and rip off each and every one of the posters, dumping them all in the trash bin where they belong.

How dare they exploit my sister's diary like this?

To use her name, her photo, with these words ...

Shameful.

I'm burning up with rage, but the volcano inside only really explodes the moment I spot Dylan slapping the posters all over the wall to my left.

I'm not gonna let this fucking slide.

26

DYLAN

I'm happily slapping all these posters around my dad's playground when some girl comes storming at me out of nowhere.

And with some girl, I mean a certain purple-haired violent little Valkyrie on a mission.

Before I can even so much as blink, she's right up in my face.

SLAP!

The sting of her hand burns on the skin of my cheek.

Everyone in the hallway stops and stares. Some even snigger, but she seems dead-fucking serious.

Very sexy.

"Where the fuck did you get the nerve?" she growls at me.

I rub my cheek. Damn, she's got some power shots for a small girl. "Hello to you too."

She steals the poster I put on the bulletin board and holds it up in front of me. "Give me one good reason I shouldn't smack your ass into the fucking hospital right now."

Is that a challenge?

A devilish smirk forms on my face. "Nice pickup line. Ten out of ten, really gets me going." I wink.

She rips up the poster into tiny pieces and throws it at me like confetti. "Is this your idea of helping out?" she growls. "Stealing my sister's fucking diary and putting her private stuff all over the school?"

My God, she really is going for the full frontal attack here. I'm impressed. And weirdly aroused as well.

I raise a brow. "Calm down. People are staring at you."

A handful of people have gathered around us, but her eyes focus solely on me.

"Do I look like I give a fuck?" she yells back, her tits practically bursting out of the laced black off-the-shoulders top she's wearing.

Oh yes ... so very fucking sexy.

"You'd better take every one of these posters down before I—"

"You'll what?" I interrupt, and I grab her arm. "Hurt me?"

I'd love to see her try, though.

I wonder how much pain she could give me.

Fuck me. The thought already has me riled up.

But now is not the time for pleasure.

I pull her away from the crowd to a secluded corner, where I shove her against the wall. And I fish my lighter from my pocket and hold it right up in her face. "Simmer down, little slut."

"Or what? You've already embarrassed me beyond repair," she growls back. "That's my sister's face and my face out there being slandered."

The fire burns her cheek. "It's not just you," I growl back. *Didn't she see the other posters?* "We used lots of pictures from the diary."

"*We?*" she parrots.

She turns her head and looks around until she finally spots Alistair casually handing out the posters to passersby. She hadn't even seen him in her blinded rage.

And when their eyes connect ... oh boy, it's like fireworks going off.

Amazing.

"Motherf—"

I grab her chin and force her to look at me. "This is necessary."

"Necessary? You call pasting my sister and her face all over campus 'necessary'?"

"Yes. Trust me."

I know what it looks like. But I'm not at liberty to tell her exactly why, or she may ruin our whole idea.

"Trust you? Why? Give me one good fucking reason."

Her round lips curl up the same way they did when she tried to confront me in that auditorium where she pulled the fire alarm. Like they're about to bite into me, yet at the same time, they look so fucking ...

Delicious.

And I wonder if I could.

If Felix would kill me if I did.

But fuck it.

I slam my lips onto hers.

Her lips taste of lemongrass tequila and rainbow Skittles, sour, sweet, bitter, fresh, all wrapped into one tasty package that I can't get enough of as I claim her mouth.

God, her lips feel so good against mine.

I've kissed many girls, but never one I've wanted this much.

And one who despises me this badly.

No wonder Felix hates her so much.

Suddenly, my lips sting, and I pull back only for her to bite down, hard.

Blood oozes on my lip, and I lick it up. "Bad girl."

"You're a fucking bully, and you know it," she snipes. "You had no right."

"What? To kiss you?" I muse.

Her cheeks flush briefly, but she quickly snaps back to her brazen self. "You really have a death wish, don't you?"

I raise a brow. "No. Did you forget about our deal?"

Her nostrils flare. "Yeah, well, a deal only works if both parties hold up their fucking end."

I tilt my head. "What do you think we're doing, smart-ass?"

"Kissing me after putting those horrible posters all over the school?" she quips.

"Horrible? I beg to differ. They're poetic if you ask me." I grin. "Poetic justice."

"That's my fucking name and picture along with the word whore. In what fucking world is that poetic?"

"In the same world where you begged us to help you out," I muse.

"You call this helping?" She's like a volcano about to erupt, and I'm here for it.

"I'm doing what I'm supposed to do," I retort. "That's all."

"Who told you to do this? To print out my sister's diary and paste it all over the school? Huh? Was it Felix?" she rebukes. "For what reason?" When I don't answer, she sneers, "Figured."

She kicks me in the nuts. Again.

And fuck me, this one hurts worse than the last one.

God, this girl packs a punch, all right.

"You deserve that," she hisses.

"True, I do," I reply, my tone fluctuating.

She runs off.

Fuck.

Lost her again.

Groaning, I grab my package as a wave of nausea overcomes me. But when I look up, Alistair is right there, staring at me. "What the fuck happened?"

"What do you think happened?" I snarl back. "She knows. Okay? And now she's gonna go straight to Felix."

He shrugs. "Not my problem. His idea." And he continues putting the posters all over the walls like it's nobody's business. "He knew this was a possible consequence."

"But everyone fucking saw," I say.

"They already knew we were bastards anyway," he says, winking. "Now let's finish up."

***

PENELOPE

I bang on the frat house doors. "Open up!"

I keep going until finally someone does. "What do you want? Jesus."

Some burly dude with bad frizzled hair blocks my way. I don't know who the fuck it is, but I don't even care. "Where is Felix?"

"Not here."

"Fuck that." I try to push past the dude, but he easily shoves me away.

"Whoa, don't even fucking try."

"Let me in," I growl. "I need to fucking talk to him."

"Who? Felix?" He snorts. "Tough luck, I already told you he wasn't here. He's at a party down the street."

"What makes you think I believe your fucking lies?" I spit back, putting my hands against my side. "All of you motherfuckers are the same."

He laughs at me in a condescending way. "Oh yeah, what's that, then?"

I lean into his face. "Liars. Bunch of fucked-up assholes."

"Go on." He grins. "Give me your worst."

"Fuck you and that fucking bird's nest on your head."

He snorts. "That all you got, little rat?"

My eyes widen. "You know ..." I grasp his collar. "Where is he?"

He grips my hands and forcefully shoves me away until I fall down onto the pavement. I groan with pain but try not to let it get to me. But as I get up, the dude is clearly making fun of me.

"Fuck you. I'll fucking find him, and when I do, you'd better pray for his fucking soul," I say, and I spit in his direction.

"Good luck with that," he retorts, slamming the door shut.

Fuck that.

I charge at the door and slam it with my fists but give up after a few times. Of course, every passerby on the street is looking at me like I'm a lunatic, but I don't care.

If Felix isn't here, I'll go fucking find him at the party instead.

I storm down the street to where that dude was looking until I find the frat house blasting noise across the yard. Everything's covered in cans and drink cups with beer spillage and chips lying all over. Seems like they've been partying all morning, and it doesn't look like they intend to stop either.

So much for studying.

I head straight for the building with a bunch of those posters tucked away in my pocket. The music destroys my ears the second I step inside. It's fucking hot and sweaty in here, with lots of people dancing and talking. It's as if the entire campus is here.

I steal a cup from someone's hand and dip into the crowd before they can even say hey. I bring it to my nose, but the mere scent of rum makes me cringe. It's a good cover, though, so I keep my cup close as I make my way through the bustling party, looking for a familiar face.

I don't fucking care how long it takes to find him. He's gonna pay for what he did.

Most of the noise drifts up from the basement to my right, so I walk down the steps into a damp, dark area, where nothing but a few disco LEDs light the faces of the people dancing. A remix of Camilla Cabello's "Shameless" starts playing. The bass is low, thrumming, just as my heartbeat as I slide into the crowd, watching out for every corner of the room.

But he's nowhere to be seen.

Suddenly, a pair of hands land on my ass, and I turn around, only to be swept up by someone I don't know, grinding away at me.

I push him. "Ew, get off me."

"C'mon, let's dance," the guy says, pressing himself and his bulge up against me. "That's what you came here for, right?"

I step on his foot, and he releases me, but when I attempt to get away, he grabs my arm. "Where are you going? I wasn't done yet."

Out of the shadows, a dark, sinister figure appears, his eyes finding mine first before a hand shoots out from the crowd to grip the guy's wrist. In his other hand, a knife, the tip edging into the guy's waist.

Felix.

I gasp in shock at the bestial rage in his eyes.

"You heard her. Let. Her. Go."

27

PENELOPE

A standoff ensues. It lasts mere seconds, but it's enough time for Felix to push the knife so deep into his tattooed skin that blood rolls down. "Unless you want me to carve you up."

Fuck. That was hot, even when it shouldn't be.

My heart pounces in my throat as the guy's hand suddenly comes off my wrist with ease.

He just stands there, blinking rapidly at both the knife and Felix himself.

And the guy runs off within a split second, disappearing through the crowd to get away as fast as possible.

Away from the one person I've been trying to find.

Felix focuses his gaze on me, but doesn't release me from his grip. Instead, he pulls me close to him and shoves the knife underneath my chin. "You've got guts showing up here."

But I don't frighten that easily. "You think a little intimidation will scare me?"

His top lip quirks up but only briefly. Then he tucks the knife into his pocket. "Do you even know where you are?"

I shake my head. "I don't care."

"You should. You're standing on Phantom territory."

"Phantom?" I frown.

He leans in again and whispers, "They don't like the Skull & Serpent Society."

"Then why are you even here?" I rebuke.

"I was trying to find someone ... until I saw that asshole touching you."

I try to push him away, but he won't let me go. "Like I give a fuck who these frat houses belong to. I'm not part of your little frat business, so leave me out of it."

"You became part of it the moment you made a deal with me," he says, his voice darkening as he grips my chin and forces me to look at him. "And they would probably kill to have a slice of you."

Grinding my teeth, I reply. "So what? It's not like you give a shit."

He tilts his head to whisper into my ear again, the scent of his cologne penetrating my nostrils as harshly as his fingers did when he and his buddies used me in the forest. "Fourth lesson ... *no one* touches what's mine."

Wow. I didn't know he was this possessive over me.

I gulp and swallow back my pride as my pussy throbs, and I push my legs together.

"I'm not your—"

He squeezes my throat until I can't speak. "Toy? You are mine in every sense of the word."

His tongue dips out and drags a line all the way up from my neck to my ear.

I try to squeak, but no sound comes out.

"And if you try to deny it, things will only get harder for you ..."

He presses up against my white pants with his bulge, and I can feel his hard-on growing against me. "You should be grateful I'm even allowing Dylan and Ali to touch you. Now tell me why you came here."

Grateful? Like it's some kind of privilege to be fucked by all three of them?

Fuck.

When his fingers loosen up a bit, I suck in a much-needed breath. "You know damn well why I came looking for you. How fucking dare you put my sister's diary all over the school for everyone to see?"

"I'm surprised you saw the posters so quickly," he says.

I raise a fist, but he catches my hand just in time and keeps it in the air.

"Pretend we're dancing."

"Why should—"

He pulls me up to his chest and twirls me around, showing me off to people who were looking at us. And after another twist, they look away like nothing's going on.

"They're not staring at us anymore," he says. "Good girl."

"Give me one good reason I shouldn't scream at the top of my lungs right now," I growl.

He leans forward to whisper into my ear, "Then you'll never find who chased your sister to her death."

My breath falters.

He bends me so far I can barely stay standing, if it wasn't for his hand firmly pressed into the small of my back. "Those posters are there for a reason. I don't need to tell you why. You just need to accept that we're using them for a purpose."

"Fuck that, you'll have to give me something better," I quip. "Why did you print out her face and slap on that horrible quote? Why is Nathan there and a bunch of other people from her diary? And why is my face on there too along with a fucked-up line about me not being innocent?"

He lifts me again and pulls me so close that all the air is knocked from my lungs. "Hate me all you want, it won't change anything."

"Tell me why," I growl. "At least give me my dignity."

He snorts and shoves me up against a wall. "You already lost your dignity the moment you came to me and begged." He tugs at my hair until my face turns upward, and he leans in to press an actual fucking kiss onto my skin. "And I would hang those posters a thousand times over if it means I could hear you say those words again. So beg."

I'm so fucking angry I could scream, but if I did, everyone would look and kick us out. And Felix said he was here for a purpose. What if it's tied to those posters? Even though it's beyond fucked up what he made Dylan and Alistair do, there must be a reason. I have to believe it, or else all my pain will have been for nothing.

My fingers push against his chest, but he grabs my hands and pins them above my head to the wall. Then he plants another deep, sultry kiss onto my skin, turning up the heat, and I can't stop the moan from spilling from my mouth when he grinds up against me.

"Please ..."

"Go on," he murmurs.

"Stop."

He pulls away, his eyes narrowing. "You trying to back out of our agreement, Pen?" He makes a tsk sound. "I expected more from you. You know I won't allow it."

"No," I say. "I just need you to stop trying to hurt me."

He tilts his head, and a deadly smirk slowly forms on his face. "I'm not going to stop until I have what I came here for. And what I need is for you to suffer in silence while I do what I do best."

"And what's that?" I ask. "Bully girls?"

"Destroy people."

He says it with such a stone-cold look that I feel the chill in my bones.

"And that includes me," I say under my breath.

"If it gets me what I want," he replies.

"What the fuck do you even want, Felix?"

He stares me down like only a cold-hearted killer could. "Revenge."

The air is thick with electricity, and all I can think about is how much I want to steal his knife and ram it straight into his heart ... and then let him rail me up against this wall.

Fuck. I hate how confused he makes me.

"You wanted my help? You got it," he growls. "Then take it like a good girl." He narrows his eyes and leans in. "And get out of my way before I finger fuck you in front of this entire crowd."

I swallow. Hard.

Suddenly, his phone rings, and it distracts us both.

He pulls away from me and answers, "What do you want?"

"He dialed the fucking phone." I can hear Dylan's voice blasting through the speakers.

"Put the burner phone against your phone. I wanna have a word."

"Who?" I ask.

He shoves me aside and walks off through the crowd, leaving me breathless and infuriated at the same time. A toxic combination.

But I'm not going to let him get away that easily.

When I spot him going up the stairs, still clutching that phone to his ear, I run through the crowd as fast as I can, chasing after him. I catch up halfway toward the building's exit. He just put down his phone, so the conversation is finished, but I missed half of it.

Shit.

Right before he reaches the door, I sneak sideways past him and block the exit.

His nostrils flare. "Move."

"No. If this has something to do with those posters, I want to know what this guy wants and why you would do such fucked-up shit."

He gets up in my face, planting a fist against the wall to my left. "You can't handle it, little girl."

"Do I look like a little girl to you?"

He towers over me. "Yeah. You shove your nose into business it doesn't belong."

"You made it my business the second you used her stuff and my photo." I fold my arms and plant my feet firmly against the sides of the wall. "Now I'm coming with, or we're both going to be stuck here together."

He grumbles out loud, borderline raging in front of everyone. "You wanna see? Fine, I'll fucking show you." Then suddenly, he puts his hands on my waist and lifts me. I squeal as he throws me over his shoulder.

"Put me down!" I yell as he marches out the door. "I can fucking walk."

My cheeks flush with heat when I stare right into the eyes of all the other people still partying up ahead in the hallway.

"You couldn't fucking stay away, could you?" Felix growls at me. "Fuck, you're just like your sister. This is on you."

Just like my sister?

Why the fuck would he bring her into this?

"Hey, I didn't ask you to fucking carry me out of the house like this!" I say, incensed he'd even go as far as to accuse me.

"If you don't move, I'll make you," he retorts. "Simple. Effective."

"Embarrassing," I add as everyone who stays behind in the house to party practically laughs at us from the porch.

"Lesson five, Penelope ... Actions have consequences. And I will be the one to fucking punish you for misbehaving."

SLAP!

I yelp as his flat hand lands on my ass.

"Wow! And in front of all of these people too!"

"I told you, I don't care who sees," he replies. "And I don't fucking care how loud you scream. You're coming with me now."

"I can walk," I growl back.

He snorts. "I'm sure you can. You've been walking in my way for days."

I roll my eyes as he carries me across the street and all the way back to the Skull & Serpent Society. I don't know why or what's the point, but maybe he decided to meet up with whoever he called.

The door's already open, and Dylan waits for him. "Sweet. You brought along a snack."

A snack? Me?

He licks his lips.

"Zip it," Felix snarls back. "She wants to fucking watch."

Dylan's eyes widen. "What? You're joking, right? You know what happened when Eve—"

Felix grabs his face by the cheeks. "Quiet."

"Eve what?" I snap, and I fight my way out of Felix's grip when he's distracted.

I only make it down by falling to the floor on my hips, and it hurts like hell on this hardwood flooring. But good God, am I glad he's no longer carrying me like some kind of caveman.

"What did my sister do?" I ask.

"Doesn't matter. Come." Felix grabs my wrist and drags me through the hallways.

He throws open a door underneath the staircase that leads into the basement.

And it's so dark down there I'm starting to worry this is just his way to get rid of me.

I gulp. "Where are we going?"

"You made yourself part of my business. Now you'll get to see it firsthand," he replies.

He tries to push me downstairs first, but when I take my first step, I freeze.

I smell something ... a kind of metallic burn that I can only describe as ...

Blood.

Adrenaline courses through my veins as I go down slowly, with Felix following suit.

Down there, between all the stacked-up boxes and underneath a grimy light, is a guy seated on a chair.

Nathan.

His hands are chained to the armrests, his legs to the feet of the chair, both with thick metal rods that got ripped off the ceiling. Black tape covers his mouth. Water droplets slowly fall onto his head from the ceiling below, while blood drips down his chin, his face covered in bruises.

Oh God.

My hand immediately flies to my mouth to stop the squeal from leaving my body.

They tortured him.

I knew these boys were sick, but I never realized how deep it went.

How far they could go.

And now I'm not even sure this is the worst they could do.

Felix grabs my shoulders from behind. "You wanted to know who I was talking to. Now you know."

Nathan?

They did all this in a matter of minutes?

Alistair jumps off one of the crates in the back, making me jolt up and down from the scare. "That's why we hung those posters with that number."

"A prepaid phone," Dylan adds.

"It's also why we needed to hang up yours and your sister's pictures around the university as well."

"So no one would think you were only aiming for him," I mutter in disbelief.

"Exactly. Don't want the rest of the school to get suspicious," Alistair replies with his hands in his pockets.

"Little Nathan here was missing in action for quite some time," Dylan muses. "Turns out he was hiding out at that Phantom frat house he apparently belongs to."

"Where we were? That party?" I ask, my eyes widening as I gaze at Felix.

"I was searching for him there," Felix says. "Until you came along and tried to interfere."

With a smug smile on his face, Dylan says, "Doesn't matter. He saw the posters when he went out, and he took the bait like easy prey, so I dragged him back here."

Felix pulls aside my hair to whisper into my ear, "And now you have what you wanted." His teeth grind near my ear. "Revenge."

I suck in a breath, unable to let it go.

Alistair walks out from the darkness beyond the crates, his body and face and neat white shirt covered in blood. He drops the hammer near Nathan's feet, who begins to whimper.

Seems like they already gave him a beating.

"Well, hi there, little slut," Alistair says. "Nice of you to join us. Your idea?" He looks over at Felix.

"She wouldn't stop," Felix replies.

"Since when do you cave?"

"Since she needs a lesson," he spits back. "Prep him."

Alistair grabs Nathan's face and rips the tape off so harshly it makes his skin break out in blood.

"Fuck! That hurts!" Nathan yelps.

"It'll hurt even more if you don't do what we say," Alistair says. "Now are you going to answer all our questions? Or do you want us to rough you up some more?"

"My face is fucking botched up!" he growls. "You're not gonna get away with this!"

Alistair grips his face so tightly his lips get squashed together. "Better hope you give the answers we're looking for, or Felix will have his way with you."

The fear is locked into Nathan's eyes as Alistair steps away.

Felix steps forward and grabs the hammer, then glances at me over his shoulder. "Well, Pen? How far do you want me to go?"

All of their eyes are on me, and it almost feels like this is all a test.

A test to see how far I'm willing to go to get justice for my sister.

If I'll say something or let him rip into Nathan.

But they don't know I already promised myself I would go to hell for her.

And it's Felix's dark, heavy voice that reminds me there's no going back.

"Go on then," I say. "Make him speak."

28

FELIX

I watch Penelope's face with keen interest.

I knew bringing her here would be a risk with a heavy price, but it's a price I was willing to pay to see her reaction.

She wants to know how depraved we can get? She hasn't even seen the worst yet.

This is going to be one hell of a show.

I brace my feet against the concrete floor and smash the hammer into Nathan's leg.

He yelps in pain, crying bloody tears, but I whip up his face so he looks at me instead of the ground. "Did you fucking push a note underneath her door?"

"I forced the fucking girl in that Alpha Psi sorority do it for me," he screams back, his face all red from the pain he's attempting to swallow.

I grip his preppy-ass by the collar and growl, "Tell me why you threatened her."

I tower over him and let it sink in, then turn my head toward Pen.

I want her to look into my eyes and witness the cruelty. The vile, twisted desires coursing through my veins. I want her to see it all.

"Having regrets yet, Pen?" I ask.

She shakes her head even though I can see it's hard for her to watch Nathan squirm in his seat.

"Answer me."

"No," she replies, feet firmly planted on the ground, her arms rigid by her side. Like she's bracing herself for what's to come.

WHACK!

I smash the hammer into the same leg, breaking it sideways.

"FUCK! My leg! You broke it!" Nathan squeals like a pig, but I'm only interested in Pen's reaction, the look on her face. But instead of looking terrified, she looks confident. As though nothing could ever shake her.

I'm impressed.

For a little rat, she sure has a lot of guts.

"Stop him!" Nathan barks at Alistair and Dylan, but they don't even bother to reply. "Why won't you stop him? He'll kill me."

"Maybe I will," I muse.

"Why? Why are you doing this?" Nathan begs. "Just because of some fucking prank?"

I snort. "A prank? Good one."

His face contorts. "You don't even fucking know her. Why do you even care?"

I tilt my head. "You think I don't know her?" My eyes narrow as I bend over, leaning on my own knees as I stare into his eyes. "I've seen the darkest parts of her soul. And now I'm going to make you pay for reminding her they exist."

I slam my fist into his broken leg and watch him suffer with pleasure.

I crack my knuckles as I listen to his groans of anguish.

God, nothing gets me going quite like a good beating.

"You hurt what belongs to me, Nathan," I say, cracking my other knuckles.

"Fuck you, you know she's going to face the same fate as Eve!" Nathan growls.

I glance at Pen over my shoulder.

She's staring at him, but her eyes are glossed over, like she's not really here.

Like her mind's gone off to that day ... the day we all watched her sister jump off the cliff.

Only this time, she's holding her hand and jumping off with her.

So I raise the hammer and break his fucking hand to snap her out of it.

WHACK!

He cries out in agony. "Please, stop!"

"You threatened Pen. Admit it," I say.

"Yes!" he yelps.

I grab him by the face. "Did you do it to Eve too?" My voice is unhinged, but my emotions are too.

"No!"

"Liar! What did you do to her?" I growl, holding the hammer over his other hand. "Are you the reason she jumped?"

"No! I don't know why she jumped." He closes his eyes. "Please, I swear to God, I'm telling the truth. Don't do this, please! My parents depend on me to make it through university, and I'll never be able to finish it without functioning hands."

"You should have thought of that before you messed with her," I retort.

"It wasn't my idea!" Suddenly, his eyes widen, and he swallows. "No, no, you didn't—"

"Hear that?" I grab his collar. "Now we're finally talking."

"I lied," he says.

"No, you spilled the truth by accident. Now tell me whose idea it was."

"No one," he says. "I just don't want you to hurt me. I'll say anything you want me to." He's really sweating it now. "Don't you know torture only makes people tell you what you want to hear?"

"Hmm ... and what is it you think I want to hear?"

"That I'm sorry?" he mutters.

I raise a brow. "Are you? You scared her."

"I didn't mean to. I just wanted her to stop searching."

"Right ... You ..." I mumble.

"Yes, me."

"Because there was no one else involved who told you to do this, right?" I pet his cheek with the hammer.

He visibly gulps. "No, no. I was just trying to get out of responsibility."

He glares at Penelope over my shoulders. "Please. I'm sorry. Make him stop."

My nostrils flare.

I'm done with his lies.

I drop the hammer, and he literally breathes a sigh of relief.

Too early.

I fish my knife from my pocket, grab his hand, and slice off his finger while he screams for mercy, the sound like music to my ears.

God, I've fucking missed this.

He squeals like a pig. "My finger! My finger! Oh my God!"

I hold it up to the flickering light above us, admiring the view of flesh and bone, dripping with fresh, warm blood, right on top of his head.

"You're insane!" he shrieks.

I grab him by the hair and make him look up at his own goddamn index finger. "No, you are, for lying to my face." I lower the finger until it's right above his face. "Now, let's see ... what should I do with this? Send it to your parents?" He shakes his head in fright. "Your little sister who was begging you to pay attention to her?"

"How do you know about her?" His skin turns pale. "Did you go through my phone?"

"You think we wouldn't?" Dylan pitches in. "You underestimate us."

"No, no ... I think I know what to do with this," I say, dangling his finger above his face like a wet noodle. "Maybe I should fucking feed it to you."

His eyes widen, and he vomits all over himself.

I only manage to just pull away before he covers me.

"Fucking gross," I snarl, stepping away.

"Oh God," he groans.

"Yeah, better pray to fucking God, all right," I reply, and I wipe off some of the blood that managed to land on my expensive shirt. "You ruined my clothes."

"You cut off my finger!" Nathan cries.

"You prefer dying?" I say, clutching my knife.

He vehemently shakes his head.

I move the knife underneath his chin. "You deserve it, though ...."

"I didn't make that fucking girl jump!" he says. "You've got the wrong guy!"

I'm about to slice this motherfucker's neck.

"Wait," Pen suddenly says.

I turn to look at her.

Now she chooses to put a stop to it?

"You're not going to ... kill him, are you?" she asks.

My eyes narrow. "Suddenly grew a conscience?"

"I think he's covering for someone. Killing him will only make it easier for that person to get away with what they did. And you said he was part of the Phantom frat house. They'll surely come after you guys when they find out." She pauses. "He's paid the price for what he did."

She has a point. A good one too. Which I wish she hadn't made because I was really looking forward to butchering this asshole.

I look down at my own bloody shirt, the scent of blood riling me up. It's not nearly enough bloodshed for threatening the girl who belongs to me. But it'll have to do for now.

I point my knife right at Nathan's face. "You tell one fucking soul about what happened in this basement, and I will make sure to cut out your tongue and slice your throat personally. Do you understand?"

He nods a few times, shaking heavily.

"Get him out of my sight," I growl over my shoulder at Dylan.

Dylan frowns. "What? You're not f—"

"Do it," I interject, and I step away before I do something we'll all regret.

"Okay," Dylan responds, and he starts untying Nathan together with Alistair, who helps him get Nathan under control. They tie his bloody hands together with a piece of rope and escort him up the stairs.

Out of my sight.

Away from my cruel intentions.

But I've got my fucking souvenir.

I stare at the bloody finger and tuck it into my pocket, then turn around to face the girl who wanted to know so badly what I was capable of.

"Did that scare you?" I ask.

She shakes her head, but when I step closer she shakes a little. "I just never expected it to go this far."

I stand before her in all my bloody, fucked-up glory, tracing a line from her cheek down to her chin, blood staining her skin.

"This is what you asked for. What you begged me for ..." I say, savoring the tense look she gives me. "I would've killed him for you."

She shudders as I grip her face and pull her in to claim a kiss from those sweet fucking lips that have been begging me to claim them.

The thrill of the chase has left me in a frenzy, and without the ability to quench that thirst.

Because my prey still walks ...

So I kiss her instead, aiming all my wicked desires at her.

And fuck me, is it long overdue.

Her lips are tantalizing, nothing short of fucking perfect for me. And I stake my fucking claim by piercing her lips open with my tongue and licking the roof of her mouth and her tongue.

God, that fucking tongue could fucking kill me if I let it.

The way it moves reminds me of how she wrapped it around my shaft not too long ago, and the thought makes me as hard as fuck, my bulge straining against the fabric of my pants.

Fuck.

She's too much.

I pull away and look at the bloody markings on her face. My fucking territory.

"You remind me so much of her."

Her lips part. "What?"

"Get out before I satisfy my cravings with you," I growl.

She's frozen for a sec, her eyes glimmering with fear.

"I'm doing you a fucking favor. Now take it." I point at the stairs.

She immediately runs off, her feet tiptoeing up the staircase, the sound a delight to my ears.

Normally, I'd bolt after her for a good chase.

But I'll tame that beast inside me, for now.

29

ALISTAIR

In the dark, we drive the fucker all the way to Priory Forest, where all the good parties take place. Not the kind of half-assed, damp-ass parties these fuckers from Phantom throw.

We carry Nathan out of the car, his body weighing a ton. Near The Edge we dump him, his head hanging over the balance, where Eve once jumped to her death.

A fitting punishment for threatening her sister, if you ask me.

Dylan unties him and shoves him farther over the edge. "And remember, fucker, if you talk about this to anyone ..." Dylan points a finger at his temple and pretends a gun goes off. "Your brain splatters all over the walls of the university."

"I have a broken leg, and I'm missing a bloody fucking finger!" he screams. "What the fuck do you expect me to do, huh?"

I shrug. "Go to a doctor for all I care. Tell them you accidentally cut it off when you were trying to saw a tree or some shit."

"Saw a tree? In what fucking world would I ever do that?" he retorts. "No fucking rich kids cut down trees in their spare time."

I step away. "Beats me. I'm trying to help you. Be grateful."

"Help me?" he squeals. "You fucking lured me to your fucking basement, tied me up, and beat the shit out of me. What the fuck is wrong with you?!"

Dylan laughs. "A lot, thank you for the compliment."

"You're fucking sick bastards," Nathan spits, clutching his hand as it oozes blood.

"Damn right, we are," Dylan replies. He throws his arm around my shoulders. "Let's go."

"Wait!" Nathan yells as Dylan and I turn around. "You're just gonna leave me here?"

"Yup, that was the plan." I glance at him over my shoulder. "Unless you want us to finish the job."

He slams his mouth shut, his hand tightening around his finger like he's trying to stop the bleeding.

"You'll fucking pay for this. You know that, right?" he yells as we walk off.

"Whatever you want, pretty boy," I reply, not even giving him a single look.

This fucker has stolen enough of our time.

It wasn't even worth it because we're still not any closer to the answers.

"And now we've got one hell of a job to clean up the mess we made," I muse.

Dylan frowns. "What? Why?"

"Because those fucking posters won't take themselves down."

A smug grin forms on his lips as he stares me down. "Don't tell me you actually care." When I don't reply, the grin on his face only grows deeper. "Alistair King ... having a crush on a girl who's supposed to be our fucking toy?"

I thrust my elbow into his side, making him groan, but I fucking love that sound. "Don't get your fucking hopes up I'll ever look elsewhere for my fix, though."

Our eyes connect, that stupid grin of his giving me all the energy I need right now. "I know."

But I don't know if I would call it a crush ...

Or if it's just morbid curiosity.

***

PENELOPE

I hide away in my room for the next couple of days, only coming out for the bare minimum of classes I need to attend before I get kicked out of school.

Nothing in this world is worse than having to go out there and possibly run into one of *them*.

Those three boys of the Skull & Serpent Society are even more fucked up than I thought.

But what's even worse is the fact that I wasn't even scared of what they did. I wasn't scared when I saw Nathan tied up to a chair like a goddamn victim. I wasn't scared when Felix hammered him to the point of breaking his legs. And even the goddamn finger he held up in front of my face wasn't enough to scare me away.

There was only a single thing I feared at that moment ... My own exhilaration.

The power.

The way Felix literally asked me, *me* out of all people, if he should stop.

Every time I close my eyes, I can see him in my mind, slamming that hammer into Nathan's knees, cutting off that finger, blood dripping down his fingers and onto my skin as he looks at me and tells me he would've killed him for me.

My fingers instinctively reach for my skin, erupting into tingles. I've already washed off the blood, but I can still feel the stain on my body, growing and growing until there's no point in denying the fact that I'm slowly falling into the trap they so easily laid out for me.

Because God, when he kissed me, I swear it felt like the world stood still.

Why?

Why did he do that?

And why do I even care?

I sigh and lie down in bed. It's past midnight, and Kayla's fast asleep. Staying awake now would only hamper my ability to study.

So I close my eyes and force myself to stop thinking about it.

I can't do anything cooped up in here anyway.

Suddenly, something creaks in the corner of the room, and my eyes burst open.

The window is open, but I can't remember if I opened it.

I crawl out of bed, shivering from the cold draft that enters, and I quickly shut it tight.

But when I turn around to walk back to my bed, I stop in my tracks like a train driver smashing the emergency button.

Because a figure in a dark hoodie hovers over Kayla.

I run to my cabinet to grab my bag and fish out my knife, but as I point it at him, he lifts his head and plants his finger on his lips. "Shh ..."

My eyes widen, and I mutter, "Alistair?"

He approaches me, and I shiver again as his frame towers over me. In the dark, he's quite intimidating, especially because he can apparently sneak into my room without me even noticing.

He reaches for the knife, but I refuse to let go as his hand snakes around my wrist tighter and tighter. I try to aim for his chest, but the closer I get, the more he pulls until I bump into him.

He slowly turns my wrist sideways until I have no choice but to let go.

"What were you doing to her?" I say through gritted teeth.

He leans in and whispers, "Checking if she was asleep." His grip tightens around the small of my back as he pulls me into his embrace. "Sit down."

I frown, confused. "Why?"

But before I can even say anything else, he's already pushed me down onto the bed.

His curly hair blocks his eyes, but I can still feel his stare bore into me from underneath that black hoodie.

"Do you do this often?"

He tilts his head. "Only when I want to."

I suck in a breath. "How many times have you been inside this room?"

"Countless."

A shiver runs up and down my spine.

"When I was asleep?"

He nods.

I should be terrified. Scared out of my mind.

Instead, I'm intrigued.

I thought he didn't like me, and that he only agreed with Felix's scheme so he could get some free ass, but maybe he's been hiding his true intentions. I wouldn't put it past a guy like him.

He's the kind of guy who lurks in the background, always waiting for the right time to take what he wants.

And that time is apparently now.

"If you want to talk, can't we do this during the day? It's the middle of the night. I need sleep."

His neck muscle flexes. "The night is more private."

Private? Oh boy.

"What do you want?" I ask, swallowing.

"I want ..." His hand rises to meet my face, the tip of his index finger barely grazing my cheek, but his touch still leaves tingles on my skin. "I want to apologize."

My jaw slowly drops.

Am I dreaming, or is this real?

"For those posters." His fingers slowly crawl across my skin as though he's admiring every inch of it just by touch. "They hurt you, didn't they?"

I nod.

"Will you forgive me?" he asks, his voice raspy.

I frown. "I ..."

I'm bamboozled by his sudden request. I never thought these guys would actually feel remorseful over their bullying. But maybe Alistair has been hiding his emotions for the sake of the group.

His lip twitches. "I don't know why I care." His finger moves toward my lips. "But I *want* to know." His voice cracks. "Desperately."

"I ... can forgive you," I mutter, transfixed by the way he's touching me.

His finger drags my lip down until my mouth opens.

"Can you forgive me for what I'm about to do?" he asks, sliding his finger onto my tongue.

His free hand slowly lowers his zipper, and it's at that point I realize what he wants.

"I need to know why," he mutters, pulling out his dick, the girth still making my pupils dilate. "Why it's you."

Why it's me?

What does he mean by that?

But before I can ask, he's already lowered my head over the tip.

And I don't know why, but I start licking.

Maybe it's because I feel like I owe it to him for fucking up Nathan.

Or perhaps I'm grateful for him saying he's sorry about the pain he caused.

Or maybe, just maybe, I'm overcome with desire at the thought of sucking him dry.

The groan that follows another lick makes me viscerally aware of my surroundings. Kayla is right next to us, and she might hear.

"She's still sleeping. Don't worry," he mutters, his hand sliding through my hair, "she won't know about the fun we're about to have."

He pushes deeper into my mouth, and I struggle to take his girth. He's not long but wide, big enough to fill up the edges of my mouth, and my eyes begin to water as he thrusts inside.

He groans with delight, and I'd be lying if I said it didn't make me wet.

Focus on doing what you need to do, Pen.

This is just an exchange. Nothing more, nothing less.

"Lick," Alistair commands, but it's so hard when he's inside me. "Faster."

Still, I do what I'm told because of the way he says it. His voice isn't harsh but smooth like you just *want* to do whatever he tells you. Like he's in complete control and knows it.

And I can't help but stare up into his eyes as I take him deep, struggling not to cough.

"That's it," he says. "Look at me when I'm inside you."

The satisfying moan that leaves his mouth makes my body tingle.

Like I'm becoming ... greedy.

And I lick him as best I can in the dark of night, knowing no one is watching me except him and only him.

His every groan sets my body on fire. It feels so powerful to be the one in control of his pleasure. I never thought it could affect me as much as it does right now, when I'm all alone with Alistair with no one to intervene. Like a big dirty secret I need to keep hidden.

I lick his shaft, watching him revel in the sight of my lips wrapped around him, but then he suddenly grips my hair and thrusts in deep.

I gag and heave as he touches the back of my throat.

His finger moves to his lips. "Shh ... don't want to wake her up. So be quiet and obedient for me, okay?"

And with tears in my eyes, I nod.

"Good girl."

And he thrusts back in like there's no other time he could ever do this, forcing me to hold back the cough and take it like he said I should.

But my body still inches back, desperate for air, and I crawl backward on the bed. However, he follows me there, crawling right on top of me until I have nowhere left to go.

"I'll make it easier for you," he says as he sits on top of my belly and pushes my hands up, locking them in place beside my pillow. "Stay."

He leans back and fishes something from his pocket. I can't see what it is, but my mind goes completely blank the second his hand dives into my pajama pants and into my panties, fingering me.

"You're wet," he says, licking his lips. "Just like before when we fucked you on the grass in front of Priory Forest. Do you remember that, Penelope?"

I briefly nod before he suddenly shoves something between my pussy lips, right on top of that sweet spot. Something that buzzes.

"I still think about that night every time I shower," he murmurs, rolling the item around my clit. "Every time I go to bed." He slowly inches forward and pushes the tip of his length against my lips again, opening them up. "Every time I make myself come."

Every time? He thinks of me?

I don't know why it entrances me, but it does.

"And I want to know *why*."

He thrusts in on that last word, leaving nothing unscathed. And I'm helpless against the onslaught of thrusts in my mouth and the lust swirling through my veins from the buzzing between my legs.

"Do you think of me too, Penelope?" he asks.

I don't know how to respond, if I even could with his big dick in my mouth.

"Or do you only think of them?"

He thrusts in with no remorse.

I try to shake my head, but I'm not sure if I'm only doing it to tell him what he wants to hear, or if I truly believe it.

Because a dark part of me I buried deep down inside my soul craves more.

More. More.

My legs squeeze together.

Fuck, it's coming soon.

"No coming yet, Penelope," Alistair groans. "Suck me like you sucked him first and maybe I'll let you."

Fuck, this is hot.

Even if I don't want it to be.

It's panty-melting hot.

And I struggle not to make a sound as he pushes my buttons and forces me to face my own limits.

"Can you take me as far as you took him?" he asks.

I gasp for air when he finally pulls out for a moment. "I can try."

"Give me *everything* you have," he says. "Everything you gave *him*."

Who is him?

Is it Felix ... or Dylan?

He slams into my mouth, and I can't even think straight as the buzzing thing between my legs kicks up the pace.

"You don't have my permission yet," he says, his voice gruff but soft, like a confident owner subduing their pet.

And it sets me off so much I have to physically hold back the orgasm.

"That's it, I want you to suck my fucking soul out of my body," he groans, his tongue dipping out to lick his lips.

He grips my face and fucks me like I'm a doll for him to use, riding me like he owns me. His balls tighten against my neck, and his veins pulse with energy, until suddenly ...

An explosion of hot liquid fills my mouth.

"Now come," he says as my eyes roll into the back of my head.

And I fall apart right there and then on his command, with his cum shooting down my throat, a whole glass load I have no choice but to swallow completely. Ecstasy floods my body, a mixture of both fear and excitement as though my mind can't choose between this being heinous or delicious.

When he pulls out, I suck in a much-needed breath, my lips still covered with his seed. But he still pulls farther away, only to grab my face with both hands so he can kiss me full on the lips.

What is happening?

My eyes open wide as his tongue swoops around mine, licking the roof of my mouth. I'm flabbergasted he doesn't care that he's tasting his own cum. But I'm even more amazed at how much I yearn for his lips as he steals my breath away again. Only this time not with lust but with butterflies taking over my body.

How?

He leans back, his lips still touching mine as he looks me in the eyes. "Now I understand."

I frown. "What?"

He understands what? That ... it's me?

Is that what he's referring to?

But I still don't know what he means.

Suddenly, Kayla snores loudly and wildly throws herself to the side of her pillow, and I lean up to look.

Alistair remains calm and steady as he slowly leans back and pulls the item that was buzzing from between my legs. A bullet vibrator small enough to hide in your pocket. The perfect, dizzying weapon to get a woman to cave.

Kayla seems to have quieted down, her face turned to us as she snores away into oblivion.

Alistair briefly smiles before he crawls off me and tucks his length back into his pants while I struggle to even sit up on my own bed.

"Thank you," he says, his back turned to me.

I don't even know how to respond. Why would he thank me? "This was a part of the agreement we made. I only did what I was supposed to."

His eyes flash underneath his hoodie. "This wasn't just for the agreement." He clears his throat. "But I will do my part." He pauses. "Do you trust me?"

I nod. "I don't have a choice."

His fist tightens. "I wish things could be different. Maybe if we'd all met under different circumstances ... if your sister ..." He abruptly shuts his mouth and looks away.

And I can't blame him.

When he mentions her, all I want to do is hide underneath my blanket and pretend the world doesn't exist.

His frame grows taller in the moonlight as he approaches the window again. "I get it now," he says. "I would kill for you."

But before I can even gasp for air, he's already jumped through, and disappeared into the night.

30

PENELOPE

After taking a shower, I try to sleep, but it's impossible. Vicious, kinky fuckery has taken over every dream I have, every waking thought. I turn and toss and after every dream I wake covered in sweat and with a pounding heart. But worst of all is the throbbing in my pussy, reminding me of how badly I've grown addicted to the games these boys play with my body.

Sighing, I roll around in bed, only to find out the sun has already risen.

Great, there goes my night. I've only slept a couple of hours, at most.

Suddenly, my phone buzzes, pulling me from my thoughts. I fish it from underneath my bed and check. It's Dad.

Dad: How's it going there? Still unsure about everything?

Penelope: Studying is fine. Hard time with some boys. But doing my best with what I have. Still searching.

Dad: Don't push yourself too hard. I don't want you dead too.

Penelope: That won't happen.

Dad: I will protect you.

Penelope: I know.

Dad: Message me if you need me, and I will be there.

Penelope: Thank you.

His comments always make me smile. He's so protective over me. Always has been.

But me going to Spine Ridge University has even put him on edge, out of all people.

I'm the only daughter he has left. I can't disappoint him.

I get up from the bed and put on my short black dress and pumps before I walk out the door and head straight for the Skull & Serpent Society on the opposite side of the street.

When I get there, I take in a deep breath and force myself to put my big girl panties on.

This place is nothing but trouble, but I have to push on for my sister.

I ring the doorbell. The wait feels eternal. After a while, none other than Alistair opens up.

His usual solemn gaze makes place for surprise.

"Pen. You're here."

My face grows warmer and warmer as the inevitable blush seeps in.

"You expecting someone else?" I ask to break the ice.

I mean, I wouldn't put it past them to keep fucking other girls. I mean, we didn't specify exclusivity or anything.

"No, I'm just surprised you'd come back here after ..." His brow rises. "You know."

Now I'm blushing even harder, and fuck me, I never blush.

Why is this happening?

He suddenly grabs my shoulder, leans in, and whispers, "Don't worry, I haven't told anyone. It can be our secret."

Secret. I like that.

"Well, come in, since you're here anyway," he says, pretending like nothing ever happened. He opens the door farther so I can walk inside. "So what brings you here?"

"I need to speak with Felix," I respond, sneaking a peek over his shoulder. "Is he here or in school?"

"We don't have classes today. Or this entire week, for that matter," Dylan suddenly chimes in as he walks out of the kitchen carrying a bagel. "Courtesy of my dad while he figures out what to do with the private hospital bill sent to him by Nathan's parents."

My jaw drops. "You got suspended?"

He takes a sip of his coffee. "Temporarily. Just to stay low. Keep out of Phantom's way after what we did." He takes another big sip, still staring at me. "For now."

"They'll get over it." Felix's voice resonates from across the hall. "Nathan didn't need that finger anyway."

He's casually leaning against a doorpost with his arms folded, wearing a smug face like he's actually proud of what he accomplished.

Meanwhile, I'm still deciding who's more fucked up; the person who cut off the finger or the person who told him to do it: Me.

Shivers run up and down my spine as our eyes connect.

"Where did you leave it anyway?" I ask, morbid curiosity making me talk before I realize it.

"In a little box," he casually replies.

"He takes trophies." Dylan shrugs.

"Trophies ..." I shudder.

Felix steps forward, walking until he's right up in my face. Always in my aura, too close for comfort. But being in his vicinity also has something empowering. Something viciously addictive. Like he oozes violence I can siphon away from him.

His eyes have only grown more bloodshot since I last saw him, and it makes me wonder if he ever really sleeps. At all.

His hand rises to grab a strand of my hair. "You're wondering what trophy I'd take from you, aren't you?" My lips part, but I don't know what to say, so he leans in to whisper, "I'd take the one thing you wouldn't ever give to me freely ... Your heart."

I lean away.

"Out of all the things that could scare you, that's the one?" he says, a smirk slowly appearing on his face.

For some reason, it makes me blush.

I don't ever fucking blush. Not for anyone.

Until he came along.

"Why did you come here, Pen?" he asks, twirling my hair around his finger. "Is your pussy hungry for more cock?"

My eyes widen. "What? No, I—"

"Wait, you fucked her?" Dylan suddenly interjects. I turn to look at him, and he narrows his eyes at me. "When?"

"None of your business," Felix barks back, releasing my hair.

Dylan steps forward. "Did you forget our fucking deal?" He's right up in Felix's face now, intimidating him. "She belongs to *all* of us."

Felix snarls back, "I've already marked her."

Dylan pushes him. "Fuck off. You don't get to claim that."

Alistair snorts. "I can't believe you guys are fighting over this. Did you forget we made an agreement with her?"

"You should've fucking told us you fucked her in private," Dylan says.

Alistair and I quickly exchange glances.

They're all talking about me like I'm not even here, and the rest of the boys who live in this frat house have now also come out of their rooms to see what's going on.

Suddenly, Felix whips out a knife and points it right at Dylan's face. "You wanna fight, pretty boy?"

"Is that supposed to be an insult, shovel face?" Dylan retorts, pulling out his own knife too now. "C'mon then. Show me what you've got."

Are they really fighting over me?

My face flushes with heat.

Until Felix suddenly swipes the knife in Dylan's direction, who barely manages to dodge.

"Stop!" I yell, and I push myself between them. "Don't fight over me."

Felix's fist tightens around the knife as he stares down Dylan, who's throwing daggers with his eyes instead of the knife in his hands.

"Yeah, Dylan ... don't fight over her. She obviously already belongs to me," Felix says, tilting his head.

I can tell he's really enjoying this, and for some reason, it makes my pussy clench, but I ignore the feeling as I'm far too busy trying to stop these two from murdering each other.

"Fine," Dylan finally concedes and tucks away his knife. "You want her? Then you can deal with your shitty plans by yourself."

He turns around and storms past Alistair and out the building.

Alistair sheepishly stares at both of us before he runs out the door too, following Dylan.

I guess those two are more tightknit than I originally thought.

"Well that escalated quickly," someone in the back says.

"Leave us," Felix says.

All of the people watching go back to the room they were in like they never even came out in the first place. Quiet as a mouse.

I guess that's the kind of power he holds.

Felix grabs my hand and tugs me along, but all I can focus on is how his hand feels when it touches mine, how I can feel every vein, and even his pulse.

Goose bumps scatter across my skin.

Why?

Why do they affect me like this?

He takes me to the back, into a private room with a fireplace and a pool table in the middle, along with a lofty couch and a giant TV.

He goes to the bar in the left corner and grabs two glasses, filling them both with some expensive-looking liquor. I stand in the middle of the room, awkward as hell, wondering why the fuck I'm even here.

Every time I'm in the vicinity of these boys, I lose all train of thought, and it's infuriating.

Felix walks toward me and holds out a glass. "Drink."

"Oh, I don't want anything, thanks."

He stares me down. "I didn't ask."

Well, pissing him off is the last thing on my to-do list after I saw what he's capable of.

Reluctantly, I take the glass from his hand.

"Sip," he says.

I bring the glass to my lips, and he watches me intently, his eyes taking in every inch of movement from my lips, to my tongue to even my throat as I swallow down a tiny bit of the hot concoction.

"Good girl."

I almost choke on it.

"Stop," I splutter, and I put the glass down on the pool table.

"Hmm. That pool table costs a ton," he replies. "I wouldn't put that there."

"Or what?"

"I've hurt people for less," he says, taking a sip himself. "You were there."

Now I'm really starting to feel the chills.

"Is this your way of forcing people not to talk? By intimidating them?" I say.

"No," he replies, and tilts his head. "I don't need to force you to do anything. I just have to say 'good girl.'"

I'm stunned as the blush appears on my cheeks, but I quickly force it to go away. "Look, what we have is an exchange. A deal. That's all it is."

He raises his brows and steps forward, right up into my face. "You sure about that, little slut?"

"Positive," I reply, swallowing from the burn still lingering in my throat.

He leans over, his finger drawing a line down my cheek the same way he did in the basement. "Is that why your lips opened so easily when I kissed you?"

"I ..."

I can't even formulate the words with him so up close, those deadly eyes haunting my very soul. God, I can't look away, not even if I tried. His lips inch closer and closer until mine start to lean in. I'm desperate to feel again what I felt that night, that pure, out of this world ecstasy.

"You're a bad liar, Pen," he whispers, and he leans away right before I almost fall into him.

Fucker.

"You're manipulating me," I say through gritted teeth.

He takes another casual sip of his drink. "Call it what you want."

"Look, I didn't come here for you to taunt me."

He saunters to the red leather couch and flops down, still swirling that drink while staring me down. "Then tell me why you came here if not to be fucked by me."

I'm trying to keep my composure here, but he's making it damn hard on me.

"I'm still no further in trying to find the one who bullied my sister and made her jump."

His grip on the glass tightens. "We already roughed up Nathan. You want me to kill him instead?"

I shake my head. "I don't think he did it. It sounded like the truth when he said someone told him to do it."

"I can cut off more fingers to make him talk," he says. "How many fingers do you think it'll take? Two? Four?"

He takes another casual sip like it's the simplest thing in the world for him to torture people.

But I'm not surprised. I knew what I was getting myself into when I came to this university, to this frat house, to these boys ...

"I don't think he'll talk. Whoever made him do it probably threatened him with death," I say. "Why else would he protect the guy?"

Felix's nostrils flare as he stares at the wall, his face growing darker with every passing second.

"I'm still no closer to finding out the truth, though. And I paid a heavy price with my face on those fucking posters."

"You knew the price was high," he says, his voice sharp, murderous.

Felix gets up and grabs one of the cues in the pool table, then lines up all the balls and shoots.

One shot is enough for him to put at least five balls in a corner.

Impressive.

"I need you to do more," I say.

His eyes focus on me briefly before making another shot.

All of them disappeared into the holes.

Fuck, he's really good.

"More?" His eyes narrow as he goes to grab the balls again and places them onto the table. "And have you ever thought about what this could cost me?"

I take in a breath. "I'm willing to pay the price."

His eyes flicker with greed. "All right." He holds out the stick to me, waiting. "Go on. Grab it."

I finally cave and take it from him. When I turn around, he's right there near my ass, feeling me up. And it's so damn hard to focus on one of the balls let alone all of them as I struggle to place the cue without shivering.

But I'm still devoted to ignoring him as I hold the cue in front of the ball and shoot.

Right then, his finger jabs up my ass.

I miss. By a long shot.

And I jolt up and down from the sudden finger thrust.

"What the fuck was that?" I gasp.

His brow rises. "Have you played before?"

"Yes," I reply.

"Doesn't look like it."

I grimace. "Not with a finger shoved up my ass. Of course, I'd fuck up."

A filthy smirk forms on his lips. I don't see that smile often, and I get the feeling he's showing it more and more when he's around me. And I have to admit, it looks good on him.

He leans in and grabs me by my ass, pulling me closer. "You should try playing with something else shoved up your ass."

My eyes widen. "What?"

Did he actually say that out loud?

Before I can ask, he walks off to a cabinet in the back, only to return with a strange bottle and a sparkly diamond-looking butt plug.

Oh God.

"Bend over," he says, his voice raspy, raw.

And I swallow back the lump in my throat. "You've got to be kidding me, right?"

He holds it up in front of my face as his hand lands on my thigh, possessively squeezing my flesh. "I don't do jokes. I thought you knew that by now."

"So what then?"

His eyes go half mast. "I do you."

My cheeks heat, but I push back the embarrassment. "I'm not some—"

He plants a finger on my mouth. "Toy. Mine." He hisses into my ear, "Now bend."

He spins me around and flops me down onto the table with ease.

"I didn't—"

He lifts my dress. "You agreed to our terms." He bends over me, his bulge pressing against my ass as he whispers, "Now do you want to do it the easy way, or the hard way?" He holds up a bottle of lube.

I shudder at the thought. I've done some ass things before with a previous boyfriend, but I never went this far.

"Use your words." His voice is commanding. Obsessive, almost.

"Easy."

"Then beg for it," he groans.

It takes every ounce of self-control not to pummel him in the face as I grit, "Please."

"Good girl," he says with a low voice, and I hate it.

I hate how it fucking makes my pussy thump.

He rips down my panties and slathers on the cold lube, rubbing it out before positioning the diamond plug against my ass.

"This is going to hurt ..." he says, pressing the palm of his hand on my ass. "And I'm going to enjoy every second of it."

I yelp when he pushes it in, slowly at first, but faster the farther he gets in. My nails dig into the pool table, tears staining my eyes, but I force them to stay at bay.

I'm not crying for this fucker.

I know he loves my tears.

"Such a good fucking slut for me," he murmurs as he plops it in until the base. Then he slaps my ass, and it reverberates everywhere. God, that thing enhances everything.

"You like to humiliate me, don't you?" I retort as I lie here on this pool table with his hands still claiming my body like he owns it.

"No," he says as he pulls me up from the table and props me up against it, eyes boring into mine. "I *live* for it."

"Why? Why do you hate me so fucking much?" I growl.

"Hate?" His eyes narrow as he leans in so close I can feel his breath on my skin. "No, Pen, this is possession." He presses himself up against me, growing hard against my dress while his hands are all over my ass. "You like being told what to do, don't you? You're just like your sister."

My eyes widen and flicker with interest. "Why are you pulling her into this? It almost sounds like you know more about her than you're letting on."

"She was a friend," he says.

Did she involve herself in these fuckers' business?

If she was truly their friend, she must've known how fucked up they were, right?

"My sister would never—"

"Maybe you didn't know your sister as well as you believe," he says, and he pulls away again.

But I can still feel his handprint on my ass.

"Now play."

My nostrils flare, anger bubbling to the surface.

Not just because I know he's fucking hiding something from me about my sister.

But also because of how lusty he just made me feel.

I lift my panties back up and pat down my dress, then turn around to grab the cue and focus on the game.

He wants me to play? I'll play.

I put the cue near the balls. "If she was such a good friend, why did you let her die? You were there too. You did nothing to stop her from jumping."

Right when I shoot, he says, "Neither did you."

I miss again.

"I saw you at the edge, standing there while her body flew down." Enraged, I turn around, but he's right there in front of me, blocking the way out. "You suspected us. But has it ever occurred to you we might suspect you?"

3 1

PENELOPE

I gasp. "What?"

He grabs a few strands of my hair and tucks it behind my ear. "You think you're innocent? Prove it."

I can't believe he's even suggesting this. "She was my fucking sister," I say through gritted teeth.

"Who says you didn't push her to jump?"

He stares directly into my eyes, and it terrifies the living shit out of me. Not because I'm afraid of him but of the words he just said ... and how much they resonate in my blackened soul.

It feels as though tar creeps up my body, pulling my feet through the ground while consuming me from the inside out.

Because who says I'm not guilty?

Guilty of all the things I accused these boys of?

Felix leans in to whisper, "Remember what you told her? What you promised you would do together?"

I can't breathe.

How does he know?

I can't even think straight until the tear that formed in the corner of my eye finally rolls down.

"Die."

***

Last year

"You're going off to that university without me," I say to my sister, who sits on her bed with her books all in front of her like she's admiring what's to come. "Then I'll be all alone."

"I'm not dead," she says with a grin, and she opens her arms. "C'mere."

I jump on the bed and hug her so tight we both fall down onto her pillow.

"God, I'm gonna fucking miss you," I say.

"I'll miss you too, lil Peepee," she says.

My jaw drops, and I snatch her pillow from underneath her and smother her with it. "You did not just call me that." She keeps laughing, so I press harder. "You haven't called me that in ages!"

"You deserve it for being a pouty little bitch," she says.

I take the pillow off and say, "What, you want me to be happy you're leaving?"

"Yes!" she exclaims. "You'll have this whole place to yourself!"

I snort. "Dad's got the whole place wired up, and there are cameras everywhere. I can't ever do anything without him finding out."

"I'm talking figuratively." She rolls her eyes. "You can have my room if you want."

I put the pillow away. "What? Really?"

She holds out her pinky. "Swear on my life."

"So you're really not planning on coming back?"

"Nope. I wanna get my own house after I'm done with university. So I promise, it's all yours."

I take her pinky, and we swear on it. "I'll still fucking miss you, of course."

"We can always talk over the phone," she replies.

"Yeah, but it's not the same." I lie down beside her and sigh as we both stare up at her glow-in-the-dark star-studded ceiling.

"You know, it's hard on me too," she says. "I'll be going there all by myself. Without you there ... it'll probably feel empty. Like there's no one there that I truly know." She takes a deep breath. "And that scares me sometimes."

I lean up on my elbow. "You told me that before. Like you feel trapped and alone."

"Yeah, exactly."

"But this is supposed to be something exciting. You've always wanted to go to Spine Ridge university. Now you can finally go live your dream."

"That's what I keep telling myself too. I'm lucky. I'm just kind of worried something might happen."

I put a hand on her arm. "What do you mean 'something'?"

"Nothing. It's just some kind of intuition thing. I can't pinpoint it."

"Are you feeling depressed?"

"What?" She snorts. "No, not at all, I—"

She's been there before because of all the bullying at our high school. That's why I had to redo my senior year at high school, and she barely made it through. It could happen again at her university.

"No, I won't allow it," I say, shaking my head.

"You're not there," she responds. "And what if something does happen? I feel like I might spiral again ..."

"Eve. Look at me. You are not going to do anything weird, okay?" I tell her. "If you're feeling like that again, you gotta tell me."

"No, I didn't say that. I just—"

"I know. But I want you to know, if you ever get these thoughts again, you call me, okay?"

She nods.

"And if you ever feel so bad about yourself that you want to end it—"

"Pen," she interjects.

"No, let me finish," I say. "I need you to know, I will be there, right by your side."

Her eyes widen. "What?"

I grab her pinky again. "Swear to me you will tell me if you get to that point, and I will be there. I will jump in front of that train with you. Okay?"

Her eyes well up with tears. "No, you can't do that."

"Yes, I can," I say. "Because I fucking will, okay? I won't have you leave this world without me."

Tears roll down her cheeks.

"Swear on it. If we die, we go together," I say, and I mean it.

I don't want her to do something she'll never get a chance to undo. And I know her.

I know how volatile her mind is.

Because she and I have the same mind.

We are one and the same. Two parts of one whole.

My twin.

"I swear I'll tell you, and we'll die together," she says. "And you'll be there for me, right?"

I nod. "Always."

***

FELIX

Present

The cue almost breaks in her hand. "How? How the fuck do you know that?"

So I grab the cue too. "I told you ... we were friends. She told me."

But she refuses to let go. "I don't believe you."

I snort. "How else would I know?"

I know it's hard to believe Eve would tell me that she had a suicide pact with her sister, but it's a cold hard truth she needs to know.

I lean in, grinding my teeth. "Who says you're not responsible for her death? I think you intended to finish it together that night, but you left her to jump on her own."

Her eyes flicker with rage.

In an instant, she raises her hand and slaps me across the face.

The sting is instant, harsh, just like the look on her face.

"Fuck you. How fucking dare you ..." she seethes. "That's why you hung those posters? Why you bullied me? Used me? Degraded me?" Her voice becomes unhinged. "Out of revenge?"

My hand rises, but I can't bring myself to even touch her, let alone punish her for slapping me.

And that doubt oozes through to my bones, making me feel something I've never felt before.

A kind of weakness.

The same weakness my victims show when I slice them up.

A weakness I can't fucking afford.

Her face contorts. "I *love* my sister to death. I wanted nothing more than to save her. And I would've gladly died to save her."

"So you admit there was a pact," I reply.

She releases the cue and marches off. "I'm done with this conversation."

"Don't you fucking leave, Penelope," I growl, but she ignores me. "Tell me the truth."

But when she turns around, all she gives me is a big middle finger.

"The deal still stands, Penelope. You can't walk away from it," I say, following in her footsteps.

"Watch me!" she yells back. "If you think it's me, then we're done here."

Right before she opens the door, I block the way and stare at her. "You still belong to me. Do not take out that fucking plug."

She glares at me without fear, then pushes past me to head straight for the exit, and it infuriates me to the point of slamming my fist into the fucking wall and roaring out loud.

32

ALISTAIR

I'm reading my Economics Basics books on a bench outside the school when a particularly incensed-looking girl wearing a black dress comes storming right at me.

"Where's Dylan?" Penelope asks, breathing heavily, like she just ran a marathon. "I tried texting him, but he's not replying."

"Not here." I close my book. "Weren't you just with Felix?"

"He's an insufferable asshole," she growls.

I snort. Well, I can't argue with that.

"You left the frat house with Dylan, so you must know where he went, right?"

"He went off with some chick. Said he was gonna get drunk and smoke some pot."

"And he left you here?" she asks.

I shrug. "I'm not interested in getting high right now. Besides, he wanted to be left alone." I pat the bench. "I am curious why you're so mad, though."

She folds her arms. "Like you don't know."

"No," I retort. "Tell me."

"You and your buddy hung those fucking posters. You know why I'm upset."

"Yeah ..." I narrow my eyes. "It was a necessary evil to catch Nathan."

"That wasn't the only bullying you guys did. And all that just because you think I made my own sister jump?"

So he told her, huh? No fucking wonder she's so mad.

I stop patting the bench. I don't think she wants to sit with me right now. Even though I would've loved her to. Maybe we could've finally had an actual conversation.

"Felix doesn't trust you," I say.

"No shit. I don't trust him either," she replies.

My brows rise. "Can you blame him, then?"

She opens her lips, but nothing comes out.

"Your sister was our friend too," I tell her.

"You guys keep saying that, but you're a little hard to believe when you've been using me to satisfy your wicked needs," she seethes. Her hands are planted firmly against her side, but I can clearly see her cheeks turn red.

"Yet you're the one who keeps blushing whenever you talk about it," I say.

Now she's blushing even more.

Lovely.

A perfect picture I'll remember for my next drawing.

I grab my phone and snap a pic.

"Hey, what are you doing?" she asks, shocked. "Why are you taking my picture?"

"Just because," I reply.

"Delete it," she says.

"No."

She lunges at me and tries to steal my phone, but I pull back and grasp her wrist midair. "Give me that," she says.

"It's mine," I say.

She jerks her hand free, and I quickly tuck my phone into my pocket.

"Why do you even care?" she asks. "It's just a goddamn picture."

"Because I want to keep it," I reply.

She gives me a strange, confused look. "Okay, fine, then. Keep it. What are you gonna do with it? Jerk off to it?"

Hmm. Now she's giving me ideas. "Maybe."

She rolls her eyes. "Pervert."

"Aren't we all?" I reply.

"Look, you wanna keep that pic? Fine, but you gotta give me some-thing in exchange." She taps her foot. "If you don't know where exactly Dylan is right now, at least give me a time and place where you'll know he'll be so I can talk to him."

"Have you tried his phone?"

She sighs out loud and shows me her conversation with him, which, for the past ten minutes, has all been one-sided. "He's ignoring me."

"He's probably feeling a little butt hurt," I reply.

"Over what?" She frowns.

I lean in. "You."

Her lips part, but she just stands there, frozen to the ground like she can't believe what I said. "But I'm just ..."

"Something they want to fight over," I fill in. "And I get it. It's not often they meet a girl as vicious as you are."

She snorts. "Me? Vicious?"

I smirk. "How many knives do you own? Two?"

"Five," she answers.

The smirk on my face only grows. "Or more."

"So?"

"That's not normal."

She shrugs. "To me, it is."

"Why? Who gave them to you?"

She narrows her eyes at me. "What's with the questions all of a sudden?"

I lean back against the bench. "Nothing. I'm just trying to get to know the girl we made a deal with. That's all."

She swallows, tucking her hair behind her ear. "Um ... yeah, sure."

"I mean it," I say, looking up into her eyes.

Her cheeks turn that same reddish hue they did before, and it's a sight to behold, especially because my words did that.

She wiggles around in an odd way and almost grabs her dress near her backside.

"You okay?" I ask.

"I'm fine. Look, I just need to speak to Dylan."

"Why?"

"Because I need him to continue our search for my sister's bully, okay?" Her voice sounds strained. "That's the deal we made."

"Can't you ask Felix?"

Her nostrils flare. "He can go fuck himself for all I care."

I laugh. "Cute."

"What?"

I pause and check out her outfit, a fitted black dress that accentuates all the curves of her body. As if she's dressed to seduce.

And fuck me, it's working all right.

"You're cute."

Now she's blushing even more.

"I would've helped you myself ... if you'd asked." I fish my phone from my pocket again and text her an address. "There."

She waits for the ping and then checks her phone. "What's this?"

"Dylan will probably be there tonight. He hates missing out on parties. It's another bonfire. Some guys from the Gehenna House are throwing it."

She frowns. "Gehenna?"

"Hell or Hell fire," Alistair says. "It's biblical."

"Jesus Christ, what a name," she scoffs.

"I know, right?" I say. "Violent bunch."

She raises a brow. "More violent than you guys?"

I shrug. "Well, more on the sexually deviant side. Rituals and stuff."

"Okay ... Anyway, I thought Dylan was supposed to stay home and stay low for a while?" she asks.

I shrug. "Where there's fire, there's Dylan."

"Near The Edge?" she asks.

"Nope. The Hot Springs."

She nods. "Okay, thanks."

"You're welcome."

She tucks her phone back into her pocket but doesn't immediately run off. "You're much nicer than them."

"Thanks, I guess," I reply, laughing it off. "I'm just giving the bare minimum."

"Yeah, but they won't even give me that."

My muscles strain against the bench, but I hold back, for her sake and mine. "Felix will come around."

She grinds her teeth. "I don't care."

"Yeah, you do," I say. "I've seen the way you look at him."

Her pupils dilate. "What? No, I—"

"You just hate that he uses you to his heart's content without feeling anything," I say. I tuck my hands into my pocket and look away. "I assure you, he does."

I don't need to look at her to fucking feel her eyes bore a hole into my chest.

"He sure has a shitty way of showing it, then," she says.

"Felix doesn't remember what love is. His family never showed him." I look at the wind blowing through the trees beyond the school grounds, carrying their leaves toward the edge. "He hasn't felt it since ..."

I pause and let the wind carry my words away silently.

"Since when?" she asks.

"Nothing." I shake my head. "Just go find Dylan. He'll make sure to hold up his end of the deal. As promised."

"And what about you?" she asks.

I turn to look at her, the fantasy of running my fingers up those thick thighs briefly invading my thoughts, but I brush it off.

Now is not the time or the place. Out here in the open in broad daylight ...

I'll wait my turn.

My gaze slowly rises to meet hers from underneath my curly hair. "I'll be there when I'm needed ..." I lick my lips. "And in return, you'll be waiting naked the next time I sneak into your room."

She gulps.

I shrug and pull out my book again, continuing my reading. "Good luck."

She swiftly walks off in her high heels and that tight little dress that barely covers her ass. But every once in a while, she sneaks a peek across her shoulder, wondering if I'm still watching.

But I'm always watching.

33

PENELOPE

I wait in my room, wiggling around uncomfortably until the clock strikes eight.

Then I get up and march out the door.

With every step I take, I can feel this plug burying itself in my behind, my pussy contracting with each movement. Every step reminds me of him.

Fuck.

No wonder he didn't want me to take it out.

I've contemplated it a million times, but every time I attempt it, I stop halfway through pulling it out. All because I can see his angered face right in front of me and hear his commanding voice in my head ...

If I don't do what he wants, I'll be the one who broke off the deal.

And what's to say he won't kill me if I do?

I've seen too much. I know too much about those boys to back out now.

This is it.

So I keep my head high, walking right out of the Alpha Psi sorority with a butt plug stuck between my cheeks.

It's bustling outside. There are a lot of parties going on around campus, and sometimes I wonder when people actually have time to study. But I have bigger problems on my hands than getting this semester on track.

I walk across the street, minding my own business, when a dude randomly jumps out at me from the bushes. I scream and punch him in the face, but he's not at all shocked.

"Whoa, calm down, chick," he tells me, drunkenly slobbering out of a bottle of beer.

"Get your hands off me," I growl at him, and I shove him aside.

"Fuck you, I just wanna have some fun," he says, stalking behind me. "And you look like you have plenty."

"I'm not interested," I say through gritted teeth. "Move along to whatever fucking party you were headed toward."

"That's no fun. I wanna come with you," he says. "What's your name, girl?"

"Leave. Me. Alone," I seethe as he walks right beside me.

Instead, he grabs my waist and pulls me closer. "I don't think so, girl. Don't you know it's dangerous to be all alone in the streets at night?"

Suddenly, he's pulled backward, and I barely escape his grasp before I'm pulled down too.

One second.

One second to turn around and a dark figure has already snatched the bottle from his hand and smashed it right into his face.

"It's dangerous all right ..." I recognize that voice.

Alistair?

His face is hidden behind a thick hoodie, but those glimmering eyes that find mine in the dark definitely belong to him.

"With me around."

I suck in a breath, not knowing what to do or even say as he hunches over the lifeless body of the dude who just harassed me.

Was he here on accident?

Or was he following me?

He gets up from the ground, hands tucked into his pockets, eyes lowered as he turns to face me. "Walk away."

I shake my head. "But you just smashed his head in."

"I'll take care of it," he replies, grabbing the guy by his arms as he drags him to the bushes.

A chill runs up and down my spine at the sight of the lifeless body on the ground.

Did Alistair just ... protect me?

He pauses to look at me. "Go."

And I don't think twice before I spin on my heels and bolt off, headed straight for the bonfire.

But I can't shake the thought that I'm being watched. Followed. Stalked.

I head beyond the gates of the university and walk off the beaten path to where I spot a fire burning in the background. Ali said Dylan would be there, and I have no reason not to believe him.

I head straight into Priory Forest, taking every step as carefully as I can because I don't want to fall down and risk this plug going in even deeper. Even though I know that shouldn't technically be possible, it still feels like it could.

When I get closer, some girls run past me wearing actual fucking bikinis. In the middle of fall.

An actual fucking pool party in the woods.

Ridiculous.

The blasting music lures me closer, and from between the trees, I can see Dylan basking in the natural spring with three other girls. He's got his hand wrapped around one of their asses while another girl pushes her boobs up against him while attempting to kiss him.

Suddenly, our eyes connect, and I hide behind the tree, mortified he saw me looking.

"I know you're here, Pen," Dylan yells over the music. "I can see you."

Fuck. Fuck. Fuck!

I ram my forehead into the tree trunk out of embarrassment.

"You gonna come out, or you gonna stay behind that tree forever?"

Fine.

You can deal with this, Pen. Just ignore his taunts.

Sighing, I come out and face him. The girls he's holding giggle when they look at me.

"She a friend of yours?" one of them asks.

"You could call it that ..." he muses.

"Nice party you got over here," I say, looking around at all the people literally slow-dancing to some filthy music. Some people hide beyond the trees, kissing and fucking around with their fingers and hands in places they shouldn't be in public. But no one here seems to mind.

Is this what *Gehenna* parties are like? Mindless orgies?

"Wanna join us?" Dylan asks, tilting his head. "There's plenty more room."

I fold my arms. "No, thanks. I just wanna talk."

His brows rise. "Talk? That's boring."

"Yeah ... don't be a bore," another girl says, and she kisses him on his jawline.

The mere sight makes me want to vomit.

"Shouldn't you be with Felix right now?" Dylan asks.

"He told me why you guys kept bullying me."

"A bully? Me?" The smirk that follows is insufferable. "I only did what I had to."

Sure. "Out of revenge?"

"If you want to call it that." He clears his throat. "So you're here because you're mad at Felix?" His eyes narrow. "Interesting."

"I'm mad at all of you, but I still need you to uphold your end of our deal."

Dylan's eyes light up like the bonfire behind him, though. "All right. I've got time."

"I don't," I reply, hoping he gets the sense of urgency.

We're still no closer to the truth, and those fuckers are busy partying, playing games, and getting drunk and high.

"So tell me what you want from me." Dylan spreads his arms, both girls clinging closer as they toy with his platinum hair and buff chest. "I'm here."

I roll my eyes. I'm not gonna say it out loud in front of all these people. "You know what I need help with."

"What you need help with ... orgasms?"

The girls laugh, and I'm fucking mortified.

"Dylan," I warn.

"What? Not the answer you're looking for?" The grin on his face grows stronger. Sexier. I hate it. But I hate more that it reminds me of that butt plug stuck in my ass.

"I need to find... someone."

Is he really going to make me say it?

"You're looking at him," he retorts.

Some girl smiles and pecks him on the cheek.

"Want something from me? Ask."

I swallow away my pride. "Will you please help me?"

I know they want me to say that word.

"And why would I do that?" he responds. "This is so much more fun."

Fuck. I should've known he wouldn't do what he promised.

He leans sideways and kisses one of the girls full on the lips, biting them, only for his eyes to find mine while he claims hers.

And for some reason, it makes my pussy thump.

Fuck.

"Jealous?" he asks when he's done with her.

"You wish." I blow out a breath as my body erupts into goose bumps, the cold really getting to me now.

"You know I can see it in your eyes, right?" he says, and he suddenly gets up.

His naked chest glistens in the moonlight, water sparkling across the many intricate designs tattooed all over his arms and hands, one of them being the Skull & Serpent House symbol. There's even a tattoo on the side of his belly; a woman begging on her knees while holding a cross. And it's becoming really, really hard to look away.

Especially since he's not wearing anything underneath.

And I mean nothing.

His cock dangles in the water in all its pride and glory, and no one seems to care.

"I don't know what you see in my eyes," I retort, trying to keep it together.

"Possibilities," he replies, taking a step toward me.

But it's the way he looks at me that makes my feet feel glued to the ground.

He playfully lifts his brow. "Like my tats?"

"You wanted to tattoo someone praying to God?"

"No," he retorts, staring at me with hawk-like eyes. "It means not even God can stand in my way of making a woman beg."

Wow.

That literally made me gulp.

"Leave us," he rasps over his shoulder, and the girls immediately crawl out of the natural spring with disappointed looks on their faces.

But he only seems to have eyes on me as he walks closer and closer until he's in the middle of the water, his hard-on growing firmer with every step.

And for some reason, it's suddenly becoming hard to breathe.

"You want me to ... help you."

I nod.

"I can do that," he says. "But what will you do for me in return?"

Fuck, I knew he was going to do this.

"I already asked you. I said that—"

"I don't need your begging," he interjects, his eyes glazing over my body from the tip of my toes to the top of my dress and higher. "Take it off."

"What?" My eyes widen.

"All of it."

"No," I say, gasping. "Everyone's watching."

"No, they're not," he replies, and when his eyes dart to the people in the crowds, I follow his lead. Everyone's kissing and dancing, minding their own business. Even the girls he just shooed away like they were nothing but playthings to him.

"Now, it's your choice, of course," he murmurs as he wades back to the corner he was sitting in. He spreads his arms across the rough corners of the spring, half-mast eyes homing in on mine. "You want my help ..." His voice lowers in tone. "Take it all off. Now."

I swallow and focus on him, wondering if I can do this. If it's worth it.

But I made that choice long ago when I agreed to their wicked little deal.

So I step out of my shoes and kick them aside, then take off my little bag. I slowly peel away the dress from my shoulders until it drops to the ground, all while his eyes remain on my body.

The obvious smirk on his face is so sexy it almost makes me forget I hate him. "I said all of it."

I run my tongue along the inside of my mouth, incensed. "I don't have a bikini."

He lifts a single brow. "So?"

Fuck.

My nostrils flare.

I don't think I can get out of this one. It's either his way or the highway.

So I slowly hook my fingers behind my bra and take it off, dropping it to the ground. He grabs a bottle of champagne nestled between a bush and two rocks and puts it to his lips, gulping it down while watching me. Some of it dribbles down his chin and chest, and when he finishes, he wipes his mouth, his hand still lingering near his bottom lip as I hook my fingers underneath the fabric of my panties and slowly push them down. And when they're on the ground, he literally licks the top of his lip.

I wish he wasn't so goddamn hot.

"Come here," he says, tilting his head.

I try not to look at the other people here because I know they can see me naked as I step into the water. The warmth distracts me from their gazes as I walk farther and farther, goose bumps crawling all over my skin because of the heat.

"Closer," Dylan commands, his arms still widely spread across the edge, one hand still clutching that bottle like he intends to finish the entire thing himself.

Or hit me with it—as Alistair did moments before I came here to protect me.

I swallow and push the thought to the back of my mind, focusing on the here and now.

When I'm right in front of him, his eyes travel down from my eyes to my breasts, which are barely hidden by the water. And he groans with delight, the sound making goose bumps erupt on my skin.

"Open your mouth," he says. When I do, he adds, "Wider."

He leans in and pours some of the champagne directly into my mouth until it runs over.

"Go on ... have a taste," he muses.

I have trouble swallowing, and more spills over.

But I'm stunned the moment he inches closer and presses his lips to my neck, right where the droplets roll down, licking them all up one by one. "Don't let it go to waste."

I manage to gulp it down and suck in the much-needed air. His hot, tantalizing lips are still on me, claiming every inch of my skin like he intends to mark me as his.

"Did Felix make you feel good?" he groans into my ear, then tugs at my earlobe with his teeth.

I struggle hard to keep the moans at bay. "He takes what he wants."

"That's not what I asked ..." he whispers, and he flips me around until his length pokes into my back and his hands snake around my waist. "I asked if he pleased you ... when he fucked you in private."

I can barely breathe as he pulls me back toward the edge, his hard-on poking my thigh as he drags me onto his lap while placing the champagne bottle back where he got it. "Because I will."

His hand dips between my thighs, and he starts rubbing me right on that sweet spot that makes me want to gyrate on top of him. Good God, he knows exactly where and how to touch me without even a hint of effort, like it comes natural to him.

"I could make you scream in front of all these people if I wanted to."

"Is that what *you* want?" I ask. "To degrade me?"

"Degrading is Felix's kink," he murmurs, his other hand sliding up to my breast to fondle it. "He wants to own people."

"And what's yours?" I ask, but it's becoming harder and harder to even speak without wanting to moan.

He bites my earlobe and sucks on it, then whispers, "To be watched."

My eyes immediately travel through the dark of the night to all the people surrounding us, and I feel like I'm caught in the limelight. I've never done this before in public with so many people watching, but the longer he fondles me the less I begin to care.

"But that isn't the only thing," Dylan adds, shoving a finger inside. "I also like to share."

I knew that the moment they chased me in the woods in those Halloween outfits.

"You're all a bunch of fucked-up bastards, aren't you?" I say, trying not to let his fingering affect me, but it's so damn hard.

He lets out a low, rumbling laugh. "Oh, you haven't even seen the worst in me yet."

34

DYLAN

She's here and mine alone for the seizing.

Fuck, I've waited a long time for this.

I finally have my chance to take what I want from her with no interruptions. And I'm not letting this moment go to waste.

I grasp her nipple and squeeze, then tug so harshly she has to swallow her mewl.

Fuck, that heavenly sound makes me as hard as a rock.

"Told you I could make you scream," I whisper, winking when she turns her head to gawk at me. "Don't pretend you're surprised. You knew what you were looking for when you came here."

My hand dives down to her ass, but when I find something hard, I pause.

"What is that?"

Her cheeks turn fiery red. "Umm ..."

"Stand up," I say.

After some hesitation she does what I ask, and I can clearly see the sparkling butt plug between her cheeks.

"Did you insert that butt plug?" I ask.

"Felix," she responds.

A wicked grin spreads on my cheeks.

Is this his way of apologizing? He really knows me well.

I slap her ass. "Sit on me."

"What?"

225

"You heard me. Sit."

"On your d—"

I grab her by the waist and pull her toward me, sinking her down on my tip.

"Oh my God, but there's already something inside me," she mutters as I lower her slowly.

"And you'll take my cock along with it like a good girl," I reply.

She struggles against my thickness, but I push her down until I'm buried to the hilt. A stilted moan escapes her mouth, making my cock throb inside her. But good God, does this pussy feel like fucking heaven.

No wonder he wanted to have her all to himself.

Greedy motherfucker.

"That's it. Take it deep," I groan as she adjusts to my size.

"Fuck, it's so full," she mewls.

I start thrusting in and out of her, lifting her ass up and down on my lap inside the water.

"Not used to a plug, whore?" I respond. "You'll get used to it soon enough when we start fucking all your holes."

She attempts to turn around, but I grab her nipples and squeeze while fucking her tight little pussy.

"Don't even think about it," I groan.

"You'd better hold up your end of the deal," she says, panting. "Or I'm leaving you with blue balls."

"Oh, don't worry, little slut, I'll fuck up the entire world for a pussy like this."

Moans slip out of her mouth as one of my hands slips back down her belly, and I start flicking her clit while thrusting into her. People all around us are either too busy dancing or fucking around just like us to even remotely care. And I don't mind. I have enough of an audience just from the person staring at us from behind a tree. I lick my lips as she bounces up and down on my cock while my eyes connect with the person.

Because nothing in this world is a bigger thrill than being caught in the act.

And fuck me, I could explode right there and then.

But I want her to come for me first. I want to feel her contract around my length, be the one to make her get to that point. She came to me and me alone, which means she knows she can get something from me that Felix won't give her.

"Fuck," she groans.

"You like that, don't you? Getting fucked in front of all these people," I whisper.

"No one is watching," she murmurs, gazing around. "They're too busy dancing and kissing."

"Look over there," I say, and I briefly point at the trees before resuming to toy with her sensitive bits.

When she gasps, I know she's seen it.

The person watching us.

"Oh God, we gotta stop," she mutters.

"No," I reply, holding her down. "You're going to come for me. And I'm going to fucking fill you up while they look."

I roll my fingers over her little swollen clit until I can feel her contract around my shaft, and then I ram it in deep. She moans, her nipples growing taut from the orgasm. I can feel the butt plug's edges against my length, the tightness of it all pushing me over the edge.

And I moan into her ear as my seed jets into her.

But fuck, once wasn't enough. I need more. So much fucking more.

No wonder Felix wanted her so badly.

"Fuck, I can't believe I just did that," she mutters.

"I'm not finished yet," I groan, and I beckon the person behind the tree to step forward. "Come and join us ... Ali."

***

PENELOPE

My whole body feels as cold as ice, even in this warm water. Because

I just fucking came all over Dylan's length. I couldn't stop it. I didn't even want to.

But I didn't know Alistair watched us this whole time.

He steps out from behind the tree, rubbing his bulge, pre-cum staining his pants.

Oh God.

My cheeks heat in a flash as I can feel Dylan pull out of me and the cum that was inside me mixes with the water, floating to the top.

Alistair's eyes fixate on mine as he stops in front of the hot spring. Gawking at me, he bites his lip.

I take in a hampered breath.

He takes off his shirt, revealing his pierced nipples, continuing until nothing is left to the imagination. Underneath is pure, lean muscles, leaner than Dylan and Felix, but more pronounced as though he's only trained them for one purpose: A hunt.

Still wearing his pants, Ali steps into the water. The music goes darker, deeper, louder, a slowed techno mix song I don't know, but the sound only adds to the sexiness. Especially when Alistair approaches us, his eyes flicking back and forth between Dylan and me.

He licks his lips, gawking up and down my body.

"You want her, don't you?" Dylan asks, and he presses a kiss onto my cheek, only to gaze at Alistair. "Then take her."

He grabs the bottle of champagne and pours the contents all over my face and chest.

I gasp as Alistair grabs my breast and covers my nipple with his mouth, sucking up the champagne straight off my body.

Holy fucking shit, this is hot.

Ali's tongue dips out to lap up all the champagne while Dylan starts to rub my clit with his tip, and fuck me, it's making me want him inside me again.

How do these boys do this? How do they make me want something I shouldn't?

It should be illegal.

Dylan's lips are on the back of my neck while Alistair sucks the champagne off my chin, then moves to my mouth. His kisses are like dipping your tongue into liquid chocolate. Succulent. Irresistible.

And I can't help but part my lips and let him claim my mouth with his tongue while Dylan's hands slide between my legs, picking up the pace. Fuck, are we going to do this again? In front of all these people?

"Fuck," I groan as Alistair takes his lips off mine.

Alistair zips down his pants underwater. "Fuck her, Dylan," he whispers, licking the rim of my lips. "Take her hard while I watch."

"Fuck yes," Dylan groans, and he shoves inside with no mercy.

He's already hard, ready to go again, and I'm helpless against the onslaught of desire flooding my body when these boys start to ravage me.

Dylan in the back, thrusting in and out of me, the butt plug adding to the sensations, while Alistair greedily kisses my lips and tugs at my nipples.

My arms instinctively wrap around his neck, wanting to get closer. But when he pulls back, my lips are still puckered, desperate for more, but all he does is smirk and tug harder on my peaked nipples until I moan out loud.

"That's it, little whore, scream for us," Dylan murmurs into my ear, rolling me over his bulge on his lap.

God, I've never done anything more fucked up and erotic in my life, and I'm here for it all.

"Harder," Alistair tells Dylan, and he picks up the pace. Alistair gazes at Dylan over my shoulder, their eyes connecting as he leans in and begins to rub his tip against my clit.

"Fuck yeah, that's it, pleasure her with your dick," Dylan groans, still inside me.

Alistair is really getting into it, sliding his length up and against all my sensitive parts.

And I can't believe I'm being two-manned right now.

Alistair begins to moan against my cheek, his size throbbing against me, and it's the hottest thing I've ever heard. Men don't usually moan for me.

Until I open my eyes and realize he's looking at Dylan.

I lose grip, and Dylan suddenly flops out of me, his length rubbing my mound.

Only for Alistair to grab ahold of his shaft and rub his own against it.

Holy fucking shit.

Are they ... frotting?

I glance at Dylan over my shoulder, but his gaze perpetually flicks between me and Alistair until he places his chin on my shoulder, and Alistair leans in to kiss him full on the lips.

Fuck.

This is why they gawk at each other every time they've used me.

They want each other too.

Is this why Alistair said he wanted to know "why it's me," and that he understood now?

Was I ... between them?

With two hands, Alistair has a grip on both their dicks, jerking both of them off at the same time underneath me, rubbing them against me with everything he has. All while I'm still between them.

"Fuck yes, Ali, jerk me off against her. Cover her in filth," Dylan murmurs, and Alistair goes even faster.

Their moans set my body on fire in ways I never thought possible.

Suddenly, Alistair pushes both his tip and Dylan's into my pussy.

I gasp, but he covers my mouth with his as they both push inside farther, deeper, burying themselves to the hilt.

Two in one.

Fucking hell.

I never thought it could fit.

But I need it. Good God, I need it so fucking much.

"See? You can take it, little slut," Dylan whispers into my ear as they both fuck me like madmen.

Our twisted moans mingle into one as I start gyrating on top of them both while Alistair alternates kissing Dylan and me, and I can taste them on my tongue, feel them inside me, twisting, knotted, thrusting inside me with every inch of throbbing flesh until both of them release themselves inside me with a howl and a groan.

My pussy thumps, and Alistair rubs me until I finish with them still inside me.

When they pull out, their cum bubbles to the surface, and Alistair dips down to literally scoop some of it up with his tongue. Then he smashes his lips onto mine, forcing me to taste them together.

And fuck me, it's making me want to have another go.

"Swallow it all, slut," Dylan groans behind me.

Suddenly, someone clears their throat. "Having fun?"

35

⁂

ALISTAIR

I tear away from Penelope's lips, an unfamiliar voice pulling my attention.

Two guys stand at the edge of the spring, staring us down like they own the fucking place with their hands on their sides. And Dylan does not seem amused.

"What the fuck do you want?" Dylan growls.

Penelope clutches me tightly, hiding her naked body behind mine when I spin around to face them.

"Sorry, this water's taken," I say, quickly tucking my dick back inside my pants and zipping up.

One of the guys, the pretty one with the chiseled face, snorts. "I wouldn't want to step in that pool of death if I was offered a million fucking bucks for it."

"Oh, fuck no." Dylan pushes Pen aside and walks to the middle of the spring to confront them, all in his bare naked ass. "You got beef with me? Just because I'm fucking around?"

"No." The big, muscled guy folds his arms. "I'm wondering if she's the girl worth dying over."

Penelope shivers behind me. "What are they talking about? Who are they?"

"I don't know," I reply. "But I have an idea."

"Nobody's dying tonight," Dylan retorts. "It's a fucking party. There's enough booze for everyone.

Dylan gets out of the spring with his half-hard cock dangling freely, but that doesn't stop him from walking up to them and picking his clothes off the ground right in front of the dude's feet.

Ballsy.

"Yet it will never be enough to satisfy my craving ..." the too-pretty-to-be-here motherfucker says, cracking his knuckles. "For blood."

Fuck. This is gonna go bad real quick.

Dylan snorts and puts on his shorts, lacing the belt through before responding. "Why? You jealous of all the ass I get?"

The dude's eyes narrow, and his nostrils flare. "Nathan."

Oh fuck.

Dylan gets up in his face, but he doesn't seem the least bit intimidated. "You've got some nerve saying that name out loud to me, Phantom scum."

The crowd around us grows quiet. Some stop dancing and kissing and stare while others immediately leave. A dark cloud hangs over this party, and everyone here knows what's coming.

"No one invited you to this party, snake," the guy replies.

"There is no fucking party without me," Dylan hisses back. "What's your fucking name?"

"Kai Torres," he replies. "Now I'm gonna give you a choice. Hand over the girl, or suffocate."

I can see Dylan's body growing rigid, his fingers curling into a fist.

Fuck.

"Don't!" I growl. "Remember what your father said."

"You scared?" The Phantom boys laugh.

Until I add, "Don't do it, Dylan!"

And their smiles dissipate instantly.

Dylan raises a fist.

"Wait!" Pen suddenly yells, and Dylan's fist stops halfway through the air.

"Penelope ..." Dylan warns her.

"If I'm the one he wants," she says, stepping forward. "I'll take responsibility."

"Fuck no," Dylan rasps.

"You don't make the fucking rules here," Kai retorts, then he looks at her. "Come here."

Penelope quickly grabs a towel lying on the side of the spring and wraps it around her tits before getting out of the water. The fabric barely covers her body, the bottom of her ass along with that beautiful plug still visible, and I just know those fuckers can see it too.

My fist tightens.

We were supposed to lay low. Quiet. Not make a scene.

Guess we won't be living up to what Dylan promised his dad after all.

"What do you want from me?" Penelope asks. She swallows, bravely facing them with her head held high. "If you leave them alone, I'll do what you want."

Why would she do this? She was there, but she didn't participate. This feud is all on us, yet she's willing to throw herself in front of us.

He whistles loudly. "Everyone. Out."

All the partygoers swiftly grab their stuff, panicked by Kai's sudden dismissal.

Kai suddenly grabs her by the throat. "Nathan's in agony because of you."

"That wasn't her," Dylan says through gritted teeth. "It was us."

Kai pulls her closer to him. "Yet he overheard Felix telling her he would've killed Nathan for her ..." Kai grins as he grabs her wrist so she can't escape. "Sounds to me like she's the one responsible."

It's taking every ounce of self-control for Dylan not to attack right now. And even I'm on edge.

Kai grabs Penelope's chin to force her to look at him. "And she'll be the one to pay."

"Let her go," Dylan growls.

"Or what? She offered herself to me," Kai replies, and he turns around. "C'mon, Josh. Let's get the fuck out of here and play with our shiny new toy."

"Oh yeah ..." Josh replies, and he tears the towel off her body with ease. " I wonder if she cries as ugly as her sister did."

My eyes widen.

Oh fuck.

That'll do it.

I jump out of the water and onto the edge, swiftly putting on my clothes before I approach Dylan.

But he's radiating energy. Like something took over his body.

"What did you just say?" Dylan rasps under his breath, his eyes lowering.

Yup. It's definitely happening all right.

"Why are you talking about my sister? What did you do to her?" Penelope asks Josh as he drags her away. "Did you bully her?"

"Enough," Dylan says through gritted teeth, cracking his fingers without even touching them.

"Did you say something, snake?" Kai glances over his shoulder. "Yeah, thought so."

Suddenly, Dylan lunges at Josh, fishing a knife from his pocket mid-air, only to thrust it into Josh's shoulder.

Josh cries out in pain. "You motherfucker!"

Within seconds, Dylan's pulled it out again only to jam it straight into Kai's arm, who releases Penelope from his grip, and she falls on the ground.

All the people who were still around start to scream and run away from the party.

"Pen, run!" Dylan roars at her.

But she's frozen to the ground.

Fuck. I gotta intervene.

Dylan's eyes connect with mine and then with her.

"Ali. Take care of her!" he yells as he bolts off with the bloody knife still in his hand.

And the two Phantom fuckers chase after him.

Just as he wanted.

"Dylan!" Penelope yells, frantically looking through the woods. "They're coming!"

I help her off the ground. "You okay?"

BANG!

Penelope's eyes widen.

I turn to look at where the sound came from, but I'm pretty certain I know what it was.

Gunfire.

"Stay here," I tell her.

"Fuck no," she says, quickly grabbing her dress and swiftly putting it on, then grabbing her little bag. "I'm coming with you, and we're gonna take those fuckers down."

It's not a question. It's a command.

And I can't fucking help but oblige.

***

DYLAN

I'm running through the woods as fast as I can, circling the bonfire while simultaneously avoiding anything these Phantom fuckers throw at me. Knives, sticks, fucking rocks they picked up off the ground.

Until Kai pulls out a gun.

BANG!

The shot fires and ricochets off the tree right beside me.

I skid to the right and jump over a bunch of rocks, headed straight toward The Edge.

I should've brought my fucking gun. Fuck. Too much is at stake.

I have to lead them away from her.

I don't want her getting caught in the crossfire.

"Get back here, you fucking son of a bitch!" Josh shrieks. "If I catch you, I'll chop your fucking dick off!"

BANG!

Another shot fires into the rock I briefly hide behind before I run farther up the hilly area near The Edge. A path leads underneath a large overhanging rock, and I bolt through it, only to head left immediately, climbing up the steep hill.

Kai's right behind me, shooting into the bushes at random.

"Come out, come out, wherever the fuck you are, snake!" he yells. "You know I'll fucking catch you."

When they're right underneath the rock, I jump down. I land right on top of Kai, and we fall to the mossy ground, tumbling around in the leaves.

"Motherf—Get off me!" he growls. "I'm gonna fucking kill you!"

He attempts to aim at me, and I grasp his wrist. I'm not going down without a fight.

But this fucker is strong, and I can barely hold on, the gun getting closer and closer to my face.

Josh wraps his hands around my neck, tugging hard, and I'm fucking choking trying to hold on to Kai's wrist so he won't fucking shoot me.

Suddenly, someone drags Josh away from me, and I can finally fucking breathe again.

Now it's time to snuff out theirs.

BANG!

The gun goes off, the bullet flying straight past my ear, grazing my skin.

Blood oozes down my neck, but I ignore it and fight for control.

"Dylan! Catch!" I briefly turn my head because the voice catches me off guard.

Penelope.

Fuck. What is she doing here? I told her to run.

She throws me her knife, and I catch it just in time before Kai shoots again.

I slice through his face.

"FUCKKKK!" he screams, grabbing his eye. "My eye!"

I snatch his gun from him and slam him in the head with it, knocking him out. Blood pours from the wound as well as his ear. He might be dead, but I don't even fucking care. All I'm focused on is getting that fucker Josh.

Alistair's got both hands wrapped around Josh, who's kicking and jabbing him wherever he can. Penelope fishes another knife from that little bag of hers and holds it over his neck so he'll stop thrashing around.

"Let go of me, you fucking snake!" Josh growls.

"You threatened me," Penelope hisses. "I don't take that lightly."

"Nathan deserves retribution," he barks back.

I wipe Penelope's knife on my pants. "And what about Eve?"

An unquenchable fire begins to rage inside me as I crack my fingers while walking toward him. "You fucking bullied her until she cried?" Pure fury courses through my veins as I approach him.

"You ..." Penelope stammers, the knife trembling in her hand. "You could be the reason she jumped."

"Hey, I can't help that bitch killed herself," he responds through gritted teeth. "I'm not responsible for what bitches do."

Tears well up in her eyes. The knife in her hand drops to the ground. The pain on her face is too much to take, even for me.

Fuck laying low.

My nostrils flare. "And I'm not responsible for what I'm about to fucking do to you."

I thrust the knife deep into his abdomen, twisting and turning it until his guts spill out.

He groans in pain when I pull out, blood gushing from the wound.

"Pin him to the ground," I tell Alistair.

Alistair kicks him in the shins, knocking Josh over. His body lands on the muddied ground with a thud. I pick up the knife Penelope dropped, clutching them both, before I grab one of his hands. "Grab his other hand."

Alistair doesn't even say a word and just does as he's told while Penelope stares at us, still silently trembling from what she just found out.

Some random asshole from the Phantoms made Penelope's sister cry. Fuck knows what they did to her that was so bad she couldn't bear it. Just that one act could've been the catalyst to why she jumped from The Edge.

All of it culminating to this point in time.

Alistair and I drag Josh to a clearing farther up, away from the trees, with Penelope right behind us watching our every move.

I won't ask her to help. But I also won't allow her to stop what I'm about to do.

Josh is groaning loudly. "Fuck, it hurts."

The music from the party is loud even this far away. "Rip Roach" by xxxtentacion blasts through the skies, amping me up.

"Don't move," I bark at him, and I pin his hand above his head. "This is gonna hurt even more."

I jam the knife straight through his hand and into the ground.

He shrieks like a banshee, whipping his head and other hand around.

"Hold him down!" I yell at Alistair, who smacks him in the face with a fist.

Josh's eyes roll into the back of his head, and Alistair pins his hand above his head while I ram Penelope's knife straight through.

He howls in pain, kicking around with his feet.

"My hands!" he shrieks.

"Dylan ..." Penelope rasps behind me.

When I turn to look, I spot the gun Kai used to shoot me in her hands.

I must not have noticed her picking it up while Ali and I were busy dragging this fucker back. I get up, ignoring the screaming fucker behind me. I walk to her and hold out my hand. "Give it to me."

She shakes her head. "No. I want to do this."

Fuck.

I knew there was a chance she'd risk it.

That was why I told her to run.

But I should've known girls like her don't turn the other way when on the road to trouble. She faces it head-on.

She goes to her knees in front of Josh, who's bleeding from every hole we created.

"Please," he begs, shaking his head. "Please, don't do this. I'm sorry. I'm so sorry."

Without saying a word, she aims for his dick and shoots.

He cries out in agony. "My dick!" And he vomits all over himself.

She gets up and chucks the gun at me, the look on her face stoic, emotionless, like it came easy for her.

And my jaw actually drops.

That was ... sick.

A smirk forms on my face.

Impressive.

I tuck the gun into my pocket while she pulls a medium bottle of whiskey from her bag, clearly snatched from the party.

Perfect.

When she's about to take a sip, I steal it from her hands.

"Hey, I need that," she says.

"Watch," I say, and I splash the contents all over his body.

"What are you doing?" Josh mutters, coughing up blood. "Oh God, please, don't do this, I don't wanna d—"

"Die?" I interject, pulling out my lighter. "Too late. You're already a walking corpse."

"Wait, no, no, no, I'll do anything you want, I—"

In the middle of his sentence, I set fire to him.

His shrieks are like music to my fucking ears as he's being roasted alive, unable to even crawl away.

A perfect ending for a miserable little bug like him.

Alistair whistles as he plucks some branches off trees and picks off some freshly fallen twigs, tossing them all on top of Josh. The fire intensifies when I pour on some more alcohol, emptying the bottle, then throwing that onto the pile as well.

The massive fire is much bigger than any bonfire in the neighborhood, and my God, is it a sight to behold. My fiery fucking heart is all pumped up from this blaze, and I loud from the sheer adrenaline.

I'm sure some people who fled the scene wonder what the fuck is happening here. And I don't fucking care. They can fucking watch him burn.

I glance at Penelope, flames dancing in her eyes. "You wanted our help ... you got it. Catch." I toss the knife back at her, and she actually catches it. Maybe I truly underestimated this girl ... and the darkness in her heart.

"Go home, Penelope," I say. "And don't tell a fucking soul about tonight."

36

PENELOPE

I head back to my room in the sorority and close the door.

The silence is overwhelming, but I can still hear the screams inside my mind.

I killed someone.

Not on accident.

Actual fucking murder.

I raise my hands, gazing at the blood on my fingers. His blood.

Blood of the person who hurt my sister.

And good God, does it feel powerful.

A big grin spreads on my face, and I bury my face in my hands, rubbing the blood all over my skin while laughing.

The bathroom door opens up, and Kayla steps out, only to pause like she's suddenly turned to stone.

"Pen..." She shudders, her eyes widening. "Is that ... blood?"

The smile on my face dissipates. "I ... hurt myself while walking back from a party."

She clutches the bathroom door, her hair still wet from the shower. "That doesn't look like an accident. Did someone hurt you?" She walks toward me, clutching her towel. "Oh God, should I call for help?"

When she grabs my wrist, I jerk away, and her face contorts in confusion. She sniffs. "Why do you smell like a fire?"

"There was a bonfire," I reply.

It's not a lie. But also not the full truth.

She swallows, visibly shaken. I must look like a serial killer's escaped victim.

Maybe it's not even that far from the truth.

"I'm fine," I say, adding a gentle smile. "Don't worry about me."

I try to pass by her, but she blocks my way. "No way. This ain't right, Pen. Whatever you're going through, you can't do it by yourself." She pauses. "I'm your friend. Let me help."

Man, that just fucking shatters me.

I know she's my friend.

I *want* her to be my friend, and I *want* to confide in her so desperately that I have to physically force my lips to stay shut.

I can't fucking involve her in fucking murder.

"I can't," I say through gritted teeth. "I don't want you to get hurt."

"So it's something real bad," she says. "I knew it. It's those boys, isn't it?"

I shake my head. "This wasn't them. I promise."

She frowns. "But they're involving you in some crazy shit, aren't they?"

I sigh. "Look ... just believe me when I say, it's best if you don't get involved."

I head into the shower and lock the door behind me before she tries to convince me again to tell her all about what I did tonight.

But I'd rather die than have another innocent soul involved in all this darkness and all this depravity.

I look at myself in the mirror, at the blood staining my skin. A mark of honor.

I straighten my back and lift my shoulders, breathing out a sigh of relief.

One down.

Plenty more to go.

But I will hunt them down one by one until all of those fuckers from her diary are burned alive.

Just as that fucker Josh.

Dylan was right.

He got what he deserved.

**

My dreams are riddled with blood, sex mingling with violence, a twisted and volatile combination. My sleep is restless, and the moment I wake up, I'm drenched in sweat.

I sit up straight in bed and look around, but Kayla's already gone. I stare at the window, reminding myself I'm awake. But what happened weren't dreams or nightmares, they were reality.

Suddenly, I'm pulled from my thoughts as my phone buzzes.

Crystal: Are you coming? It's time for our shared class, but you're not here?

My eyes widen.

Shit. Did I forget because of everything that happened?

I scramble to get my schedule off the floor, and fuck me, she's right. It starts in two minutes.

I jump up from my bed and throw on some proper clothes. A black hoodie and a pair of gray leggings. Inconspicuous, just as I intend to be when I walk through that school.

I run out the door and rush down the stairs.

"There she goes again," someone jokes from the kitchen, but I pay no attention to it.

I know I'm often late. I don't mean to be, but I guess it's what happens when you're busy trying to find your sister's bullies while simultaneously trying to juggle three horny sicko boys.

I head straight for the main building and bolt inside, then pretend I was walking slowly even though everyone can see me breathing like a crazy person.

"Pen! Here!" Crystal waves from across the hall.

I wave back and smile, but the smile on my face immediately dissipates when I spot someone familiar with a bandage wrapped around his hand, a plastic boot on his leg, and a cane in his hand walk straight toward her.

My stomach drops into my shoes.

He's already back at school?

How? Why?

I would've expected him to stay away for a long time, but now he's here in the flesh.

But the worst part is that he's staring right at me with deadly fire in his eyes.

Does he know we killed his Phantom friend?

I swallow.

Too late to turn back now and pretend I was never here.

Sweat drops form on my back as I approach them.

She's talking to him like she already knows him, and it surprises me.

"Hey Pen, how are you? I haven't seen you in days," Crystal says. "You're barely on time for class."

"Yeah, Pen ... where've you been?" Nathan tilts his head.

I leer up at him from underneath my hoodie. "I could ask you the same thing, Nathan."

"Hospital," he says, and he holds up his bandaged hand. "Got a gnarly wound that needed sutures along with a fracture."

"What happened?" Crystal asks.

Adrenaline surges through my veins.

Fuck, and here I was thinking the basement was the worst part.

Wrong.

It's the aftermath.

What's he going to say?

How long will it take until everything we did will come to light?

Will Crystal and Kayla hate me?

My body buzzes with anxiety.

"Oh man, I hope it doesn't hurt too much," Crystal says. "How did that even happen?"

Nathan homes in on me. "I got into a bad fight at a party. Some fuckers tried to accuse me of something."

Is he intentionally insinuating he wasn't the one who put that fucking note underneath my door?

"But I'm not easily intimidated," he adds, his eyes narrowing.

"Maybe it's because you were at a party with a rival frat house," I say. I know I'm taunting him, but I can't help it. "Can't have been a smart thing to do."

He steps closer. "Are you trying to blame me for getting injured?"

"It's what they always tell us when some boy touches us without our permission."

He's right up in my face now, but I'm not scared of him.

If he chooses to spew the truth right here, right now, then I'll show everyone that fucking note. He threatened me.

"You think you know what it's like to lose a limb, Pen?" he spits in my face.

"Wow, guys, calm down," Crystal says.

"I know what it's like to lose my fucking soul," I growl back.

"Sold it to the devil, huh?" he retorts. "So do you happen to know what happened to my buddies, Josh and Kai? They've suddenly vanished overnight."

Flames erupt in my body when I hear their names. "Doesn't ring a bell, asshole."

"Guys, why are you fighting? You weren't even involved?" Crystal asks, but she pauses and then looks at me. "Right, Pen?"

I take in a deep breath. "Right."

Nathan snorts, shaking his head.

Suddenly, his eyes shoot up toward the hallways and his pupils dilate. He immediately bolts off into the class room to our right. But the second I try to turn around to see what scared him off, a hand lands on my shoulder, and a dark voice whispers into my ear, "Talking with some friends, Pen?"

I'd recognize Felix's grip and voice anywhere.

"Remember what I said ..." he adds.

"I didn't say anything," I reply, but he's already moved on to Crystal.

"Who are you?" he barks, folding his arms.

She stutters, overwhelmed by his presence. "Uh ... C-Crystal."

"Crystal who?"

"Murphy," she adds tentatively.

His eyes twitch.

"She's a friend," I offer.

"She'd better be," he says, tilting his head.

Crystal takes a step back when he gets up in her face, but I curl my hand around his arm and pull him back. "Felix."

"What?" he snaps.

"Can you act a bit more civilized?" I hiss at him.

He leans in and tells me with a low murmur, "You should be glad I didn't kill Nathan."

"You wouldn't," I mutter in disbelief.

"Believe me when I say I would gut him like a fish right in this hallway in front of everyone. Just for daring to fucking open his mouth at you."

A blush spreads across my cheeks, and I struggle to even form a single word. "I-I..."

Suddenly, he slaps my ass. "Still wearing that plug?" he whispers into my ear.

Now my whole face turns red as I nod. "I only took it out to go to the bathroom."

"Good girl," he whispers, pressing a quick kiss on my neck. "Because you're still mine, even if you don't want to be."

What?

Why is he acting like he didn't fucking piss me off, questioning if I killed my own fucking sister? I won't let him gloss over that.

I push myself out of his grip and stumble off, dazed by how lusty it suddenly made me when his hand landed on my ass. "Class is starting. I have to go."

I'm not gonna let him do this. Especially not here in this fucking hallway in front of one of my friends.

"Yeah, you go study like a good fucking girl, Pen," he says, loud enough for everyone in this hallway to hear. "I'll see you in the Skull & Serpent Society after you're done."

I'm so fucking mortified I just grab Crystal's hand and storm into the class. But I still can't shake the image of that smug smile on his face right before I slam the door shut.

"Sorry, we're late," Crystal tells the teacher.

"Thank you, Miss Murphy. Please, sit, both of you." The teacher sighs, waving at a few chairs in the back. "I've wasted enough time."

"Sorry," I say as we make our way to the back of the room while all the other students stare at us.

It's only been a few minutes, but I know we're late.

Boys.

Always those fucking boys.

"You okay?" Crystal asks. "What was that all about with Nathan?"

"Ah, nothing," I reply. "Just some fighting going on between some of the frat houses."

"The Phantoms and the Skull & Serpent?"

I nod.

"They've always had feuds, but no one's ever gone to the hospital and disappeared for several days over it."

She's fishing, and I don't know what to tell her without spilling the beans, which I'm definitely not going to do. Involving Crystal in this mess is the last thing I want.

"Probably, yeah," I mutter.

"But you're 'friends' with Felix and those other boys, right?" She makes air quotes with her fingers. "You must know something. I mean, he sure seemed protective over you."

"Oh, you don't wanna know, trust me," I reply.

"If you don't want to tell me, that's fine, I just—"

I turn to look at her. "I don't want you to get hurt."

Her lips part, but nothing else comes out.

"I'm sorry," I add.

"It's okay," she replies. "I get it."

I place a hand on her arm. "You're my friend. And it's best if you don't know too much."

She nods a few times, but she still pulls back from me and focuses on the teacher instead, which is probably for the best.

I blow off some steam and grab my books while I try to pay attention to what the teacher says, but it's hard to focus when my phone keeps buzzing in my pocket.

I pull it out and check my messages.

Dylan: Did you talk?

Penelope: No, did you?

Dylan: I need you to come to my dad's office. Now.

Penelope: I can't. I'm in the middle of class.

Dylan: Walk.

Penelope: No. I'll flunk.

I put the phone away, but it keeps going off, and it's annoying the shit out of me.

Alistair: Stop ignoring us.

Penelope: You in on it too now? I told you, I haven't said a word to anyone.

Alistair: People are talking. They know the Phantom boys are missing.

Penelope: Yeah, well it wasn't me. What did you even do with ... you know.

I don't want to say bodies. I don't ever know who's watching.

Dylan: Not here.

Penelope: Then where? I need to know if it's even safe to walk around on campus.

Dylan: You're safe when you're ours.

Fuck. That doesn't help me one bit.

Penelope: Nathan literally came to "talk" to me. You call that safe?

I suddenly get pulled into a group conversation with all three of them.

Dylan: Nathan's back? You need to fucking tell us those things, Pen.

Penelope: It literally happened three seconds ago. There was no time. Chill.

Dylan: I don't care how long it's been. Stay away from him. I'll deal with him.

Felix: No need. I was there, watching.

Alistair: You stealing my job, bro?

Felix: Fuck off.

Dylan: Looks like someone's still mad.

Alistair: Don't make it our problem, dude.

Felix: You boys did something, didn't you? Tell me. Now.

Dylan: Not safe over text. We'll talk after class. Pen's coming too.

Penelope: I'm not interested in watching you three fight.

Felix: Pen...

Dylan: You're coming, or I'm dragging you.

Alistair: I'm going to enjoy this.

I roll my eyes.

Penelope: Fine. Better be worth it.

Felix: We're doing all of this for you, Pen. Don't fucking forget.

I put my phone back down. I'm not interested in being schooled by them, and especially not by Felix. I'm still so fucking mad at him for even thinking I could hurt my sister.

Class can't be over quick enough.

***

When I finally get to the Skull & Serpent Society, one of the dudes who opens the doors immediately escorts me to the private library. The same one where I almost choked on Felix's cum, and the mere memory makes me squeeze my legs together.

"In here," the guy says, and he pushes me inside and closes the door behind me.

But I'm completely frozen to the floor when I realize I'm not alone with Felix, Dylan, and Alistair.

"Well, hello there. And your name is?"

It's the fucking dean. Dylan's father.

37

PENELOPE

"Penelope," Felix answers for me. "A friend."

"Penelope who?" he asks.

"Uh ..." Fuck. "Richards."

He narrows his eyes. "Richards. Hmm ..." The man looks me up and down, tucking his hands into the pockets of his expensive suit. "Interesting." He turns back to the boys. "Why is she here?"

"Because she was with us that night," Dylan says, rolling a lighter between his index finger and thumb. "She can vouch for us." His eyes land on mine. "Can't you, Pen?"

"Um." I'm really confused what's going on here. "What?"

His father's eyes narrow. "Are you being roped in to lie for these boys?"

"No," Alistair adds. "It's the truth. You were at the bonfire near the Hot Springs too, the other night, weren't you? We were dancing."

My eyes widen.

Oh fuck.

They're using me as an alibi.

"Yeah, I was with them. Why do you ask?"

The dean's face is stone-cold, so much different from how Dylan behaves. "Two boys from that Phantom frat went missing, and I need to know if they're involved." He narrows his eyes at me. "After what happened with Nathan Reed..."

Why do I feel like he's trying to implicate me?

Fuck, how much does he know?

Dylan frowns. "I told you, we didn't—"

"Shhh!" His father interrupts him with a single finger. "I don't want to hear it. I already paid for the hospital expenses as well as the damage." He adjusts his coat. "The family chose not to sue the university. But it won't regrow a lost limb. You should feel lucky money was all they wanted."

I swallow. So he does know.

"We already told you we had nothing to do with it," Felix retorts, folding his arms. "Nathan's lying."

"I don't fucking care who's lying," the dean seethes. "This ends now."

When no one replies, he finally turns around and walks in my direction. "If you value your time here at this university, you'd better stay away from these boys."

A chill runs up and down my spine as the man marches past me and out the door.

"Wow …" I mutter.

That man held a kind of power, not just in his stride but in his attitude as well.

Because there hasn't been anyone able to completely silence these boys, until now.

"Tell me about it," Dylan scoffs, jumping up from the couch.

"What the fuck was that about?" Felix suddenly blasts through the room at Dylan. "What the fuck did you tell your father?"

"Nothing, I told you," Dylan quips. "I don't fucking know how he knows. Maybe Nathan told his parents and they told my father."

"He threatened Pen, though," Alistair adds. "If he tries to implicate us, we can always throw it in his face. That would get him kicked out of here, and his parents wouldn't be too happy about that."

"Why do you think his father paid them off?" Felix says through gritted teeth. "It's the only reason we got away after letting him live." Now his eyes focus on mine. "We're in deep shit now, though."

"What are you looking at me for?" I ask. "You called me here, not the other way around."

He gets up in my face. "What did you do last night?"

I'm burning up just from the intense look in his eyes. "I was at a party."

"With them," he says through gritted teeth.

"You wouldn't help me. We found one of my sister's bullies."

His nostrils flare. "I knew it." He stares at Dylan and Alistair. "Those two Phantom boys ... it was you."

Alistair throws his hands in the air. "I'm pleading the Fifth."

Dylan turns on his lighter and fishes a smoke from his pocket, setting it ablaze. "We made some fucking fireworks."

Felix closes his eyes, rubbing them, but it won't take away the fire literally emanating off his body. "You killed them."

"Well, one of them died, that's for sure," I say. "The other one just got pummeled in the face."

But the lethal look in Felix's eyes the moment he opens them instantly makes me regret it.

"Don't worry, Ali and I took care of it."

"Just as they agreed they would, according to the deal we made," I snide.

He tried to blame me for my sister's death and refused to find the real people responsible.

Felix leans in until he's only a hair's length away from my face. "So you let *them* kill for you?" He points at Ali and Dylan.

It's almost as if he considers it an insult.

I swallow. "It wasn't intentional."

"Why?" he growls.

"Because Josh touched my sister," I reply.

"Josh ... Josh Walton?"

"Yes," Dylan answers.

"He admitted it to my face," I continue, "and then tried to do it to me too."

"I saved her," Dylan says from the back. "You're welcome, by the way."

Felix's face twitches and he towers over me, then snorts. Shaking his head, he marches out the room. "I need a fucking drink."

254 ~ CLARISSA WILD

Wait, what? He's not running off, is he?

I follow him out of the library and straight into the same room we were in before with the bar and the pool table.

"Felix." I try to draw his attention, but he keeps marching on until he's at the bar.

"Why are you running off?" Dylan asks, coming in right behind us with Alistair.

Felix grabs a glass and fills it with whiskey, chugging it down, then taking another.

"Hand me one too," Alistair says as he approaches the bar.

"Felix ..." I mutter.

Felix slides him a glass and pours it in, but slams the bottle down so harshly it makes me jolt up and down.

"Don't," he grits. "Don't say my name like it belongs to you."

His eyes light on fire, a burning brighter than the night he tortured Nathan. And it's making me hold in my breath.

"Like you say mine as though I belong to you?" I retort. "I'm still my own person, even with this deal we've got going on."

Alistair swiftly takes his glass off the bar and takes a sip.

"Is that why you had them kill for you?" Felix asks, his voice dark and heavy.

"She didn't ask," Dylan intervenes. "Those fuckers interrupted us when she was naked."

"Naked?!"

The glass he's holding shatters in his hand. Shards embed in his skin, but it doesn't seem to faze him.

His words come out through gritted teeth. "You fucked her?"

Dylan makes a funny face. "Well ... she could take a whole lot more than just me."

Felix's blazing eyes settle on Alistair.

Alistair frowns, lowering his glass. "Wait ... you didn't know?"

"But you put that plug inside her," Dylan says. "I thought you meant it as a gift."

I turn to look at him, equal parts disgusted and intrigued they'd consider me as a reward you could deliver to someone. "A *gift?*"

"That was meant for me and me alone!" Felix says, storming at Dylan. "You motherfucker, you fucked her without me?"

He grasps Dylan by the collar and lifts a fist.

"Get your hands off me," Dylan barks.

"You touched something that belongs to me."

What?

"She belongs to all of us," Dylan replies. "That's the whole fucking point of that fucking agreement we have with her!"

"I allowed her to be shared," Felix says, his voice booming through the room. "That does *not* mean you can just go off and fuck her when I'm not around."

Is this ... what I think it is?

"What the fuck did you do with her?" Felix asks, threatening to hit him again.

"Felix, calm down," Alistair says.

But Felix ignores him. "Did you stick your dick up her pussy? Did it feel good to fuck her when I wasn't even there?"

Oh my God. He wants me for himself.

Dylan smirks. "You jealous?"

Felix punches him in the face, and I cover my mouth with my hand. "Oh my God."

"Fuck you," Felix growls, shoving Dylan away.

Fuck, they really are fighting over me. That wasn't supposed to happen.

"Yeah, well fuck you too," Dylan retorts, spitting the blood out in his face. "You don't deserve her."

"Guys, let's not fight about this," Alistair says. "I don't think it's worth it."

"Yet you fucked her while I wasn't around too, didn't you?" Felix replies. "You're a part of the problem."

"Last I checked, we're all a part of this agreement, and she wanted us both," Alistair says. "Shame you don't like sharing. I do."

Dylan snorts. "You should've seen her face when she came all over me and licked up Ali's cum."

My whole body flushes with heat just thinking about it.

"Don't," Felix rasps, practically breathing fire.

"But you weren't there," Dylan adds.

"For good reasons, it seems," Alistair chimes in.

"We're not the problem here," Dylan says, shoving a finger into Felix's chest. "You are."

"I'll make you my fucking problem," Felix growls.

"Guys," I mutter.

But they pay no attention to me.

Dylan wipes the blood off his lip. "You'd better give me a good fucking reason not to kick your fucking ass right now."

"You wanna try me?" Felix taunts, cracking his knuckles.

"GUYS. STOP!" I step between them and spread my arms, staring down Felix. "Stop it."

I mean as much as I enjoy three guys fighting over me, this is not going to help anyone.

Felix eyes me down for a second, and I contemplate hitting him where it hurts by telling him how fucking hard I came. But I'm not gonna stoop that low.

"We agreed I would do whatever you told me. All three of you. And in exchange, you would help me find everyone responsible for my sister's misery." I swallow away the lump in my throat.

"And I did my part," he replies, stepping closer. "Until you ran away."

"I went to the only people who *would* help me," I retort.

He briefly eyes Dylan and Alistair again.

"Hey, don't look at us. You were the one who chased her off."

"Did you both forget she might be responsible for Eve's death?" he says, his face contorting. "You saw the fucking text message. You know about that fucking death pact she made with Eve."

He walks to the cabinet and fishes out the diary I've been missing, holding it open on a specific page where I pasted a photo of me and my sister as a memorial.

He pulls it away, ripping off the glue that kept it all together, revealing only a part of the text I pasted inside. The last text *she* sent me.

Her final goodbye.

But her words are misconstrued. Butchered, because of the glue keeping part of the photo from coming off.

I've done everything that's been asked and more. It's never going to be enough. And I refuse to go through life ... broken. Split in half by a decision that wasn't mine to make.

So I will stop it now.

This bonfire near The Edge will be the last night spent at this godforsaken university—

Tears well up in my eyes seeing these words again. "You don't know what you're talking about."

"You put this in the diary, didn't you?" Felix asks. "Like a little piece of truth buried along with all the lies. Just like the death pact you made with your sister."

"Stop," I hiss.

"Is it true?" Alistair asks as he approaches.

This is why they tormented me. Why Alistair and Dylan hung those posters. Why they tried to corner me in the stairwell. Why they chased me into the woods with those creepy masks.

Why Felix tried to break me.

I shake my head and rummage in my pocket to fish out my phone, then pull up my sister's face. God, I haven't seen her in such a long time that it hurts to look. But this needs to end now.

So I turn and show Dylan and Alistair the real text.

I can't do it anymore, sis. Please don't be mad at me. I've done everything I could and more. It's never going to be enough. And I refuse to go through life ... broken. Split in half by a decision that wasn't mine to make.

So I will stop it now.

This bonfire near The Edge will be the last night spent at this godforsaken university for me.

I love you, sis.

And whatever you do, don't ever get involved with those boys of the Skull & Serpent Society.

xoxo

Eve

Dylan reaches for my phone, and I let him take it so he can have a closer look.

"Oh ... wow."

Exactly.

"Let me see," Alistair says, and he snatches the phone out of Dylan's hands. "Oh boy. Felix ..." he mutters.

I turn to look at him, but all he does is stare nonchalantly, shaking his bloody hand like it means nothing to him.

"You believed a lie," I tell him to his face. "A lie you told yourself was true."

38

FELIX

Fuck.

I've never regretted a single thing in my life.

Until today.

"She told me you and her made that pact," I say, trying to make sense of it.

Dylan snatches the phone back from Alistair and holds it up to my face. "Does this look like she's fucking guilty?"

His voice fluctuates in tone so much it almost sounds like he's just as mad as she is.

"Look at it," Dylan barks. "And tell me you think she still did it."

I grind my teeth as I stare at the text.

"Eve literally told her she loves Pen," Dylan adds.

"This text ... this is why you guys did all that shit to me?" Penelope mutters.

Alistair suddenly grabs her hand and leans in to whisper something. I can't hear it, but I see his lips move, and all they say is, "I'm sorry."

She nods as he squeezes her hand. "Thank you."

Dylan grabs my hand and shoves the phone inside. "Look. At. It."

And I can't fucking look away from the text that was clearly sent from Eve's phone to Pen's. The emotions inside it reminding me of the girl she was right before she made the jump.

Solemn. Angry. Distraught.

All for reasons I never understood.

And I misconstrued those words as blame.

Blame on her sister for ruining her life to the point of wanting to end it all.

And when she came to this school, I made it my life's mission to make her suffer just as much as Eve did for all the wrong reasons.

Because Pen was right.

It wasn't her.

My lips part.

"You could've asked me, you know," she says, her nostrils flaring. "Instead of stealing that diary, the last thing that I got from her after she decided to end her life."

Her strained voice physically hurts to listen to.

More than any of these shards embedded in my skin ever could.

"I knew it was a bad idea to ask for your help." She grimaced.

"No," I say under my breath, putting the phone on the bar.

"You knew I needed someone fucked up and with no restraints to find the one responsible," she says. "But if you three are determined to fight over me out of jealousy, then we might as well cancel our agreement right here, right now."

"No," I say again.

"You're mad at them for doing exactly what you all said you would," she replies. "And you're mad at me because I proved to you I'm not lying and that you were wrong."

"Penelope ..." I grumble. "Don't make me say no again."

"Then are you going to do what you're supposed to?" she asks. "Or are you going to remain unreliable?"

Okay. I'm about ready to fuck this whole thing up, including her.

I approach her, and Dylan attempts to step in, but Penelope holds up her hand to keep him at bay. With just a single hand, she's managed to control both him and Alistair.

And I realize I haven't given her the credit she's due.

"Look at me."

She tentatively raises her catlike-lined eyes.

I tip up her chin. "I was the first to fuck that pussy raw."

Her lips part, and she sucks in a hampered breath.

My gaze lowers. "And I'd kill every last son of a bitch on this campus if they ever fucking laid a finger on you."

A whimper escapes her mouth, and she immediately shuts her lips after.

But I heard it. I definitely fucking heard.

She's much more like us than she lets on.

A twisted little girl with dark, fucked-up needs just like ours.

My thumb presses onto her purple lips, pulling them down as I slowly lower it, rubbing her lipstick all over her chin.

"You're mine, Penelope."

Dylan steps behind her and places his hands on her waist. "Ours."

My nostrils flare, and it only makes him grin.

"An agreement is an agreement, after all." Dylan leans in to press a kiss on her neck. "Where's the fun if we can't share?"

He sinks his teeth into her skin, and fuck me, the moan that follows makes me want to gut him like a fish.

I've never felt this possessive over something or someone, yet this little spicy fucking slut managed to pull it right out of me.

Fuck.

"Do you want her?" Dylan asks as he snakes his hands underneath her hoodie and grabs her tits while she looks at me with desperation.

My jaw clenches as I will my cock to go down.

"Then give her what she wants," he adds. "And it could all be yours."

"Felix ..." she whimpers when he twists her nipples underneath that hoodie.

And fuck me, I want nothing more than to rip it all off and show her I can do it better than him.

What the fuck has she done to me?

My knees cave in on me as I kneel before her.

"I've been a fucking fool," I say. "But don't you ever question my fucking loyalty."

I rip down her leggings and panties in one go.

She tries to swat me, but I grasp her wrist and force it aside, gazing up into her eyes with a kind of greed I've never felt before. And I bury my face in that sweet fucking pussy.

But I fucking need it. I need it more than I need my fucking ego.

I want it more than anything in this entire fucking world right now, so I'm taking it, whether she wants me to or not.

"Don't move," I groan as I lick her little clit until it's swollen. "I'm fucking famished, so let me eat this pussy of mine."

She tries to jerk free from my grip, but my hold on her wrist only grows tighter, while my other hand grabs her ass and pulls her closer.

"Sounds like you missed her," Dylan says.

"Shut it," I growl at him as I swivel my tongue back and forth while he plays with her tits from behind.

She grinds her teeth. "Get your fucking tong—"

"What? Here?" I shove my tongue right up her slit, and she sucks in a breath.

"Don't," she hisses.

"Or what?" I retort, my tongue grazing past her sensitive bits. Not close enough to hit that spot, but close enough for her to want to lean in. "You're gonna try to slap me again?"

"I'm not gonna forgive you," she growls.

"I don't need forgiveness ..." I reply. "I need mercy. Because I can't fucking stop, and I won't."

My fingers dig into her ass, her breath picking up when I inch closer to her tight little holes. I can feel the hard diamond nudging against my hand. I thought she'd remove the plug after she ran like hell, but she kept it in, despite the fact that she didn't trust me anymore.

Even when I revealed my true intentions, she was still too committed to the deal, too afraid to say no to me for fear of what I might do.

And that ... that's sexy as hell.

"God, you rile me up like nothing else," I groan against her skin.

Her hands find their way to my hair, taking hold, but her grip only entices me to lick harder and faster. More and more, her taste is so fucking addictive, I can't get enough.

Dylan suddenly pulls her hoodie over her head and grabs both her nipples, twisting them until she screams.

"That's it. Scream our names, little slut," he groans.

"Dylan!" she gasps. "Oh God, yes."

Fuck yes, that's the word I was looking for. Finally, she admits she wants it.

"You crave this as much as we do," I groan against her pussy lips, swiveling my tongue around her swollen nub until her legs start to quiver.

"I-I ..."

I slap her on the ass. Hard. "Don't you fucking deny it."

"But I'm only doing this so—"

SLAP!

Dylan's hand whacks her tit, making her moan out loud. "Don't you dare, Penelope."

"But the agreement," she mutters, glancing over her shoulder at Alistair, who's jerking himself off right through the fabric of his jeans just from watching us.

Dirty motherfucker.

"We'll fucking help you, all right ..." Dylan groans at her. "But first I'm going to help myself."

When I hear a zipper go down, I stop and glare at him. "Don't."

He frowns. "What? We're doing this, aren't we?"

I get up and lick my lips, the taste of her wetness too delicious to pass up. "I put that fucking plug there, and I'm the one who's gonna take it out." I grab her thighs and pull her toward me. "And my cock will be the first to fuck her there."

"What?" she gasps.

But before she can even say another word, I lift her in my arms and carry her to the pool table.

"Alistair, underneath her," Dylan barks.

"Fuck yes," Alistair mutters, and he flops down onto the table before I even have a chance to say anything.

"Better make it fucking worth my time," I growl at them.

"If we're gonna fuck her, better fuck her right," Dylan retorts, and he grabs the bottle of whiskey and takes a big gulp before planting it down onto the pool table's edge.

I put Penelope down on top of Alistair, face-down, then tear off what's left of her leggings and shoes and chuck it all into a corner.

"Wait, what are you doing?" she asks, glancing at me over her shoulders.

While I grab some lube, Dylan grabs her face and kisses her, and I fucking hate to watch, but I have to remind myself this is what I agreed to. Alistair even pulls out his hard-on, rubbing it all over her. I don't fucking care what he does with himself. All I care about is that she comes over and over again until she goddamn passes out from the orgasms.

As she plants her hands on the pool table and attempts to get up, Dylan pulls out the lighter and holds it over her neck. "Don't fucking think about it, Pen. You're ours now."

Fear flickers in her eyes, but when I swipe one finger along her slit, I can feel her get wetter and wetter.

She likes the scare.

The thrill of the threat.

And nothing in this world is more intoxicating than a girl who knows how to scream.

"I'm gonna take your fucking ass, Pen, and it's gonna fucking hurt," I grumble. "But you're going to fucking love every inch of my cock inside you."

I climb onto the pool table and perch myself behind her. As I spread her ass cheeks, Dylan tips up her chin and kisses her right on the lips, and a twinge of jealousy cuts through me like a dagger, but I ignore it.

"Alistair, fuck her pussy. Remind her who she belongs to," Dylan says, grinning.

I throw him a glare, but he challenges me with an equally possessive look across her shoulder, and it almost makes me want to lunge at him right across this pool table.

But her ass is right here for the taking, and I am not letting her out of my sight again knowing she could run away at any moment.

I pull out the plug, and she shrieks. "God, that was fast."

I press my lubed-up thumb into her ass. "You'll be begging God for mercy by the time I'm done with you."

The fear in her eyes makes my dick strain in my pants.

I pull it out, veins protruding as I position near her hole. Alistair pushes his length inside her with ease, and it makes me want to fucking jam this bottle of whiskey into his eye.

Instead, I thrust into her ass, claiming her like I was fucking supposed to before she ran off to be with them instead. But I'm not going to let them have her all by herself. I'll fucking win her back and make her mine, forever.

***

PENELOPE

I'm ravaged by an onslaught of lust building in my body as Felix thrusts into my ass and Alistair into my pussy, the feeling so tight and full I can barely take it. Every ridge of their lengths pushes against my insides, and Felix's piercings add so much pressure that I want to moan. But the second I open my mouth, Dylan plunges inside, stifling my sounds.

"That's it, Pen. Take it deep like a good fucking girl," he groans, plunging in and out of my mouth like it belongs to him.

Three of them taking me all at once, just like in my depraved fucking dreams I never dared to speak about out loud. But it's real and dirty and so fucking sexy that I want to die.

"So fucking tight," Felix groans, plunging in and out of me. "How often has this fucking ass been used, Pen?"

I can't even reply because Dylan's destroying my throat.

When he takes his hard-on out, I suck in a deep breath. "Never," I swiftly reply because I know I won't have much time.

Dylan slaps my face and rubs my spit all over. "Don't lie, slut."

"I'm not, I swear," I retort. "I've never—"

"Then this ass belongs to me," Felix groans, thrusting in so hard I see stars.

"You motherfucking possessive son of a bitch," Dylan retorts before he thrusts right back into my mouth.

I can feel both of them colliding inside me, pushing and shoving each other out of the way as they fight for control, fucking my pussy and ass until I can't even tell who's where. And it makes my mouth fucking water.

"That's it, make it nice and wet, Pen. Slobber all over it like the slut you are," Dylan groans.

Good God, could this get any filthier?

I moan when Alistair starts to suck on my nipples as he hits that sweet spot.

"Yes, take their fucking cocks deep," Dylan says. "Come all over them like the good whore you are."

Fuck me. It's too much.

I explode all over Alistair's shaft, Dylan's words and Felix's thrusting too much to take.

And I moan as Dylan briefly pulls out, but it sounds more like a hampered cry.

Felix groans along with me. "You're a sick little twisted bitch, aren't you?" He grabs a fistful of my hair and pushes inside slowly, then pulls out. "Just..." *THRUST.* "Fucking..." *THRUST.* "Perfect."

I can't even catch my breath from that rolling orgasm before Alistair goes right back into fucking me again.

Dylan spreads my saliva all over his length, and I open my mouth in anticipation.

I shouldn't be this needy or this horny, but I can't stop myself.

Despite the fact that these fuckers are monsters.

They're my monsters now.

And I'm the only one who can control these wicked desires brooding inside them as they unleash all of it onto me.

Saliva and pre-cum cover my whole face as I'm hammered in all holes by three of the most fucked-up guys I've ever met. And with Alistair's mouth going crazy on my nipples, all my senses are going haywire.

One of them begins to roar with lust, and I moan along too. Felix explodes inside me, and shortly after, Alistair does too. I can feel both of them throb inside me and fill me up to the brim, and it makes my eyes roll into the back of my head.

"That's it, Pen, take it all," Dylan groans, and he too buries himself to the hilt in my mouth until his seed jets out.

I struggle to swallow it all as it keeps on coming and coming.

"F-Fuck," he groans as my eyes grow red from the pressure inside me. "Swallow it all like the cum-slut you are."

God, I should hate it when he talks to me like that. Despise it, loathe it.

Instead, it makes my clit throb.

Wildly.

My tongue struggles against Dylan's length, but I still manage to push it all to the back of my throat and gulp it down.

Finally, he pulls away, and I heave and suck in a breath. In the back, I can feel Alistair's length slowly fall out of me while Felix retracts it, still hard.

"God, that was heavy ..." I mutter, completely entranced.

Dylan spits on my face and wipes it all over. "We're not fucking done yet."

SLAP!

I shriek as Felix's hand leaves a sizzle on my ass.

Felix's voice darkens. "Next round."

39

DYLAN

Alistair and I flip her around with ease, so her ass is now pointed at me, and fuck me, the sight of it covered in cum is something else.

I grasp the bottle of whiskey and chug down the last few drops, cheering with delight at the kinky fuckery unfolding. And without a second thought, Alistair's mouth is immediately on her slit as though he's made it his life's mission to suck her off.

"Lick her until she fucking squeals," I say, and I part her cheeks and shove my half-hard cock into her ass.

She squeals with delight as we alternate licks with thrusts, driving her mad.

I could see it in her eyes before when I took her mouth ... she loves being used, beat, choked, defiled. Like a girl who never learned to accept how fucked up she really is until she met us.

And fuck me, it's the best thing in the entire fucking world to have a girl who actually fucking loves to be degraded and watched.

"Yeah, you like this, don't you?" I say, slapping her ass.

She moans with delight as Alistair's tongue swivels around her clit.

Her ass feels as amazing as her pussy did when I fucked her in the hot springs, but watching Alistair lick her brings it to a whole different level.

"Open your pretty little mouth for me, Pen," Felix says with a low voice, pushing against her lips with the tip of his dick. "Show me how hungry you are."

She parts her lips just like he tells her to, and he rams inside with no remorse.

The way he fucks her gets me going, and I pump into her ass as hard as he plows into her mouth, leaving no second to spare.

"You came inside her, didn't you?" I groan at Ali, whose eyes are on my dick as it thrusts into her ass. "Clean her up then."

He eagerly laps her up, suckling and swirling around, getting her nice and wet. She moans with delight, practically bouncing against me. And I just know she's enjoying this as much as I am.

"Take it," Felix groans. "Take it like a good little slut."

She gurgles from Felix's sheer size thrusting into her mouth. He doesn't fuck a lot of girls, but when he fucks, he fucks to destroy.

And I fucking love watching him do it.

"Don't," he growls at me. "I don't need your fucking eyes."

"Fine." My brows rise. "I've got something more appetizing to look at anyway." And I let my gaze travel down to the tongue lapping up Pen's juices.

"Open your mouth, fuckboy," I groan.

And he lets me fucking thrust into him too.

His fingers swivel across her pussy as his tongue focuses on my dick, and I can't help but fucking bury myself to the base.

"F-Fuck," I groan. "I've missed that."

When I take it out for a second to allow him a breath, he says, "Me too."

And I fucking know he's been waiting on me for ages.

But I need my fix, and he knows.

Girls, boys, it doesn't fucking matter to me. If it has a hole, I'm game as long as I get what I need from them.

But Ali knew he always came first, and I knew he was always there when I was drowning in my own desires.

Until she came along.

Every time I saw her, I grew hard just from the thought of burying myself inside. I knew the moment I met her I needed to have her, even when he wanted me just as badly.

And I have to admit ... jealousy looked good on him.

But I don't play those kind of games.

I just fuck.

And right now, I need him to shut up and do as he's told.

"Don't fucking talk," I say. "Lick." And he sticks out his tongue. "Good boy."

***

PENELOPE

Felix grabs my chin and forces me to look at him. "Eyes up here."

Those intense hazel eyes make it so hard to look away.

I can feel every inch of his length in my throat, coated in both pre-cum and saliva. Every time he hits the back, I almost become cross-eyed.

"That's it, choke on me," he groans as I heave and cough.

The salty mix of both him and Dylan is intoxicating. Suddenly, Alistair's tongue rolls all over my clit again. And God, I can barely keep it together as Alistair licks me like he's never had anything tastier in his life.

"Fuck yes, lick both of us off," Dylan groans, plunging right up there between us.

I moan out loud from the sheer pleasure, and Dylan throws out a wicked laugh. "So fucking horny ... I'll fucking give your pussy something to come for."

I gasp when he grabs the bottle of whiskey standing on the pool table, and I pull away from Felix.

"What are you—"

He shoves it into me, and I shriek from the cold.

"That's it. Scream, slut, scream," Dylan says.

"I didn't say you could stop," Felix growls as he grabs me by the hair and directs my mouth right back over the tip.

Good God, it's so fucking wrong, yet I'm sloshing with wetness as

Dylan plunges the bottle in and out. It's dangerous as hell, and I know I shouldn't be doing this, but I can't stop either.

Even though I told myself I only did it for my sister, that I fucking hated Felix for even daring to suggest I was the one who caused all of her despair, I'm slowly becoming addicted to every wicked, fucked-up thing these boys do. So I turn off my brain and focus on the pure ecstasy between us. And as Felix pushes in to his base, my eyes roll into the back of my head.

"Fuck, I'm gonna come again, and you're gonna swallow it all," he groans, thrusting in so hard I almost lose control.

Because for some reason, every thrust, every groan, makes my pussy throb.

And this glass bottle, despite being dangerous as hell, adds fuel to the fire burning in my body.

"Oh God," I mutter between thrusts.

Suddenly, Dylan groans, busting all over my body, and Alistair immediately swivels across my clit, causing another orgasmic tsunami wave.

I moan out loud with Felix deep inside me as my pussy contracts around the bottle.

"Fuck yeah, she came again, all over the fucking bottle," Dylan says, laughing like a devil. "Lick it all off her, Ali."

He pulls out the bottle, making me gasp.

Felix howls and buries himself inside my throat, grasping my hair as he shoves me over the edge so far I see stars.

I can feel him combust inside me, dick throbbing, cum running down too far to let it all out again.

And all I can think about is ... how?

How do they have so much energy to keep on going, again and again?

Felix pulls out his half-hard cock and puts his hand on my mouth. "Swallow it all." He doesn't remove it until I've done what he asked, then he leans in and whispers into my ear, "Good little Penelope."

And fuck me, that literally made my clit thump.

Suddenly, the door in the back slams open, and to say I'm shocked is an understatement. I'm lying here on full display, completely naked, and here is this motherfucker just walking in like it's nobody's business.

Dylan, Felix, and Alistair all stop doing what they're doing as if everyone's frozen in time.

"Well, this is getting interesting," Dylan says.

"You'd better have a good fucking reason to interrupt us, Foley," Felix growls, tucking his length back into his pants.

This "Foley" guy's eyes briefly connect with mine, and they twitch when he sees my tits.

His eyes immediately flick to Felix. "You told me to come to you the second the dean announced something," the guy says. "Well, it's much, much worse."

"Well, c'mon then!" Dylan growls at him, shoving his package back into his pants as well and zipping up. "If it was so important to ruin our fuck session, fucking spill it."

The guy swallows as he firmly clutches the door. "Someone found a fucking body. They're locking down the university."

The whiskey bottle clatters to the ground.

40

FELIX

I zip up and march straight toward the door of the pool room with Dylan and Alistair barely on my tail after cleaning themselves up.

"Felix?" Penelope calls out as she crawls off the pool table and puts on her clothes. I hate having to ignore her, but right now, I've got bigger troubles.

"What are you doing?" Dylan calls. "Felix, where are you going?"

"I'm gonna talk to your fucking dad," I reply, pushing past Jason Foley.

"Whoa, whoa." Dylan runs in front of me and blocks the hallway. "You can't just barge into his office."

"Watch me," I say through gritted teeth.

"Why? What do you think you can even do?"

"Stop him from getting the police involved," I retort. "Ali, Dylan, you're coming with me."

"Wait, what?" Ali frowns. "Fuck no, I'm not going in there when—"

I grab his collar. "You were the ones who got us into this shit. Now you're going to get us out of it."

"Hey, I was just following his lead." Ali points at Dylan, who taps his feet and sighs.

"Thanks, asshole," Dylan says.

Ali shrugs. "What? It's the truth."

"I don't fucking care who did it." I shove him away. "But I need this to disappear. Stat." I ram my finger into Dylan's chest. "Now you're gonna tell me exactly what you did to that fucker."

"We nailed him to the ground," Dylan says with a low voice, his face darkening. "And burned him."

Penelope walks out of the pool room and watches us fight, the mere sight of her making me grind my teeth. "Was she there?"

"She helped us do it," Dylan says.

My blood thickens with anger. "And then what?"

"Well, we buried him," Alistair replies. "After Pen left."

"Obviously not deep enough," Dylan says, shrugging like it's no big deal.

"What about the other one?" I snap my fingers. "The dude you pummeled?"

Alistair's eyes grow big. "I don't know. We just left him there."

"He wasn't moving," Dylan adds.

I grasp him by the collar and seethe at him, "You fucking idiot! One of those fuckers might have been alive and you didn't even fucking bother to tell me?"

"Chill the fuck down, dude. He was bleeding from his ear when we left him. I didn't think he'd survive," Dylan says through gritted teeth, and he grabs my hands and rips them off his body. "And if you wanted a fucking say in it, maybe you should've been there."

My nostrils flare as the thought of punching his gut crosses my mind.

But something in Penelope's eyes stops me from doing just that.

"Come with me," I bark as I turn around and march out of the Skull & Serpent Society. "Both of you."

"I'm coming too," Pen utters.

"Stay in the house," I growl at her.

"Fuck that. If they're gonna interrogate people, I need to be there."

I turn around to face her. "Why? So you can rat us all out?"

She folds her arms. "So we can align our stories and make sure none of us spills unnecessary info." She tilts her head. "In case you forgot, I was there too."

Fuck, I almost forgot about that.

If anyone saw her there, she'll be implicated too, and people will start to ask questions. And I don't know if she can handle it.

"Did anyone else see you guys with those two dudes?" I ask.

Dylan snorts. "Oh, plenty. Though most ran off when the fight broke out."

I roll my eyes and slap my hand against my forehead. "Could you have been any more unsafe?"

"What?" Dylan scoffs. "What was I supposed to do? Just let them casually walk off after telling me straight to my face they assaulted Eve?"

"And don't forget they tried to take Pen too as payment for what we did to Nathan," Ali adds.

Fuck. Just the mere thought makes me want to rip this fucking decorative rifle off the wall and hunt down any motherfuckers who dared to lay a finger on either of them.

"C'mon," I growl.

Several police cars drive onto the property, and the school seals the gates shut. It's been a long time since I last felt this uneasy.

Everyone's looking around at all the police cars being parked on school grounds, drawing quite a lot of attention as well as gossip.

Beyond the gates, several ambulances as well as a coroner are parked near Priory Forest. All the students flock near the gates to watch the scene unfold, and we run toward the front, pushing past most of the students until we can finally see what's going on.

"Uh-oh," Dylan mutters.

A body bag is lifted onto a stretcher.

Several students gasp in shock.

"Fuck," Alistair says, taking a deep breath. "Too late."

A girl with a curly bun and bouncing tits pushes past the crowds, storming straight to Penelope, and grabs her arm. "Pen, did you hear? They found a fucking body on the school grounds," she says, but it's only when her eyes travel to meet mine that she finally realizes whose company she's in. "Oh ..."

Pen throws me a quick glance before focusing on the girl. "There's the ambulance picking him up." She points at the gates, and Kayla's eyes follow her finger.

Her face loses all color. "Fuck, so it's true."

They both stare at the body as it's hauled into the vehicle.

"Who is she?" I ask, narrowing my eyes.

"Kayla," Penelope sneers. "My *friend*."

She says it like I was about to cut the girl into thin strips.

"You're actually with them? I thought you said it was just a one-time thing," Kayla whispers, but I can hear her. "I heard some rumors about a fight in the woods between ... them." She eyes Dylan. "And you were there too."

Penelope's whole face glows red, and Kayla sees too. She grabs Pen's arm and drags her away from the crowd, so I follow suit. "So you *were* there? Did you see the actual fight?" She slaps her hand in front of her mouth. "Oh my God, don't tell me you're involved. I told you they were dangerous."

I step between them, towering over the girl. "That's enough."

Kayla's eyes flash between mine and Penelope's, but she doesn't budge. "If you lay even a single hand on me, I'm gonna rat you guys out like no tomorrow." She grabs Penelope's hand from behind me. "And I'll make sure she's protected from the likes of you."

She's got a lot of balls, that's for sure.

Dylan snorts. "It's cute you think that threats work on us."

I lean in. "I don't even need to lay a single hand on you."

I flick my fingers.

"Kay, I love you, but ..." Penelope swiftly releases Kayla's grip and takes a step back. "It's safer if I go with them."

She frowns. "Those sick boys? Safe?"

"She *wants* to be with us. Just like she *chose* to be our plaything," I add with a smirk. "So I'm gonna give you one fucking second to turn around and walk away."

Kayla's expression turns even more horrified. "Or what?"

"Shoo," I growl, my hand slowly drifting to the pocket where I keep my knife, but her eyes follow. "Before I change my mind."

Her whole body begins to shiver, and she suddenly bolts off toward her sorority, but not without throwing another glance at Pen.

"I'm sorry, Kay!" Pen yells after her. "You didn't have to be that much of an asshole." She punches me in the side so harshly my knees almost buck. "She's my fucking friend, and I'm not gonna lose her because of your possessive ass."

"She was a threat, and I got rid of it," I hiss back, grasping her by the hoodie. "Ditch her."

"Over my dead body."

"She's a liability who knows too much," I growl.

"I don't fucking care." She folds her arms, despite the fact that I'm gripping her clothes tightly. "I trust her."

Grinding my teeth, I try to focus, but all I can focus on are those plump lips just begging me to show her who makes the fucking rules.

And something about that makes me irrationally angry.

Why do I fucking care so much?

"You trust too easily," I retort.

"I trusted you," she says, momentarily catching me off guard.

She ... trusted me?

And I fucking broke that trust when I tried to go after her instead.

My nostrils flare. "And look where that got you."

"Felix Rivera ..." A stern voice makes me look up. "Put that girl down."

Dean Caruso comes walking up to the crowd, and he doesn't seem the slightest bit amused.

As I place Pen back down on the ground, her whole body begins to tense, and even my veins pulse with adrenaline. But worst of all is the fact that the entire crowd is staring at us now.

Dean Caruso glares at all three of us. "Follow me."

"Who? Him?" Dylan points at me like I'm the one to blame for his murder.

His father snarls, "All of you."

Sighing, I glance at the boys before we follow him inside.

"But we haven't gotten our stories straight yet," Dylan says.

I shove my elbow into his side and whisper-growl, "Shut up. People are listening."

All around, people stare at us for all the wrong reasons as we walk toward the big building in the back and head inside under heavy scrutiny.

"What's gonna happen? Is he gonna kick us out?" Pen asks.

When I glance at her over my shoulder, Ali's hand snakes through hers, and it makes me want to fish this dagger out of my pocket and throw it right at his heart.

Fuck. Since when did I become so fucking possessive I can't even look at someone else holding her hand? Have I gone insane?

I shake it off as the dean walks us up the stairs to the top level of the building. Along the way, a multitude of students looks at us and visibly gossip, unafraid to be speaking about us in public. They all knew we were dangerous before. No one just ever expected the cops to get involved.

A familiar face bearing a smirk at the last staircase makes me halt and stare.

"Nathan ..." My body feels like it's about to combust. "You're responsible for this?"

"I didn't do anything. I'm gonna enjoy this, though," Nathan replies, grinning like he's on drugs.

And fuck me, I'm gonna end this motherfucker's life.

I immediately go for my knife, but Dylan grasps my arm and stops me midway. "Don't."

"Listen to your buddy there, Felix," Nathan spews. "Or this might get a whole lot uglier."

"Nothing as ugly as your fucking stump of a finger," I retort, tilting my head when the anger flashes across his face. "I guess my snake Nessie will enjoy a tasty meal soon."

His pupils dilate, and he charges at me, punching me in the face.

Dylan's father growls, "Hey! Get off him!"

A police officer standing near the stairs jumps in and separates us, drawing his gun at Nathan. "Step back!"

Nathan stops midair with a second punch and glares at the police officer before lowering his fist. And I can't help but fucking smile at him.

He hisses, "You motherf—"

"Not another word," Dylan's father quips, and he nods at the police officer. "Show him the exit, please. I don't want any more fighting on these school grounds."

The police officer grabs Nathan by the arm and pushes him farther down the stairs, forcing him to break eye contact.

I know that fucker hates me for what I did to him, but he deserved it after threatening Penelope and possibly even hurting Eve.

And I thoroughly enjoy tormenting every single inch of his soul.

But if he's the one who ratted us all out to the dean to settle a score, I'm gonna make sure he pays.

We're alone with Dylan's father, who turns to us like a bull getting the whip. "You motherfuckers better give me one good reason not to kick you out of this school right now."

"Uh ..." Dylan mutters. "Maybe because I'm your son?"

He glares at his son before sneering at all of us, "My office. Now."

"Wait, me too?" Penelope asks.

His eyes narrow at her. "*All* of you."

We follow him up the stairs and into his office, but the second the door closes on us, Alistair practically loses all the color in his face.

Because next to the dean's chair is the police chief in charge of the entire city as well as this school.

And Alistair just mutters, "Hi, Dad."

41

ALISTAIR

Staring into my dad's eyes after committing a murder was the last thing I wanted to do, but here we are.

"Wait ... that's your father?" Penelope whispers behind me. "What's his name?"

"Diego King," I reply, but all I can focus on is my dad standing there like he wants to take my name out of his will.

"Dad, I don't know what—"

"Sit. Down," he interrupts, and he slides two extra chairs our way. "All of you."

"What's going on?" Penelope asks as she sits down on one of the chairs.

Dylan grabs the one in front of the desk and throws his feet up. "Well, this is gonna be interesting."

Dean Caruso slams his fist onto the desk, causing his feet to fall off. "How many times do I have to tell you to fucking behave?"

Felix grabs the chair next to Dylan and sits on it with legs spread wide while I grab the one my father scooted over and sit beside Penelope, ignoring his burning gaze.

"You're all a fucking disappointment," Dylan's father murmurs as he sits behind his desk and grabs the wood like he needs to crack it in two to make a point. "I knew you guys were doing some fucked-up shit with drugs and alcohol, fucking girls left and right ..."

"Girls?" Dylan's brow rises, and he and I briefly make eye contact.

"But actual fucking murder on these school grounds?" Dean Caruso continues, ignoring what Dylan said.

"Are you accusing us of something?" Felix asks.

"I know it was you three. Don't fucking deny it," Dean Caruso says. "There's no one else in this school as fucked up as you." He clears his throat. "I should know because one of you is my spawn."

Why does he make it sound like Dylan is trash? All I see is a guy who has uncontainable desires, and sometimes his sparks just start to fly.

"Hey, I don't see any proof," Dylan retorts.

"We found the fucking body," my father says through gritted teeth. "Don't act like you don't know. I saw you staring at the ambulance."

Dylan shrugs. "What happened then?"

"He was burned to a crisp," my father replies.

"Interesting." Dylan briefly glances at both Penelope and me.

"But you know all that since you're the one who set it on fire," Dean Caruso says.

Dylan's brow rises. "Again, where's the proof?"

My father stomps forward and places a bunch of papers with photographs all over the desk.

"This. This is what you two have done."

Damn. Josh looks even worse than I remember.

"Doesn't ring a bell," Dylan says.

"Let me ring it for you then," my father growls. "There was a party in the woods near the hot springs, and people saw you two fighting with some Phantom boys." He points at both Dylan and me.

"What? Why would you believe some random people?" I retort, trying to deflate the situation. "I was literally studying."

I mean, it's true... for some part.

"So why am I even here?" Felix asks, frowning.

"Because you're the ringleader, and I know you're always involved even when you're not there," Dean Caruso replies.

Felix grimaces. "That's not even remotely fucking legal."

"Killing someone isn't either, so here we are," he adds.

Felix stands. "We didn't do a fucking thing."

"Sit. Down," Dean Caruso barks, his voice as low as his eyes, as he tries to subdue Felix.

And fuck me, this is about to turn into a fucking fight right here in the dean's office.

"It's true," Penelope suddenly says.

My face turns stone-cold as I focus my gaze on her, realizing what she just did. And I'm not the only one. Both Dylan's father and my father are now glaring at her.

"They protected me," she adds. "Josh tried to ... use me against my will." She swallows.

"And then what?" my father continues.

Everyone's looking at her now, trying to make sense of her story.

"Some guy named Kai was there too," she says.

"That Phantom house freshman?" Dylan's father asks.

Dylan nods.

"Kai attacked Dylan and Alistair," she says. "We had no choice but to defend ourselves."

My father makes a face at her. "So you set Josh on fire?"

She shakes her head. "No. There was a lot of fighting between Josh and us, and then he pulled out a gun and threatened us. So Dylan knifed him down."

Fuck, why is she telling him this? And it's all a jumbled, dishonest mess too.

My whole body shakes right now, and I wish I could wrap my hands around her neck and silence her. But my dad would drag my ass to jail right away.

Fuck.

If only Felix hadn't dragged us into this mess to begin with. I could've just lived out my life knowing I at least had Dylan to fall back on.

But now ... chances are none of us will make it out of here without shackles around our wrists.

"Kai then came after us too, but he fell while running, and he hit his head on a rock, so he started bleeding from his ear. That's when the fight finally ended."

My eyes widen.

What?

"Alistair, Dylan, and I ran off and hid in the bushes to escape while Kai got up. But when he couldn't find us, I saw him torch Josh's body and bury him."

What the fuck is she doing? These are half truths and half lies.

My father's eyes narrow. "Hmm ..."

"I swear, that's all we did. Kai killed his own housemate so he could frame us," she says with the most sincere voice I've ever heard. "As revenge for not being able to take their shit out on me."

"So you got assaulted?" my father asks. "And these boys defended you? Is that what you're trying to say?"

She nods. "We didn't mean for anything to happen at that party. Those Phantom boys just showed up out of nowhere."

"Where's your proof of all of this?" my father asks.

Penelope pulls up the sleeves of her hoodie, revealing bruises on her wrists.

Goddamn.

Maybe I was wrong about her.

"I tried to fight them off, but I couldn't. Not without their help."

My father grabs her wrist and inspects it up close. "And you saw Kai burn Josh's body?"

She nods.

"And what did Kai do after?"

She shakes her head. "I don't know. We all left as quickly as we could after what he did. We were scared we'd get caught. And now we did." She swallows. "Please don't lock us up. We didn't do anything wrong. They only tried to defend me."

I hold my breath.

Is this really going to work?

My father glances at all of us. "Then where is Kai now?"

I make a face. "I haven't seen him."

"Me neither," Dylan chimes in.

Everyone looks at each other.

Because we all know what this means.

If they haven't found him where we left him, then he's gone. Which means he's going to talk.

"Look, all of this is news to me, so can I just go?" Felix says, yawning.

"Stay," Dylan's dad barks at him. "As long as Chief King isn't done with you, you're staying here."

Felix rolls his eyes, but my father ignores him.

"So you're all telling me some guy named Kai from the Phantom house burned one of his own housemates so he could frame you for his murder, all because you two wouldn't let him take advantage of her?"

We all nod.

"That's about it, yeah," Dylan says.

My father rubs his forehead and sighs out loud. "All right."

Wait. He believes it?

Wow, that's a first.

"Joseph, this is going to be one hell of a case," he mutters, turning toward Dean Caruso.

"I don't want to go to jail, please," Penelope mutters. "I'm the victim."

My father raises his hand. "No one's going to jail."

Our jaws collectively drop.

"Wait, what? I thought you said you suspected us?" Dylan asks.

"Do you not want me to believe her story?" He narrows his eyes.

Dylan gulps. "No, sir, it's the truth."

"Then be happy you'll get off with a warning." My father grabs the papers off the desk. "Now, if you'll excuse me, I have some work to do."

"But what about the body?" Dylan's father asks. "We can't just ignore it."

"Let me deal with that," my father replies. "I know how to fucking handle things."

Dylan's father leans in to speak with a soft voice, but we can all still hear him. "This will come back to bite us in the ass. Josh's family won't let this rest easily."

"I'll take care of it. The case won't be going to court. I'll make sure of it."

Is he suggesting he'll tamper with evidence?

"I'll leave you four to Joseph," my father says, eyeing me in particular. "And I'll speak to you soon." I feel uneasy when he rubs my hair like I'm still a kid.

When the door closes, Dean Caruso doesn't seem too pleased. "You do realize how lucky you are?"

"So we're definitely off the hook?" Dylan asks, crossing his legs in a way that looks like he's getting comfortable.

"You wish." Dylan's father grabs a stack of papers from his cabinet and throws them all onto our laps. "Ten thousand words on how to make this school a better place."

"Ten thousand?" Dylan quips.

When he throws the stack on Felix's lap too, he responds, "Whoa, I didn't do shit. Why are you giving me flack too?"

"Because it's about time you boys learned your actions have consequences."

"Wait, but is that suspension still on, then?" I ask.

"Yes," he retorts. "Five days remaining. The next infraction will be mandatory community service here, and if you still haven't learned your fucking lesson, it will be expulsion."

My eyes widen. "I don't want to get kicked out."

This education is the only thing that will get me someplace beyond the fucking Mafia my father is involved in.

"Then make it fucking count," Dean Caruso replies. He grabs a cigar from the box on his desk and lights it up. "Now get out of my office. All of you."

We don't wait a second longer before we all bolt out of there and rush down the stairs, but as he slams the door shut, Dylan quickly grabs Penelope's hand and spins her around.

"You lied for us," he whispers.

A brief smile flashes across her face as she whispers, "You killed for me."

Dylan smirks. "Well, I'll be fucking damned. There's my girl."

Felix towers over both of them, but the look on his face makes me want to take a step back. "What did you just say?"

Penelope gazes at him.

Uh-oh.

***

DYLAN

My phone rings, distracting everyone. Which is good, judging from the lethal look Felix gives me.

I ignore him and put my phone to my ear, answering, "Hello?"

"Hey, my little man."

Oh fuck. It's Mom.

I swallow and turn away from the boys. "Hey, what's up?"

"What's up? You normally never greet me that way."

"I know, but I'm not alone," I hiss into the phone.

Alistair snorts. "Who is it, D?"

I try to wave him off, but he just laces his fingers through mine like he finds it funny. "Cute."

I throw him a glare.

"Your mom's calling?" Alistair asks.

"Dylan, I'm throwing a dinner party tonight, and I want you to come," Mom says. "And don't tell me you can't tonight because I know your father has suspended you. You have nothing better to do anyway."

I frown. "He told you?"

The boys snort behind me, and even Penelope seems amused.

"Is he getting a scolding?" she asks Ali.

"Sounds about right," Alistair replies.

I try to shush them, but it's no use.

"Your friends are there with you?" Mom asks. "Bring them over too."

"What? No, no," I quickly say. "They don't like—"

"My food? Nonsense. Bring them," she says in her stern voice. "I won't take no for an answer, Dylan."

Oh God. Why did my father tell her? I'm so fucking embarrassed.

"Mom, I—"

"And bring that girl too I keep hearing in the background."

I throw a glare at Penelope, who's giggling like a schoolgirl. She immediately shuts her mouth.

"The more the merrier," Mom adds.

"You sure Dad approves?" I ask.

"He's the one who suggested it," she says. "He just called."

I roll my eyes. Of course he did. If he can't punish me with the justice system, he'll punish me by forcing me to spend "quality time" with my family instead.

"Who's gonna be there?" I ask.

"Well, all of our friends, of course," she replies. "Including your friends' family. So make sure you dress your best. I'll see you tonight, honey!"

She hangs up before I can even rebuke her words.

Goddammit.

Sighing, I put the phone back into my pocket. The others are still laughing at my misery.

"Yeah, you laugh now."

"Your mom's forcing you to come home again?"

I pat Felix on the shoulder. "Yeah, except this time, she's expecting you and your whole family as well."

His eyes widen.

"And Penelope, too, of course," I add, winking.

"What?" Penelope's eyes widen.

All the color leaves Felix's face. "What did you tell her?"

"Nothing," I reply. "Who do you think told her?"

Felix's fist balls as he turns to look at the staircase where my father's office is. "Motherfucker ..."

"Guess that's one way to keep us in check," Alistair jokes.

"Get your fucking smokes out, guys," I say. "It's time to pretend we're regular old boys."

42

FELIX

I tap my foot and sigh out loud as I stare at the Alpha Psi sorority house, waiting for a certain someone to finally walk out the front door.

She's taking forever, and I don't fucking like waiting around out on the streets. It's too obvious, too easy to become a target.

Impatiently, I check my watch, wondering how much longer she'll be. I wasn't even going to go to this dinner party to begin with, but Dylan practically begged me to come so his parents wouldn't hurt him.

And I can't ever resist a bit of groveling.

Clearing my throat, I lean against the side of the car.

The window rolls down, and Dylan sticks his head out. "Any sign yet?"

"Nope."

"If we don't make it on time, my mom's gonna kill me," Dylan says. "You know that right?"

"Go buy a coffin, then," I reply.

"Dude, really?" Dylan scoffs, adjusting his sunglasses. "Can't you call Pen or something?" he asks.

I fold my arms and casually lean back. "Can't you?"

He makes a smug face. "It's against the law to use your phone while driving."

Since when the fuck does he care about the law?

One of these days, my fist is going to meet his smug jaw again and knock out some teeth.

When the door to the sorority building finally opens, we both look up.

"My God ..." Dylan mutters, lowering his sunglasses.

Out steps Penelope, her hair curled up into a bun with loose hairs framing her face, lips in a dark-red hue, her eyes smoky and dark.

Dark enough to appease my blackened soul.

The corner of my lip slowly inches into a smirk as she steps out onto the porch in a Victorian-looking bordeaux-colored dress with black lace on top, platform pumps, and a black teardrop choker around her neck.

That was definitely worth the wait.

"If it isn't perfection herself," Dylan says, licking his lips.

I press the button inside his car so the window rolls up again.

"Don't be like that," he snarls.

"Stop drooling," I growl back.

Now Alistair's window rolls down. "Beautiful."

I narrow my eyes at him. "Since when do you like her so much?"

"Since you don't pay attention," Dylan says.

I avert my eyes again as I have much better things to look at that carry the name Penelope. Though the way she's dressed now, it feels like whore would be a much more fitting name.

My whore. And no one else's.

Well, maybe these two clowns here in the car. If they behave.

"Penelope," I say as she approaches me.

"Felix," she replies, her brows rising in a fucking arrogant way.

And even though I hate to admit it, it looks good on her.

"You look ..."

"Nice?" she fills in for me.

"Appetizing."

Her cheeks grow redder than the blush she applied.

But I doubt she realizes we can all see.

Dylan suddenly opens his door and steps out when she's only a couple of feet away. He shoves me aside and grabs the passenger door handle, throwing it open wide while holding out his hand. "Your personal carriage awaits, milady."

My nostrils twitch as I turn to smack his hand away from the door.

Penelope grins. "How chivalrous," she murmurs as she gets inside and turns to look at him. "Almost makes me forget how vulgar you are."

Dylan's face slowly unravels, and it's the most majestic sight I've ever seen to the point that it makes me laugh.

Rarely anything ever makes me laugh. Not since ...

Dylan slams the door shut. "Slut."

"I can hear you," she retorts through the window.

"Good," he adds.

"You gonna sit down too, or do I have to shove your ass back inside?" I tell him.

He raises his hands. "Fine, fine. Jealous much?"

"Of that interaction?" I snort. "Hardly."

He sits behind the wheel while I park myself next to him and shut the door.

Behind me, Penelope seems befuddled by the other girl in the back seat while Alistair sits between them.

"Um ... you didn't tell me we weren't alone," Penelope says as Dylan starts the car and drives off. "Who's this?"

Giggling erupts from the other side of the car, and my eyes instinctively draw to the noise. "Lana. Be nice." I glance at her through the rearview mirror, and she looks right back at me with that same familiar stare.

She bites her lip in defiance. "I'm always nice."

I narrow my eyes at her. "Just as I'm always nice, right?"

She rolls her eyes and blows a bubble with some of that awful bubblegum. "You wish."

"This is Penelope. She's—"

"A friend," Penelope interjects.

My eye twitches.

I don't like how she made that sound.

Penelope reaches out her hand. "Nice to meet you, Lana."

"Want some gum?" Lana offers.

"Oh, thanks, that's nice of you," Penelope says.

"Don't do it," Alistair mutters, eyeing her. "It's poisoned."

"Wait, what?" Penelope stammers.

Lana shoves her elbow into Ali's side, making him grunt in pain. "Of course not, asshole."

Penelope snorts as Lana gives her a piece of gum. "I like you already."

This fucking conversation.

I roll my eyes.

"Same, girl," Lana says as Penelope begins to chew on the gum.

Dylan swerves through the streets while Lana curls her long black hair around her finger, taking care not to coil her red ribbon that's attached at the top. "I take it you're railing my brother, then?"

Penelope's eyes widen, and she almost chokes on the gum, swallowing it down.

"Lana," I sneer, warning her with a look.

Lana makes a rude hand gesture. "What? It's the truth, isn't it?"

"It's none of your fucking business," I growl.

"Fuck that. Family's always my business." She crosses her arms and looks out the window.

"Okay, well, that went amazing," Alistair jokes.

"Don't fucking start a fight now. I'm trying to drive," Dylan barks.

"God, I hate that I have to even go to this stupid fucking dinner," Lana says, rolling her eyes. "I have a giant fucking test tomorrow morning, and now I'm gonna have to stay up late to study."

"Then why did you come?" I retort.

She raises her brows. "Do you really not know the answer?"

"And here I thought you wanted to spend some quality family time," I respond.

She throws out a stilted laugh. "With your friends? Good one."

"I thought you liked me," Dylan pouts.

"Dylan, I like you, but please ask your mom not to invite the whole fucking friends list next time," she replies. "Fucking please."

"Lana ..." I warn her. "That's enough."

Her nostrils flare, and she looks away again, curling her finger around her long black hair. "Fine."

As the car continues to drive, everyone in the back sits with their legs together like they're afraid to even touch. And I've never in my life had a more uncomfortable car trip than this one.

When we finally reach our destination, Lana throws the car door open and pertinently steps out, slamming it shut behind her.

The fucking attitude of that girl will be the end of me one day.

I stare at Penelope through the rearview mirror.

"That's your sister?" she asks.

"Not by choice, or he would've picked a different one," Dylan jests, and I shove my elbow into his guts until he coughs wildly.

"Okay, I'll see you inside," he splutters, opening the car door.

Penelope just gives me an awkward look before she too gets out.

"Well ... that was awkward," Alistair muses.

"Thanks," I say, as I get out too and leave him alone in the car.

Penelope adjusts her dress and checks her makeup in a tiny mirror she fished out of her clutch. "So your sister, huh? Damn, you two are like peas in a pod."

I stop in my tracks and turn around, frowning, "What did you just say?"

She shrugs. "That arrogance and the temper ..."

I shove her against the car and plant a flat hand against the metal, blocking her way out. "I do not have a temper," I growl.

She smirks in my face.

Actually fucking smirks.

And it makes me want to punch the fucking car ... and kiss her at the same time.

"Told you," she says.

I grab her throat with my free hand, squeezing around her veins until she struggles to breathe. "If you dish it out, better be prepared for the consequences, Pen," I whisper, leaning in to lick her neck. "Are you ready for that?"

"Won't change facts," she mutters through her gasps.

"My sister is *nothing* like me."

She snorts. "I've known her for two seconds, and I've seen all I need to know."

My grip on her throat tightens, and I can feel her heartbeat slow down, her eyes struggling to stay open, and the sight gets me hard as hell.

And we haven't even gotten to the fucking dinner party yet.

"You're a masochist, aren't you?" I murmur near her ear. "You like the humiliation and pain."

The more I push my fingers into her veins, the softer her posture becomes until her head tilts back and her thighs spread, yielding to my body as if she turns to mush.

So I slide my hand down the car and snake it down her legs instead, creeping underneath her dress until I find that spot that makes her shiver. And I don't even need a fucking answer from her mouth anymore. Her body tells the truth.

"And you're a fucking sadist," she says when I finally release the pressure a little.

My fingers are still clasped around her neck as I lean in close enough to feel her breath become more ragged with each encroaching inch. And it's like fucking cocaine sniffed straight into my brain. Addictive.

"A sadist you fucking love to be used by," I say, my lips hovering close to hers. "And if you don't watch your mouth, I will stick my fingers inside your fucking pussy right here out in the streets."

Her jaw drops. "You wouldn't."

My lip twitches. "Wanna bet?"

"Guys? You coming, or what?" Dylan calls from the gates to the property his parents own.

There goes the fucking moment.

"Coming," I growl, without ever taking my eyes off hers, and then whisper, "And you will too before this night is over."

I push myself off her and march to the gate, leaving her in a puddle of her own wetness.

Just like she deserves.

43

PENELOPE

I'm sweating like crazy already, and I haven't even gotten to the dinner part of the night.

God, how does he do this every single time?

I was almost hoping he would actually go through with it.

I swallow away the lump in my throat and adjust my dress again, which got all scrunched up from the way Felix just casually swiped his finger along my pussy. But worst of all is the fact that I was already wet, and he fucking knew.

Fuck that fucking arrogant smug face of his.

I really have to stop letting him get to me. Even though I know, deep down, he's as right about me as I am about him. The people you hate are the people who know you the best, and that's exactly why you hate them.

I sigh out loud and make my way to the property's gate.

The place is giant and opulent. Not that I'm amazed, considering who Dylan's parents are and what they do. Not their real jobs, but the secret society hiding behind it is what brings in all the money. I don't need to see it in action to know it's happening right under our noses. Half of the people who go to Spine Ridge U are family of criminals.

I walk through the rose garden along the pebble path up to the big road where a ton of cars are parked underneath an open garage. A lady stands at the front door smiling happily.

"Welcome back, Mr. Caruso!"

"Hi," he says awkwardly, as he sneaks past her as quick as he can. How unlike him.

"And hello, Mr. King and Mr. Rivera."

"Save it," Felix barks as he walks past her.

The lady's face looks like she's just stood in the snow for an hour.

I glower at Alistair, who simply shrugs. "That's him."

Does he have to be such a asshole to everyone, though?

We go inside the mansion, and I gawk at all the beautiful tapestries, the vintage paintings and artwork scattered through the hallway, and all the expensive-looking wines in the back. Dylan's father is a collector, that's for sure.

"Welcome, welcome," a voice calls from the back. Dylan's father approaches us with a big smile. "Your mom's already finished dinner, so we're just waiting on you in the dining room."

"Mom finished dinner?" Dylan scoffs. "We have cooks for that."

"Dylan," his father warns and leans in, "do not insult your mother."

He rolls his eyes. "I'm just surprised. That's all. Can't wait."

Dylan passes by his father as if he's got a stick up his ass.

"What's with him?" I whisper to Alistair.

"He hates family things. Don't ask."

"I can't wait to taste all the amazing dishes she created," Lana tells Dean Caruso, and it makes his face beam.

"Thank you. At least someone's excited," he says, and he beckons us back to the room. "Let's go inside."

We follow Dean Caruso to the room, but I bump into Felix on the way, who's stopped midway through the doorway.

"Felix ..." A low voice emanates from the room beyond, and I peek over his shoulder to see a man sitting behind a large dinner table, his chiseled face outlined by thick, black stubble, hair slick and combed back, eyes narrow and partially blocked by a pair of glasses, his posture self-assured. Completely the opposite of Felix in every way, yet that voice sounds ... similar.

Felix clears his throat. "Dad."

Aha.

Wow, I did not see that one coming. They don't even look alike.

Felix marches over to the opposite side of the room and parks his ass down on a chair as far away as possible, and it makes me so goddamn curious as to why.

"Welcome, welcome, everyone," a lady says as she waltzes in through the door in the back of the room carrying two big plates filled with delicious food. Her black hair is tied into a curly knot, and a small but extravagant hat sits on top. That must be Dylan's mom. "Food's almost ready. You can sit wherever you like. Feel free to make yourselves at home!"

"Thank you, Mrs. Caruso," Lana says.

Mrs. Caruso has a bright smile. Her face looks almost pristine, and it almost makes me want to ask her about her skincare routine.

"That looks lovely, Jeong-Suk," Felix's father says as she puts down the plates.

"Oh, this isn't even half of what I have prepared," she muses, giggling. "C'mon everyone, sit, sit!"

Alistair and Dylan find a seat near Dylan's father, but I can't help but swerve to Felix's side and sit down beside him.

"So that guy is actually your dad?" I ask.

"What about it?" Felix grabs a knife and starts twiddling with it.

"Nothing. I'm just ... surprised."

"Surprised?" He side-eyes me.

"Well, you two look nothing alike," I reply.

"No." He turns around again, like he's trying to avoid having to even talk to anyone, let alone me.

"He's all by himself. Shouldn't we sit next to him?" I ask.

"No thanks."

Wow. Cold.

"You don't like your dad?" I ask.

He turns to me again, his nostrils flaring. "Does it matter?"

I shrug. "I don't know."

"I'd much rather sit here," he says. "Where it's quiet."

I look at the man again as he's tasting some of the snacks Mrs.

Caruso put out, like the crispy fried cookies covered with peanuts and honey glaze. "He doesn't look like the type to get ignored by his son."

"You really wanna go there?" Felix says through gritted teeth.

"Are you always this cold?" I rebuke.

"Talk to Dylan if you want the heat," he retorts.

I ignore his obvious taunt. "Did your father come here all by himself? Where's your mom?"

Suddenly, he punctures the table with the knife. "Do not. Speak. About my mother."

Everyone looks at us.

Literally, everyone.

And it's gone so quiet I can hear my own heartbeat.

"Felix, not at the table. Please." His father smiles. "We're guests at a friend's house."

Felix's face contorts, and he rips the knife out of the table only to scoot back and march off.

"Jesus," I mutter.

"Ignore him, it's sensitive," Lana says as she hovers over my seat. "He hates these kinds of family things. Reminds him too much of something we don't have."

She smiles before following Felix outside.

"Sorry," I say to everyone at the table.

"It's fine," Dean Caruso says. "Let's just keep the spirits up."

Mrs. Caruso walks in on her high heels with even more plates. "Dinnertime!"

Everyone starts talking again as she puts down copious amounts of food, and my mouth begins to water at the sight. Two hot pots on the table are filled with broth along with all sorts of meats and vegetables, as well as dipping sauces. And my favorite, Kimchi.

I take some leaves and put on some veggies and Kimchi and roll it up into a ball before shoving it into my mouth.

"Goddamn, this is delicious," I murmur.

Mrs. Caruso laughs. "I thought I'd need to explain how it works, but I see you've already got the hang of it."

"I had a Korean friend when I grew up who invited me to her house for dinner so many times. Well, I invited myself over."

Everyone laughs.

"Sounds like you, all right," Dylan jests as he takes some of the meat and dunks it into the hot pot.

Every bite is delicious. "Oh my God, I love this."

Mrs. Caruso chortles. "Well, I'm glad you're enjoying yourself. What was your name again? I didn't quite catch it."

"Penelope," I reply.

"Penelope ... what?"

The whole room goes quiet for a second.

"Richards," I mutter between slurping some of the broth in my bowl.

I swallow when everyone looks at me.

"And how did you meet my son again?" Dylan's father asks.

I put my spoon down. "Well ... I, uh ..."

Why does it feel like I'm being interrogated all of a sudden?

"We helped her with a couple of bullies," Dylan muses, putting some wrapped leaves filled with meat and sauce on his father's plate. "Now eat. You're scaring her away with all your questions."

"Oh, nonsense," Mrs. Caruso says. "I'm so glad she's here."

I take another sip of the soup before they decide to kick me out because it's just too good.

"I finally get to meet my son's girlfriend."

I spit out almost half a spoon all over the table.

Now everyone looks at me like I've made a scene. And maybe I have. I mean, half my plate is covered with broth.

I grasp a paper towel and rub it all over. "Sorry."

Mrs. Caruso looks surprised. "So you're not his girlfriend?"

"Mom!" Dylan gasps. "You know I don't ..." He makes a sign with his hand in front of his neck to make her quit.

Good God, this is embarrassing.

"Oh, right, you don't *do* that," she muses, waving her hand around. "You're '*flexible*.'" She makes air quotes.

"Flexible," his father parrots, and a bulky laugh follows. "Just say you're a player and deal with it."

"Dad …" Dylan rolls his eyes. "Do we really have to do this now?" He grabs more meat. "I just want to eat Mom's lovely dinner."

"Aw," his mom gloats, and she immediately runs over to his chair and gives him a big fat kiss on the cheek.

Lana and Felix come back into the room and they sit back down again, breaking the awkward spell. I wonder if they talked in private.

"So what is it that you do, Mrs. Caruso?" I ask, trying to be nice. "I know Dylan's father is head of Spine Ridge."

"Oh, I work in finance," she mumbles. "I also do some work for our trust, which regulates some of the funds that go into the school."

"Ah, so you're both part of the board that runs it?"

She looks up at me like she's surprised I even know about it.

"Interesting," Dylan's father says like I'm saying something suspicious.

"I just wanted to know everything about Spine Ridge before I started studying there."

"An eager student," Felix's father says.

"You're on the same board too, if I'm not mistaken," I tell him. "I saw a photo with all the members on the website."

"Correct," he replies, adjusting his tie.

Lana clears her throat. "Dad's also the owner of a luxurious brand of clubs called—"

"RIVERA," I fill in.

"I'm impressed," Felix's father says, narrowing his eyes. "You've clearly done your research."

Felix grabs my knee under the table and squeezes so tightly that I struggle to even breathe. "Stop," he whispers into my ear. His hand slides up just a little, but enough for me to break out into a sweat. "Before I make you."

"So you're studying business then?" Felix's father asks me.

I nod. "It wasn't my dream education, but I wanted to honor my sister's legacy after her death."

It's almost as if she suddenly rose from the dead. That's how quiet it is at this table.

"Can you pass some of the Kimchi?" Alistair asks Lana after a moment to break the ice.

She rolls her eyes and casually hands him the plate without even looking at him.

"Thanks, L," Alistair says with a grin.

"L?" Lana grimaces. "No. Fuck no."

"Lana," her father warns. "No swearing at the table."

She grumbles to herself. "This is why I hate these kinds of parties."

"Why? Just because they use it to grill the new girl?" Dylan jests.

It becomes hard to swallow.

"Relax," he muses. "I'm just messing with you."

"Of course you are, D," Lana retorts, narrowing her eyes at him. Then she turns to glare at me. "It's not a joke. They want to know what you're doing with them. And I want to know what you're doing with my brother."

"What?" I mutter, completely confused where this is all coming from.

"He's never been this obsessed over anyone, so spill," she says, jamming her fork into the meat on my plate before shoving it into her mouth. "You can either talk, or I'll use force."

Suddenly, a knife is thrown across the room and pierces the wall behind Lana.

"Don't." Felix's dark voice makes me turn to look at him.

The whole room contains so much tension that I'm starting to wonder if we're having a dinner party or a brawl to the death.

Felix's father puts down his fork and knife and stares at Felix with a disappointed look. "What did I just say about this?" When Felix doesn't answer, he gazes at Lana too.

Lana rolls her eyes again. "No weapons at the dinner table."

Weapons?

Felix's father adds, "Or butter knives." And he sticks his knife into the butter. "Now pass me the buns, please."

Jesus Christ, this is one weird party.

Felix grabs some perilla leaves and fills them all with only cooked meat that he just shoves into his mouth, chomping in an annoyed and hurried way.

"Why did you bring me here again?" I ask under my breath.

"Does it look like I wanted to?" Felix replies.

Ah, so he does listen to someone.

My eyes land on his father.

"So I guess you're all a violent bunch, then?" I murmur.

Felix shrugs. "Blood runs thicker than water."

"Then why do you hate your sister so much?"

She laughs beside me. "Oh no, we don't hate each other." She reaches for him and pats him on the shoulder. "This is brotherly love."

Felix shoves her hand off. "I can't fucking wait for this to be over."

"Can we just have dinner, please?" Alistair muses, happily munching away at his food. "It's too delicious to fight over."

Lana completely ignores him. "You know they're just trying to figure out where she belongs, right?" Lana muses at her brother.

"Who? Me?" I ask.

"Who do you think?" she retorts. "You're the only new girl here."

New girl. Interesting.

"Well, after Eve of course."

My eyes widen.

Eve? Lana knows her.

Has she eaten with this family too?

"Okay, I've had about enough," Felix says, and he puts down his fork and knife, violently scoots back his chair, and marches off, chucking a napkin to the floor.

"Where is he going?" Dylan's mom asks.

"Toilet," Lana quickly replies, and she picks up the bowl of Kimchi. "Kimchi?"

I scoot back my chair and run off too, following Felix.

I don't know where he went, but I'm pretty sure it's not the toilet.

I run off on my high heels through the giant mansion until I'm suddenly pulled to the side in a small, dimly lit hallway. I shriek, but a strong hand covers my mouth.

Felix.

He puts a finger in front of his lips, then slowly lowers his hand off my mouth.

But not away from my face.

"What are you doing here?" he asks.

My heart beats in my throat. "I could ask you the same thing." His nostrils flare, and when he doesn't say anything, I add, "Did you run off because of what she said about Eve?"

His fingers instantly wrap around my throat, squeezing the life out of me. "Don't talk about her. Not to them. Got it?"

I nod, and he slowly releases the pressure, but his hand still hovers very close to my veins, like a looming threat.

"She's been here too," I mutter. I don't need him to answer to know it's the truth.

"Dylan's family occasionally invites over their inner circle for dinner. Even friends."

So I'm a part of the inner circle now?

He grabs my hand and tugs me into a bathroom behind me, shutting the door.

"It's not safe to talk," he growls. "You don't know who the fuck our families are and what they're capable of."

"None of them seemed scared by violence," I reply. "I think I can take a good guess."

"Then don't fucking talk," he growls. "Not to anyone unless they ask."

I frown. "Why? You scared I'm gonna tell them about our deal?"

His grip on my wrist tightens to the point it almost starts to hurt. "Think very carefully about what you're gonna say, Pen."

"They know about ..." I mutter, wondering if I should finish my sentence. "They think I'm Dylan's girlfriend, right? Are they trying to see if I'm a good fit?"

He nods.

"They don't know you guys ... share." I swallow. "What else don't they know?"

"Lots, and I want to keep it that way," he replies.

I jerk free from his grip. "If you want me to act like I enjoy it here, you can at least talk to me."

"About what?" His eyes narrow.

"I don't know ... pretend we're normal or something. Tell me about your family before you take me to them."

He closes his eyes and sighs. "You don't want to know, trust me."

"I do, actually," I reply, as he rubs his forehead. "What about your sister, for example? You two seem to hate each other. Why?"

"It's complicated. She's my li'l sis, and I need to protect her. She hates it. But at the same time, she acts like a fucking floozy with the wrong guys." He groans. "Never mind."

He's still rubbing himself like he hates even talking about them, but I'm glad I'm getting at least some information. If these guys are fucking around with me, I might as well get to know them. Who knows, maybe the information will be useful someday.

"God, I need a fucking drink," he mumbles.

I bet he does. "You looked like you were about ready to kill when I mentioned your mother."

His fingers part, revealing a half-mast, widened eye, almost like he's homed in on me, ready to strike, and it makes goose bumps scatter on my skin.

"My mother ..." He lowers his hand and gets up close and personal. "Is dead."

"Oh." I avert my eyes. "I'm sorry."

He plants his hand on the wall beside him. "My father killed her."

I look into his murderous-looking eyes that don't even bear a hint of fear or anguish, and my lungs stop sucking in the oxygen they so desperately need.

His mother ... killed by his own father? Why? And how would Felix be okay with that?

Suddenly, the door opens, and Dylan leans against the doorpost. "Hey there, *girlfriend*."

He invites himself in and shuts the door behind him.

Felix turns around, incensed. "Why the fuck are you here?"

"Checking up on y'all," he muses, folding his hands behind his head. "What are y'all doing?"

Felix raises his brow. "What does it look like?"

Dylan shrugs. "I don't know. Seemed to me like you just want some alone time with my girlfriend." He grabs my hand like he owns me. "Best keep up the charade, right?"

Felix slaps his hand away and stands between us. "Don't even fucking try."

The door opens again, and this time, Alistair's peeking in. "Whoa, what's going on in here?"

"Jesus Christ, why are you following us?" Felix growls and tries to shut the door, but Ali pushes his way inside first. "Goddammit. When I said I had enough, I meant all of you."

"Fine," I reply and push past him. "I'll leave then."

He grabs my wrist before I can even lift a finger at the door handle. "You. Stay."

He turns to face me, the look in his eyes madly possessive.

"Why? You wanted some time alone." I swallow just from the way he looks at me—like he could almost eat me alive even though we all just ate. "You don't need me."

He's so up in my face that I'm forced to step back, but when I bump into the toilet, there's nowhere for me to go but down.

His grip moves from my wrist to my chin. "You are *everything* I need right now."

His thumb brushes along my lips, and when he parts them, I don't even protest.

A need to satiate an unquenchable thirst fills his darkened, stained eyes. And when he pushes me back, my body instinctively walks along, unable to look away. I hit the wall in the back of the bathroom, and suddenly, the air is too thick to even breathe.

"On your knees," he growls.

44

PENELOPE

My pussy thumps when it shouldn't, but something about his voice drives me to obey.

And I sink down and squat in front of him as he unzips his pants.

This is the deal we made. Anywhere, anytime, I am theirs, and I submit to their every dirty fucking fantasy.

And right now, that's me on my knees in the Caruso family bathroom, where everyone can probably hear us. But Felix doesn't care as he pulls out his length riddled with piercings, the ampallang in the head already dripping with pre-cum.

"Open that pretty little mouth, Pen," he says.

"Here? In Dylan's parents' house?" I reply. "Really?"

"I don't fucking care. You're mine, wherever the fuck I want." He swipes his finger along my lips, then dips it into my mouth. "Aren't you, Pen?"

I nod, not because I want to, but because I'm obliged.

"I need to release myself, and this slutty girl is always ready to receive," he groans, pushing his fingers so deep into my throat I gag. When he hears the sound, he pulls out and shoves his dick inside instead, leaving no room for me to breathe.

But when I look up into his eyes, I don't see the same hatred I saw before. Something is different about him this time, as though he's trying to swallow back words he refuses to speak out loud and wants to take it all out on my mouth instead.

And for some reason, I want to let him.

"That's it, take it deeper," he groans. "I know you can."

"Well, if we're gonna do this now," Dylan rasps, zipping down. "Might as well join in on the fun."

I gag when Felix pulls out, rubbing his shaft as I suck in the oxygen. Dylan steps in and pulls out his hard-on too.

"Fine," Felix growls. "But I'm not stopping. She's fucking mine."

"Oh, don't stop on my account," Dylan says, pushing his tip against my lips too. "Why not make her take two at the same time?"

My eyes widen. "What? No, that's not—"

"You can take it." Dylan grabs my head and shoves my face over both of their lengths.

Tears well up in my eyes as I struggle to keep them in my mouth.

"God, your tongue ... it's fucking divine," Dylan groans. "Roll it around."

I do what he asks, but it's tough when you're trying to take two at once.

From the corner of my eye, I spot Alistair gawking at us, rubbing his half-hard dick he pulled out. He loves to enjoy the show like the voyeur he is. The more I lick, the harder he gets, and to me, it's almost like a game. I play to see how much harder I can get him before he tries to intervene.

Am I just as fucked up as them? Maybe. But when I focus on a task, it feels like I've gotten back an inkling of the power they stole from me.

"Look at me, Pen," Felix rasps, gripping my neck as he shoves Dylan out of the way and plunges in deep. "I want you to look at me when I bury myself inside this mouth."

With tearstained eyes, I look up into his and find hunger and greed. All the pent-up rage, all the violence inside them, nothing scares me as much as the way he wants to own me. It's as if he wants to possess me. Lock me up in a cage and throw away the key.

And my fucked-up mind isn't even sure it cares.

What the fuck is happening to me?

"Fuck," Dylan groans, as he steals me away from Felix, not even letting me catch my breath before he buries himself to the hilt.

He throbs in my throat, and tears roll down my cheeks when he pulls out again.

"Cry more, Pen." Felix brushes them away with his cock only to rub it all off on my tongue. "Show me how much you hate me for taking it all out on you."

So I was right. He's mad at me, at us, at everyone, but probably most of all his father, and he wants to fuck out all of his fury.

But every time they both slide across my tongue, I still whimper. My cheeks still flush, and my pussy still throbs, despite all this being so damn wrong and bad for me.

Felix treats me so roughly that the tears can't help but roll down my cheeks. And he plucks up each and every one of them with his dick, only to thrust them right back into me like some kind of goddamn payment for being his whore.

"This is too fucking hot," Alistair groans, his thickness glistening with pre-cum.

"I think she's getting hot too from all that cock in her mouth," Dylan groans, his eyes slowly gliding down my dress. "Aren't you, Pen?"

"Fuck yeah, let me have a taste and see," Alistair says as he lowers himself to the floor, crawls underneath them, and softly slides his finger into my panties.

I gasp when he circles my sensitive spot.

"Fuck, she's dripping," he says, licking his lips.

He rolls over onto his back and slides underneath me, tugging my panties aside.

I pull away from the two boys. "Wait, what are you doing?"

"Oh no. Eyes up here," Felix growls, and he grasps my chin and forces me to look at him. "No talking. Just open your mouth and be a good little slut for us."

He rams back in like there's no time to waste, and I struggle to take it, especially when Dylan joins in too.

Suddenly, Alistair's tongue hits that spot between my legs, and I quiver so hard I almost collapse.

"Oh fuck, she tastes so good," he says, practically moaning while he laps me up.

And fuck me, I can't think straight.

"You like his tongue, huh?" Dylan says, slapping my face. "Of course you do, little slut."

"Suck," Felix commands, and I almost instantly do what he asks.

Not just because I know I have to, but because Alistair's licking makes me insane.

The salty pre-cum coats my tongue as I gobble both of them down.

Suddenly, Alistair's tongue thrusts into me, and I gasp and moan at the same time while both of the boys are still inside my mouth. My knees can't take it anymore, and they start to shake vehemently.

"You can't take it, can you?" Dylan smirks. "Sit, then."

"What?" My eyes widen.

"You heard me," he says, biting his lip. "Sit."

"Sit on my face, Pen," Alistair groans from underneath me.

And he drags me down until my feet cave in on me and my knees buckle to the floor. He moans as he swipes his tongue along my slit.

But what really undoes me are his words.

"Ride my face like you own it."

***

ALISTAIR

God, I've rarely tasted anything so fucking divine.

I need to have more. More. So much fucking more.

I lap her up like there's no one in the fucking house except us, hungrily, greedily licking and sucking at her little swollen nub until she moans with their cocks still in her mouth.

I'm addicted.

Addicted to her needy sounds.

Addicted to the way she looks when she mewls with delight.

Addicted to the very taste of her.

With every waking thought, I'm consumed by this fucking girl ... and I don't fucking understand why. But I don't care anymore. All I crave is this fucking pussy, rubbing all over my mouth and nose.

"Fuck yes, that's it," I groan, circling my tongue around. "Make yourself come on my mouth."

"Oh God, but what if they hear?" she moans.

SLAP!

Dylan's flat hand lands on her titty. "Do we look like we fucking care?"

"But your parents—"

Another slap follows.

"My parents can go fuck themselves if they disagree. I'll do whatever the fuck I want, and what I want right now is to hear you gag."

He plunges into her again. I don't need to see it to know what's happening because I can hear it from her stifled moans, and I can feel it from the way she gets wetter and wetter.

"God, you're so fucking wet," I groan.

"Just like a good little whore should be," Dylan muses. "Now moan so the whole fucking world knows."

"Oh, fuck you," she spits.

Even though she tells us to fuck off and pretends she hates us, every time we fuck with her, she's as wet as can be. She's lying to us, but most of all herself when she says she doesn't want it.

"Keep saying that, and I might just do it," Felix growls at her.

He rams into her throat before she can even reply.

"My turn to destroy her," Dylan says when Felix pulls out again, only for him to take her throat next.

She can barely stay put, but I keep her up with my hands on her waist while she rolls around on my face. The harder they plunge into her, the fiercer her movements get, almost like she's in sync with them. And I'm getting so turned on that I begin to thrust into the air.

"So hungry," Felix groans. "Have your fucking dessert, then."

He grabs her face, and I can hear him moan before unleashing his load into her. "Swallow it."

Her pussy contracts around my tongue as I lick her while she swivels back and forth across my chin. She writhes, and I can feel her come undone.

Dylan growls, "Take my cum too, whore."

And he blasts away inside her, clenching his ass while clutching her face.

And fuck me, the sight as well as the wetness flooding out of her is too much to take. "Fuck, I can't hold it."

A loud groan emanates from deep within my chest as I spurt out my seed all over the bathroom floor.

"Fuck, you just came?" Dylan says as he pulls out of her and stares down at me. A big grin forms on his face. "Without anyone touching you?"

"I don't need that," I say between breaths as I continue to lick up all of her juices. "All I need is this pussy right up in my face."

Dylan laughs. "Oh, now you've got her blushing all right."

"Stop it," she says, swatting away at him.

Felix catches her wrists. "Did you swallow it all?" She opens her mouth to show him. "Good girl."

I crawl out from underneath her, but when I come to my feet, Felix grabs her face and kisses her full on the lips in front of us. I'm surprised. He's normally never this affectionate, not with anyone. Not even with Eve.

I grab a tissue and clean up, but Dylan swiftly comes my way and kisses me before I can even turn around. "If they're kissing, I want some action too," he murmurs.

A knock on the door makes us all stop. "Hello? What's going on in there?"

"Lana," Felix mutters under his breath while Penelope pulls her dress back down.

He quickly tucks his dick back into his pants and presses a final, obsessive kiss on Penelope's mouth before he opens the door.

"What do you want?"

Lana peeks over his shoulder and briefly glances at all of us. A filthy smirk forms on her lips. "You know I can hear you moan, right?"

Fuck.

"What are you even doing in here?" she adds. "Jerking each other off?"

"None of your business," Felix says, and he narrows the gap between the door and him.

"Dad told me to come find you," she says.

"You found us," Dylan muses, stepping forward. "Good job. Want a cookie?"

Lana looks mortified. "Fine, stay here and fuck around in the bathroom for all I care. I'm just relaying the message."

She rolls her eyes and walks off.

"She saw all of us in here. What if she tells your dad? Dylan's dad?" I ask.

Felix shrugs. "They think she's your girlfriend anyway." He looks at Penelope over his shoulder. "Might as well keep up the ruse."

"Wait, what?" Penelope mutters.

"Dylan!" Jeong-Suk's voice blares down the hallway.

"Fuck," Dylan rasps before he jerks open the door and walks off.

When his mom gets angry, shit's about to get dangerous.

I swiftly grab Penelope's face and press a kiss to her lips. She seems shook I even went there, but I want her to know I didn't just do this for my own pleasure. I enjoy seeing hers.

"Don't forget ... you're not just his, but mine too," I say before I walk off.

Felix side-eyes me, but I pay no attention to him.

He agreed to share her, and I'll be damned if I let him try to take her away from me.

I grab some tissues and hand them to her, and she cleans her face, which was still covered in saliva. "Thanks," she murmurs.

"Let's go back," I reply.

We all walk out the door and head back to the dining room, but the moment I take one step inside, I freeze.

"Alistair!" my father's voice booms through the room. "So you haven't dropped dead in the bathroom after all."

Everyone's staring at us, and I fucking hate it.

"You're here," I mutter.

"Of course I'm here. Do you think they'd have an amazing dinner without me?" my father jests, laughing.

"Where's Mom?" I ask.

"She's sick at home, so I came alone," he replies. "C'mon, boy. Sit down, and let's eat."

"What were you doing in that bathroom anyway?" Dean Caruso asks, casually taking a bite of his food.

Dylan rubs his lips together as he stares me down, softly shaking his head.

Lana's glaring at us three from her seat at the table. "Yeah, what *were* you doing in there, boys?" Her brows rise as she and Felix exchange lethal looks. "It sounded like a lot of heavy moaning."

"Moaning?" Jeong-Suk drops her wrapped leaf on the table.

"I was sick," Penelope intervenes.

Dylan's father frowns. "Sick? I hope it wasn't from the food."

She shakes her head. "No, I've been having stomach issues. The boys ... helped me lift my hair and clothes," she lies.

Lana tilts her head and glowers, but I ignore it.

"I'm fine now, though," Penelope adds.

"Well, that's good to hear, darling," Jeong-Suk replies. "Do you still want some food, or are you good for now?"

She smiles. "I'll sit with you guys."

"How generous of you," Lana taunts.

"Lana," Felix warns.

Lana rolls her eyes again. "My God, it's too ridiculous."

"C'mon, boy, sit," my father says, pointing at the empty chair. "Your food's getting cold."

Penelope sits beside Felix, and I sit next to my father, who took the only empty chair left at the table.

He hugs me out of the blue and almost squeezes the life out of me. "C'mere, boy. So glad you all decided to come."

"It's not like we had a choice," Felix says, toying with his food.

"No?" Jeong-Suk mutters as she cooks more veggies in the hot pot. "Dad kind of—"

"Dylan," his father warns. "Not. Another. Word."

The entire table grows quiet.

"Let's just enjoy the lovely food Mrs. Caruso cooked for us," he adds, looking at all of us.

"So does this mean we don't have to write that essay anymore?" I ask.

Dylan's father glares at me while Dylan draws his finger across his neck, telling me to quit it. Too late.

"This dinner is not an escape from your punishment," his father says, lowering his fork and knife. "You're all still suspended for the week. And that essay is still due in full."

A collective sigh fills the room.

"Now sit and eat. Mrs. Caruso made an amazing dinner, and if any of it goes to waste, I'll add another essay."

45

PENELOPE

After the boys complete their suspension, and we've all written our ten-thousand-word essay, Dylan's father finally lets us off the hook.

The following days, everyone around this campus looks at me like I'm a devil in disguise. Whispers of my story about those Phantom boys have gone all around the university, and even though most believe my story, no one really dares to get close anymore.

All because I'm a part of the clique who got caught up in that unresolved murder case.

As I walk down the hallway, Dylan and Alistair walk out of a classroom where Felix waits for them, leaning against the wall. He hands Dylan a cigarette while holding up his own, and Dylan lights both before they all walk down the hallway in my direction.

A devious smirk grows on Dylan's face when he spots me while Alistair remains aloof, as always. But Felix's eyes scare me most of all. Possessive. Greedy. An all-consuming stare that could bore a hole into my chest and rip out my heart while it's still beating.

They're headed straight toward me, but instead of turning around, I face them head-on, just as I did the first time I met them in these same hallways.

And when they get close, Dylan runs to me and wraps his arm around my neck so tight I might choke.

"Hey, cute little rat," he says, rubbing my hair so it's all messy.

"Oh my God, I told you not to call me that," I retort, shoving him, but he won't let go, and for some reason, it makes me laugh too.

"Okay, little slut," he rebukes.

My jaw drops. "We're in public."

"So? Doesn't make you any less ours," Felix says as he stands behind me and leans over, holding the cigarette between his index finger and thumb. "Want a smoke?"

I shake my head. "No, thanks. My uncle died of lung cancer. I've seen what it does."

Felix shrugs. "Suit yourself." He takes another whiff, then casually puts his hand on my waist.

"No smoking in the hallways, Rivera!" a teacher yells from down the hall.

Felix just raises his brow and keeps smoking until we get to the teacher, after which he chucks it on the ground in front of him and stomps it out. "There you go. It's all yours now."

"Insufferable little—"

"Did you forget who's on the fucking school board?" Felix says, shoving his hands into his pocket, which I know is a sign he's getting pissed.

"You know the rules—"

"I'll make sure that rule is fucking changed," Felix interjects. "And the day it does, you won't find out because you'll be fucking gone."

Then he walks off like it meant nothing at all, even though the teacher seems horrified that he'd even have that kind of power.

When I spot Kayla talking just beyond the grand doors of the building, I leave the boys and run up to them. "Hey, girls. Sorry, I'm late for our usual picnic."

They eye me as though I've risen from the dead. "Are you sure you want to come?" Crystal peeks over my shoulder. "Seems like you've been busy."

I shrug. "They won't get in the way." I glare at them over my shoulder. "Right, boys?"

Dylan shrugs. "Ali, wanna go get some burgers?"

"Fuck yeah, I'm game," he replies, and they walk off together while Felix remains with me.

"You're not going with them?" I ask him.

"No," he retorts, hovering behind me like a goddamn ghost. "Someone's gotta keep tabs."

I frown. "Tabs?" *Wow, offensive.* "I'm not a fucking toddler."

His brow rises. "I don't care what you think."

My eyes narrow as I lean in. "I don't need to be watched."

He leans in too now, getting eye to eye. "Did you forget about the Phantoms? Kai's still out there. You've got a target on your back now. I'm watching."

I grit my teeth. "Fine." I point my finger at his chest. "But I don't want to hear you insult any of my friends, got it?"

He grabs my finger and gently brings it to his lips, sucking on the tip. "Command me some more. I might grow to like it."

I heat like a kettle about to whistle. "Oh my God." I rip my finger away before I blush, and I turn around, determined to ignore him.

"Seems you two have got some marital problems," Kayla jests.

"He'd wish he could put a ring on this finger," I retort.

"C'mon, the others are waiting," Crystal says.

Felix grumbles behind me, so I throw him a glance, but he doesn't open his mouth. Good. I don't want him to ruin the one good thing I've got going for me.

"Does he have to come?" Kayla whispers to me.

I nod. "Sorry. Something about the Phantoms. He's worried about me after ... well the incident at the hot springs." I roll my eyes.

"I heard some guys tried to take advantage of you," Crystal whispers. "Is that true?"

Rumors travel fast here. "Sort of."

"I'm sorry," Crystal adds.

"Nothing too bad happened," I say. "Ali and Dylan were there to protect me."

"Ali? Nickname basis already?" Kayla shoves me with her elbow. "You're getting too close for comfort, girl."

"Hey," Felix snarls at her, and we both turn around to look at him. "Don't touch her."

Kayla grimaces. "You're a lovely fucking dude, aren't you?" she scoffs. "Asshole."

He steps closer to her. "I'll show you how fucking lovely I can be."

They're up in each other's faces again, so I jump between them. "Stop. Just fucking stop, okay?" I bark at him. "If you can't fucking behave around her, then leave."

"No," he says through gritted teeth.

"Why not? Nothing's gonna happen." I point at my friends in the grass. "Who's gonna try to do something in the middle of the day while we're having a picnic? Not even the Phantoms are that stupid."

"I would rather cut off my own finger than leave you alone," he grits.

It doesn't just make Kayla's eyes widen. Everyone in our vicinity is staring at us.

He'd go that far just to keep me safe?

I can feel my cheeks heat again, and I hate it.

And judging from the penetrative stare in his eyes, I already know arguing with him will be futile.

"Fine," I growl, folding my arms. "Sit with us. But quietly. I don't want to hear you moping around."

"Lead the way," he says, eyeing Kayla too.

She rolls her eyes and turns to walk away, and I follow suit.

"Sorry about that," I tell her.

"I don't get what you see in them. I really don't," she says.

"I'm sorry they treat you like shit. I've already told him he needs to quit that." I swallow. "You guys are my friends, and they just need to accept that, end of story."

"So they're all like hanging out with you or something?" Crystal asks.

I tuck a strand of hair behind my ear, laughing it off because I don't know how to answer this without sounding ridiculous. "It's complicated."

"With those boys? For sure," Kayla says, rolling her eyes.

Crystal laughs. "They sound like a handful to me. But at least they're protective over you."

"Protective?" Kayla snorts. "More like stalkerish."

Felix grumbles again, but he doesn't say a word. Good. I don't need more trouble. I've got enough as it is with him following me everywhere from now on.

We walk up to the rest of the guys sitting in the grass, and they all look up in surprise like they never expected to see me here.

"Hey, Pen. Long time no see," Jeremy says.

"Pen! Not covered in gunk today, I see," Calvin says, and Jeremy punches him in the knee for saying that out loud. I'm just glad I didn't have to do it myself.

"Look who's with her," Jeremy hisses at him.

Calvin's eyes lurch up to Felix's, and he loses all the color in his face. "Um ... why is he here?"

"He's her stalker," Kayla announces like it's not a joke at all.

"He's a friend. He won't be a bother, I promise," I add.

Calvin almost chokes. "*Friend*?"

I turn to look at Felix. "He'll just sit in a corner, far away. Right, Felix?"

He rolls his eyes and sighs. "I'm not letting you out of my sight."

I'm so fucking embarrassed he just said that out loud like it's a normal thing to do because everyone heard.

"Oh my God," Jeremy mutters.

Calvin snorts. "Oh, she's got it good."

"You can just ignore him," I say as Felix sits down on the farthest tip of the picnic blanket, his nostrils twitching like the mere smell of their food sets him off.

"Tough luck," Kayla jests. "Fucker is like a statue."

"Oh, c'mon now, he can't be that bad," Crystal says, smiling at me. "She likes him so there must be something nice about him."

Okay, now I'm really blushing. "He just helps me."

"With what?" Calvin asks.

Oh Jesus. How do I answer this?

"He ..."

"He's her silent protector," Kayla jests, putting her finger in front of her mouth. "Like a goddamn ninja warrior."

The boys laugh, and Jeremy says, "Cringe."

"I wouldn't put it past him to suddenly ninja kick the shit out of someone just for looking at her, though," Calvin says.

"Come here and find out," Felix retorts.

"Felix," I warn him, so he folds his arms and looks away again, annoyed as hell. "As I said, ignore him."

"Wow," Calvin mutters. "I'm impressed."

"Eat your fucking sandwich," Jeremy says, and he stuffs the sandwich Calvin brought into his mouth so harshly half of it falls onto the blanket.

I laugh. "Good thing I brought plenty more." I pull out my big shopper and hand out some sandwiches. "On the house."

"Wow, thanks, Pen!" Crystal says as she takes one. "That's so nice of you."

"I just wanted to do something to make it up to y'all. You know, for disappearing on you so much." I look over my shoulder at Felix who just sits there, staring at me. "And for him being an asshole to you, Kayla."

She smiles at me. "It's not your fault. I totally blame him." She throws him some shade. "We should meet up at a club later. Maybe we can get rid of him there."

"Oh yes!" Calvin exclaims. "I know just the place downtown. Delectable. It's like a drag bar."

"Perfect," Kayla responds.

"That's an exclusive one," Jeremy responds. "No way we'll get inside without tickets. And I don't know anyone on the inside."

"Well, we can try," Crystal says.

"I know a better place," Felix suddenly interjects, and everyone looks at him like they can't believe he's about to suggest something. "Club RIVERA."

Kayla's jaw drops. "What? But that's—"

"My father's," he fills in, tilting his head. "And very much exclusive ... unless you know someone on the inside."

I frown.

Why would he suggest that?

Though, being there would probably be one of the safest locations, far away from Phantom hands, and it would make it easier to stay on the lookout for Kai.

"Wait ... are you seriously suggesting we go to your dad's club?" Calvin asks, his jaw almost on the ground. "Holy shit."

"Calvin, you cannot be serious right now," Jeremy says, rolling his eyes. "Really? You're simping over a RIVERA club?"

"What? They've got the best snacks, and I don't just mean the food." He licks his lips. "I need to see that shit for myself."

"Sellout," Jeremy mutters under his breath.

"Like you don't want to see some hung horse dancing on stage," Calvin rebukes.

"Wait, is this real? Are you trying to invite us?" Kayla asks, pointing at all of us while gawking at Felix. "Your sworn enemies?"

"You're not my enemies," he retorts. "Or you would've known, trust me."

Kayla rolls her eyes. "Thanks. That totally makes me feel better."

"Why not give it a chance?" Crystal asks. "It can't be that bad if it's like the most exclusive club in town. Besides, we need to celebrate after you aced that last test." She bumps into Kayla and wraps her arms around her neck. "C'mon, Kay. Can we go? Please?"

Kayla sighs out loud. "Okay, okay."

Crystal cheers and plants a kiss on Kayla's cheek. "We deserve a night out."

I eye Felix. I don't know why he's doing this. It almost feels like he's got an ulterior motive.

But I don't want to disappoint my friends.

So with a smirk on my face, I say, "All right ... if Mr. Rivera personally invited us, I guess it's time we paid that club a visit."

46

PENELOPE

That night

I sit down at a circular table with my friends, enjoying the very racy show in front of us. A girl twirls around the pole in a scantily-clad bikini as the music blasts through the roof of this posh place. The front end of the club was filled with people dancing, but we're in a secluded backroom meant only for VIP customers.

Lucky for us, Felix's father owns the place, so he got us all into the special section with private dancers and lots of expensive liquor.

And even though I'm enjoying the show, I can't help but glance at all three of them as they walk into the room. Felix's tight, pitch-black long-sleeve shirt barely covers his muscles, and the gray jeans he's sporting underneath are probably worth more than the watch on his wrist. Dylan casually drapes his jacket over his shoulder, looking fine as fuck with that tousled, platinum-blond hair and a black necklace dangling from his neck over that expensive white shirt of his. Alistair's donning that same fishnet outfit on top of a black shirt I saw on the bonfire night, and I have to admit it looks very good on his lean muscles.

They all look damn good, and it makes me swallow away the lump in my throat.

Dylan sees me looking, and I swiftly look away, but he still makes his way to our table.

"Pen," Kayla says, nudging me. "Your boy's coming over."

"He's not my boy," I hiss back.

"Who's not your boy?" Dylan asks, raising a brow.

My cheeks flush. "Doesn't matter."

Dylan leans over the couch we're all sitting on, and Calvin chuckles so loudly that Jeremy actually has to jab him with his elbow.

"I can be your boy if you want me to."

Kayla's jaw drops, and Crystal actually mutters, "Oh my God."

"Dylan," I hiss, "stop embarrassing me."

"You think I'm embarrassing you?" he muses as he leans forward and curls my necklace around his finger, slowly pulling at it until I'm forced to lean in too. "I can make it far more shameful right here, right now ..." He pulls me in until he's so close to my ear I can feel his breath on my skin. "I could lick you on this couch and make you come so hard you'd be begging to God and screaming my name in front of all your friends."

"Stop," I murmur, even though my breath hitches in my throat at the thought.

"Only if you ask me nicely," he mutters.

"Please ..." I tack on, hating myself with every fiber of my being. And him. Definitely him.

My eyes flick over his shoulder, where Felix is chatting with someone in the back. A girl with long black hair that's laced with a red ribbon at the top, as well as serious anger management issues. Lana.

As Dylan leans back again, I tilt my body to the side and watch some dude grope Lana while dancing with her. Felix pummels him in the face.

I gasp, and it immediately makes Dylan turn to look.

The guy who got hit first tries to punch Felix back, but when Felix pulls out a knife, he walks off, enraged.

"Oh ... Of course." Dylan doesn't seem surprised even the slightest bit.

"What?" I say.

"Oh, Lana always attracts the wrong crowd," Dylan says, folding his arms. "But Felix can take care of it."

Felix grabs Lana's wrist, but she jerks herself free, pointing at his chest as they engage in a heated argument.

"I thought they hated each other," I say.

"They don't. They've just got a complicated relationship," Dylan casually replies as he watches them. "But Felix won't let anyone lay a finger on her unless they deserve it."

Maybe Felix doesn't have a heart of stone after all.

"He cares about his little sister," Dylan adds, and he looks my way, winking. "But don't tell him I said that, or I'll never hear the end of it."

"Gotcha," I mumble.

He snorts. "Oh, and don't tell Lana I called her little. She'll kill me."

"Do you have any brothers or sisters?" I ask in the spur of the moment.

Dylan glances at me. "A little brother. Why?"

I shrug. "Just curious."

"He's in high school. And I'm not sure if I'd ever allow him to attend our university."

Fair point, considering what happens at Spine Ridge.

Lana walks off into the big club room, away from the private section, leaving Felix with a hot head. He blows off some steam and marches toward a different table across from ours, where Alistair casually sips a drink.

"Well, that's my cue," Dylan mutters, and he pushes himself off the table. "Have fun with your friends." He throws them a look and grins, then saunters off with an arrogant swagger to him.

"Your boy sure is something special," Calvin muses.

"Oh God," I say, burying my face in my hands. "He's not *my boy*."

"No, all three of them are, aren't they?" Jeremy says.

Crystal gasps. "What, really?"

"You mean you didn't know?" Jeremy gasps. "I'm surprised."

"Can we please stop talking about those boys? Let's play a game instead," I say, smashing some money on the table. "Drinks on me for the first person who dares to tip the dancer on stage in her underwear."

***

DYLAN

"Bro, you sure this is such a good idea?" I ask Felix as we settle down on our usual couch while Penelope and her squad of geeks remain seated around a table in the back near the stage.

I can't stop looking at her off-the-shoulder black dress that scrunches up in just the right way around her waist. Like an appetizing teaser just waiting for me to take a bite out of.

And with me, probably every other man in this club is thinking this very same thing.

I clear my throat and focus on Felix. "Inviting them here seems like a dangerous move."

"I'll keep an eye out," Felix says. "If any Phantoms show up, I'll shut the place down."

"Your father's clients come and go," Alistair says, and he orders three shots from a server.

"If they try to bother Penelope or her friends, I'll intervene," Felix says. "They'll have to listen, or I'll have them kicked out."

"Not sure your father's gonna like that," I muse as I lean back in my seat.

Felix glares at me. "I don't fucking care what he thinks."

"Wow, it's almost like you want to impress her," I joke.

The murderous look on his face gives me life.

I glare right back at him. "And here, I thought Alistair was the only one falling for her."

Add some more oil to the fire, yeah.

"Dylan," Ali scoffs. "Really?"

"What?" I throw him a glance. "It's the truth, isn't it?"

"I said we would share," Felix growls. "I never said you could fucking fall in love with her."

"Chill. I'm not," Ali responds. "I'm just enjoying what we have together."

"There is no 'together.'" Felix makes air quotes with his fingers. "Only the agreement. Once it's done, it's over."

I frown. "Whoa, hold on, you mean to tell me you just want to ditch this little thing we've got going for us? Now that it's finally getting juicy?"

"You can get juicy with any other fucking woman. Or man, I don't fucking care," Felix growls. "Just don't get fucking attached."

Ali snorts. "You're just trying to escape your own feelings."

Felix almost lunges across the table. "What did you just say?"

"Felix," I warn him. "Relax. We're here to party, not to fight."

"I'm here to watch," Felix snarls back. "And you're distracting me."

He turns around in his seat and focuses on the group of girls. But I know he's only trying to tell himself that he's not at all butt hurt by Alistair's comment. Ali always knows how to find his limits within the snap of a finger. That's how he gets to me too.

But this isn't about what Ali says, and he knows it.

Unfortunately, it always takes a long while for Felix to realize what he truly wants.

And by then, it's usually too fucking late to take it.

The server comes back with our drinks, and I greedily grab my glass and chug it down while staring at the hunk whipping out his hard-on on stage toward the girls. They're all squealing like they've never seen one before, and it makes me laugh.

From this side of the room, all I see is a very thick, muscular ass that I could just take a bite out of, and I lick my lips in excitement.

"Getting horny already?" Ali jests.

I raise a brow at him. "Oh, c'mon, can't I even enjoy the view?"

He smirks. "That's why I brought you here."

I bite my lip and place my hand on his thigh, squeezing. "Maybe we should invite him to a little bit of fun later."

"Since when are you two dating?" Felix suddenly asks.

"Who needs to date when you can just fuck around?" I muse, taking a quick sip of his shot when he isn't looking.

Felix snorts. "You sure Ali would agree?"

I turn to look at my best friend, but he seems to retreat into his shell like he always does when he doesn't want to be involved in the conversation.

I sigh out loud. "I'm not exclusive. None of us are." I fold my arms. "You know that."

Felix turns to look at me. "Prove it."

I won't say no to a challenge, especially from him.

"All right." I run my tongue across my inner cheek. "Watch."

I gaze at a girl dancing around the table next to ours, where a private party takes place. She's been throwing looks at our table ever since we sat down here, but I haven't flirted back until now.

I run my tongue across my lips, watching her dance, and when our eyes finally connect, I throw myself back and spread my legs, then wink.

She grins and continues to dance, but after a while, she picks up her drink and makes her way over to our table.

"Hey," she says. "You three having fun over here?"

"Not nearly enough," I reply.

Alistair rolls his eyes.

"Come sit with us," I say, patting the couch.

"Well, if you insist." She flops down between Ali and me, her drink sloshing around on the floor. "Whoops!"

"You sure about this, Dylan?" Alistair asks, visibly annoyed.

"Felix asked me something. Of course I immediately oblige," I jest, throwing a quick glance at Felix, who seems just as annoyed that it comes so easy to me.

I turn to the girl. "So what's your name, beautiful?"

She giggles as I begin to twirl her hair. "Farah."

I grab her glass and place it on the table, then take her hand. "A gorgeous name for an even more gorgeous girl."

"You always this smooth?" she jests.

"Only when I want to be," I reply with an elegant smile as I pull her closer. "I like the way you danced over there."

"Oh ... you wanna dance?" With a wink, she gets up, dragging me along with her. "C'mon."

Alistair looks displeased as I let her tug me along, but I just shrug and make a face at him. He knows what I'm like. Any hole, anytime, anywhere. That's my motto.

But if I can stick it to Felix and prove to him that I'm not fucking exclusive with anyone, it's the icing on the cake.

The music blasts, and I twirl the girl around and pull her close. Her hair sticks to her red lips, her tits right up in my face, barely covered by the short glittery dress she's wearing. A perfect distraction for the night.

And I dance around with her to the sultry, heavy bass, dragging her so close to me I can feel her body grow clammy and her breath unsteady.

From the corner of my eye, I see Felix shake his head and Alistair blowing out a breath, then grinding his teeth. I know he doesn't like to share ... but he can't ever tell me no, either.

"Think you can do better, Felix?" I yell across the room.

His nostrils flare even more, and he gets up and marches right at us. And the smile on my face couldn't be any bigger when he starts to dance behind Farah.

He spins her around while my grip loosens, and he grabs her body and dances with her like he owns the fucking place.

But my eyes are drawn to Penelope, clutching a glass as her face contorts with anger. Disgust.

She jumps up off the round couch and storms off through the exclusive room's exit with one of the girls following suit.

And fuck me, that'll do it.

I pull away from Farah and leave her on the dance floor. Felix follows quickly. "Hold up ... you're just gonna leave me here?" the girl asks.

"Yup," I reply.

"But we were dancing," Farah says.

"And now I'm done," I say as I make my way back to our side of the room.

"What about you?" Farah asks Felix.

But he flips her off.

The girl stomps off, but I don't fucking care. She was just a game to me, just as everything else in this life. But that game got ruined the second I saw Penelope sitting there with her arms folded, her face looking like she could almost eat mine.

Fuck.

Nothing ever gets to me, so why would it now?

"Well, that went well," Felix says when we return to our couch.

"I won. That's all," I reply.

Alistair places his glass down and stands up. "But at what cost?"

I approach him and grab his face with one hand. "You know I'll always return." And I kiss him hard, just as I always do after I finish with my toys. He bites my lip, but I suck on the blood and kiss him even harder.

"I hate how jealous you make me," he growls.

"And I love seeing you jealous," I retort. "Now shut up, and fucking kiss me."

***

PENELOPE

I head straight for the first bathroom I find in this posh place, and it's filled to the brim with people. The music is way too loud, and I need a break from all that noise.

Even the bathrooms here look expensive as fuck with purple-and-gold wallpaper, several gold-lined paintings of half-naked ladies, and floors made of thick marble slabs.

I lock myself in a stall and sit on the toilet, breathing in and out to calm myself.

But the longer I'm here, the more I'm convinced it isn't just the loud music and the dancing people who've got me overstimulated.

Because all I can think about is that image floating through my head of Dylan and Felix dancing with that girl.

I shake my head, grumbling with frustration at myself.

Fuck that. It shouldn't bother me this much. We made a deal, nothing more, nothing less. My body for their help. It doesn't mean anything. *They* don't mean anything to me, and I don't mean anything to them.

"Penelope?"

Lana's voice makes me look up as my fingers dug into my skin so badly it started to bleed.

"Are you in here?" she asks.

"Yeah," I reply.

She softly knocks on the door. "You okay in there?"

"I'm fine."

Don't let them get to you. That's why they did it.

I take another big breath and open the door again, walking out with my head held high. "I just needed a break from all the noise."

I mean, it's sort of true.

I grab the lipstick from my small bag and redo my lips in the big mirror in front of the stalls.

Lana stands beside me and rakes her fingers through her long black hair, then adjusts her little red dress and readjusts the red ribbon in her hair. "You've got more balls than I do."

I frown as I apply a second layer of lipstick. "What do you mean?"

"If I saw my boyfriend dancing with some other girl, I'd probably knock them out." She snorts.

"Boyfriend?" I mutter. "Oh no, Felix and Dylan aren't—"

"Stop lying," Lana interjects. "I know what you are to them. It's what they do." She chews on her gum. "They've been doing it for a while now. Even in front of your sister. Everything's a game to them."

"What?" I pause midway through smearing the lipstick on my top lip.

"You know they fool around with everybody, right?"

"No, I mean the sister part," I stutter.

She throws her hair back. "Oh, everyone in your school knew they were fucking around. I heard it from some friends who go there. They were a real foursome for like three months."

The lipstick in my hand drops to the floor.

A foursome?

They ... fucked around?

With my sister?

Her eyes flick to mine, and she frowns. "Wait ... you didn't know?"

I feel light-headed. Sick. Absolutely sick to my stomach.

"Hello?" Lana mutters when I don't say a word.

But instead of answering her or throwing up into the toilet next to me, I bolt out the door.

47

FELIX

"Where's Penelope?" I ask as I look around the room.

Dylan's lips tear away from Alistair's as he turns to look at me. "I think she went to the bathroom. I thought she'd be back by now?"

"No."

Fuck. Something doesn't feel right.

I push myself off the couch again. "I'm gonna go check."

Her buddies are still on that same couch. What's taking her so long?

Not to mention the fact that I haven't seen Lana in a while, either. If she's talking to Penelope behind my back, I'm gonna give her a fucking ear-splitting headache over it.

I'm antsy, and my nerves feel like they're on fire as I march out the door, ready to beat up whoever's trying to sneak her away from my sight. If some Phantoms got in, I'll pummel them into next year.

I make my way through the club, past all the dancing people, but when I spot Lana coming out of the bathroom, I shove my way through. Some people throw me angered glares and frowns, but I don't give a shit. I'm the owner's son. They don't like it? They can leave.

"Get out of my way," I growl.

When I finally get close enough, I grab her arm and turn her to me. "Where's Penelope?"

"What? Why should I—"

"She was in that bathroom with you," I interject.

She frowns. "I don't know where she is. She ran off."

"Tell me why." My grip on her arms tightens. "What happened?"

"Get your hands off me." She tries to shake me off, but it's not happening. "I was just talking to her."

"What did you say to her?" I bark.

She glowers at me. "I told her about you and your boys and Eve, and that you'd been fucking around with her."

My pupils dilate.

Fuck.

Why the fuck would she tell her that?

"I thought she knew," she mutters.

I shove her away.

"Jesus Christ, Felix," she cries, but I'm not listening.

Fuck. Fuck. Fuck!

I don't even fucking care what Lana is saying anymore. I need to find Penelope. Now.

"Felix!" Dylan calls from the back as I push through the sea of people. "Where are you going?"

"Penelope's gone!" I yell back.

His eyes widen, and he immediately beckons Alistair, then follows suit. But I'm far too busy trying to get out of this crowded club to care if they're coming or not. Every second is another one wasted.

She could be halfway across town by now.

If I don't find her soon, things will go south pretty quick.

"Fuck!" I yell out loud when I finally get to the door.

"Everything okay, sir?" one of the guards asks, popping open his umbrella to hold it over my head because it's raining.

"Did you see a girl with purple hair run past?" I ask him in a hurry.

"Um ... I think so. Maybe," he mutters.

I grab him by the collar. "Tell me where she went. Now."

He points in the direction of a one-way street that leads to the outskirts of Crescent Vale City. "That way, sir."

Fuck. That's exactly the direction I hoped she wouldn't take. It has only one remaining point of interest she could possibly go to.

I don't even thank him before running off directly into the pouring rain. I can't waste any time.

"Felix, wait!" Dylan yells behind me, but I can't fucking wait for them. "Where are you going?"

I glance at him over my shoulder. "The cemetery."

His eyes widen. "What, the one—"

"Where her sister was buried," Alistair fills in as they finally catch up with me. "But why?"

In front of my car, I stop and look at them both. "She knows about Eve and us." I unlock it. "Get in."

***

PENELOPE

Raindrops trickle down my face, mixing with the tears as I stare at my sister's headstone. Her name is carved out onto the slab the same way it's carved onto my flesh.

I pull away my dress sleeve to look at her name so beautifully drawn in ink.

Beautiful, just like her.

Unlike this sullen grave.

"Eve ..." I mutter as my knees begin to buckle. "Why? Why didn't you tell me?"

I can't believe it. It can't be fucking true.

My sister ... being in a foursome?

With the Skull & Serpent boys?

Imagine her walking around with them on campus, touching each other, kissing, and making out in secret. I shiver at the thought.

That was not the Eve I knew.

My Eve was unwavering in her convictions. She wanted to make the world a better place. She hated people who did others wrong. She was the spitting image of my mother with my father's soul.

Yet why do I find it hard to dismiss Lana's words?

Why do they make me obey?

When my knees hit the mud, more tears roll down my cheeks.

"You wouldn't keep this a secret from me," I mutter to Eve's grave. "You're my sister. Sisters tell each other everything."

I wish more than anything she could talk back to me. That I could hear her voice one final time, whispering to me that it's all a lie and that she's okay.

That she didn't die, she just slipped away.

I bury my face in my hands, unable to look at her name without feeling destroyed.

All of the clues were right in front of me.

And whatever you do, don't ever get involved with those boys of the Skull & Serpent Society.

Over and over, the note's words repeat in my mind.

I should've known. It was right there in front of me all this time.

I wish I could read her texts right now. Just one last time.

But my phone's dead, and I can't bring myself to leave to go charge it up somewhere.

CRACK!

The sound of twigs breaking puts me on edge.

I swiftly turn to see what it is.

Two, no, three guys emerge from trees that cover the area in the dark of the night.

"Penelope ..." Dylan's voice fluctuates in tone.

I stand, unabashed and unafraid, and fish out my knife. "You *lied* to me."

Felix just stands there, staring at me with that same arrogant and stoic look on his face like he doesn't give a care in the world, and it hurts. It fucking hurts.

"You told me she was a friend," I growl.

"That wasn't a lie," Felix says.

"You fucked her!" I scream.

My voice is unhinged, just as my heart, but I don't care who hears.

These fuckers destroyed me. Used me. Played with me.

And for what?

Just so I could find the one who bullied Eve to death.

Yet the more I look at them, the more I realize they may have been lying to me all this time to cover up their tracks.

"Did you bully her into selling her body?" I ask. "Is that what it is?"

Alistair shakes his head, but I don't believe him.

"Stop lying to me!" I yell. "You're the reason she died!"

"No," Felix barks sternly.

And I hate the way he looks at me, so full of contempt like he hates what I'm saying.

But he knows as well as I do what they're capable of.

He just can't look at the man in the mirror.

And I hate how he continues to lie, even now.

Felix pulls those other two with him and makes them do what he wants. He was the start of all my misery ... of my sister's downfall.

So I point my knife right at him as I go straight for the heart. But the second the tip of my knife hits Felix's chest, I pause. My hand begins to shake.

He's not stopping me.

His arms are still in his pocket, even when confronted with a blade.

Like he's accepting death with open arms.

And I can't fucking push myself to puncture his skin, no matter how badly I want to.

"Did you enjoy seeing me get hurt? Is that why you seduced me too? Just to torture me like you tortured her?" I ask, my voice breaking as much as my spirit. My face contorts as the tears begin to stream down my face. "You killed her."

"No," Felix reiterates.

"Yes! Stop lying!" I yell right up in his face. "She jumped because of what you guys did to her. The same thing you did to me! What did she ask you to do, huh? Did you try to *help* her too? Find some fake enemies to hurt?"

"No," he says again like it comes easy to him. "But I wish we would have."

I grimace. "I should cut out your fucking heart. She deserved better than you."

"She did," Alistair chimes in. "She did deserve better than us."

"No one chooses who they fall in love with," Dylan adds, stepping closer.

"Don't get close, or I'll fucking do it!" I yell, pushing the blade farther into Felix's chest.

"Do it then," he says, locking eyes with me alone. "Kill me."

His hand snakes around mine, pushing the knife farther and farther into his chest.

"So you admit you hurt her," I say through gritted teeth.

"I admit ..." he mutters, eyes stone-cold. Deadly. "We loved her."

My pupils dilate. "What?" I shake my head. "No."

When his lips part again, I break even more than I thought I could. "And she loved us too."

I shudder in place as my hand tremors. "No ..."

"It's true," Dylan says. "We all loved her."

"To the point of obsession," Alistair adds. "Something I never truly understood until I met you."

"No, you're all lying," I say, slowly stepping back as they all back up Felix. "She was a good girl."

"Like you?" Felix quips.

"That's different. I'm trying to get revenge," I quip.

"And she was trying to find acceptance in the way she was," Dylan rebukes, smirking. "A spicy little pepper just like you."

"Bullshit," I spit.

"I wish it was. With us together," Alistair says, rubbing the back of his neck, "it felt like we had something special."

"But it was taken from us as much as it was taken from you," Felix says, his sanpaku eyes even more chilling now that I know the truth.

"Don't you dare," I grit. "You didn't even come to her fucking funeral."

"Oh no?" Felix tilts his head. "I remember locking eyes with you."

"You didn't come to say goodbye. You weren't at the service!"

"Because my father told us not to," Dylan says. "To avoid anyone thinking we had any relations."

I frown and glare at him. "Your father knew?"

Dylan rubs his lips together, sucking up the raindrops. "He found us naked in a classroom."

"If everyone knew we were a thing, people would blame us for her death," Alistair says, throwing his curly, wet hair back.

I can't wrap my mind around all of this. I really can't.

And when Felix takes a step toward me, I keep the knife pointed at him in defense. "Don't."

"After all this, you still don't believe us?" he asks.

I shake my head. "No. She warned me about you. She knew you were trouble."

"She was right about that." Dylan snorts. "That's what you get for being a kinky fucker."

"No. She still thinks we bullied her sister," Felix says.

"Damn right you did. You were there too that night, on the cliff, when she jumped. You didn't fucking stop her," I growl.

He steps even closer, raindrops rolling down his forehead. "Neither did you."

"I tried!"

"I would have jumped after her if I knew what she was about to do," he growls back.

When I keep shaking my head, he shows me the palm of his hand. There's a particularly weird tattoo on there, a circular line that moves from the outside of his hand to his knuckle. I've always wondered what it meant but never thought it mattered.

Until now.

"Dylan," he barks. "Show her."

Dylan moves his fist in line with Felix, but ninety degrees turned so Felix's knuckles point at the side of his hand. And right there, an overlapping circular tattoo line makes a half circle.

Alistair is next, pointing his fist to an empty space while pushing the side of his hand into Dylan's knuckles, making the tattoo three-quarters of a circle.

And my breath begins to falter.

It's the same tattoo as my sister had.

48

FELIX

"You've seen it before," Alistair says. "Haven't you?"

Penelope nods, but she can't even say a goddamn word.

"She has the final piece of the circle," Dylan says.

"She was a part of us," I say, stepping closer.

Tears well up in her eyes. "Why ... why would she lie to me?"

The knife in her hand steadies, but I'm not afraid, not even as the tip penetrates my skin. Still, I inch closer and wrap my hand around hers. Slowly, she yields to my grip as I lower her hand.

Suddenly, she falls into me, bawling her eyes out.

And I just stand there, not knowing what to do with her.

I haven't seen her cry like this. Not even as we chased her, bullied her, stalked her, used her, fucked her, hurt her. Not ever ... until now.

I look up at Dylan, who makes big eyes and smashes his lips together like he wants me to do something. But these things do not come naturally to me.

After a while, I lift my hand and pat her on the back.

It only seems to make her cry more.

The knife rolls out of her hand onto the ground, and her arms wrap around me.

And fuck me, it's been too long since I've felt this kind of embrace.

It's the kind of hug I've only had from two people in my entire life.

Her and Eve. And it's the kind of hug that can ignite a long-extinguished heart and set it ablaze, even in this cold, rainy weather.

I don't know what to tell her except ... "I'm sorry."

I don't say these words a lot, but today, they matter.

The scars we bear are deep and gnarly, and they still hurt even today.

She looks up into my eyes. "What?"

My lip twitches. "Don't make me repeat that."

"I know what you said. You've just never said it before."

"Then don't take it lightly," I say.

She wipes some of her tears away, her eyes smudged and stained with mascara. "It's so hard to believe."

"She meant a lot to us." I grab her chin and tilt her face so she keeps her gaze fixated on me. "*You* mean a lot to us."

"We just didn't want you to snoop in our business and find out about Eve," Alistair says. "Because we knew it wouldn't take long for the entire school to find out."

"And my father would kill me if that happened," Dylan adds. He raises a brow as he clutches his waist with both hands. "But you're much more like your sister than we thought."

She pulls away from me and holds up her hands. "Whoa, wait a minute, this is all a little too much to take. You're all telling me you knew I was her sister, yet you still wanted to fuck around with me?"

"We didn't set out on it," I reply, running my tongue across the inside of my cheek. "But you made it impossible to stay away."

She takes even more steps back until she's almost on the trail leading out of the cemetery. "Why didn't you tell me?"

I walk closer, but she backs up, almost like she's still afraid of me.

Of us.

And the thought alone makes me both angry and excited as hell.

"Would you have believed us?"

She rubs her lips together before shaking her head. "You didn't give me a chance."

Dylan approaches too, extending a hand, but all it does is make her move farther back. "C'mon, Pen. Don't do this."

"You fucked my sister ... and now you're fucking around with me too," she says through gritted teeth.

I hate the way she speaks about us.

Like all we care about is some ass.

My nostrils flare. "Say it again like that." My hand turns into a fist. "I fucking dare you."

"I'm not here to be her replacement," she says, swallowing. "I won't let anyone fuck around with me."

"You are *not* a replacement," I seethe, angered she'd say that out loud. "You ... you are so, so much more to us ... to me ..." I take in a breath, having a hard time with myself because I've avoided even thinking about this.

In fact, I almost convinced myself it wasn't true.

"Even more than Eve."

She shakes her head. "I don't believe you." Her face contorts. "You danced with that girl."

"I danced with that girl to take my mind off you," I interject. "To prove to myself I was still the same coldhearted asshole I ever was."

Her eyes widen in shock.

"Wow ... Felix Rivera has actual feelings?" Dylan jests. "Never thought I'd see that day."

"Shut up," I snarl.

When she turns around, I growl, "You run now, and I will make you remember who you belong to."

"Fuck you," she says, and she sticks up her finger.

That'll fucking do it.

She runs off through the trees, and it takes just one glance over my shoulder to know we're all going for the chase.

As I run after her with Dylan and Alistair on my heel, my feet burst with energy. We pass through the trees and jump over graves, getting closer and closer. Adrenaline shoots through my veins, and by the time I catch up with her, I'm a fucking torrent of desire.

"Mine," I growl as I grasp her foot and stop her in her tracks.

She tumbles to the ground, and I pin her down, crawling on top of her.

"Let me go," she snarls as she writhes underneath me.

"No," I reply, grasping both wrists and pinning them above her head.

Rain pitter-patters down onto her face, mixing with her tears and running mascara, making a hauntingly beautiful sight.

Both Dylan and Alistair hover over me. Her face contorts the moment she realizes she has nowhere to run, nowhere to hide. There's no escaping us.

"Why?" Her desperate voice is like a plea for mercy. And even though I love the sound, it's almost as if she's begging me to want to use her in this context.

But that's no longer an option.

"Why can't you let me go?" she mutters, her pouty, red-stained lips so attractive I almost want to lean in and kiss them just to take away the pain. "Why do you even care?"

I lick my lips. "Because you're ours, and it's time you understood what that means."

She grimaces. "I can't believe I fell for the same trap my sister did."

A trap?

"She didn't fall into any trap," Alistair says. "She found us."

She frowns. "So what ... you did all that kinky shit to her too?"

I nod slowly so she understands what kind of relationship we had.

"Everything and more," Dylan says, licking the raindrops off his lips. "And you know what? She liked it."

She shakes her head. "No, that can't be true."

I tilt my head. "Maybe you didn't know your sister as well as you thought."

"She was more than just a sex doll," Penelope quips.

I slam my fist into the mud, splattering it all over as I growl at her, "Do *not* call her that." Her eyes widen at my sudden rage. "Just because we used her as a slut does not mean she's nothing more than that. Not to us."

She shivers, but I don't know if it's from the cold or from what we've just told her.

"But you call me the same thing," she mutters.

"Exactly," I say.

The air is thick with tension as she holds her breath, despite wanting to say so many things all at once.

I know she hates me.

She'll continue to hate me into eternity, and I knew that going into this.

But then why does my fucking heart feel like it's being stabbed by a million of those fucking knives of hers?

I lower my head so she can't see my eyes.

Because, dammit, they would betray me.

I grasp her face and kiss her once, peering into her eyes to search for a reaction. But they're riddled with questions even I don't have the answers to.

I told myself I wouldn't do this again.

That Eve would be the last, and I'd rather die fucking around with random girls than fall for even one of them. If you continue to lie and tell yourself none of it matters, you'll start to believe it.

But even that was a lie.

A slow, decrepit smile spreads across my cheeks.

I give up.

"You want to know why I won't let you go?" I whisper into her ear.

She nods.

"Because I *need* you."

Her breathing falters.

And I hate how weak it makes me feel.

"For all my fucked-up cravings."

She shudders.

"And if someone else even thinks of touching you, it makes me want to gouge out their eyes and split open their brains for even daring to think about it."

"What?" she mutters.

I lean back to look into her eyes. She looks at me like she can't believe it, and I don't blame her because even I find it hard to believe. The last time I felt this madly possessive over someone was with Eve.

But with Penelope ... It's even worse.

I want to own her. Mark her. Kill anyone who dares to take her from me.

And it makes me fucking wild.

My fingers slowly rake through her hair, grabbing a few strands to take a whiff.

I can definitely smell her fear, her arousal as I sit on top of her, the palm of my hands slowly moving down her arms. She's not even fighting back anymore.

"I don't want to share you," I whisper, "but you know as well as I do that they won't ever accept it if I keep you to myself."

I groan as my tongue darts out to lick her skin, her taste so fucking addictive I could lick her up all day and still not have enough.

"I fucking need you, Penelope," I say. "I need you to uphold your end of the deal ..." My tongue travels down in a line from her earlobe to her neck, licking up every droplet of rain until none are left. But I need more. So much fucking more. "I need you to scream for me and only me. Can you do that?" I bite down on her skin until my teeth draw blood, and she cries out in both agony and bliss.

"Fuck ... so fucking perfect," I murmur, licking up her blood.

"Wha—"

But before she can finish her sentence, my lips smash onto hers.

And I don't fucking care who sees.

***

PENELOPE

I'm stunned.

He needs me?

Did he actually just say that out loud?

No, that can't be right. He must mean my body.

After dancing with that other girl, he just wants to finish his urges with me.

But then why is he kissing me like this? Greedy, hungry, like he wants to destroy me with not just his words but his tongue too. Like he wants to own my fucking soul.

His tongue sweeps past the roof of my mouth as he lays claim to my mouth while his hand slowly snakes around my throat. But I'm not afraid of him.

If he wants me as badly as he says he does, he won't hurt me.

Even when he bit me, he didn't go deeper than the moment I screamed as if the sound of my voice stopped him from going too far.

What if he really does want me?

The thought flashes through my mind, but I ignore it as his lips make it hard to focus. His hand squeezes my throat while he groans into my mouth.

"God, I hate it. I hate what you've done to me."

What I've done to him?

Suddenly, he lets go and crawls down my body, jerking up my soaked-through dress.

"What are you doing?" I mutter.

"I'm gonna fucking lick your soul out of your body."

RIP!

I squeal, but Alistair slams his hand onto my mouth and whispers, "Don't make a sound. Unless you want someone to see you like this." He bites his bottom lip.

I shake my head and look down at Felix, who's torn my underwear to shreds.

But the second his mouth lands on my pussy, my eyes almost roll into the back of my head.

"Fuck, you're already wet for me," Felix murmurs against my skin, and he swivels his tongue back and forth across my slit.

"Hey now, don't take her all for yourself," Dylan says as he steps right next to me. "Let us have some fun too."

Felix's lips only tear away from mine to glare up at Dylan, and oh boy, I don't think I've ever seen him this enraged. "Don't interrupt my meal."

Fuck. That's hot.

I can literally feel the heat rising in both my cheeks and my core.

Don't let it get to you, don't let it—

His mouth covers my clit, and he sucks so hard my toes curl.

"I can feel you moan through my hand, Penelope." Alistair goes to his knees in front of me and zips down. "Keep making those sounds. Even when you can't breathe anymore." He slowly removes his hand, only to part my lips and push his thick, bulging hard-on inside.

"You'd better be fast," Felix grumbles. "Because I'm not gonna hold back, and if she fucking bites your dick off, that's on you."

Felix amps up the pace, and my moans become faster and heavier with every stroke of his tongue. But when his fingers join in, I'm about ready to die and go to heaven. He thrusts them inside while moaning against my pussy, lapping me up like I'm his last fucking prison meal.

It's wrong, so fucking wrong, but I want more, so much more.

And when Alistair thrusts into my throat, I take him all the way down, moaning like the whore they say I am.

And for a split second, I wonder ... how long?

How long until our deal is over and all that's left are hungry eyes and a body yearning for attention?

No, don't think like that.

You've had lovers before.

Suddenly, Felix's fingers touch that spot deep inside that makes my pussy contract, and I explode into an orgasm out of nowhere, wetness spilling from me as fast as my eyes open wide.

"That's it. Drown me with your wetness," Felix groans, licking it all up like he actually enjoys it.

No, I was wrong. I've never had lovers like this before.

Never.

Never before. Never after.

Because nothing, absolutely nothing, compares to this.

Can I ever do without?

"Alistair."

Dylan's voice abruptly pulls me from my thoughts.

"Eyes up here."

Both our eyes go to Dylan, who has already pulled out his ample length and is jerking it off. The slow hardening of his pierced shaft makes me gulp, and Alistair's length throbs inside my mouth like it's yearning for a cock too.

Dylan steps over my body and grabs Alistair's hair, forcing his face to his hard-on. "Keep fucking her mouth, and I'll fuck yours."

Dylan thrusts into Alistair's mouth without warning, and Alistair's length pulses inside me again, and fuck me, it's the hottest thing ever to watch him suck while I suck him.

A mixture of saliva, rain, and sweat covers my face, yet I don't even care.

"Don't stop," Alistair moans. I'm not sure if he means Dylan or me, but I don't even care at this point.

Felix continues to pump away inside me, alternating fingers with tongues and sometimes both together, making me delirious with need.

"Fuck her tongue like you own it," Dylan rasps.

And I moan when Alistair pushes harder, faster, deeper, just from his commands.

It's as if being told what to do makes him want to please, just like me.

And even though I hate that part about me, he seems to have accepted it's a part of himself.

Maybe I should just give in, too.

My eyes burst open, but I can't even process my own thoughts as I'm being pounded by Alistair's thickness, watching Dylan's face scrunch up as he's about to explode.

But right before he does, he pulls out of Alistair's mouth and shoves him away. I cough, choking on my own saliva as his dick pulls out too.

"I want my fucking turn with her," Dylan groans.

Felix pulls out and lifts his head. "Lift her."

"What?" Dylan frowns. "Why not let me have my way first?"

Felix's eyes narrow. "Do what I tell you to fucking do."

Dylan clenches his jaw, but still he moves into action, forced to obey the fucking ringleader who doesn't want to share.

What kind of a mess have I gotten myself into?

Suddenly, Alistair and Dylan hoist me up by my arms and hold me in front of Felix, whose smug face makes me hate myself for enjoying what he did with his tongue so much.

Felix steps back and sits down on a tomb with his hard-on on full display right through his soaked gray jeans, muscular pecs visible straight through the fabric of his black long-sleeve shirt, his wet hair contouring his harsh face, half-mast eyes dark and intense.

And then he beckons me. "Straddle me."

I lick my lips, contemplating if I should do what he says ... or run away.

But where has it ever gotten me?

Only right back into their arms.

There's no escaping them or this onslaught of lust whirling through my body, taking over my brain.

So maybe I should just ... give up.

Don't stop.

Don't look back.

Don't fall.

Run.

My sister's words ... finally, I understand them.

I let out an exasperated sigh.

My conscience.

My ego.

My heart.

All of it flew away with that single breath.

And I feel free as a bird.

I walk toward Felix with my dress still scrunched up, my pussy on full display as I stand before him in the pouring rain. He zips down his jeans and pulls out his long, fully pierced cock, the metal still a sight to behold.

His hand rises to fondle me, and he grips me by the waist and pulls me closer, closer, down, down, down, until the tip as well as that piercing touch my entrance.

And then I slowly lower myself.

The feeling is divine, and even though I've felt it before, it never felt as good as it does now that I'm ... free.

Free of my own criticism, free of consequence.

There's only me and them, their cocks and my willing, lusty body craving release.

"That's it, Penelope. Break for me," Felix groans, gripping my waist with both hands while he pounds into me. "Does it feel good to be my little slut?"

I moan when his piercing touches my clit. "Fuck, yes."

And I'm done denying it.

The grin on his face almost makes him unrecognizable compared to his usual stoic face. "Then spread your fucking ass cheeks." His hands slide up my dress until he exposes my ass. "And show them how badly you want to be their slut too."

49

ALISTAIR

My mouth salivates at the thought of taking her like Felix takes her, but Dylan beats me to it. He walks up to them and places his hand on her ass, then pushes the tip against her. He spits down, spreading it all over, before pushing farther and farther inside.

Penelope's mewls make my bulge throb, and I swallow away the lump in my throat as I watch them bounce away.

Good God, nothing is sexier than watching the two people you crave fuck around together.

I walk up close and circle the grave, gawking at their fuckery like no one is watching. But I love to do it. I live for this, and my hand instinctively moves to my length to tame my desire. I cannot help but gravitate closer until my body is right next to Dylan. I can feel all his muscles tighten as he thrusts into her, and I whisper into his ear, "God, I love watching you fuck her. It gets me hard."

"You dirty bastard," Dylan groans, but he doesn't stop.

Instead, he pushes into his base and wraps his arms around her to clutch her tits from behind, pinching them until she screams.

Right then, Felix kisses her, sucking up all her noises so no one but us can hear her.

I rub myself while I wrap my arm around Dylan and watch him get hot and heavy with her.

I thought I'd hate watching him with her, but I was so fucking wrong.

All it gives me is more to watch, more to enjoy, more to share. I want to touch him and her at the same time, both equal parts of my obsession.

"Make it dirtier," Dylan growls. "Spit on her."

I open my mouth and dribble on her ass over his shoulder.

"Good boy," he groans, and he leans sideways to kiss me too.

And fuck me, if I could live like this with them every day until my death, I would do it in a heartbeat.

***

PENELOPE

Two guys are railing me at the same time in the pouring rain.

I never thought I'd do this.

Or that it would feel so damn good.

My clit hums with desire as Felix plows into me again and again while I bounce up and down on his lap. My arms are locked around his neck, his eyes on me like I'm the only girl in the world for him, and something about that makes me feral with greed.

"Are you mine?" he growls.

I nod, sweat drops rolling down my back as Dylan continuously thrusts into my ass.

Felix's hand snakes around my throat. "Say it."

"I'm yours," I whisper.

He squeezes my throat until I feel light-headed. "Louder."

"I'm yours!" I yell.

And I don't give a damn in the world who hears.

I've already broken my soul into pieces and given away the shards.

Now I am nothing but a vessel for their desires.

A toy for them to use and play with until they discard me, and I'll beg them to do it.

"Now fucking take my cock like a good fucking slut and ride it like you own it," he says, his penetrative gaze making me want to nod.

We move in sync as Dylan pounds into my ass, Alistair adding saliva on command. And I can feel myself unraveling before them.

We're fucking around in a cemetery, on an actual fucking tombstone, without a care in the world.

"Fuck, I'm gonna blast my load inside your ass," Dylan groans, and he plunges in so deep that it hurts.

So I lean in and kiss Felix instead, burying all the pain inside his mouth with my tongue lashing away at his. But he takes my kiss like he knew it was coming, grabbing my face as his tongue dances around mine. I can taste my own wetness, but I don't give a damn. All I want is for them to take away every fiber of my being until I'm nothing but strings to pull.

Use me, corrupt me, ruin me beyond repair.

Because that's what I signed up for.

That's the deal I made with the devil himself.

Felix's lips tear away from mine, despite my desperation, and he murmurs, "That's it, Penelope. See what you've become. See what we made you. What you've turned into."

"Our. Little. Slut," Dylan says, thrusting with each word. He groans out loud, and I can feel him explode inside me. "Fuck!"

"Don't you fucking stop riding me, Pen," Felix warns.

And I keep going because he tells me to, because I've lost all sense of self, all sense of control ... and it's the most magical thing in the world.

I can hear Dylan and Alistair kiss and moan behind me. "My turn," Alistair says, and he pushes Dylan away only to grab my ass for himself. "God, I've waited so long for this."

He doesn't hesitate before he thrusts in too, his girth so large I can barely handle it.

"You can take it, Pen," Alistair says, his hands softly caressing my ass cheek. "I know you can."

I'm a sucker for encouragement, and I practically float away the second he buries himself to the hilt.

"Good girl," Alistair groans.

My lips form an o-shape as I struggle to keep it together.

"Don't come yet, Pen," Felix says, and he pulls my hair until my head tilts back and exposes my neck. Rain pitter-patters down onto my skin, and he licks up all the individual droplets like he's thirsty for more. "Take all of us until you can barely hold it."

"Fuck," I rasp as they're both buried deep inside me.

I can feel them throb right next to each other.

If this is what people mean by rearranging guts, I get it now because this is it, and I'm practically salivating for it.

"Please," I mutter.

Felix bites his bottom lip as he stills inside me. "Please what, Penelope?"

"Please ... I need it. More. Faster."

"Your wish is my command." Dylan steps behind Alistair and spits on his own dick before ripping down Alistair's pants and thrusting into him as well.

And to say I'm fucking stunned would be an understatement.

They're fucking on top of me.

"Oh fuck," Alistair groans.

I don't need to see to know what's going on as I can feel Alistair bouncing against me while whimpering, and the sound is such a turn-on, I automatically begin to gyrate on Felix.

"Oh God, it's too much," I mutter.

"You can do it. Take his dick like a good girl, Pen," Dylan commands me. "While I pound this fucker's ass."

I can't believe Dylan can go again already, but at the same time, I shouldn't be surprised. I knew these boys were sexual deviants. I just didn't know how bad they were until it was too late to turn back. And now I'm here for the full ride, ready or not.

"Fuck, faster, Dylan," Alistair groans as he plunges into me with equal fervor.

It's like a game to them to see who can come harder.

"Fuck, I can feel your cum," Alistair groans.

"Slather her with it," Dylan replies.

Ali pulls out, only to coat my ass with their mixed juices before he pushes right back in.

Felix leans back on the stone and plants his hand underneath my belly button as though he's feeling himself through me. But the pressure it adds feels so fucking good that I can feel myself coming undone.

"Oh God, I can't hold it any longer," I mutter.

"Hold. It," Felix growls.

"The fuck I will," Dylan retorts even though Felix wasn't talking about him. "I'm gonna come in his ass too."

I can feel Alistair being pushed up against me, pounded by Dylan as he fills him up to the brim. And Alistair explodes along with him, howling as though his soul has left his body, and I'm right there with him.

"Now," Felix groans.

And I fall apart against them both, the wave of ecstasy between my legs too much as I collapse onto Felix, my mouth colliding with his.

And while Alistair pulls out, Felix buries himself deep inside me, coaxing out my last moan while he jets into me.

"Fuck!" Felix roars.

But the all-consuming, devouring kiss that follows ... that's what gets me the most.

It's as if all the atoms in the universe have collided and split apart just for us.

A kiss so possessive and needy it sucks my very life essence out of me, and I don't even care if it kills me.

"Who's there?"

A loud voice makes me tear my lips away from Felix, and I look up at a bright, shining light not far in the distance.

"Oh fuck," Dylan mutters as he tucks everything back into his pants and zips up. "The groundskeeper."

Felix pushes me off him and zips up before grabbing my hand. "Run!"

"Hey! What the fuck are you doing?" the groundskeeper yells when he spots us.

We dash off through the trees, adrenaline coursing through my veins as all three boys are in pursuit. But instead of feeling like I'm being hunted, I'm haunted by the visceral look in their eyes.

And I realize they're not the only ones obsessed.

50

DYLAN

"Come back here!" the groundskeeper yells, but we outrun him with ease as he chases us through the cemetery gates.

Every other second, I glance over at Penelope, whose face radiates with deviance, the same kind that floods my veins whenever we break the rules. Everything wrong feels so damn right, and I know she can feel it too.

Laughing, we escape the property as the groundskeeper stays behind, and we run all the way to the car parked out front. I open the passenger door, and Penelope, Ali, and I jump inside, squeezing into the back while Felix hops behind the wheel.

"Hold on tight," he growls as he puts the gear into reverse, and the wheels begin to squeal.

We race off, leaving behind an irate man at the gates yelling his socks off. None of us can hear what he has to say, nor do we care.

I know Felix can drive like a champ. That's why he's always behind the wheel when shit gets real.

"WHOO!" I cheer as we swerve through the streets. "That's what I'm talking about."

"You all really enjoy being delinquents, don't you?" Penelope muses.

I place a hand on her knee, my fingers digging into her skin as I say, "And you loved it."

She scoffs. "It's not like I have a choice."

I grab her chin and force her to look at me. "You had a choice." A wicked grin spreads on my lips. "And you made yours long ago."

I slowly lean in, my eyes glancing between her and the rearview mirror through which Felix is glaring at me. But it doesn't stop me from claiming her mouth right in front of him. And he can't do anything to stop me.

She tastes like heaven and hell at the same time, a toxic mix I can't get enough of, and if I could, I'd fuck her all over right here in this car.

But we're all soaking wet, and I need her to recoup some energy before we go again.

"God, you undo me," I mutter into her mouth.

My tongue is wild for her. The last time I felt this way was with Eve, and even that didn't come close to the visceral reaction my body has to Penelope. She fires up my body like nothing else, and I could turn the whole world into ashes and flames just from the mere thought of losing her.

But I'm not alone.

Two others in this car share the same feelings, and I get the sense somehow, someday, this will all explode in our faces.

I inch back and watch as her lips lean into mine, desperate for more.

Lovely.

Her eyes open, and the look on her face sours as she realizes I was looking at her pretty lips begging me for a kiss.

"Asshole," she hisses.

I smirk. "And you love it."

"I'm surprised you care," Penelope says, and she raises a brow. "Don't you have a boyfriend?"

I slyly gaze over her shoulder at Alistair, who licks his lips. "Oh yeah ... but he doesn't mind."

Alistair's hand slowly slides across her thigh until he touches my fingers, and he grips her chin with his other hand to steal her away from me with a kiss that's apparently so good she moans. And it makes me want to rip her out of his arms.

"I'm not his, and he's not mine," I say, pecking her neck instead. "But you ... you belong to all of us."

"Simmer down back there," Felix barks.

"Jealous?" I mutter, gazing right back into his stern eyes through the mirror.

"Shut up," he growls, and he kicks the car into gear, speeding like crazy.

"Oh well, if we can't kiss her ..." I lean in and grab Alistair's face, kissing him instead right in front of Penelope.

"Wow, it's getting steamy in here," she muses.

My lips unlatch from Ali's. "Might even be able to dry up."

"Dry up at home," Felix retorts.

Penelope suddenly gasps. "Wait, what about the club? Shouldn't we go back? I left my friends all by themselves. I thought we were going back."

"They'll be fine," Felix replies, tightening his grip on the steering wheel. "I'm gonna take you home. Safe."

She swallows and sits back, despite the fact that I could swear she was about ready to rip his ass out. But something about his choice of words has subdued her.

"Okay."

Wow. I never thought I'd be here the day she'd simply give up.

I sit up straight to look at her. "What, no protest?"

She shakes her head.

Felix glances at her through the mirror. "Good girl."

Her cheeks turn a reddish hue, and I almost can't believe it was that easy. Why does she suddenly listen to him without fighting? Did something happen back there in the cemetery?

"But I am gonna text them, though," she says.

I roll my eyes. I should've known she cares way too much about what other people think of her.

"What will you tell them?" I say, bucking my hips. "That you got banged so, so good in a cemetery?"

She shoves me with her elbow, and I groan with pain and excitement.

"I'm telling them how sorry I am and that the entire bill is on me to make up for the fact that I left," she replies.

"Oh, how chivalrous of you," I muse as she tucks her phone back into her pocket again.

Alistair squeezes her knee. "Are you okay?"

"I'm fine," she replies, shivering again.

"Dylan," Felix growls, eyeing my coat lying in the back.

I immediately lean over and cover her with it. "You should've told me you were cold."

"I said I'm fine," she says.

"You still don't trust us, huh?" Alistair mutters, slowly rubbing her knee.

"I don't trust you with myself," she replies, glancing at us. "I trust you to kill."

Felix's eyes narrow. "Is that all you see in us? Murderers?"

"I see what we agreed to," she replies. "My body for your help."

The car comes to a stop in front of the school grounds, and the gates slowly open for us. They recognize my car's plate number via an automated system, which makes it easier to get on and off the property. Unfortunately, it also allows my father to block us from exiting when he hates us.

We drive onto the property, silence filling the car until it becomes awkward as hell.

Suddenly, Penelope practically jumps over my lap to stare out the window, hands glued to the glass.

She gasps.

We all do.

Because the house she belongs to, the Alpha Psi sorority house, is on fire.

51

PENELOPE

I practically fall out of the vehicle as it stops in front of the sorority. I push my way past Dylan and jump out, watching the flames lick up the ceiling of the building with horror in my eyes.

What the fuck happened?

Firefighters are on the scene, dousing the flames with water as best they can, focusing on one particular room to the left. The rest of the rooms seem unscathed from the outside, but who knows how long the fire has been raging, destroying everything in its path.

"Penelope!" Kayla yells as she runs up to me. "Tilda called me, and I came home with Crystal as fast as I could."

"What happened here?" I ask, gazing at the roaring fire.

"I don't know, someone said there was a small explosion, but no one saw anything."

My pupils dilate. An explosion? That means it's ...

"Someone wanted that room to burn," Dylan mutters as he creeps up behind me.

"Jesus, Pen, where were you?" Kayla asks, gripping my dress. "You're soaked." She eyes Dylan. "You both are."

"I was at my sister's grave," I say.

She releases my dress. "Oh. I was just wondering why you'd leave us like that."

"Sorry," I mutter, entranced by the flames.

"Oh my God, this is like my worst nightmare," Crystal says as she approaches us, and she pulls us both in for a hug. "I hope no one got hurt. I'm scared."

"It's okay," Kayla says. "The firefighters are doing their best."

"Whose room is it?" I ask.

"Not ours," Kayla replies. "But you should have seen the flames before. They've already doused most of them."

Felix and Alistair step out too, and Kayla looks up with suspicion in her eyes. "You boys only bring trouble. You need to stay away from her."

Felix raises his brow in a menacing way.

"Why are they even here?" Kayla mutters as we stop hugging.

"They helped me get through a tough spot," I say and smile at her. "I don't want this to sour our friendship." I look across my shoulder at the three boys. "Can you please accept them for me?"

"They're not gonna go anywhere, are they?" Crystal muses.

"I'm as stuck with them as they are stuck with me," I reply.

Dylan winks at me while Alistair takes a step back and puts on his hoodie, but Felix seems the most annoyed of all that both Crystal and Kayla are looking at him, and not in an amicable way.

After a while, they've extinguished the fire, and all that's left is smoke and ashes fluttering down the building. The firefighters talk among themselves, arguing about an item one of them is holding, and it makes me anxious.

"What do you think they found?" Crystal asks.

"It can't be good," Kayla replies.

"The fuse," Dylan mutters.

"What?" I frown.

"That fire wasn't an accident," he adds.

I swallow. "How do you know for sure?"

He points at the building. "The fire was contained to that room only."

"So?"

Felix clears his throat. "That was your sister's room."

All the blood leaves my face, and I feel like I'm about to puke.

I immediately walk toward the firefighters.

"Penelope!" Kayla yells.

"Penelope, come back here," Felix hisses at me, but I ignore him.

I try to listen to what the firefighters are saying about the item they found, but it's hard with all these loud sirens.

"Are you sure?" I can hear Tilda, the sorority leader, say.

"Positive. We'll have to file a report."

Tilda sighs. "Okay. And where do we stay now?"

"The building needs to be inspected for safety first. That'll take at least a week."

"A week?" I hear audible gasps from the other ladies who live in the building.

Dean Caruso approaches out of nowhere.

Was he here all this time? Watching the fire, just like us?

"Don't worry, ladies. I will immediately ask my contacts so they can set up different accommodations for you." He sighs out loud. "In the meantime, book a hotel room and send the receipts to my office. But only for one night. I'll get something up and running tomorrow."

He's talking to the crowd like there's nothing to be worried about. But I am fucking worried.

And when his eyes connect to mine, I know this won't end well for me.

"Everyone back to their houses. Show's over," he announces to the crowd gathered to watch the fire, but his eyes are still locked on me.

"Tilda, I'll leave this to you," he says.

Tilda gazes at the firefighters. "Can I borrow this just a second?"

They nod. "One minute."

She takes the item and walks over to me. "Penelope ... I'm sorry, but you can't stay in our sorority anymore."

My eyes widen. "What? You're kicking me out?"

When she nods, Dylan steps in. "Hey, she didn't do anything."

Tilda holds up the item. It's a piece of fireworks, badly burned, but a piece of laminated plastic is stuck to the shell. Beneath it was a piece of paper with my first name written.

This has to be a cruel joke.

It just has to be.

"What?" I mutter.

"Since your name is on this, we have no choice."

I'm incensed. "You're accusing me of setting this fire? I wasn't even here."

"She was with us," Felix says from the back, folding his arms.

Tilda briefly acknowledges him with a glance. "We don't know who did," Tilda says with a stern voice. "But your name is on this thing, and I cannot take the risk."

"That isn't fair to her at all," Dylan interjects, but I raise my hand to quiet him.

I don't need them to fight for me. I can do that myself.

"I'm sorry, Penelope. But enough is enough. You've already broken the rules, and I warned you there was a limit to my patience," she says. She turns around and hands the fireworks back to the firefighters before returning to me. "I need you to leave the property. When the house is open again, you may return to get your things. But you won't be allowed to join us again."

It hurts so bad that tears sting my eyes, but I refuse to let them fall.

I'm not the culprit of this blazing fire, but I sure as hell will go down from it with honor.

"Fine. If that's the way you want to deal with this," I turn away from her, closing my eyes as I walk away.

Kayla and Crystal follow suit. "Wait, Pen, you can't be serious, right?" Crystal says.

"You're just gonna let Tilda kick you out?" Kayla adds. "I know you didn't do it."

"I didn't, but that won't matter to her. She needs someone to blame, so I'll play the fucking martyr."

I look at the boys. Those boys whose influence reaches far beyond the walls of this university. Whose deadly encounters leave behind countless enemies, all set on revenge.

It's because of them, and they know this. I can see it in their eyes.

I take in a deep breath.

"They aimed for my sister's room," I say. "So it's a vendetta against us both. That, or they aimed wrong."

"Doubt it," Dylan says from a few feet away.

"Are you telling me they were trying to ... kill you?" Crystal asks, her face turning as pale as snow.

"It's a possibility," Felix fills in for me, and he steps forward. "Which is why she's coming with us." Felix's fingers slowly dig into my shoulder as he grips me tightly. "She'll be safe at the Skull & Serpent Society."

Kayla snorts. "I find that very hard to believe."

Dylan's whole body tenses up. "If anyone ever tries to put a finger on Penelope, I will fucking gut them myself."

Kayla's pupils dilate, and Crystal holds her gasp.

They've never said it out loud before, especially not in front of my friends.

And it's as if the world has gone completely silent.

Felix squeezes my shoulder again. "C'mon. Let's go."

"Wait." I pull free from his grasp to hug Kayla and Crystal.

"I just want you to be okay."

"I'll be fine, don't worry about me," I reply as I lean back. "Talk later."

"Text me every day so I know they haven't murdered you," she says.

I chuckle as we stop hugging and I make my way back to the boys. "Will do."

"Murder ... her?" Crystal repeats with a shaky voice.

"I was joking," Kayla muses, but I can tell from the way she's looking at me as I walk off she definitely was not. But Crystal doesn't have to know.

52

PENELOPE

The boys drive me back to the Skull & Serpent Society and park the car on the property before hopping out. Dylan opens the door for me and holds out his hand. "Milady."

I snort. "That's awfully chivalrous, even for you."

When I take his hand, he says, "I thought it'd be a nice contrast after I just rearranged your guts." He pulls me close to him, too close, and I can barely breathe when he smirks in my face. "Do you like it?"

I don't even know how to respond. "Um... Yes?"

His eyes narrow. "Are you getting flustered, Pen?"

Fuck. Now I really can't stop the heat from flooding my face.

"You're really yearning for a beating, aren't you, Dylan?" Felix says as he slams the door shut.

"I'm just having fun," he retorts.

"By bullying me again?" I jerk my hand away from his.

"Bullying?" He scoffs, still keeping me close to him. "I prefer the word tease."

"Enough playing around," Felix barks as he marches to the door. "Get inside."

"Woof," Dylan barks back, and the glare Felix throws him is so funny it even makes me laugh.

"He's right, though," Alistair says as he walks up to us. "The Phantoms have obviously made her their target. It's too dangerous to stay out here."

366

He's right.

Those fireworks in my sister's room were definitely a message to me.

This means we're getting closer to whoever caused her misery ... and now mine.

I swallow as Alistair steals my hand away from Dylan and drags me along with him. "C'mon."

"Hey, wait for me," Dylan growls, jumping up the steps to the building.

We head inside and go through the main hall where the big staircases are. The last time I was here, it was dark and filled with sparkling lights and lots of people dancing around. Now it's like a ghostly anteroom with doors and windows on all sides, all closed off.

"Jesus, this place needs some light," I mutter under my breath.

"Felix doesn't want people to snoop from the outside," Alistair says.

I frown. "It's a multistory building. Who's gonna snoop on the second or third floor?" I point at the window at the top of the stairs, where thick curtains block the light.

"No need," Dylan replies, and he flicks a switch.

A giant chandelier in the hallway turns on and brightens it with pretty crystals glittering onto the walls, and I stop and stare for a moment at its beauty. That light alone is expensive as fuck, and it makes me wonder how much money has been sunk into this society ... these boys.

Alistair lets go of my hand and wanders off to the other side of the hallway. "If you need me, I'll be in my room." He adds a wink.

"C'mon, I wanna show you my room," Dylan says, and he drags me along with him before I even get the chance to reply.

"Dylan ..." Felix rumbles from the other side of the hall.

Dylan ignores him and pulls me into a different room. It reminds me of a hollowed cave, with steps lowering into an area where a red, velvety arch in the wall outlines a beautiful beige king canopy bed with a white curtain all around. To the left of the bed is a fireplace and to the right a door through which I can see a big bath. Soft lights with intricate Moroccan designs fills the bedroom, and the furniture looks so soft I could probably fall asleep on them and never wake up.

"Wow," I mutter.

"Better than sex, right?" Dylan muses, and he jumps onto his bed and splays himself in a playboy fashion, rubbing the bed like he wants me to join him. "But what's even better is this bed plus you."

I snort as I approach him. "You've got to be kidding me, right?"

He raises a brow, and it only makes me laugh harder.

I clutch one of the bars of the canopy bed. "This actually works on girls?"

He frowns. "Are you actually bullying me for a change?" He gets up. "I can't believe it. Come here, you little rat."

He lunges at me and hoists me onto the bed while I squeal and laugh at the same time, and he rolls me around until he's on top of me.

"Wait, but we're completely soaked!"

"I don't care. I've got you now," he says, pinning my hands above my head. "Just like I caught you the day you ran at the Halloween party."

A hot flash runs through my body. God, I hate to be reminded of that day. Not because I despised it, but because of how every time I think about it, my clit still thumps.

"You weren't alone," I reply. "It would've been much harder for you if you were."

"Oh." His eyes flash with curiosity. "Are you suggesting I wouldn't have been able to trap you myself?" His grip on my hands tightens. "What would you have done to avoid me then?"

"I have knives," I reply, swallowing away the lump in my throat.

"And you think that would deter me?" he retorts, biting his bottom lip. "The challenge only gets me hard."

I lift my knee, pushing against his bulge, which throbs from the touch, and even I have to admit it feels powerful to be the one to cause that kind of reaction. "You wouldn't be able to handle me on your own."

He groans with delight and pulls out his lighter, hovering it so close to my breasts I can feel the heat burn through the fabric. "I like your tenacity, Pen. I like how fearless you are in the face of pain." And he leans in to press a kiss against my neck, turning off the lighter the moment it almost threatened to burn through my dress.

Suddenly, a loud clearing of a throat has us both turn our heads.

Felix stands in the door opening, clutching the doorpost with one hand, with a possessive, almost unhinged look on his face.

"You're really doing this now?" he growls.

"Yes, what about it?" Dylan replies.

Felix's nostrils flare. "She's wet."

"Not just from the rain," Dylan retorts with a smirk.

He grips Dylan's door so harshly I can almost hear it break. "Get off her. Now."

I can practically see the fumes coming from Felix's mouth when he talks, and my God, it actually makes my heart thump in my throat.

"You really know how to sour a mood," Dylan says, sighing out loud as he rolls off me.

I sit up straight and adjust my hair, pretending nothing was going on, because I get the feeling he's not just mad at Dylan.

Felix suddenly lunges at me and grabs my wrist, hauling me with him.

"Hold up, what are you doing with her?" Dylan says.

"Just because she's cold doesn't mean you can burn her," Felix says through gritted teeth.

He drags me through the hallway all the way to his room, where he kicks open the door and pulls me inside, slamming it shut behind him before locking it.

One hand slams into the wood beside my face. "Do not push me, Pen."

I frown. "I didn't—"

"If you ever let him touch you like that again ..."

"Like what?" My eyes narrow. "Like he could actually be more than just someone who uses me for my body?"

The muscles in his arms tighten as though it takes everything in him to hold back. "You belong to *me*."

I hold my breath as he closes in on me, his free hand traveling up my body without touching me. I can still feel the electrical current between us, and I know he can feel it too.

"I'm only willing to share if I'm there to watch."

My eyes narrow. "You're jealous?"

His eyes darken as he clenches his jaw. "Don't mistake my possessiveness for jealousy. I *allow* them to play with you."

I snort. "But only when it pleases you."

He pounds his fist into the wood, making me jolt.

But then he grabs my face and smashes his lips on mine.

It's not a sweet or gentle kiss, but an unholy one, full of unspoken desires. An all-consuming kiss that makes my toes curl and my knees buckle.

When he pulls back, my lips still yearn for more.

He looks into my eyes for a moment, but it feels as though it lasts an eternity.

His hands still linger on my face, the look in his eyes mesmerizing to the point that I feel like I can't breathe when he looks at me.

"You've unlocked something inside me I thought I killed off."

I don't know if that's a compliment or a threat.

"No matter what I do, what I say, who I fucking play with ... everything reminds me of you."

Who he plays with? What is he talking about?

Or does he mean that girl at the club?

I swallow away the lump in my throat.

"Enough with your games," he says, and he pulls away, only to grasp my hand and drag me along with him. "Time for a shower."

"What? But we just came out of the pouring rain," I splutter.

Too late. He's already turned on the faucet, and the water splashes down right on top of me and onto my dress. My eyes instinctively close with the rush of the water.

Great, now I'm wet again.

"Let's get this off."

My eyes burst open. He's right in front of me, underneath the same water, with his expensive black long-sleeve shirt and pants still on. A knife in his hands glitters in the bathroom light.

He cuts through the fabric around my shoulders, then peels away the off-the-shoulder dress, slowly pulling down the fabric until he's exposed my breasts.

RIP!

He cuts through the rest in a way that's almost too meticulous. Like he's thought about how to do it. Studied it.

His Adam's apple bobs, and I don't know why I focus on it, but I do. And when he slowly sinks to his knees to take off the rest, leaving me bare, my entire body erupts into goose bumps.

He pulls off my heels and chucks them aside like they're only in his way.

But he won't let go of my foot.

"You're playing a dangerous game, Penelope," he mutters.

He leans in, planting a kiss on my foot.

"A game that has no winners."

His eyes bore into mine as he drags his lips up to my knees, and I hold my breath in anticipation, my pussy throbbing with excitement again.

God, it's only been an hour since we last fucked around in the cemetery, yet I already feel like I could go again.

Is this what my sister felt when she was with them? Is this what they did to her? Why she felt like she couldn't escape?

Their greed is suffocating.

And they make me want to offer the leftover oxygen in my lungs for free.

"If Dylan got you so riled up already, then I will be the one to take care of it. I can't have you falling for them," he says.

Falling for them?

Does he mean Dylan and Ali?

The knife is pushed into my calf, right above where he's kissing me. "So if you won't play by my rules, then let's play by yours."

I can't even reply because his tongue is everywhere, stilting my breath.

"We made a deal, you and I," he mutters, kissing his way up my thighs while dragging the knife up with him. And I'm equal parts terrified and aroused. "So tell me what you need me to do."

When his tongue swipes my slit, I moan out loud.

The cold blade pushing up against my inner thigh silences me. And he pauses his kisses and looks up, knife digging into my skin. "Tell. Me."

"Find my sister's bullies," I murmur as I gaze down.

Right then, his tongue dips out to lick me again, and I almost lose my balance. I steady myself against the walls while the water clashes down on me.

"What else?" he says, lapping me up.

"Punish them," I say.

His tongue is relentless.

His voice is dark, commanding, "Be specific."

"Hurt them," I say.

His mouth covers my most sensitive parts, circling me like he's intent on making me come again, and I don't think I'll be able to stop it, even if I wanted to.

"How?" he asks.

"What?" I mutter.

And he actually pulls back, leaving me bereft. "If you won't give me everything you have, I won't give you mine."

God, my clit thumps just from the fact that his tongue hovers so close, and I hate him for edging me like this. God, I hate it, and I love it so much.

"Cut out their tongues," I murmur.

And he immediately goes to town on me to the point that I struggle to even let out a moan.

"More," he groans.

"Slice off their fingers," I say.

"Yes," he says, rolling his tongue around until my legs begin to quake.

"Rip out their eyes."

Suddenly, he thrusts the handle of the knife into me, and I gasp, only for it to turn into a moan as he starts fucking me with it while his tongue continues to roll around. The sharp end of the blade must be cutting into his skin, but he doesn't seem to have a care in the world over pain.

A mixture of rage and animalistic lust floods my body as he continues licking me, and I can barely keep it together.

"Now finish it," he growls.

"Kill them," I whisper.

And his tongue dives into me so deep along with the knife I mewl with delight. "Fuck, I'm coming, Felix!"

"Yes, finish all over my mouth," he groans, lapping me up like he can taste the revenge on my wetness.

My hands on the wall can barely hold me up. He rises to his feet and catches me just before I fall, planting me against the wall, before his lips crash into mine again.

The knife tumbles out of me and clatters onto the tile floor, but I don't give a damn.

All I want is more of these kisses, more of his touch, more of everything so depraved I would sell my soul to receive just a crumb.

"I will bring them hell for you."

His voice is dark, heady, and so mesmerizing that I'm becoming obsessed.

God, now I understand what they did to her.

I tear off Felix's clothes and throw them to the side, pants and shirt and everything between him and me. But when our lips momentarily unlatch, I gaze at all the intricate tattoos on his body, at the Skull & Serpent tattoo he wears too, just like Dylan and probably Ali too, and many more. Because what was hiding underneath those high-buttoned shirts and thick black hoodies was a neck tattoo of a phoenix going from his chin all the way down to his chest.

Along with a Medusa right underneath.

A tattoo people usually only get when ... they've been assaulted.

Fuck.

I suck in a breath as I touch it, but he flinches when I do. "Sorry."

"Don't be."

"Is this ...? Were you ...?" I mutter.

"It was a long time ago," he says, clenching his jaw.

So it's real? That really happened to him?

Wow.

Out of all people, he was the last I would guess to ever be ... a victim.

There are many more layers to this man than I originally thought.

A tortured soul hell-bent on giving the world exactly what it gave him.

Desolation.

His hand grips mine. "Don't pity me."

"I wasn't—"

"I know what I see," he says, his nostrils flaring. "I've looked at you long enough to recognize every fucking emotion on your face."

I gulp.

Was he always that obsessed?

Or did I just never notice because I was too busy to make him the object of my hatred?

"I'm sorry, it's just ..."

"You don't expect it with someone like me."

I nod. I always thought he was impenetrable, hard as steel, cold to the bone.

But maybe he wasn't always that way.

Someone *made* him that way.

"Life is cruel," he replies. "I learned that lesson at a very young age." He swallows. "And if people take something from you that's precious ... you annihilate them."

He turns off the shower, but I'm far from finished with showering. Or from cooling down.

With a hard-on, he marches out of the shower only to return with dark-red towels. "Catch."

He throws me one that barely covers my body, but I make do and dry myself off. He returns with one of his shirts when I'm about to wrap it around my body. "I don't have women's clothes, so this will have to do."

It's one of his.

I put it on, and it's oversized for me but just big enough to cover my butt. But the smell ... it reminds me of him.

A blush spreads on my cheeks.

When he walks off, I follow him back to his bedroom, wondering why we aren't finishing him too.

But I'm far too busy gaping at his room, which is so different from Dylan's. I've been here before, but it still doesn't fail to mesmerize me. And now that I'm not being chased, I can finally have a real look around.

It's dark and gloomy, covered in skulls, but the place is gigantic, with two big window panes in the back where a lofty bed stands. Across the room are several tables filled with half-filled liquor bottles and empty glasses—a testament to someone drowning in their agony.

I rub my lips together and walk through the room. Plenty of expensive-looking leather seats are scattered throughout, along with a bench and something that looks like a cross with straps on it. Every piece of furniture has a skull pattern on it. Exactly what I'd expect from someone who loves death.

I gulp.

In the back, near the window, is a wooden table with a small enclosure on top.

The creature inside it draws me in.

It's a snake.

And it's eating a dead rat.

"Nessie."

I almost jump up and down from the scare.

He's right behind me, wearing nothing but a towel around his waist.

"Our pet snake," he adds.

I frown and smile at the same time. "A pet?"

"Snakes can be pets," he responds.

"No, I mean, *you* have a pet?" I snort.

His eyes narrow. "Is that so hard to believe?"

I shrug, still smiling because he's right. It is kind of hard to believe from a frigid man like him. Though I suppose this kind of pet suits him perfectly, especially with that tattoo.

"Actually, no," I reply.

My finger dips into the cage to touch her body, which feels strange.

"Do you want to hold her?" He lifts her out before I can even reply, then places her on my neck. "She won't bite."

"Gee, that's a comforting thought," I mutter, feeling her slither across.

He tilts his head and watches me for a moment. "You're not scared."

"No ... should I be?"

A smile gently tugs at his lips. "Maybe you aren't exactly the same as Eve."

I make a face. "She was scared of snakes?"

I didn't even know that. How did I not know?

He pulls Nessie off my shoulders again and places her back in the cage. "Maybe she didn't tell you everything about her."

I lower my eyes and sigh. "I wish she would've confided in me. Maybe then I wouldn't have had to go through all this trouble."

With a single finger, he lifts my chin and forces me to look at him. "Maybe there was a reason she didn't. She was trying to protect you."

"From what?"

I shudder in place.

"Us."

Too late.

53

FELIX

Her body erupts into goose bumps.

But I don't want her to be afraid. We're way past that now.

"She was also trying to protect you from the others," I say.

Turning around, I grab my sweatpants from my stack of clean clothes and put it on under her watchful eye, knowing she's probably staring at my ass. I don't care.

"Others? Do you mean the Phantoms?" she asks after a while.

Suddenly, someone slams his fists against the door. "Hey! Open up!"

Dylan.

My fists ball.

"I'm not playing around. You're having sex with her, aren't you?" he growls.

"None of your goddamn business," I rebuke.

"Wow!" He slams his fists on the door again. "You tell me not to and then you go around behind my back?"

Penelope looks at me like I'm making a fuss out of nothing with her arms crossed. "C'mon. This isn't fair to him."

She approaches me and holds out her hand.

I just stare back.

Suddenly, she lunges at me and steals the key right out of my pocket.

I try to catch her, but she springs right out of my arms like a fucking mouse jumping away from the cat, and she immediately runs to the door.

"Penelope," I warn. "Don't open that door."

While staring me straight in the eyes, she still shoves the key into the lock.

Goddammit.

She's testing me.

Seeing how far I'll let her go.

And the truth is ... further than I wanted to.

The bad part is, she knows now.

Grinding my teeth, I watch her open the door.

"You're gonna pay for that later," I say through gritted teeth.

"I can take it," she retorts, then she turns to Dylan. "We're not fucking."

"I heard you talking about Phantom. What's that all about?" He looks over her shoulder, and his eyes connect with mine. "Are you telling her everything?"

I guess now that the cat's out of the bag, there's no point in keeping all this from her anymore.

Nodding, I turn around. "The Phantoms aren't the only other house on this campus."

Dylan walks into my room like he owns the place and picks up my vape to fill it with some of the new stuff I bought.

Penelope follows him. "Wait, what didn't you tell me? Who else is there? And what do they want?"

I lie on the bed and sigh out loud. "Dylan, go ahead and tell her since you already invited yourself into my room."

He takes a whiff and sits down on my chair. "This university is far more than just a college. A lot is going on underneath the surface, more than most people know."

She looks like she's cracking her pretty brain over this.

"This college isn't just for the rich," he says, smirking. "People buy their way in. People from the criminal circuit."

She sways her hand around. "And you know this ...?"

"Because my father is on the board that pays for all of it," I fill in. "But you knew that already."

Dylan smirks. "So you know what kind of people our families are."

"All of you?" she asks, confused. "But what about Ali? His father is the head of the—"

"Police. A rat," I interject.

She swallows. Probably finally starting to realize why Ali's father let us off the hook so easily. "So literally everyone in this school is corrupt?"

"Not everyone," he replies.

She frowns. "But how do you know who's the criminal and who isn't?"

"That's where the different frat houses come into play," Dylan responds.

"So you're telling me these houses are like gangs?"

He nods. "You can think of it like that."

Her eyes narrow. "So you're all part of a gang?"

Dylan shrugs. "We prefer to call it a society."

Penelope yawns and slaps her hand in front of her mouth when I notice.

I rub my forehead. "Enough."

"No, no, wait, I want to know more," Penelope stammers.

"You need to sleep," I say, patting the bed.

"Yeah, time to sleep." Dylan walks toward her and grabs her hand.

"Dylan," I warn as I sit up. "She's staying here."

"What?" Penelope mutters. "But you have like other rooms, right?"

"Yeah, let me show you," Dylan says, and he attempts to drag her along with him.

So I march up to them and grab her hand, pulling her to me. "You're staying with me," I say, looking at both of them intently. "I need to keep watch."

"Why?" Dylan scoffs. "Those Phantoms won't come here."

"Are you sure about that?" I retort.

Dylan makes a tsk sound. "Whatever. I know how to stake out."

"You fall asleep too easily," I say, putting both hands on her shoulders. "I'll watch."

He pauses and stares at me for a moment. He knows I'm right.

"Fine," he says. "But you'd better remember this agreement is between all four of us." And he gawks at us both before walking out the door and slamming it shut behind him.

Penelope lets out a breath. "You two ..."

"Ignore him," I say as I pull her back onto the bed. "Come. Sleep."

I lay her down on the second pillow on my bed and put the blanket over us, wrapping my arm around her waist so she stays put.

"Hmm ... okay," she murmurs.

"What?" I reply.

"Well, this is just awkward."

"Why?"

I can feel her body heat against mine, and my cock twitches against my sweatpants, but I ignore it.

"Well, you haven't even ... taken what you wanted from me."

Her hand slowly drifts beneath the blanket, but I grab her wrist just before she touches my shaft. "Not now."

Her breath catches in her throat. "But you always—"

"Then you don't know me as well as you thought you did, either," I interject.

She relaxes again.

"Just sleep," I tell her.

"But I'm not that tired," she replies.

"It's the middle of the night. Of course you are," I reply. "Stop lying to yourself."

She sighs. "What about you? Are you going to sleep?"

"No sleep for the wicked."

"So you're just gonna lie here beside me and wait until I fall asleep?" she asks.

"No. I'm going to make sure this room doesn't turn into Eve's old room."

She sucks in a breath. "But you can't stay awake forever."

"Watch me," I growl back, and I push her closer to me so her head rests in the crook of my neck.

Each strand of her hair pricks at my skin, but the scent ... God, her fucking scent brings me back.

"Close your eyes," I mutter. "I'll stay here and watch over you."

"Okay ... good night."

I don't trust this agreeability. She's the girl who always fights back, yet ...

Has she started trusting me?

My body grows rigid against hers.

I can't repeat the same mistakes.

I can't fucking let it destroy me again.

54

PENELOPE

Every breath he takes, I can feel deep within my bones.

Like a watchful guardian, he stays put, silently waiting until I fall asleep.

But all I can focus on are those muscular arms wrapped around my waist and that tight snugness his body provides, like a warm, velvety cocoon shielding me from whatever darkness is out there.

How could I ever sleep like this?

My heart is going a million miles an hour like it's running a marathon all by itself. Every time he moves, my entire body tingles. And I don't understand why.

I suck in another breath and wait, but he doesn't seem to be falling asleep either.

Maybe he wasn't lying when he said he doesn't sleep.

No wonder he has such sunken-in bloodshot eyes.

I swallow away the lump in my throat.

Could it be related to the Medusa tattoo?

No sleep for the wicked.

His words reverberate in my mind.

And from this corner of the bed, I'm staring straight at the night-stand, where an overturned glass filled with a crystal-clear fluid slowly drips onto the wood, the scent of alcohol penetrating my nostrils.

Goose bumps scatter on my skin, and I close my eyes again, wondering if my sister knew.

If this is the reason she fell.

But in the back of my mind, I think I already know the truth.

Because I'm feeling it too.

***

"Penelope ... Penelope ..." My sister's voice forces me to open my eyes wide. Her fingers reach for mine just before she falls.

"Stay away, Pen," she says, but her voice is distorted and not hers.

I try to move, but my feet have sunken into quicksand at the top of the hill, the mud slowly consuming me whole.

"Eve!" I call out her name as she slowly tumbles backward over the hill.

"She won't come back, Pen." I turn to look only to find Felix grasping my hand, and no matter how hard I try to jerk free, it only gets me more stuck.

And I just want to reach my sister.

"Don't make my mistakes," Eve whispers. "Find my message."

I scream out loud as her body disappears down the ledge into the crevice of despair.

I sit up straight and pant heavily, sweat droplets rolling down my back as I focus on my environment. I'm still in Felix's bed, still in his room, still here, still safe.

It was just a nightmare.

A nightmare that really happened and keeps repeating itself in my mind.

I bury my face in my hands for a moment and breathe in and out to try to collect myself.

When I've calmed down a little, I open my eyes and look around. To my surprise, Felix is right there.

But his eyes are closed.

Has he fallen asleep?

His arm is draped over my thighs, while the other is tucked underneath his head, and I can't help but admire him for a second. Much less menacing than the killer boy who literally cut off someone's finger for sending me a threat. Like this, he almost looks ... cute.

I gulp.

He said he wouldn't sleep, yet here he is …

The sunken-in eyes on his face have reduced a little as though they were hankering for a good night's rest.

I wonder if his trauma made it impossible for him to sleep.

Maybe this is why he's so harsh on everyone, even himself.

I slowly push his arm off me and crawl out of bed. I need to get out of this clammy place and reset my mind because that nightmare was too vivid and too fucked up. And why did my brain even bring Felix into it?

I shudder as I make my way across the hall, trying to find a bathroom to wash my face in that isn't connected to one of their rooms. But the light around a door in the hallway draws me in. It's the middle of the night. Who's awake now and why?

The door isn't closed all the way, so I peek through the crack.

It's Alistair, and he's busy with something at his desk, but I can't tell what.

Curiosity prods me to open the door farther.

His arms move heavily, and his eyes keep flicking back and forth between whatever is in front of him and a phone.

On it is a picture of me.

"I know you're there."

His sudden voice spooks me a little, and I clutch the door, wondering if I should make a run for it.

"You can come in," he says. "I don't mind."

I should really leave.

But with that picture on his phone, how could I?

He glances at me over his shoulder. "I won't bite."

"I doubt that," I mutter as I step farther inside.

He smiles. "I might just surprise you someday."

I approach him, my own picture luring me in as much as the idea of finding out what he's doing in the middle of the night. The picture was taken on school grounds, where I found him studying on the bench outside while I was searching for Dylan.

"Shouldn't you be asleep?" I ask.

I gaze over his shoulders as his hands meticulously move across a thin sheet of paper from left to right. The drawing is only half finished, but I clearly recognize my own face, far more beautiful than it appears in a mirror.

"Oh," I mutter, in shock.

Alistair places the pencil down on his desk. "I can't help it." His eyes remain glued to the paper. "Images keep flooding my mind, and I can't sleep if I don't put them down."

"You drew me," I mutter.

"Is that weird?"

It takes me a while to respond because I'm stunned. Not sure if it's because I'm scared or if I'm in awe at his level of detail because, dammit, it's almost as if he does this for a living.

"No, I'm impressed."

He turns around to look up at me. "Thanks."

I smile, but my attention is drawn to the rest of his room, which is so full of clutter I wonder how anyone could ever live like this. Worn and unworn clothes, jewelry, art, and little trinkets here and there. One small crystal egg draws my attention because I have to push the button on the side. Out pops a tiny girl in tights, dancing around and around to a cute little song.

"I got it from a high-end designer store," Alistair says, breaking the spell.

"You bought this?" I ask.

"I stole it," he responds.

Like it's the most normal thing in the world.

"But why?" I ask.

"Because I like the thrill," he says.

There's so much stuff here. He stole all of it? I'm amazed.

"So you don't intend to use any of it?" I ask.

He shakes his head.

No wonder he stole that stuff at the grocery store when I caught him in the act.

Maybe that's his thing. His vice.

My eyes suddenly land on a stack of notebooks, and I pick one up, wondering what's inside.

I sift through the pages. Inside are a ton of drawings of Dylan in all sorts of poses, both with clothes and without. Enticing and sexy, almost. The level of detail is astounding and makes goose bumps scatter on my skin. Until I get to the next page ... where I suddenly see my own face.

"Wait—" he mutters.

Too late. I can't stop flipping through the pages. It's like a movie come to life.

Image upon image of my own face and body in various poses and places. On the grass and in school, with a smile and with a seductive gaze. And even the one where he was sitting on the bench, and I asked him about Dylan.

The photo he took with his phone.

This is what it was for?

My heart comes to a stop the moment I see myself naked on the page. And the next one. And the one after that.

"You drew all of these?" I ask and I turn to look at him.

He nods. "I couldn't stop drawing you."

There's even one where I'm lying in my bed, sleeping.

The pages tremble in my hands. "You were in my room more than once, weren't you?"

There's a long pause.

"Yes."

I should've known the moment I found out he stole the diary.

He's the kind who stalks. Sneaks. Invades.

When I turn around, he's right there in front of me.

"Why?" My voice comes out in a squeaky breath.

His hand reaches for my face, and he caresses it so gently I almost fall apart. "I thought I'd found my muse already, but when you came into the picture, you invaded every corner of my mind," he says.

I glance sideways at the paper lying on his desk. A half-finished drawing of me being spit-roasted on top of a tomb by two guys, one of which is him.

I didn't realize his obsession ran this deep.

"Are you scared?"

I don't know how to respond. Whether I should be afraid or impressed.

I shake my head softly, but when the palm of his hand softens against my skin, I instinctively lean into it.

"I'm just confused. I thought you and Dylan—"

"Dylan and I will always be," he interjects as his hand snakes around the back of my neck, fingers curling through my hair. "But you ... you've unleashed something inside me that I can't ignore."

Suddenly, he smashes his lips on mine, and I don't know how to react.

With my eyes wide open, I let him kiss me, his hot lips roaming my mouth like he's wanted to do this for ages and never had the chance.

It's as if all time has stopped, and all that's left is us, these drawings, and his obsession over me. He's pouring everything he has into this one kiss, and it makes my whole body turn to mush in his hands.

But I still push him away. "What if they see us?"

"Then let them." He hovers so close I can taste his breath. "They're not the only ones who can have you. You belong to all of us."

As he leans in to kiss me again, my eyes land on the diary lying right next to the drawing he made of me in the cemetery. My nightmare immediately flashes through the front of my mind again, and I push past him to grab it.

"We haven't touched it since the posters, I swear," he says, following me.

"I just ... there must be something inside that I've missed."

I sift through the pages again, turning it upside down and inside out, pondering like crazy. At the end is a soft piece of ripped paper at the seam, barely noticeable. Could more than one of the pages have been ripped out?

"Where is this page?" I ask.

"I don't know," Ali replies. "It wasn't us."

I narrow my eyes at him.

"Believe me," he says, and he grabs my hand to press a kiss on top. "I would hurt anyone who'd try to harm you like that."

I swallow. Maybe he's right. Maybe they didn't do it.

But no one else touched it, which means the paper was already ripped out before it got into my possession.

Could it still be in her old room?

My eyes widen.

"The fire," I mutter.

And I immediately run off to the door, clutching the diary tight.

"Where are you going?" Ali asks, catching up with me.

My lips part but pause midway.

If I tell him the truth, he'll stop me.

"Felix expects me back," I lie as he grabs the door. "I was just going to go to the bathroom, that's it."

His eyes narrow. "You sure that's the truth?" He leans in with a wicked smirk on his face. "Or are you just trying to run away from me?"

A blush creeps onto my cheeks because his kisses are definitely seared into my mind. But I have to stop myself from thinking about that. More important things are on my mind.

"I need to sleep," I say. "They were very clear about that."

He frowns and points at his own comfy-looking bed. "You can sleep here with me."

"If Felix wakes up and finds me missing, he won't take it well," I point out.

Ali takes in a deep breath and sighs. "All right, if you insist." But before I can run off, he grabs my arm and slams his lips on mine again, the kiss making my head spin. When his lips slowly unlatch, butterflies fill my body. "So you'll remember me."

Don't fall.

Fuck.

No wonder my sister wrote that in her diary.

It wasn't just some rambling ... it was a warning.

And I didn't take it to heart.

I swallow and nod at Ali, after which he releases me.

"Good night, Penelope," he says as I make my way down the hall.

When I glimpse over my shoulder, his door closes, and I run back to Felix's room only to sneak inside and grab my bag. Luckily, he's still sleeping. I walk toward the nearest stack of clean clothes in his closet and steal some pants and a jacket. Then I grasp a pair of sneakers that are just the right size, so I'm fully dressed and ready to head outside.

There is only one place on my mind, and I need to be well-dressed and prepared for the worst.

I can't wait until Felix and Dylan wake up to help me. What if they don't want to? Besides, they might not even let me leave. And if I don't do this now, the evidence might be gone tomorrow.

Whoever lit that fire in my sister's room had a reason, a purpose ... a target.

Me.

Which means they're trying to fucking hide something.

And I'm going to find out what.

55

PENELOPE

The moon lights my path as I make my way back to the sorority, knowing full well I'm not welcome there. But I need to know why they set fire to her old room.

I shiver from the cold and quicken my pace, hoping my muscles will keep me warm enough until I get there. I yawn, still tired from the lack of sleep, but if I wait until morning, the evidence might be gone, and I can't risk it.

When I'm finally at the building, I look up. All the lights are off, and it looks like a ghost house. Definitely no one inside. They must've all accepted the dean's offer and stayed at a hotel.

Guess they won't know I was here.

I locate the fire escape at the back of the building and jump up to grab the lowest bar. It costs all my energy to pull myself up to the second bar and latch on with my feet. But I finally manage to make it up the stairs to the second floor, where her window is.

I move along the balconies and crank open the broken-down window. The glass is already shattered with a big, gaping hole in the middle. Not something that just a fire would cause.

I push it open as far as it will go and crawl inside.

The room is ash gray, covered in soot, and the air feels like it's been deprived of oxygen.

I cough and take in the view.

Bits and pieces of furniture remain. The mattress on the bed is destroyed, with only fringes and metal left. The ceiling is blackened, just as the wooden floor, and the desk in the corner is marked by flame. Near the small kitchenette, directly opposite of the window, a bright spot on the floor is followed by the deepest burns, in a way that reminds me of an explosive.

Is that where the fireworks went off?

I approach it and go to my knees to inspect it. I'm not an expert, but it definitely looks like it.

My eyes follow the floor, searching underneath every corner and even under the bed. There must be something here that explains why someone tried to burn it. They can't have thought I was sleeping in this room, right?

But the longer I search, the less everything starts to make sense.

Rustling beyond the door sets me on edge.

I stay as still as possible, listening to the sounds, and I can feel my heart beat in my throat.

The door handle twists.

I fish my knife out of my bag.

The door slams open, and two boys I recognize stare right at me. My blood begins to boil.

Kai and Nathan.

"I knew I heard something. Guess it's not a rat after all," Nathan says. "Penelope, I'm surprised to see you here."

I immediately step back, clutching my knife. "You've got some balls, Nathan."

Kai steps sideways, his face somewhat hidden behind Nathan's frame, making me gasp. A gnarly gash from top to bottom covers his eye, leaving him partially blind. His head remains covered in bandages, probably from the blow Dylan gave him with the gun.

But my God, he looks absolutely destroyed.

"You're alive," I mutter.

"Of course I am." His nostrils flare. "No thanks to you. Luckily, the clinic downtown associated with my family took me in and treated me."

"What are you doing here?" I rasp.

"You thought we would let you walk away after what you did?" Kai seethes.

"Stay back," I growl, holding my knife in front of me.

Nathan laughs. "You think that will stop us? You're alone, Penelope. No dogs to protect you here."

"Felix is right outside the building," I hiss.

"No, he's not," Nathan says. "We followed you here."

I gasp.

They've been stalking me?

Fuck.

"You were stumbling about on that fucking staircase, though," Nathan mocks.

"Why the fuck do you care? What do you want from me?" I growl.

"You and your fuck buddies scarred me for life," Kai interjects, his face contorting.

"Maybe you shouldn't have tried to take me, then," I retort. "I didn't have anything to do with your fight with the Skull & Serpent boys, but you involved me in it anyway."

"You're the reason Felix cut off my finger," Nathan spits.

"So we came for fucking payback," Kai says. "And ended up losing another one of the Phantoms along with my eye."

"That's on you. You came for a fight, and you got one," I reply.

"They didn't fucking stay away from Eve when they should have," Kai says.

"Take my sister's name out of your fucking mouth," I say through gritted teeth.

He snorts. "You don't even know what you're up against."

"Get out," I retort.

When Nathan steps even closer, I clutch the knife tighter. "No. You're here, and I want payback for my lost finger."

"Shouldn't have shoved that note under my door, then," I growl. "You knew who you were messing with. Those boys protected me. They won't hesitate to end you."

"They're the fucking cause of all of this fucked-up shit." Nathan tilts his head. "You don't even fucking know, do you?"

"Know what?"

"Why everyone wants that fucking diary."

My eyes widen.

He knows about the diary?

And who is "everyone"?

Kai laughs. "What's the point in telling her? She won't give it to us."

"Give you what? The diary?" I scoff. "Over my dead fucking body."

Kai crosses his arms. "See? Told you."

"Why the fuck do you want it anyway?" I ask.

Kai dangles a piece of singed paper in his hands. A paper I recognize all too well because it's the same color as the pages in my sister's diary. "So we can burn all of it."

They burned my sister's room ... for a single page of the diary?

Anger seeps into my bones, causing me to lash out. And I charge at both of them with my knife. "Give me that fucking page!" I scream, slicing into the air with my knife because both of them keep dodging my slashes.

"Whoa, look at this." Nathan grabs my wrist and stops me in midair. "So much fucking violence from such a small girl."

"Let go of me!" I squeal.

"No, I don't think I will," Nathan says. "You deserve pain after what you and your buddies did to us."

"I didn't do shit!" I scream. "Where did you fucking get that page?"

"Oh, this?" Kai dangles it around like a carrot. "Found it underneath her bed just minutes before you crawled in through the window."

"Give it to me," I snarl. "It doesn't belong to you."

"No, but you know what did belong to me?" He steps closer until he's right up in my face. "My fucking eyes. And you took one of them away from me."

"You have your dead buddy to thank for that," I retort. "He provoked Dylan by speaking about my sister."

Nathan twists my arm, and Kai grabs my throat. "Don't you fucking see it? All of this fucking violence points back to you and your fucking sister. You don't even know what the fuck you're messing with."

"Then fucking tell me," I reply.

Nathan snorts. "You think we *can*? We'd be killed before we could tell even one fucking soul."

I frown. *Killed? By who?*

Kai's fingers dig into my skin. "Enough. No need to tell her anything she doesn't need to know."

Nathan leans in too, whispering into my ear. "Should've taken my warning to heart, Penelope. Now you'll follow in your sister's footsteps."

That's fucking it.

I kick Nathan in the balls and shove my head back so hard it lands right into Kai's nose, making him bleed.

"Fuck!" he groans as he grabs his nose while Nathan crumples with pain.

Not one second do I wait before I slice behind me. Right through the hem of Kai's shirt, I jam the knife straight into his belly.

"Oompf ..." He sinks to the floor as I pull back my knife.

Nathan charges at me with his fist, but I narrowly avoid it and jump him instead. I wrap my arm around his neck, holding the knife right at his throat.

"Don't fucking move," I hiss.

He swallows against the blade. "You're going to regret this, Pen. You don't know what you've gotten yourself into."

"I doubt it," I scoff, and I force him to turn around and face Kai. "Give me the fucking page, Kai. Or I swear to God, I'll kill him right in front of you."

His eyes burn with fire. I know how much they care about their fucking buddies. The houses are ride or die with their own. And there's nothing they won't do to save them.

Kai struggles to breathe as he pushes the burnt paper my way. "Fine. You wanna die?" he gurgles. "Go ahead."

Die? What the fuck is he talking about?

Kai's eyes slowly begin to roll into the back of his head. "I can't breathe ..."

"Penelope," Nathan rasps. "Let me go."

"Then choose. Follow me, or save your fucking buddy," I growl, and I push him forward, then grasp the paper off the floor.

Nathan goes to his knees in front of Kai as I run to the door. Right before I close it, he turns to look at me. "Burn it and run." I don't know why it doesn't just feel like a threat, but a warning. "Do you hear me?" he growls as I shut the door and bolt through the hallway to get away from them. "It'll destroy you!"

**

FELIX

In the dark, I lie awake. Always waiting. Always watching.

My bed is clammy. Cold and hot at the same time. Sweat rolls down my back.

The door opens.

I close my eyes and hide under the blanket.

I can't ever sleep.

Footsteps patter into the room, and my heart begins to quake.

It's coming.

Again and again.

Just like it does every night since my last birthday.

But I don't want it to.

All I want is to call out.

Leave me alone. Leave me alone.

And scream.

In the middle of the night, I sit up straight in the bed, drenched in sweat. But without the warmth to keep me comfortable.

It takes me a moment to gather my bearings as I blink rapidly.

Did I fall asleep?

That never happens, not in a million fucking years. Not without the drugs or the alcohol.

But her scent ...

I turn to look.

Penelope.

She's gone.

Frantically, I throw the blankets off and look around the room. "Penelope?"

No response.

I run to the bathroom and check there, but she's nowhere to be found.

Fuck. She's gone.

I storm out of the room and head straight for Dylan's room. She has to be there. He wanted to sleep with her so fucking badly, I just know he tore her straight from my bed.

I'm seething as I slam open his door, inviting myself into his room. "Where is she?"

Dylan's snoring half naked on his bed, and he jolts up. "Huh, what? What are you talking about?"

I throw his blanket off him to catch him in the act, but no one is in there with him.

What the ...?

"Where is Penelope?" I growl.

He frowns as he leans up. "Jesus, Felix. I thought she was with you."

"She's gone," I say, looking through his room, tearing it all apart.

"She's not here," Dylan says.

I open the bathroom door, but she's not there either. "Then where the fuck is she?"

"I don't fucking know, okay? Stop destroying my room."

"What's this fucking noise?"

I look up. Alistair's standing in the doorway with his arms folded, casually yawning.

"Penelope is gone," I tell him.

He frowns. "Huh? But she said she'd go back to your room."

My pupils dilate, and I lunge at him, grasping him by the shirt. "You took her from me?"

"No. She came to me on her own," he replies, grasping my hands. "Release me."

"Where is she?"

"She didn't want to sleep, but I told her to go back to your room. I don't know where she went after," he says. "She seemed shocked by the diary, though."

"What?" I frown. None of this makes sense.

"Apparently, a page is missing," Ali says.

My grip on his shirt loosens, and he tears away, patting himself down.

Why would she leave the fucking building when she knows those Phantom fuckers are out there?

Unless ...

"Eve's old room." I shove past him, heading out the door.

Fuck. I should've known that diary contained something important. It just wasn't in the fucking book anymore, but lingering in her old room.

Like a secret meant to stay buried.

Or found ... by a particular someone.

"What? Why would she go there?" Dylan shouts, following me through the hallways to the stairs. "The whole place burned down."

"That's where Eve kept the diary. She's looking for that missing page."

I grab a pair of clean pants from the stack near the laundry room along with some spare shoes and put them on before I head out the door.

I have to find her.

I bolt out onto the street and go straight for the sorority house, the scent of burning ashes penetrating my nostrils as I get close. The doors have been taped off and sealed shut, but I know she's in there.

I go to the back where I find a ladder that's down.

Bingo.

I jump up and climb to the top, where a window at the far end of the balcony has been pushed open, the glass shattered. I walk toward it, but when I look inside, no one's there, and the door has been left wide open.

The floor is tinged in blood. Someone was here.

Fuck. I missed her.

I race back down the stairs and rush back to the frat house. Instead of Dylan's car, I put on my helmet, grab my motorcycle from the garage, and race off the property. She has to be on the school grounds somewhere. There's no way she got away that quickly.

I drive around the campus, searching for her, ignoring anyone who calls me out for driving on my motorcycle this late at night. But I don't fucking care who wakes up from the noise. I need to fucking find Penelope.

Where is she, goddammit?

I cross the campus all the way to the forest. Near the cliff, I spot a small glimmering cell phone shining in the dark.

Penelope.

I race toward The Edge and come to a stop, then hop off my motorcycle.

She's sitting at the very ledge of the cliff, her feet dangling into the air.

Fuck.

I pull out my phone and text Ali and Dylan the location.

"Penelope ..." I tear off my helmet and put it on the seat. "What are you doing here? Why did you run off in the middle of the fucking night?"

She glances at me over her shoulder, but her solemn eyes bring a chill to my spine.

"Why didn't you fucking tell me the truth?" she rasps, her voice laced with anger and bitterness.

I frown as I step closer, confused. "What the fuck are you talking about?"

"I went to my sister's room to find remnants of her diary that she tore out." She holds up a piece of paper with Eve's handwriting on it, written in the same style as the entire diary. "You broke up with her."

56

PENELOPE

I stare down into the vast emptiness of space, wondering how deep the fall must've been. If she felt at peace with her decision. If it hurt.

"It didn't happen like that."

I take in a deep breath and turn to look at Felix. "Stop lying to me."

His gaze fixates on the piece of paper from the diary in my hands. "What's on that paper?"

I read the words out loud.

"I wasn't given a choice in the matter.

It was either do what I'm told, or quit and leave.

I cried when I said the words.

And they did nothing.

Nothing.

Nothing at all.

I begged them with my eyes, my tears to fight for me.

Instead, we broke up.

And my heart broke into a million little pieces.

303."

My teeth grind against each other as I can almost hear her scared voice pleading for help. They ignored her. Betrayed her. Made her feel worthless.

"Quit and leave? That's not—"

"Don't call my sister a liar!" I yell.

Alistair and Dylan come running out of the forest. "Oh fuck," Dylan mutters.

"Penelope? Why are you on that ledge?" Alistair asks, approaching us. "You're not planning to—"

"Why do you even care?" I bark back. "You were all there when she jumped, and you did *nothing* to stop her." I'm boiling with rage. "You're the reason she jumped. And you all lied to me!"

Alistair's eyes widen. "What?"

Dylan turns to Felix. "What is she talking about?"

"The breakup," Felix says, swallowing. "She wrote it in her diary and hid the page."

"Fuck," Dylan mutters.

"You knew, and you never told me," I say, clutching the paper tightly. "No wonder she tore it out. She was terrified you would destroy the only evidence of who caused her to jump."

"Whoa, we didn't tell her to do that," Dylan says.

"You didn't have to! She was distraught!" I yell, my tone fluctuating.

Dylan stares at me, pain seeping into his eyes.

"She pleaded with you! Begged you not to end it!" I rasp.

"It wasn't just us." Felix steps forward. "It was a mutual decision."

What?

My sister ended it?

No, that's not what this paper says.

She wouldn't do that.

"Stop lying to me!" I scream.

"It's not a lie," Dylan says. "It happened right before the bonfire."

Alistair looks at me intently, like it hurts him to even admit this. "She told us she couldn't do it anymore and that we should see other people."

"So we did," Dylan says.

"Bullshit," I growl, tears staining my eyes.

"We didn't have a choice," Felix rasps, balling his fist.

No choice? How? Why?

"But if I knew she would jump off that fucking ledge after telling us it was over, I would've forced her to stay, Penelope." His voice is laced with emotion, and it hurts to even listen.

"She begged you," I mutter.

"Not with any kind of words," Dylan replies.

"Her heart broke so badly she wanted to end her life," I say.

The air is thick with tension, and the silence only makes it more difficult.

"We should've fought for her," Alistair says after a while. "But we didn't because it's what she wanted."

"She only confirmed what we knew needed to happen," Dylan adds.

What needed to happen? What is he talking about?

"All this time, you went on a mad, fake witch hunt with me to find some bullshit bully when it was really you three."

"It wasn't fake. We didn't know she hated her decision," Dylan says. "We thought someone else drove her to do it by someone else."

"There was no one else. We searched," I growl back.

"You don't fucking know that," Felix says through gritted teeth. "Don't blame this on us, Pen."

There's more rustling, and I pull out my knife and point it right at them.

"Stay back!" I yelp.

"She's manipulating the narrative," Felix barks. "It was Eve's decision. What if she ripped out more pages with the names of her bully?"

I don't believe him.

All the fucking clues. All the people telling me those boys were trouble.

Why did I ignore it?

Felix steps closer. "Penelope, I will not allow you to chase your sister into the fucking grave. Do you hear me?"

"I'll cut you if you touch me," I growl.

His jaw tightens. "Give me a thousand cuts, and I would still hold you."

I'm momentarily stunned.

A thousand cuts?

All the pain and blood and it still wouldn't stop him from being near me?

I swallow.

They're only doing this because they get a second chance with you.

Your sister tried to warn you.

Don't let them do this to you.

Don't trust them.

I put the knife to my own throat instead as I stand and face the edge of oblivion.

Both boys stop moving.

"I swear to God, I'm gonna do it if you come closer."

"Penelope, put down the knife," Felix warns.

"Stay. Back."

But when Felix refuses to walk away, I take a step back.

A wrong one.

My foot slips on a piece of rock, and I tumble backward, shrieking.

But as I fall, a hand grips my wrist.

Felix's eyes bore into mine.

"Don't you fucking dare," he growls.

My heart races in my throat as I stare down at the abyss between my feet.

One wrong move and I splatter into a million pieces, just like my sister.

But I don't want to die.

The will to live grabs ahold of me, and I reach for the rest of the ledge, desperate to hold on to something.

"I won't let it happen again," Felix growls. "Hold on."

Alistair slides to the edge, offering his other hand as a safety net while Dylan tugs at Felix's waist to help him pull me up.

They drag me up to the cliff, where we all fall down, me on top of Felix, breathless.

Cathartic.

"Fuck, that was close," Dylan says, panting wildly.

"We did it," Alistair says between breaths.

Felix's hand rises and grabs a strand of my hair, tucking it behind my ear as the back of his hand lingers on my skin.

"You almost died," he says.

Goose bumps.

No. I can't let them do this to me too.

I crawl up from the ground and step away from them.

"Where are you going?" Felix barks.

"Away from you," I retort, walking off.

"Penelope," Dylan says. "C'mon. Let's go home together and talk it out there."

"I don't want to talk to you," I say.

"What?" Felix scrambles to his feet. "No, you're coming home with us."

"Fuck no," I retort. "You're gonna let me fucking leave. And you're gonna stay away. The end."

"Penelope ..." Alistair sighs.

"Penelope!" Felix growls, his voice thundering through the sky.

I lift my knife and jam it right into the wheel of his motorcycle.

Then I walk to Dylan's car.

"No, no, no!" he yelps.

Too late.

BANG!

The tire slowly deflates.

I glance at them over my shoulder and grit, "Leave. Me. Alone."

Felix narrows his eyes at me, but when I walk away, he doesn't follow like before.

"What are you going to do?" Dylan rasps behind me. "You can't just let her leave like that."

But no one takes another step.

Good.

It's about time they realize this won't end well for them if they do.

In fact, after the horrible misery they caused my sister, they should be happy I didn't drag them down that fucking cliff with me.

57

DYLAN

My fingers squeeze the cigarette tightly as I look around campus. I haven't seen Penelope in days, and something about that makes me antsy as fuck.

Where could she be?

I know she told us to leave her alone, and we did what she asked ... but that didn't entail her skipping out on classes.

What the fuck is she up to?

My feet tap the asphalt as I try to listen to the conversations around me, but I can't fucking focus.

"Dylan," Alistair says, bumping into me. "Hello? You there?"

"Huh, what?" I mutter.

"There's a party tonight at the Phantom house." He leans in to whisper, "Wanna fuck some shit up?"

I shrug. "No, thanks."

Alistair frowns and leans back. "Whoa. Are you serious?"

I take another drag. "Not interested."

His jaw drops. "Wow. Dylan Caruso, not interested in a party? That's a first."

I ignore him and fish out my phone to scroll through my messages until I find her.

Sex_God: Where are you?

There are dots. And then it stops. More dots. And then it stops again.

Sex_God: You have class.

More dots. Then nothing.

Sex_God: *Goddammit, Penelope, stop ignoring me.*

The messages go silent, and they infuriate me beyond anything else.

God, I normally never cared this much.

When did I start getting so fucking invested?

Just one girl managed to pull me off my axis.

"She's not answering my texts either," Alistair says.

I know she told us to leave her alone, but that didn't involve her ruining her own education.

"What the fuck is she doing?" I mutter to myself. "Hey, have you seen Felix, by any chance?"

Alistair frowns. "No, I thought you'd know. I haven't seen him in hours."

My eyes narrow. Suspicious. "He hasn't told me anything."

Ali shrugs. "I don't know. Last I saw him was at the Skull & Serpent Society. He was fixing his bike. Said he'd be busy today and told me not to bother him."

Strange because I don't recall him telling me a single thing.

Suddenly, my phone rings. A private call.

I pick up, wondering if it could be her, and she got a new phone. "Penelope?"

"You still haven't gotten rid of that girl?"

The raspy voice on the other end definitely tells me all I need to know.

"Dad ..." I grit, and I move away from the group of people we were standing with. "What do you want?"

"Since you still talk about that girl, I take it you're still in contact with her?" he asks.

"Why do you care?"

"Because someone entered the sorority house she was a part of last night and destroyed some of the evidence," he says. "And if it was her, I need to speak with her immediately."

"How do you even know it was her?" I frown.

He wasn't there, so he couldn't possibly know.

"Just because it's her sister's room doesn't—"

"I have credible sources who say they saw her entering the room with their own eyes. I'm on my way to the school now."

Credible sources? What the fuck?

"Look, I don't know where she is, and I'm not interested in helping you."

"Dylan," he warns. "Remember who you are."

Who I am. Of course, he always dangles the Caruso family name in front of my face like a fucking carrot.

But I don't need to be reminded of that.

"I have nothing to do with her. Leave me out of this."

And I click off the conversation before he can do any more damage.

***

PENELOPE

I slip into the back entrance of the school, mindful of who sees me. Anyone connected to those boys could give away my location, and seeing them is the last thing I want right now.

I just want to focus on my studies. Or at least, what's left of them.

After culling the classes that I share with Dylan, Alistair, or Felix, there weren't many left. Even the ones with Crystal and Kayla had to take the fall. But I'm sure if any of the boys see them, they'll surely ask them about me. I just can't risk Kayla and Crystal telling them where I am.

Before I know it, those boys will come and find me. Trap me in a room. Force me to yield until I can no longer run.

They've done it before, and they'll do it again.

That's just who they are.

Vicious.

Inescapable.

And I cannot let myself fall for that ever again.

I sigh out loud and move through the hallways in my hoodie,

clutching my bag tight, hiding my face underneath to make sure no one recognizes me.

But Kayla's voice still makes me turn. "Penelope?"

Fuck. Just one second was enough for her to spot me.

I turn and run off.

"Wait, Penelope!" she calls, but I can't risk it.

It's too dangerous, even for her, now that I know what those boys have done.

I glance over my shoulder to check if she's following me, but no one is there. I've shaken her off my tail. Phew.

I turn my head and walk straight into someone else.

I'm knocked back to the floor, the contents of my bag spilling out. But the person in front of me doesn't even seem to notice I've bumped into them.

A whole bunch of students have gathered like they're looking at something.

I swiftly pick up my books and try to peek between the restless feet, skittishly walking around something in the middle of the circle of people.

But when I spot a hint of blood, my fingers drop the books.

I get up and push past the people, desperate to know if my suspicions are true.

At the front, I come to an abrupt halt.

On the floor in the hallway, in the midst of a circle of people, is a body.

Cut with a thousand slices.

Eyes pulled out of its sockets.

Mouth wide open, tongue sliced off, a stump all that's left.

I gulp, and I drop to my knees.

People begin to scream.

The entire hallway swarms with people, running in and out, after realizing what they just witnessed.

But me? All I can do is stare at the nameplate on the front of the body's jacket.

Peter Young.

The same boy who was in my sister's diary.

***

Hours later

Several students who saw the body have gotten counseling and will probably need a follow-up. But it doesn't appear that anyone else saw what happened to Peter. Apparently, the body was put there when all classes were in session and the hallways were empty.

But whispers floating around talk of a snake slithering down the hallway.

And I doubt they mean the animal.

"Are you sure you saw nothing?" the police officer asks me.

I swiftly shake my head.

The police officer puts his paper away and sighs, placing a hand on my shoulder. "Look, witnessing stuff like that is tough. I know that." He tucks a note into my hand. "Give this place a call if you need someone to talk to."

He pats my shoulder and leaves. Kayla is right behind me, watching me from the sidelines, but I don't go to her. I don't dare.

If I get too close, she might die too.

The body is gone, along with the trail of blood, but I won't forget.

I saw it with my own eyes.

Those wounds ...

They weren't just inflicted by a killer.

They were my exact words.

Only one person could have done this.

It was a reckoning.

Some shuffling is audible behind me, and I flick my head in the direction of the sound. I swear I could see someone disappear into a room up ahead.

I run to it and open the door, but when I look inside, no one is there.

"Felix?" I call.

But no one answers.

"I know it was you," I say.

Still, no reply.

Did I dream it all up, or did he leave that body for me to find?

Like a message?

A gift?

A shiver runs up and down my spine.

I told him to kill for me.

And he promised to bring every one of my enemies hell.

One by one, the people who tormented me and my sister fell.

He's seen the pages, so he knows them by name.

All he needed to do was find and destroy them.

Just as he vowed he would.

And so he did.

They'll never stop.

I open the door again and exit without looking back.

I can't. I can't go back.

No matter how big the gesture.

No matter how imposing the obsession.

I have to stay away.

58

PENELOPE

A few days later

I sift through the pages of the diary, wondering if I missed something about those boys. There must be. Why else would she hide this one page?

I don't understand why Dylan, Ali, and Felix would say it was a joint decision.

Her words looked like she was desperate and distraught. Who would write these words and then still want to break up? It doesn't make any sense.

I swallow as I come across the same text.

At the bottom is a number. 303.

Why would she put this here?

Was it a mistake?

I saw it before, but I didn't think it mattered.

What if it did?

I sift through more of the pages until I get to page 303, but there doesn't appear to be anything significant on it besides a picture of her and the guys taped on top of the page, adorned with hearts and smileys.

What does it mean?

She wouldn't just put those numbers there for no reason, right?

This book wasn't just a diary. She hid that page on purpose so the guys wouldn't find it, which means it contains a message. A message she wanted *me* to find.

"What are you trying to tell me, Eve?" I mutter in the bathroom stall.

"Penelope?"

I hold my breath.

"Pen? It's me. Kayla." She knocks on my door.

I sigh and get up, closing the diary before I turn the lock.

"Hey," she says, peeking through. "Are you okay?"

I shake my head and walk out of the stall to take a much-needed drink at the sink by sticking my head under the faucet. After I've swallowed my sip, I say, "You were right about those guys. I should've stayed away, and I didn't."

"I'm sorry. I don't want to be. I just didn't want you to get hurt." She rubs my back.

"They never told me they fucked around with my sister and then broke up with her right before the bonfire."

She rubs her lips together. "I'm sorry. I didn't know they were an item too. Her death bothers you a lot, doesn't it?"

I nod at her through the mirror. "I can't stop looking through the diary, wondering what I missed. If I could ..." I rub my forehead. "If I could just talk to her and ask."

She pulls me in for a hug.

"I'm sorry, girl. I know it's been rough on you," she says. "Those guys play with everyone's heads. It's what they do. They destroy everything in their path, starting with your sister and ending with you."

I suck in a heavy breath. "I was there when she jumped."

"You couldn't have stopped her. She'd made up her mind already," she says.

"How do you know?" I ask.

She pulls me back and looks me in the eyes. "Tilda told me she heard Eve crying in the bathroom before the bonfire."

I frown. "Tilda? Tilda was there that night?"

She nods. "Not at the bonfire, but at the sorority. From what Tilda told me, it sounded like Eve just had a huge argument in the dean's office."

My pupils dilate. "Wait ... the dean's office? You're sure?"

"Tilda doesn't lie about those things. It broke her to realize she might've been one of the last ones to talk to Eve." She averts her eyes. "Before she ..."

I swallow and turn toward the mirror again, staring at myself.

At the image of my own sister's face reflecting right back at me.

303.

The numbers.

My eyes widen.

I slam the diary onto the sink and open the first page, where I placed the torn paper.

303.

"What's that?" Kayla mutters as she peeks over my shoulder. "Is that ... Eve's?"

I flip through the diary until I find the warning written on the pages. The warning I thought was meant for me.

Don't stop.

Don't look back.

Don't fall.

Run.

303.

It wasn't just a warning.

It's the fucking key.

I turn and grab Kayla's arm. "What room is the dean's office? What's the number?"

She looks distressed. "I don't know. Uh ... three? Maybe?"

"What floor?"

"Third," she says.

And it's all I need to know.

I peck Kayla on the cheek. "Thank you, thank you, thank you!"

"You're welcome, I guess?" she mutters, confused.

I shut the diary and stuff it into my bag, then run off.

"Penelope!" Kayla yells as she follows me out of the bathroom. "Where are you going?"

"I need to know something. I'll talk to you later," I holler over my shoulder. "Thank you!"

I run through the hallways of the main building, pushing past people who obviously seem pissed off that I'm butting in. But I can't wait any longer now that I know my sister left these clues in there on purpose. She wanted me to find out about her being in the dean's office that night.

But what happened in there?

What did he say to her?

Or did something else occur?

The thought of him hurting her sets me off as I rush up the stairs as fast as possible. First floor. Second floor. Third floor.

My heart is racing in my throat, and I take a moment to catch my breath before I walk toward his office. The number 303 sits on a plaque on top of the wood, drawing me in like a moth to a flame as my hand curls around the door handle.

To my surprise, it's not locked.

Maybe Dylan's father forgot the last time he was here.

I open the door and step inside. The musty air invades my nostrils as I close the door behind me and look around. Dust covers the shelves of his bookcase, and I look through them to see if I can find any reports on my sister. So far, none match her name.

I go over to his desk and sit down behind it, turning on the computer. Sweat beads roll down my back as I wait for it to start. When the home button appears, I immediately open his mailbox and search for my sister's name to see if he's had any contact with her.

But to my surprise, there are none.

Zero emails carrying her name.

This doesn't make any sense because I can see he definitely emails about his other students.

Did he delete them so no one would find any evidence?

My eyes momentarily skitter away to the notes on his desk, but they fixate on a particular small stack of papers inside a box. Because it's yellow, same color as the paper tucked underneath my door.

I grab one and feel it.

Same texture too.

On the corner of the desk lies a book with personal notes, and curiosity forces me to open it. His handwriting is all over each date, outlining all of his business for the rest of the year.

But what strikes me the most is the letters and the way they're written. The loop on the E and the curl at the bottom of the letter F ...

I fish out my phone and find the photo I took of the note shoved under my door, and my hand begins to quake.

It's the same.

The same handwriting.

The same paper. The same color. The same texture.

My heart skips a beat.

It came from here.

Did Dylan's father threaten me?

But that doesn't make any sense. He's the dean. Why would he stoop so low as to get multiple students to shove notes underneath one girl's door when he could just call her into his office and talk to her? He has all the power. He could kick me out of this school any time he wanted. I don't understand.

Suddenly, the door slams open, and I stare right into the eyes of the man whose office I've raided.

"*You,*" he asks, his voice accusatory. "What are you doing here?"

"Waiting for you," I reply.

It's part lie, part truth. Even though I hate to even look at this man, I need to know the truth.

He puts his briefcase on the table next to the door. "You broke into my office?"

"Your door was open," I retort as I get up from his seat.

"Impossible," he scoffs.

I shrug.

"You realize it's illegal to barge into my office, right?" He narrows his eyes as he takes off his coat like he's about to get busy with work. "I could expel you just for the audacity."

I cross my arms. "Is that what you threatened my sister with?"

He pauses while hanging his coat and stares me in the eyes.

"Yeah, I know about your little 'talk' right before the bonfire." I make air quotes with my fingers.

His nostrils twitch as he approaches the desk, but I'm not afraid of him or the consequences of being here. Because if even an inch of it is true, he's in deeper shit than I am.

"Tell me, what do you think it is you know?" he mutters, approaching the desk.

I grab one of the yellow papers off his desk and hold it up. "Someone pushed a note underneath my door. The same paper."

He snorts. "What does that have to do with anything? There's a ton of this kind of paper on the market."

"Your handwriting was on it."

His pupils dilate, and he leans in. "Listen here, I don't know what you've got into your head, but—"

I hold up my phone and show him the picture of the note.

He can't deny it now.

"You sent some fucking students to send me a threat."

He snorts. "Ridiculous."

"No wonder he wouldn't tell us," I snarl. "Why?"

The dean suddenly slams his fist onto the desk. "This is my office. Do you hear me? Get. Out."

I stare right back at him, determined not to budge even an inch. "No. What did you tell my sister?" I interject. "I have a right to know."

A wicked smirk forms on his face, and it's the first time I see Dylan in him. But this smile ... it's far more sinister than Dylan could ever be.

"You're just as meddlesome as she was. Always up in everyone's business where you don't belong," he seethes.

"So you admit you made Nathan put that note under my door," I growl.

"I told my son he shouldn't involve himself with the likes of you, and now look at what you've done—breaking into my office like you own the fucking place," he retorts.

"Answer me," I say.

"Or what? You gonna threaten me with that little knife of yours?"

My eyes flicker.

How? When? Where?

"Yeah, I've seen you toy around with that thing," he scoffs. "You're a child. You have no clue how dangerous that is."

"What are you talking about?" I mutter.

His eyes darken in a terrifying manner. "My son is not your fucking plaything," he grates, slamming both hands onto the desk now. "You are a threat to him. Just like your fucking sister."

My face tightens as I lean in, almost crushing my phone in my hand. "Is that why you sent that note?"

"Stay. Away. From. Him," he reiterates.

I stand up straight, unable to keep my emotions from taking over. "She jumped because of you."

His face contorts. "How dare you?"

My nostrils flare. "You made her break up with those boys, didn't you?"

He snorts. "I don't care what you call it. I told my boy he needed to quit before it got out of hand, and he didn't take my advice until it was too late."

Wait ... the dean made the boys break up with her too?

His jaw barely opens up as he grits, "I gave that girl a choice, and she didn't take it."

My eyes widen.

What?

A choice? As if dying was a fucking choice?

"You threatened her just like you threatened me," I growl. "You wanted her gone."

"She was toying with my son, messing with his heart and his head," he growls, leaning over the desk like he intends to grab me. "I allowed her to leave the school. Quietly." He pauses. "But she decided to make a fuss."

A fuss.

A fucking fuss.

That's what he reduces her suicide to.

"And if you do not stop engaging with my son, I will require you to leave as well," he warns. "Unless you want your parents to have zero children left."

My eyes widen as I step away from his desk, my heart palpitating, and I run out the door, not even once looking over my shoulder.

59

ALISTAIR

I watch the sorority girls hover near the building, waiting for the fire department to release their home. Apparently, the place has been deemed safe again, so they're just busy finalizing some paperwork as well as making sure no one actually goes into the burned-down room. Obviously, the place will need some renovation, but that's definitely not enough reason to keep a bunch of girls away from their precious things.

A girl I recognize jumps to the front of the queue, and when they're finally given the go-ahead, all the girls stumble over each other to get back into their housing like they haven't been there in ages.

Guess it's about time I visited someone.

I get up from my comfy bench and march toward the girl's sorority, but instead of going inside in the regular fashion, I slip to the backside of the building and go up a fire escape. One of them connects to a particular balcony that I frequently hop onto, and I crawl in through the window without a second thought.

A loud shriek stops me from placing my second foot on the ground.

"Jesus Christ!" Kayla looks at me like she's seen a ghost. "Alistair?"

I put my finger in front of my mouth as I put both feet onto the floor and come to a stand.

"Why didn't you just ring the doorbell?" she asks.

I raise a brow at her. "Like they'd let me in."

She makes a face. "Good point." She sighs. "What are you doing here anyway? I haven't seen Penelope here if that's who you're looking for."

I shake my head. "I actually came here to talk to you."

She frowns. "Okay, now I'm really confused."

"You're her best friend. I figured she might have told you something about why she suddenly ran off?"

She tilts her head. "Wait a minute." She points at me. "I thought she was staying at your frat house."

I rub my lips together. "She disappeared and hasn't responded to any of our texts or calls."

Her face contorts. "Oh no, that's not good." She sits down on the bed. "Oh God, what if something's happened to her?" She clutches a necklace hanging around her neck. "She must be around the school grounds somewhere, right?"

I shrug. "That's what I'm trying to figure out."

She narrows her eyes at me. "This is all because of you three boys. Always causing trouble wherever you go. First with Eve, and now with Penelope."

I avert my eyes. "Yeah, well, we kind of attract the violent ones."

"Violent?" she scoffs. "Penelope?"

"You don't know her like I do," I say, crossing my arms. "Anyway, any chance I could check the burned-down room?"

Kayla rolls her eyes. "Whatever. I'm not gonna stop you. But if someone catches you, it's your fault. Don't drag me into it." She points at the door. "It's down the hall and to the left. Can't miss it because there's tape all over it."

I nod. "Thanks." And I walk past her.

"Hey," she says, and I glance over my shoulder. "If you see Penelope again, tell her to call. I'm worried."

I nod and continue through the hall, passing by several open doors where students are putting their clothes back and rearranging their stuff like they just came from a long holiday. No one seems to notice me slipping by, which is a good thing.

I head to the room in the back with the taped-over door, but I tear it all down and go inside, closing the door behind me. The place is completely blackened, and the taste of soot lingers on my tongue.

I sit down on the bed where a new student already made her home, but to me it'll always be Eve's. But it collapses underneath me, and I struggle to even stand among the rubble.

My eye catches on an odd-looking piece of crust in the wall behind the bed, almost like a loose plate that's been pulled open and pushed back several times without anyone noticing. But the fire has singed the edges and maybe ...

My fingers hook underneath the plate, and it cracks as I pull it away, pieces of the burnt paint falling off.

Behind is a small crevice, and on the bottom lies a laminated kind of image that's survived the blaze.

I fish it out.

It's a photograph of Eve and Penelope with an adult man and woman with their hands on their shoulders.

But what makes my brows furrow is the surname on the back ...

"The Ricci family," I mutter, frowning.

That's strange.

She told us her name was Richards.

Is this picture a fabrication?

Or did Eve ... lie?

***

PENELOPE

"Here it is," my mom says as she hands me Eve's phone. "I haven't touched it since ... well, you know."

"Thanks," I say.

"What do you need it for?" she asks.

I avert my eyes. "I just need to know some things."

She clutches the front door and leans in to whisper, "You've found something, haven't you?"

I nod. "Please don't tell Dad. Not yet."

She quickly pulls me in for a hug. "Only when you're ready."

"Thank you," I reply. "I just need to know for sure first."

"Of course," she says.

"But yes, I have found the people responsible for her decision," I say as I lean back.

My mother grabs my face, and our foreheads collide for the most intimate of gazes. "Pen, give them hell."

Her words emblazon my soul. "Oh, don't fucking worry. I intend to make it hurt."

"Emilia? Who is it?" Dad calls from across the hall.

My mother pushes me back. "Go. Before he sees you. We'll talk later."

I nod and quickly run off the property right before my dad shows up.

I'm normally not the type to run like that.

I love my dad to bits, and he has a heart of gold.

But if he knew the truth ... Lord have fucking mercy on the souls of Spine Ridge U.

I go to the bus stop and hop on. I know where I'm going, but my eyes focus only on one thing.

Eve's phone. Damaged. The screen almost peeling off.

But I still managed to load up the phone with my portable battery.

The noises in the bus make it hard to concentrate, but I still go through every image, every text, every file meticulously. Something my mother didn't want to do because it was too painful to even look at it, let alone acknowledge a sliver of her still existed, like a still in time, an unreachable image, left somewhere out in the open.

My sister's phone is a gateway into her memories, and I will sift through it without stopping, even if my life depends on it.

Until I find the answer to my question.

The why.

Why she needed to end things. Why the dean wanted her gone. Why she never told them the truth.

An email, sent to herself with a picture attached on the day of her death. Just in case someone would try to empty her phone, she still left crumbs of proof scattered throughout. Because she knew I would see this one day.

That I wouldn't stop until I uncovered the truth.

The phone almost crushes in my hand.

Until I find the email she sent to the dean.

On the image included is a test with two pink lines. The same image she sent to herself for safekeeping.

I guess the saying is true ...

A picture says more than a thousand words ever could.

Just as the havoc I will wreak.

I grab my phone and call my mom. "I know the truth now. She was pregnant."

She begins to sob.

"Mom, don't cry." I swallow back my own tears. "It's okay."

There's a pause, and she sucks in a breath. "You know what I told you a long time ago?"

"The story about how you and Dad met?"

"Yes."

I gulp. "I promise, I'll make things right."

"Good," she says.

I hang up the phone and immediately contact Jeremy. "Hey. It's me. Do you have a minute?"

"Penelope? Of course. Where have you been? I haven't seen you at school. I thought you got expelled or some shit."

"Just taking a small break," I muse. "Hey, I have a question about your dad's business."

"Wait, my dad?" He snorts. "You need gas or something?"

"I'm serious."

"Okay, what do you want to know?"

"I'm going to need you to help me out here. How much does it cost to buy a couple of barrels and get them delivered?" I tuck Eve's phone into my pocket. "Asking for a friend."

***

DYLAN

That night

In the middle of the night, my door slams open and hits the wall so hard I fall out of bed with my head on the carpet.

I groan. "Fuck ... who the fuck—"

"Wake the fuck up, Dylan," Felix snarls as he pulls my pillow away from my face. Boy, that angry face of his was the last thing I wanted to see after that wet and wild dream about Penelope I just had.

"Why?" I mutter. "Why are you here?"

"Look out your goddamn window," he growls.

He nearly drags me up from the floor. I jerk free of his grip and adjust my gray sweatpants. "All right, all right, Jesus. I'm going."

Right as I take a step, Alistair walks into my room. "Have you guys seen it?"

"Seen what?" I mutter as I glance at him over my shoulder, but when I turn around again and approach the window, my jaw literally drops so hard I can almost pick it up from the floor.

The main school building ...

It's completely engulfed in flames.

60

DYLAN

We bang on everyone's doors, telling them to wake up before we head downstairs and run outside along with everyone else already awake. The fire is gigantic, swallowing the building like a gate of hell opened up underneath the ground, and the sight of it is ...

Magnificent.

Never in my life have I seen a fire this big, and for me that's a rarity.

"Wow," I mutter as we all stare at the blazing fire.

"What do we do?" Alistair mutters behind me.

"The fire department must've already been alerted," Felix says, pointing at the students near the building who gather small buckets and fill them with water from the fountain.

But each bucket they throw disappears like a droplet on a hot pan.

"C'mon," Alistair says, and he grabs my hand and tags me along. "We gotta go check if there are survivors who need help."

"I have a bad feeling about this," Felix says, but he still follows us as we head toward the fire.

The heat singes my skin, even from a distance.

Jesus Christ. How did this happen?

"Quick, fill it with water!" A fellow student shoves a bucket into my hand, staring at me. "Well, don't just stand there. Help!"

I shove the bucket into Alistair's hand and push him along. "You do it."

He reluctantly puts it into the fountain and hands it to the next in

424

line, but he continues to stare me down like he wants me to know he's suffering in silence.

"The fire department is on the way!" someone yells out.

"Has someone called the dean yet?" another person asks.

My eyes widen. "Please don't. He's gonna lose it."

The girl next to me lowers her phone. "Too late."

I groan and roll my eyes. "Oh God."

"Hello, some help, please?" Alistair barks at me, throwing me glares.

Sighing, I make my way over to him. "Fine, fine, coming."

"Felix!" Alistair yells, and he throws him a spare bucket.

"Fuck that." Felix chucks it aside. "Let it burn."

My face contorts, and I don't know whether to yell at him or laugh as he waltzes off, settles down on a ledge surrounding the fountain, and lights a smoke.

Damn that fucker. I should've known.

"Pass it on," Alistair says as he shoves a bucket full of water into my hands.

It's heavy as fuck as I push it to the next guy in line. "There you go."

"Next one!" Alistair says, shoving another one into my hands.

"Jesus, not so fast," I reply.

"What do you think we're doing? Having a pool party?" Alistair scoffs.

I splash some water at him for that comment.

"Save the fun for later!" a big burly guy growls at us while throwing more buckets onto the fire. "Bring more!"

I can hear the sirens in the distance, making me stop in my tracks.

"Listen," I say, breathing rapidly as we exchange buckets.

"The fire department," Alistair says between breaths. "Shouldn't take long now. Just keep going a little bit longer."

A car comes chasing through the gates, but I pay no attention to it as I'm far too busy shoving buckets back and forth.

"Hey, Dylan," Felix says, making me turn my head.

The bucket in my hand drops to the ground.

"Your dad's here," Felix adds, taking a drag of his smoke.

My father stares at the blazing fire with his jaw dropped. "Mother of ..." Before I know it, he has his hands all over my collar as he snarls, "Where is she?"

"What? Who?"

"The girl!" he chides. "Penelope."

I've never seen him this incensed before. "I don't know. I haven't seen her."

"She must've contacted you by now," he says.

"No. I don't know what you're talking about." I frown, clutching his hands so he'll let go. "How would you even know she'd contact me?"

"Oh please, you've been hanging out with her daily," he scoffs, pushing me away. "You should've gotten rid of her when you had the chance."

My nostrils flare. "What the fuck does Penelope have to do with any of this?"

"She's the one who lit this fucking fire!" he rages.

My eyes widen, and I don't know what to say for a moment.

That can't be true. She wouldn't fucking set the school ablaze. Would she?

Alistair puts down his bucket and comes to stand next to me.

"I don't understand ..." I mutter.

"What don't you fucking understand?" he growls. "She's responsible for destroying the school. I need to know where she is *now*."

Why would she light the school on fire? It doesn't make any sense. She wasn't mad at the school. She was mad at us for breaking up with her sister. She thought we caused her sister to jump. And I won't deny that our decision may have played a part in that.

But there is something else ...

Sirens of the fire department's arrival break through my train of thought.

"Did you talk to her?" I ask.

"She needed to go," my father says, coming eye to eye with me. "It was for your own good."

"You chased her off?" Felix snarls, marching at him. "You had no fucking right."

My father glares at him, facing him head-on. "I have *every* right. This is my university, and she put this entire fucking school as well as you three in jeopardy."

"Jeopardy?" I scoff. "Bullshit. You're basing that on your prejudice because of Eve. You don't even know if she's behind this. It's all guesswork at this point."

Alistair jumps in. "She's just a random girl. She couldn't have started this fi—"

"Random? Don't you fucking know what family she and her sister belong to?" my father interjects.

I shrug. "Yeah. Her family name is Richards."

My father leans in and sputters, "No. She's the heiress of the Ricci family."

The ... Ricci family?

My father once told me there was a Mafia family hell-bent on making the most soulless mobsters pay for their crimes by stealing their wealth and giving it to the poor.

A modern Robin Hood hunting only the rich Mafia.

My family, Felix's family, and literally everyone on the board.

And Penelope is part of it?

"Do you get it now?" he seethes.

I nod.

"That can't be it," Felix says. "She said several times her name was Penelope Richards. Even at the dinner party."

"Dean Caruso is right," Alistair intervenes, and we all look at him as he pulls a photograph out of his wallet, where both Eve and Penelope are depicted with her parents. "I found this in Eve's old room after it burned down. I just didn't know what it meant."

He flips it over, revealing the Ricci name on the back.

Fuck.

"She lied to you all," my father says. "She came here with a purpose. And now she's fucking fulfilled it."

I can't believe it.

Penelope managed to fool us all.

All of it is starting to make sense. Her fearlessness, the unhinged looks she sometimes had on her face, those knives, all the violence ... none of it scared her.

Because she'd grown up living that same truth as us.

"I've never heard of the Ricci name before," Alistair says. "What makes it so important?"

"They're enemies of literally every criminal family on the planet," I mutter. "Including ours."

"Wait, what?" Alistair's eyes widen as if he can't believe what I'm saying.

"They hate bad guys," I add.

"Wow ..." Alistair mutters. "This just got a whole lot more complicated."

"Little Pen ... so fucking deliciously evil," I say with a smirk.

My father approaches Felix who just glares at him with disdain in his eyes. "You're the ringleader," he barks. "Find her. Punish her."

***

PENELOPE

Fifteen minutes ago

I stare at the barrels standing in the basement that I broke into. It didn't take much effort, with only a single stained glass underneath some bushes to break that I could slip through, and then I was able to pull the plastic barrels inside.

The whole place is stacked to the brim with old books and notes from previous students. Information the dean probably wants to keep around.

Too fucking bad for him.

I kick over the barrels and let the contents spill out all over the notes and floor.

I fish my phone from my pocket and text my dad.

Penelope: It's done. I know the truth now.
Dad: Name.

I take a deep breath.

Penelope: Dean Caruso. Dean of Spine Ridge.
Dad: Thank you, Penelope.
Penelope: What now?
Dad: You know what we do ... Destroy.

After tucking my phone back into my pocket, I pull out the box of matches I bought at a store and immediately light one.

The fire dances in my eyes.

I can hear my mother's voice, whispering to me from the darkness.

Remember how your father and I met?

He saw me when no one else did. He helped me off the street, gave me a home, gave me love and adoration ... gave me vengeance.

Your grandma had destroyed my spirit by putting me out on the street at my most vulnerable.

So we destroyed her life ...

And burned. It. Down.

And with a smirk on my face, I throw the match on top of the oil and then jump out through the window, bolting off as the fire turns into a blaze of vengeance.

61

FELIX

Penelope ... Ricci.

Penelope "Richards" fucking lied to us.

My face darkens as I look at Dylan. "She needs to pay for what she's done." I'm fuming, overtaken by raging madness. "We're gonna find her."

After everything I did for her, all the fucking people I killed, all the bodies I piled up ... this is how she repays me?

I storm off, chucking my cigarette aside. No fucking time to waste.

"You can't be fucking serious, Felix," Alistair says as he follows in my footsteps. "You're gonna work for Dylan's dad?"

"I don't fucking care about him," Felix says. "She burned down the fucking school."

"So what?" Dylan scoffs, catching up with us. "We've burned down plenty of shit. It's just a fucking building. It'll get repaired or rebuilt."

I stop in my tracks and point my finger at him. "This isn't just about some fucking building. This is about her betrayal."

He swallows and stares me dead in the eyes. "You trust my father?"

My jaw tightens. "No. But I know where my loyalty lies."

"The board," Dylan says through gritted teeth.

"Family above all," Alistair says, rolling his eyes.

"Wait, you can't be ... no," Dylan says. "You can't turn this into a family feud. It'll be a fucking war."

I lean in closer. "I didn't do shit. She did."

"No. Fuck this. Fuck family," Dylan growls, grabbing my finger. "My father isn't telling the entire story. I just know he's hiding something."

"Yeah, well, so is she." I turn around again. "And I'm gonna find out why the fuck she'd do this."

"You don't even know if she did it," Alistair says as I march off. "It could've been anyone."

"Doubt it," I reply, headed straight for the frat house. "Only one soul alive with that much of a grudge against this school." I grab my motorcycle, which I only just got some new tires from my garage, and put on my helmet. "It's her, all right. And I'm gonna fucking find her and punish her for what she did." I kick-start the engine. "With or without you."

I race off before they try to change my mind again.

I know what I need to do.

She wants a fucking war? I'll bring it to her fucking feet.

At the gates, I come across Crystal, one of Penelope's friends, and I immediately come to a screeching halt. "Did you see her?"

She tucks a strand of hair behind her ear. "Who?"

"Penelope," I grit.

"Yeah, she just ran off down that road," she mutters, shivering in the cold of the night. "Sorry, I should've stopped her."

I quickly blast off, leaving a very frazzled Crystal clutching her nightgown in my wake.

The wind blows in my face as I drive off the school grounds while more vehicles from the fire department race to the scene. But I pay no attention to the blazing fire behind me. There's no time to lose. It's been more than just minutes since that fire started. She could be anywhere by now.

Fuck. Fuck. Fuck!

"FUCK!" I scream against my helmet.

I race down the long road leading down the mountain, checking behind every rock, every tree, every fucking twig to see if she's hiding there.

"Penelope!" I roar out loud, hoping she can hear me. "When I get my hands on you, I'm going to make you wish you'd never come to Spine Ridge!"

I zigzag down the road, narrowly avoiding a rock that's sprung loose from the mountain. Sweat rolls down my back as I try to focus with barely any light. In the middle of the night, the only guidance I have is the moonlight scattering across the road.

In the distance, I see something running through the grass, headed for the forest far beyond the road. The reflection of metallic-colored shoes flickers in the light of my motorcycle.

Penelope.

I hit the gas and go even faster, hoping to catch her before she disappears between the trees.

Behind me, fresh, barely used car tires skid across the road, and I can hear from the noise the engine makes that it's Alistair and Dylan.

But I don't have time to wait for them.

I stray from the road and drive across the grass, leaving a cleanly cut path in my wake. Right before she runs into the forest, I drive up to her, slide my bike sideways, and block her path.

"Oh no, you fucking don't."

I jump off as my bike begins to fall, and I throw myself on top of her. Together, we tumble a few feet down the slope of the mountainous area until we come to a stop in the middle of the grass with only the light of my motorcycle to illuminate the darkness on her face.

She struggles against me, fighting me off. And she loses both her shoes in the process. "Get away from me!"

We wrestle on the ground, rolling through the mud until I finally gain the upper hand and sit down on top of her.

I pin her wrists to the ground and yell, "You thought you could fucking run after what you just did?"

Teardrops stain her cheeks.

I tear off my helmet and throw it to the side, then pounce down on her again. "You burned the fucking school down!"

Her lips barely part. "Prove. It."

My nostrils flare, and I lean in. Grabbing a few strands of her hair near her neck, I take a deep whiff. "Your hair smells like gasoline. Burned." I lean back to stare into her eyes. "Just like your fucking heart."

"Fuck you." She spits in my face.

I slowly wipe off the saliva and grasp her mouth, forcefully lowering her chin. I shove my fingers inside and swipe them across her tongue. "Fucking bite," I growl. "I dare you."

The murderous look in her eyes makes me almost want to smother her in kisses.

But she ... she did something unforgivable.

When I pull my fingers out again, I pinch her cheeks together. "You know I won't let you get away with this."

"So what?" she growls. "I don't fucking care anymore."

I don't like that tone. Like she's given up.

But she isn't fucking allowed to give up until after I finish with her. "Why? Why did you do it?"

She shrugs. "You all deserved to go to hell for what you did to my sister."

"Goddammit, Pen, I already told you we didn't make her jump. Just because she broke up with us doesn't mean anything. And the school didn't have anything to do with it!" I yell back.

A wicked smirk grows on her face but quickly dissipates. "This school had *everything* to do with it. And seeing it burn is the highlight of my life."

Fuck. Dylan's right. She's just as crazy as we are.

Did I just not notice? Or has she just always hidden this side of her?

The car comes to a screeching stop behind us, and I peer over my shoulder. Dylan and Alistair jump out and run to us. And Penelope thrashes around underneath me to try to escape, but I keep her in my vise grip.

"I won't allow you to run away again," I growl.

"I'm not the fucking enemy!" she shrieks, still flailing around with her legs.

Dylan swiftly grabs one foot while Alistair grabs the other.

"Well, hello there, Pen. So nice to finally see you again," Dylan says. "Had a nice barbecue?"

She smirks gleefully. "I was taught by the best."

He gloats. "Why, thank you."

I smack him in the arm. "This ain't a fucking joke. You know what she fucking unleashed with this fire."

"Unleashed?" She scoffs. "Oh, fucking tell the world what I unleashed, Felix. Are you gonna tell them about the body you dropped in front of everyone in the school?"

Dylan frowns. "Uh ... what is she talking about, Felix?"

"Yeah, tell him, Felix," she taunts.

But she knows as well as I do why there was a dead body in that hallway. "I did what you asked. A contract is a contract. A body for a body."

"Bullshit. You just wanted to remind me that I can't fucking get away from you, just like I can't fucking get away from you now." She writhes underneath me.

I slam her down onto the ground, knocking the air out of her lungs. "I did that for *you*."

She stares at me for a moment, blinking rapidly, like she's digesting my words.

But none of them seem to land. "You think you can hide from the world, but I will expose all of you."

She fights me off again, but I grasp her hands and shove them into the grass. "You lied to us. Your last name isn't Richards. It's Ricci." I stare into her eyes. "Your family is notorious for destroying every fucking crime family they come across. And now you tried to do it to us too."

"I'd clap for you for finding out, but my hands are kind of busy right now," she muses.

My fingers squeeze her wrists. "Stop fucking around."

She raises her brow. "Why? So you can tell yourself I deserve this?" She starts to rage. "You're just like your father. He murders his wife, and you murder your girlfriends!"

How dare she? How fucking dare she bring my father and mother into this?

I plant a fist into the ground right beside her head. "My father killed my mother to protect me from her!"

Her pupils dilate, and she stops thrashing. For a moment, all we can do is stare at each other, into the void of our own making.

"What?" she mutters after a few seconds.

I didn't want to be reminded of that day.

I never do.

But she's managed to drag all my weaknesses to the surface, and that's on me.

"You have no fucking clue how much our family does for the people we love." My teeth grind together, and I tilt my head back to meet Dylan's gaze. "Tie her up."

"What?" she rasps.

Dylan nods and runs back to the car only to return with some rope we always keep in the back for emergencies such as this.

Penelope starts fighting me again. "Give it up, Pen. You knew this was coming the moment you decided to burn the place."

"Fuck you! I'm gonna scream the entire way. I don't fucking care where you take me. I'll yell until my lungs give out."

Dylan throws me a tape roll. "Thanks. Gonna need this because she won't shut up."

Tears well up in her eyes as she focuses on Dylan. "I thought you all cared about her, and you fucking drove her to her death along with your father!"

"My father?" Dylan mutters.

"He spoke with Eve the night she—"

Right then, I smash the tape over her mouth. Fuck this nonsense.

"What did she just say?"

"Doesn't matter," I say. "She's making up shit just to avoid responsibility." I turn to look at them as they tie up both her legs. "But we know the truth now. She's been trying to take our families and us down from day one."

Alistair frowns. "You really think that's why?"

My face darkens. "Bring her to the car."

Penelope moans and groans through the tape, but her words are gibberish, and I'm not gonna remove the tape to listen to what she has to say. Not until we return to our safe spot; the Skull & Serpent Society.

"Catch," Alistair says as he throws me the rope, and I tie it around her wrists.

Then we carry her to the car.

She wriggles around in our arms, but it's no use. With ease, we push her into the car's back seat, and I shut the door while Dylan and Alistair hop inside.

I fetch my helmet from the grass and haul my bike off the ground. "I'll meet you there," I yell at Dylan, who rolls his window back up, and the car speeds off.

As I jump onto my bike, hooting owls make me pause. Something about being out here during the night is ominous. Something is off, but I can't put my finger on it.

All I know is that I should've trusted my gut.

Once a rat, always a rat.

And I kick-start the engine and race off.

62

PENELOPE

I wriggle around in the ropes as best I can, but they tied them so harshly I can barely move. It's almost like they've done this before, and you know what? It wouldn't even surprise me.

I know who these boys are just as much as they now know me.

We're all part of the same crooked life, the same fucked-up story.

Only this time, they're not the ones who committed the crime. And I am damn fucking proud of it.

Still, the way Felix looked at me chilled me to the bone. I've never seen him that upset. Like he wanted to rip my heart out of my chest and stomp on it.

Or like I stomped on his.

Not that it matters. What's done is done. I can't and won't take it back.

That place can burn down for all I care. I did what I had to, to avenge my sister. But I can't let them take out their rage on me.

"Ignore the firefighters," Alistair tells Dylan.

Firefighters? So they're already putting the fire out? That's quick.

I groan loudly to capture their attention, but they ignore me.

I have to get out of here, but how? I can barely move my body except for rolling around, which is no use. And if they take me back to the society, I'll never fucking see daylight again.

Maybe I can bite through the tape. At least then, I can call for help.

I start chewing away, trying to ignore the disgusting taste of the glue that sticks the whole thing onto my face, but the material is chewy and tough to get through.

By the time I've gotten through a tiny slit, the car stops, and Dylan gets out. Within seconds, the back door opens, and my feet are hoisted out. I mumble against the tape, trying to yell. "Huuu!" Of course, I sound like a cavewoman.

Dylan throws me over his shoulder. "You get the door."

I can hear Alistair run up the steps.

Fuck.

I can't let them take me in.

I look around, hoping there's someone around to witness this, but it's the middle of the night, and everyone is either sleeping or busy with the fire.

Fuck!

"Nummm!" I groan, pushing my tongue through the tape until I create a tiny hole. "Don't do this!"

Felix's bike stops right behind us. "Dylan, wait," he says, and he gets off, puts his helmet down, and pulls the tape out of the back compartment.

"HELP!" I scream as best I can.

"Oh no, you don't," Felix growls, and he slaps an even bigger piece of tape onto my mouth.

Shit. All my effort down the drain.

They bring me up the steps and into the society house, and when the doors close behind us, my heart sinks into my shoes.

Guess escaping is off the list.

At least I got to avenge her. That's all that matters.

"Where to?" Dylan asks.

"Upstairs. My room," Felix says.

They all walk up the stairs, with Felix right behind me. Sometimes I catch a glimpse of his stone-cold eyes. And all the greediness that once shone so brightly has now been replaced with pure hatred.

I close my eyes and let out a sigh.

If I'm going to go down like this, at least I'll do so with my dignity intact.

Dylan breathes heavily as he reaches the top. "God, this isn't fucking easy when you haven't slept."

"Sleep later," Felix says. "We've got work to do."

"Work?" Alistair mutters.

Felix eyes Alistair as they march into the room. "Punishment."

Nessie, the snake, hisses at me as the boys carry me inside.

Felix flicks his fingers. "Put her on the cross."

My eyes widen.

The cross? That wooden thing I saw before?

Oh God, does he intend to use it as some sort of torture device?

I shudder as Dylan brings me to the device and sets me down, only for him to tie my legs to each end of the cross. I almost fall down, but Alistair captures my hand and pins it to the left arm of the cross while Dylan secures both my ankles. By the time they finish, I'm fully strapped in, and the ropes are gone. One trap replaced with another. Fuck.

The moment Felix pulls out a big knife, Dylan and Alistair step back.

I gulp as he approaches and lets his eyes travel over me. He zips down my coat and pushes the fabric aside, revealing my white shirt and blue shorts that I bought at a cheap store after I ran from campus.

"The damage you caused ... you thought it would go unpunished?" Felix says through gritted teeth. "Think again."

SLICE!

The shirt falls to the floor in pieces.

And even though my heart races, I keep my eyes fixated on his.

"I was finally starting to trust you," he says, "and then you ran off and betrayed us."

SLICE!

My bra splits in half and falls to the floor. His eyes slowly lower to my nipples, and I can see the muscles in his jaw tense as he swallows like he's trying to hold himself back from ravaging me.

"Felix ..." Alistair mutters.

"What?!" he barks, turning around.

"What are you doing?" Alistair asks.

"Isn't it obvious?" Felix replies, his top lip inching up into a half smile as the knife slowly creeps underneath the fabric of my shorts. "I'm going to remind her of her place."

SLICE!

Without looking, he cuts through my jeans, ripping them to shreds on one leg before slicing through the other piece. It slides off me like water, leaving me in nothing but my panties.

"But we were the ones who broke up with Eve. She has a right to be mad," Alistair says.

"Mad, yes. Burning down our fucking school? No," Felix says, turning to face me again. "That's a step too far." The cold blade against my skin makes the blood rush through my veins. "You touch the school ... you touch our fucking families' money. So now I'll fucking touch you."

RIP!

The panties slip off my body and onto the floor, and goose bumps scatter all over my skin. Two fingers immediately fondle me, and I'm having a tough time focusing.

"This was my pussy. *Mine*," he seethes, rubbing my clit over and over. "But this little fucking pussy dared to fucking destroy everything in her path. And now it's going to fucking pay."

Sweat drops roll down my back as I struggle against the restraints while he continues to rub me until I'm dizzy.

"Shouldn't we interrogate her?" Dylan asks.

"I'd rather have some fun first," Felix replies, swiveling his fingers back and forth across my slit. "See her eyes roll into the back of her head while I deny her the very thing she craves so much."

He leans in to whisper, "We may have broken up with your sister because she wanted it, but I have no intention of ever letting you go. Make no mistake, Pen. You may hate me, but you belong to me until the day you draw your last fucking breath."

His fingers dive into me, and my lips crack from the tape splayed across, desperately trying to moan.

"You thought orgasms were nice?" he grits, thrusting in and out until I'm wet as can be. "How about being denied?"

He pulls out again, leaving me hot and bothered.

Fuck. I hate it. I hate how much he knows about my body. How to make me yield.

He walks to his cabinet, only to take out what looks like a silicon rose with a nub in the middle. My eyes widen when he approaches again and turns it on right in front of me.

He licks his lips. "Your swollen clit won't stand a chance, Pen."

He presses it against my pussy, and oh my God, the pressure is just like a tongue, but it vibrates. I've never felt anything like it before, and it quickly makes me pant.

"You can already feel it building, can't you?" Felix says, narrowing his eyes.

Then he takes the rose away from my clit again, leaving me in a jumbled mess of wantonness.

With a wickedly dangerous grin on his face, he leans in to whisper, "I wanna see what you can handle."

And he pushes the rose to one of my nipples, vibrating it until it's taut, after which he covers it with his mouth, sucking then nibbling until it stings.

And I almost, almost want to moan.

Suddenly, he tears away and rips the tape off my mouth. The instant burn makes me hiss.

"Ready to fucking talk now, Pen?"

"Fuck you," I retort.

He slams his fist against the wall behind the cross, making me flinch. "Why did you do it? We let you go, just like you asked. And then you have to go and burn down the fucking school?"

"I don't owe you an explanation," I grit.

He leans in so close I can almost smell the anger seething off his lips. "That school is our legacy, our fucking heritage. And you burned it down."

A smile forms on my lips. "And it felt so, so good."

The violence in his eyes reminds me of my own when I found out what happened to my sister.

"You feel better now, huh?" he growls. "After that little tantrum?"

He's trying to egg me on, but I won't let him.

"You don't know what you've done." His fist slams into the wall again, but I'm not scared. "I should kill you."

"Do it then," I rasp.

The knife almost instantly touches my neck. "Is that a fucking dare, Pen?"

"You didn't hesitate when you let my sister die, so why stop now?" I taunt.

His nostrils flare. "You've got some nerve, begging for death."

"Pen," Alistair says, folding his arms. "This isn't you."

I laugh. "Not me? This is all me. All of it. You just didn't want to see it through your rose-colored glasses."

Dylan snorts. "Well, I am impressed, that's for sure."

"Thanks," I say with a petty voice. "That means a lot, coming from the resident pyromaniac."

His smug smile instantly dissipates. "I don't remember you being this cold."

"You didn't pay attention," I bark back.

"Jesus, put that tape back on, will you?" Dylan growls at Felix.

Felix pinches my cheeks together. "Give me one good reason not to, Pen."

"Why would I?" I mutter through clenched teeth. "When you never once told me the fucking truth about my sister?"

"Hey, we didn't intentionally keep anything from you." Dylan shrugs. "We just neglected to tell."

"You destroyed her life!" I shriek.

"It was a mutual decision," Dylan says.

"She didn't want to. Your father—"

"Enough." Felix suddenly slaps the tape right back onto my mouth again. "I don't want to listen to your lies."

"My father what?" Dylan scoffs.

I muffle out more noises, but they all fall on deaf ears.

"She's just trying to mess with your head," Felix says.

He raises his brow. "If you say so."

"She called you a pyromaniac."

"It's true, though," Alistair chimes in. When we both glare at him, he adds, "What? He likes fire."

Dylan sighs. "I do, though." His eyes lock in on mine, and I don't look away because I want him to know I believe it in my heart. "But pyromaniac makes it sound so ... evil."

He *is* evil.

All three of them are.

And they deserve hell for what they've done to her.

Felix toys with his knife, sliding it down my cheek, following the trail of a single sweat drop. "You're part of that Ricci family, which means someone put you up to this. And if you won't tell us willingly ... I guess we'll have to force it out of you, Pen."

"If we're gonna do this, might as well do it good," Dylan growls, and he walks to the cabinet to pull out a candle. "Lemme work my magic." He pushes Felix aside and lights the candle, and my eyes follow the flickering flame. "Ever been burned, little slut?"

I vigorously shake my head, desperate to avoid the fire as it licks my skin.

"Make it worth my time," Felix growls at Dylan.

"Oh, don't fucking worry, I'll definitely light up the room." A dangerous fire burns in his eyes. "With her screams."

The candle's wax begins to melt, and he tips it over right above my breast. When the hot wax lands on my skin, I swallow the shriek.

God, it's so fucking hot.

Yet the moment it lands on my skin, it instantly cools and turns to a solid again.

"Fuck ... do it again," Alistair says, biting his lip as he watches Dylan play with me.

Even after everything that's happened between us, they still want to fuck with me. Still want to possess me.

When I scream, Felix only laughs. "Scream all you want, Penelope. No one will hear."

I struggle against the restraints and mutter some words against the tape, but of course none of it is audible.

Dylan merely smirks. "Oh, you want more? Well, all you had to do was ask." He hovers the candle over my other breast, and my pupils dilate. "You wanted fire? Then feel the fucking burn."

63

DYLAN

I drip even more onto this nipple than the other, leaving her squirming against the cross.

God, I love watching her writhe.

Nothing on this earth can satisfy me as much as this.

Call me a pyromaniac, I don't care. The fire makes my fucking soul sing. And if I can use it to both punish and pleasure the woman I want more than anything but can't have, then so be it.

"This would be so much better if she'd be writhing with desire too," Alistair jokes as he sits down in the chair next to the door with a pencil and paper.

Our eyes connect, and I know what he's thinking. I wink, and he grins in response. I love how he reacts to everything I do to her with an unmatched hunger. And I'll pretty much do anything and everything to see more of it. I've always been a free spirit, but I'd let them tie me down.

Alistair pulls his zipper and passionately draws something on the paper. Probably Penelope, strapped to this cross, at the mercy of his friends.

But as he draws, he starts to touch himself. And fuck me, he's already rigid, and the glistening tip makes me swallow. Hard.

I turn to look at Penelope, who's closed her eyes, but her flushed cheeks give away she was looking at him just like I was. I pour more wax on her chest to wake her up. She shrieks, and her eyes burst open as it runs all the way down to her belly button.

"Don't look away, Pen," I say, tilting her chin up. "I can see you gawk at him. You want him, don't you?"

She frowns and jerks her head away.

"You can deny it all you want, but we both know it's the truth." I swipe a finger along her slit, dipping my finger inside her wetness. It shouldn't feel this fucking nice to punish the one girl I want to fuck so badly it almost hurts.

But I can hold myself back. The question is, can she?

A grin forms on my lips. "You hate that you still want us."

She's biting her tongue, but her legs can barely handle it as I thrust in and out. Her whole body quakes.

"You're so wet and needy. Even when you despise us." I lean in to whisper, "But only good sluts get to come."

I can feel her throbbing, so I pull out right before she explodes.

An exasperated sigh comes out through her nose.

Goddamn, I didn't think it'd be this sexy to withhold her orgasm.

But we're not here for pleasure. We're here to find out the truth about why she lit the university on fire.

I hold the candle closer to her slit. "Now are you going to talk?"

She shivers and shakes her head, sweat rolling down her body at the thought of being burned.

"No? Maybe a waxed pussy will change your mind."

I drip some of it onto her sensitive parts, and the sizzle makes her hiss and jolt against the restraints. My bulge tents in my pants, but I ignore it because I don't want to get distracted from my goal.

Alistair moans in the back, juggling between the drawing and his own gratification. "Don't stop."

"Our boy wants more, Pen ... let's give it to him." I pour on more until even her pussy can't separate the pain from the pleasure anymore.

I set down the candle and rub her with two fingers, mixing the hot wax with her wetness. "You're just as fucked up as we are," I mutter, lost in her eyes. "We could've been so fucking perfect together. If only you hadn't tried to destroy it."

I pound her with my waxed-up fingers, and she gasps when I drip more wax onto her nipples.

"Fuck," Alistair groans in the back, the pencil dropping down onto the drawing before he shoots cum all over the paper. The paper lowers, revealing Penelope, naked, covered in wax, my tongue rolling across her skin, splashes of cum all over.

Exquisite.

I glance at Alistair over my shoulder, grinning with delight. "So quickly? You horny bastard."

***

ALISTAIR

I didn't expect to get turned on so easily, so desperately.

But I guess even I have my limits.

And when Dylan plays around, things get out of hand quick.

I guess nothing gets me riled up as badly as watching the two people I want most of all being kinky together.

I roll the pencil through my semen until it's coated.

I shouldn't have liked it as much as I did. But I guess we're all fucking sadists in this room.

She's on that cross for a reason, and it isn't just to play with her.

I get up, letting the paper drop to the floor as I zip back up. "My turn."

Dylan steps away while biting his lip as I approach with the pencil. "What was that you said about Dylan's father?" I slide my own slickness across the pencil. "Maybe I need to jostle your memory."

I shove the pencil into her, and she gasps as I roll it around inside, coating her insides with my juices. And I look into her eyes, taking in all the regret, all the hatred, all the yearning, every emotion she has left. Like a drunk desperate for a last drop before the bottle is poured empty.

"If I can't have you anymore … at least my fucking cum will be there for eternity," I rasp, and I pinch her waxed nipples so hard she screams.

I don't want to hurt her, but after what she did, she leaves me no choice.

"Fuck that, we're not letting her go," Felix growls, butting in only to shove the handle of the knife inside me along with that pencil. "If we can't have her, no one can."

"Aren't we supposed to interrogate her, though?" Dylan casually asks.

"She'll only lie," Felix says through gritted teeth while staring Penelope in the eyes.

"I know, but … why would she keep mentioning my dad?"

"Because he's the one who told us to break up with both her and Eve!" Felix barks.

Penelope snorts, but the snort quickly turns into muffled laughter, so much so that all of us are now looking at her like she's gone mad.

I don't like this one bit.

I pull the knife and the pencil out of her.

"What are you laughing at?" Felix snarls, grasping her face with one hand.

"Okay, I want to know what she has to say. Now." Dylan rips off the tape and chucks it out the window.

But all she can do is laugh out loud.

"What's so fucking funny?" Dylan asks.

"You all think someone put me up to this, but it's just me. It was all me," she says between laughs. "And you don't even realize it's all your fucking father's fault."

Dylan frowns. "My father? No, he has nothing to do with whatever the fuck you're doing. He literally came to help the firefighters."

Her face changes. Stoically.

Like she's suddenly given up and thought *Oh what the hell … screw it.*

"He spoke to Eve just before the bonfire and told her to end things or she'd be kicked out of the school," she replies in a haze.

Dean Caruso spoke with Eve before she died?

"What?" Dylan mutters as he steps away while staring at Penelope with a blank face. He shakes his head. "No, that doesn't make any sense. Why would he—"

"Because she was fucking pregnant!"

64

DYLAN

I'm so dazed by what she says, I can barely even stand straight.

Eve ... pregnant?

I hit a table while backtracking and almost fall but manage to catch myself on the wood, clutching the table like my life depends on it. "No, that can't be it."

"She was *what*?" Felix growls at her.

The dead-serious look in her eyes gives me chills. "She. Was. Pregnant." She stares at me. "With *your* baby."

My heart has never beaten this fast.

Not even when killing people.

"A baby?" Alistair mutters. "Wait, how do you know? And whose baby? Dylan's?"

"No ..." I whisper in shock.

"Don't act like you didn't know," she says, her face stone-cold, despite the fact that she's the one hanging on the cross as our plaything.

"We didn't," Alistair says.

She frowns. "Why else would you take his fucking side?"

"Whose side?" Alistair asks.

"His father's!" she shrieks.

Everyone's looking at me now, and all the blood drains from my skin.

A baby? But how?

Fuck, I gotta sit down.

My body instantly gravitates toward the nearest chair.

"Eve contacted your father and asked him for help," Penelope tells me.

But my ears are ringing. All I hear is pregnant ... Is it mine?

"Fuck no, you're lying," Felix says, and he turns to look at me. "Don't let her poison your mind."

"It's the fucking truth!" she shrieks. "Swear on her fucking grave."

Felix grasps her throat. "Don't you fucking dare."

"Don't believe me?" she says with a squeaky voice as his fingers dig into her skin. "Look at her phone."

Alistair and I immediately home in on her stuff that we brought back with us when we captured her on the road down the mountain. And we both jump at it like sharks going for blood.

"Fuck, let me have it," I growl at him.

"I want to see too," Alistair says.

We fight over it like crazed animals until Felix marches over to jab us both in the waist and steals the phone from our hands. "Give it to me."

He immediately opens it up while we look over his shoulder along with him.

"The photos. Three months ago," Penelope says.

He scrolls and scrolls until we find the one picture that says a million words.

A stick with two pink lines.

Fuck.

So it's true.

She was pregnant.

Felix clamps the phone so harshly the screen fractures.

"Are you sure this is hers?" he asks without even looking at Penelope.

"She had no way out. Dylan's father didn't want her pregnant. So he gave her a choice. Leave or he'd destroy her and our family."

"How do you know my father is involved?" I ask, my voice cracking.

"There's an email. He deleted it on his side. I checked his office. But she kept the email," Penelope replies, swallowing.

Felix vigorously scrolls through the phone until he finds what he's looking for.

Eve's email with my father, where he literally threatens her with complete ruin along with her entire family if she doesn't abort it or disappear entirely.

Fuck.

I feel sick.

"That's why he made her jump," Penelope adds. "To erase the evidence."

"But the phone survived," Alistair mutters.

"And you're sure that baby was Dylan's?" Felix asks through gritted teeth, still bent over the phone like he's memorizing every inch of the email and photo.

"It could be ... all of us," Alistair mutters, and our eyes connect in a moment of shared misery.

God.

The one girl who got away ... was pregnant.

And one of us lost their baby.

"Yes," Penelope replies.

Alistair sinks into a chair, hands between his legs, head dropping between his shoulders like he always does when he feels defeated.

Felix places the phone on the table and closes his eyes, rubbing his forehead. The silence in the room is overwhelming. "Let her down."

"What?" I gasp.

"Release her," he rasps, his fingers digging into his skin so deeply I'm almost starting to worry he might break his own skull.

"But what about the punishment?" I ask. "The fire?"

"I only set that goddamn fire because your father made her fucking jump to her death!" Penelope screams.

I gaze into her eyes, and my face contorts.

If that's true ... my father is the one person we've been looking for all this time.

Her eyes fill with tears. "She didn't want to break up. He *made* her."

My father ... responsible for Eve's death?

"Oh God," I mutter, my heart aching.

"And you did *nothing*," Penelope says, tears rolling down her cheeks. "She pleaded with you with her eyes. Begged you to save her."

"Why didn't she tell us?" I mutter.

"You think your father would allow her to create that kind of rift?" Felix interjects, still in his own thoughts.

"She was terrified of him. She didn't see any other way out," Penelope says through gritted teeth. "And when she died, your father tried to cover up his involvement by erasing everything ... and everyone. Including me."

"Wait but the note—" Alistair begins.

But Penelope interrupts him. "Nathan worked for Dylan's father. He burned down Eve's old room to burn any evidence left."

Felix's eyes almost glow with violence. "Nathan was there in the fucking Alpha Psi house?"

Penelope nods. "So was Kai. That's how I got the torn page."

"Why didn't you tell us?" His hand forms a fist, and his eyes almost bulge out of his skull with rage. "I would've stabbed them both and cut out their fucking hearts."

"Because I don't fucking trust you anymore," she says, tears forming in her eyes. "Eve is dead because of all of you."

"She jumped because she didn't want a life without us," Alistair ruminates. "And we abandoned her. Because he demanded we did."

The look in Penelope's eyes kills me.

I immediately march over to her, take my knife from my pocket, and slice through the restraints, releasing her from the cross. She falls down, and I catch her in my arms.

"I'm sorry. I'm so sorry," I mutter, clutching her. "We should've listened."

She cries into my shoulder, wailing like never before, and the sound breaks my heart into a million pieces.

"I said I wouldn't hurt you again," Alistair says. "I lied. And I'm sorry." He sinks off the chair and onto the floor, kneeling in front of her on all fours like he's begging her for forgiveness.

She pulls away from my embrace and just looks at him, her lips slowly parting as if she doesn't know how to respond.

Guilt floods my body as I drop to my knees in front of her just as Alistair.

Humiliated.

All by our own doing.

"Get up," Felix growls.

But I don't even fucking care to look at him, let alone listen.

All I care about is the girl whose heart we broke by not telling her the truth about Eve and us, by letting things escalate so far she felt she had to burn the entire school down for vengeance.

The kind of revenge I can only dream of.

God, she's magnificent.

A fiery fucking goddess I want to worship.

"What are you doing?" she murmurs as I grab her foot and kiss it.

"Apologizing."

"But there's no use. It won't undo what happened. It won't bring Eve back."

"I know. And no amount of groveling will ever fix that." I gaze up into her eyes. "But I don't want to lose you too."

Her pupils dilate, almost as if she's shocked I'd admit that.

But I'm not scared to admit she owns my very fucking soul.

"Get. Up." Felix's dark, commanding voice makes my skin crawl, but I ignore him.

"No," Alistair replies. "We made a fucking mistake bringing her here and tying her to that cross."

Some rummaging goes on in the back, but I pay no attention to it. Felix is always busy, always trying to rid himself of his feelings, but I refuse to run from them.

"Did you forget who told us to punish her?" Felix says.

I know it was my fucking father. But we made the conscious choice to obey.

"Can you forgive me?" I mutter as I look up at Penelope, who's gawking at us like she's confused about what to do.

"Don't beg her for forgiveness," Felix growls, stepping forward.

And I'm almost offended he'd even suggest we shouldn't, until he opens his mouth again.

"You don't deserve it."

We both look at him over our shoulders, and he's even gotten Penelope's attention.

His fist balls. "Earn it."

He marches at us and literally lifts us both from the ground with ease, setting us on our feet. He grabs my hand and shoves a bunch of smaller knives into my hand, and a gun and a giant knife into Alistair's, then straps himself in with a bunch of weapons I've only ever seen once; when there was a giant turf war between the Phantoms and the Skull & Serpent Society.

He steps between us, focusing solely on Penelope as he grabs her face with one hand, caressing her cheek with his thumb. "Tell me what you need. Be specific."

Her pupils dilate, and her lips part, almost as if she recognizes those words.

But I don't remember him ever saying that.

Did they have a personal conversation I'm not aware of?

She swallows as they exchange looks. "Hurt him. Scar him where it hurts the most."

His face darkens in a way that only happens when he's on a murder spree, and he grabs her hand and slowly brings it to his lips, pressing a kiss on top as though he's sealing a deal.

"I'll bring him fucking hell for you."

65

FELIX

I gather all my tools and weapons, stuffing them into a bag before I throw it over my shoulder.

"Wait, what's going on?" Dylan asks as I put on my protective vest.

"War," I growl back, grabbing my sharpest knives from the toolkit I keep hidden in my room.

I don't even care to look at those two while they're groveling.

They don't deserve even an inch of her fucking forgiveness, let alone the air she breathes.

Because of her, we now know the truth about what really happened to Eve.

And I'm not going to let this go.

That baby ... it could have been mine. Or Dylan's. Or Alistair's.

But we'll never fucking know.

It's dead because of the decisions of one fucked-up man.

I'm going to fucking annihilate him.

With determination, I tuck some more knives into my belt and pocket. This is how I will repent.

"A war against who?" Alistair asks.

"Oh, fuck my life," Dylan mutters, shaking his head. "You're going after—"

"The dean," I reply, adjusting my belt buckle so all my knives are in the right place, ready to be used when I need them. And I'm gonna need *all* of them.

When I turn around, Dylan's all up in my face.

"Hold up. You don't actually want to go at him, do you?" He holds up his hands. "C'mon, Felix. We need to talk about this first."

"Talking is for guilty people to avoid responsibility," I reply. "I made that mistake once. I'm not making it again."

He frowns. "When have you ever thought things through?"

But I ignore him and focus on getting all my gear ready. I'll be nice and save some spares for Ali and Dylan too, in case they finally decide to man the fuck up.

"Felix!" Dylan tries to catch my attention. But when he blocks my way, he's got it. "He's my father."

"And he killed Eve along with her baby."

He's staring at me like I'm making the gravest mistake of my life. But there's no way back for me.

"I made a fucking vow to Penelope, and I intend to keep it, even if it costs me my own fucking life. Because *that* is what she deserves."

Penelope's eyes widen as I say the words, but I'm not ashamed.

"He's right, D," Ali says, glancing at both of us. "Your father ... he ruined literal lives."

"Felix." Dylan's right up in my face. "Don't do this. You're my friend. Don't make me your enemy."

"Then choose," I growl back, leaning my forehead against his. "Because you can either stand in my way and get crushed ... or help me bring that motherfucker down."

His teeth grind as we engage in a death stare.

But eventually, he caves.

His eyes avert, and he punches the air, grunting out loud.

Behind him, Penelope has gathered a big white shirt and put it on, covering up her private parts. "Wait, are you really going to ...?"

I tuck my last knife into my pocket and say, "I'm gonna fucking kill the son of a bitch."

I grab my collection of knives and chuck some at Alistair. "You're gonna help me."

He briefly exchanges looks with Dylan but still tucks them into his pocket, nodding.

I look at Dylan and hold out a knife to him. "Are you in?"

He stampedes around the room, looking pissed as hell, but eventually, he gives in and snatches the knife out of my hand. "This is a mistake. It has to be. There's no way—"

"Your father would rather destroy your lives and kill Eve and her baby than let you be a dad," Penelope interjects as she steps forward.

Dylan swallows his pride. "You're asking me to hurt my own damn father."

"I'm not asking anything," Penelope says, and she grabs one of my spare knives and pushes it into his hand. "I'm telling you to."

She holds Dylan's hand like it's her last lifeline, and she tiptoes around him, leaning up to whisper into his ear. I don't know what she says, but his eyes light up like she just sparked an inferno.

And fuck me, it's been too long since I last saw that side of him.

He twirls the knives around and tucks them into his belt with the same confidence he usually sports. All the conflict seems to have disappeared from his face as he steps forward and stares me directly in the eyes. "I'm ready."

I nod and march to the door together with them, but as Alistair and Dylan exit, Penelope stops me. Her hand latches around my wrist, forcing me to stay. I can't rip away. Not even when I want nothing more than to taste his blood on my lips and rip his heart out of his chest.

But her ...

Her needs are more important.

"Wait," she murmurs, and I oblige.

Not because I should but because I need to. For her.

She swallows as I look at her, my chest filling with discomfort, making it hard to breathe. I know I've hurt her. I put my trust in the wrong person, and it damaged her and her sister beyond repair.

But I would fucking die today to give her back even a sliver of her honor.

"Take me with you."

Her words slice through marrow and bone.

Fuck.

Out of all the things she could've asked from me, I did not expect this.

"No," I reply.

"It wasn't a request," she says as she puts on a pair of oversized pants along with some boots that don't even fit her. "I'm coming with you."

My nostrils flare. Even though I hate having to disappoint her, it's for her own good. "It's too dangerous."

"I don't care. I need to be there," she says, her eyes almost burning a hole into my head. "You owe it to me."

Fuck.

How could I ever say no when she pulls that?

My teeth grind together.

"I'm not asking," she says, and she turns around and grabs her bag, stuffing in more knives from my spare collection. Her bag is so full when she returns that it can barely stay closed.

It's almost cute.

I lean in and say, "Let me do this for you."

"You can do it while I watch," she replies, propping her hands against her side. "I'm coming too."

A lopsided grin forms on my lips. "I won't be able to stop you, will I?"

She flicks one of the knives open and holds it out like she's going to cut me. "Try. I fucking dare you."

I place my hand on her head and scrunch up her hair until it's all messed up. "I won't, little one."

"Little one?" She blushes and shakes her head, freeing herself from my grip.

My brow rises. "What? You prefer slut?"

Now she's blushing even harder.

I tilt her chin up. "Our agreement ends after today."

Suddenly, the door opposite my room opens up. And the person walking out of the bathroom is one of the few who could make my rage go from zero to a hundred.

Especially when only a towel covers her body.

And her arm is draped across Jason's waist.

My nostrils and eyes twitch at the same time. "Lana?"

Her eyes connect with mine as panic slowly fills hers. "Oh ..."

"What the fuck—"

I immediately charge at Jason, but she protects him with her body, stopping me from grabbing him by the throat.

"Whoa, chill the fuck out, Felix."

"Why the hell are you here?" I yell. "Naked?" My eyes settle on his, and I'm about ready to tear his dick off. "Are you fucking my sister?"

She plants a flat hand on my chest. "Listen here, asshole. I'm allowed to fuck whoever I want."

"He's from my fucking society," I retort, getting right up in his face. "You've got some nerve, Foley."

He holds up his hands. "I don't wanna get between you and your sis."

"Should've thought of that before you drilled your cock into her!" I shove him.

Lana gets between us and pushes me back. "Felix, stop! It was my choice to come here!"

"How many times?" I ask.

"None of your fucking business," she replies.

"I'm your brother. It is my fucking business to protect you," I retort.

She steps forward while Jason clutches the door like he's about to smack it in my face if I get too close.

But Lana's soft hand on my shoulder distracts me. "Felix, I appreciate that you care about my well-being. But I'm a grown-ass adult just like you."

"You're eighteen," I say through gritted teeth, then glare at Jason for even daring to touch her. "She's barely—"

CRASH!

I pull Penelope close as we duck to the floor. Something happened in my room, but I can't look as smoke fills both the room and the hallway.

Lana coughs and crawls to Jason. "Jason!"

"I'm here," he mutters.

"For now," I retort.

"Not now!" Lana barks back.

Fine. I'll use the rage for whoever the fuck just dared to attack me in my own home. I turn around toward my own room and look up at the window. Something broke through it. A metal ball, which is still spitting smoke.

But the worst part is that Nessie's glass cage has shattered, and she's crawling across the floor like it's no one's business. No one touches my fucking snake.

Enraged, I slam my fist onto the floor. "Fuck!" I help Penelope off the floor. "Someone's after us."

Penelope pulls herself from my arms. "No, that can't be right. They wouldn't attack—"

Another bomb flies in through the bathroom window, and Lana and Jason duck for cover.

"Fuck, get out, get out!" I yell, grasping everyone and running through the hallway as fast as I can.

"What's happening?" Lana asks as we walk into the main hall, which is completely covered in smoke.

"Dylan!" I scream through the house.

"Down here!" he yells. "I was in the bathroom. What's going on?"

More bombs go off, and shards of glass fly through the building. Gunshots fill the house. People scream and run for cover. Alistair's closest to the door. The blast flings his body against a big support beam, and he groans in pain.

Who the fuck would come for us in here?

Unless ...

"Dylan!" I yell. "Open the fucking front door."

"What?" he yells back. "Are you insane?"

"Do it!"

But before he can even take one step toward the front door, it's blasted open, knocking him to the floor again.

As I clutch the staircase, my jaw drops when I see who's in the door opening.

A chiseled bearded, gray-haired motherfucker with tattoos snaking up from his hand all the way into his trench coat steps inside the house with a gun pointed right at us.

An ominous voice booms through the hallways. "Get your hands off my fucking daughter."

66

PENELOPE

My eyes widen at the sight of the man bursting into the Skull & Serpent Society.

"D-Dad?" I mutter, shaking in my boots.

Oh boy.

Felix, Lana, and Jason turn to look at me like I know what's going on.

"Wait, that's your fucking dad?" Lana's eyes almost bulge out of her skull.

Felix grabs me by the shoulder. "Did you call him here?"

BANG! BANG! BANG!

Three concise shots push us apart as Felix ducks for cover behind a pillar. All three shots are buried deep into the stone.

Fuck.

"Penelope! I'm coming for you," my father growls, and he turns his head only briefly. "Engage."

More men pour into the building.

"Fight back!" Dylan yells from down below.

And out of nowhere, the boys from the Skull & Serpent Society start attacking the men my father brought.

All the doors open up, and knives and weapons are thrown around the room.

"Stop!" I yell, but no one can hear me through the onslaught of guns going off one after the other.

"Penelope, answer me!" Felix roars as he chucks one of his knives at one of my father's men, who's charging Dylan with a machete.

But I'm too occupied trying to find my dad in the haze of blazing guns and smoke bombs going off.

Felix suddenly grabs both my arms and shakes me. "Tell me!"

"No. I just told him I knew who caused my sister's death. And I gave him a name ..." My eyes widen, and I gasp out loud. "Caruso."

Felix's eyes immediately flick down to where most of the fighting is happening. Alistair and Dylan are both fighting off my father's guards, punching and cutting their way through people like their life depends on it. But most of the men only seem focused on one thing.

"Dylan," we both mutter in sync.

I run down the steps of the stairs, but Felix just jumps over the railing, his boots sidestepping the stone pillar for a safer landing. And as I come down the last step of the stairs, he rams his knife into one of my father's guards.

Fuck. Fuck. Fuck!

I have to do something.

BANG!

I duck for cover behind the pillar. A gunshot misses me by just an inch, but my hair is still singed.

When I take a peek at who shot, I notice more people coming in through a side entrance. But they're not sporting the same type of gun my father's people have.

What's going on?

More shots are audible, and Alistair passes right by me, hiding behind the same pillar I was just behind. "Penelope. You gotta run."

I shake my head. "It's my father."

His eyes widen. "What? Did you contact him?"

"I sent him a text, but I didn't know he'd come for me."

BANG!

The shot is so loud it makes my whole body shake.

"Then tell him to stop!" Alistair barks.

"I can't fucking see him!" I retort.

Frustrated, he takes a peek behind the pillar, only to be shot at. "I can't see a damn thing either. Too much smoke."

"There's people coming in from the right side entrance too," I say, pointing him in the right direction.

"Fuck, Dylan's close," Alistair says. "I gotta go help him."

Alistair runs off before I can say another word.

**

DYLAN

I hold up my lighter, and all those fuckers think I'm waving it around to scare her father's men away, and they all snort at me. But with a smirk on my face, I fish a canister of deodorant from my pocket. "Say hello to my little friend!"

And while laughing like a complete and utter maniac, I light the bitch on fire, setting the entire hall as well as the people who were pouring in ablaze.

"Whooo! Now that's what we call a barbecue!"

Some men are on fire and run off screeching like chickens. Serves them right for trying to break into our fucking society.

I turn to look across the hallway. There are bullet holes littered throughout the walls and floors, and men are wrestling and knifing each other everywhere. Felix and Penelope are across the hall, fighting men who pour in from the front entrance. Penelope's staring at the canister in my hand.

"Did you see?" I scream enthusiastically.

Her eyes are wide open, but she still nods. Her dropped jaw followed by an impressed smile fills me with pride. She turns around and stabs a guy in the guts.

I'd burn down the world to see that smile. That lust to fight.

Fuck.

And here I was, thinking that deal we made would just be temporary.

Fleshly.

But Alistair isn't the only one who's fallen.

And I doubt I will be the last.

Something itches near my leg, and my eyes veer down. A snake slithers between and up my calves.

"Nessie," I mutter, and I grab her. "What are you doing here?"

I completely forgot her cage broke from the bombs going off.

She hisses at me.

Goddammit, what do I do with her?

I can't let her get crushed by rubble or shot by those fuckers.

I swiftly tuck her into my pocket.

But the moment I turn around, everything suddenly goes black.

***

PENELOPE

Minutes ago

Right in front of me, Felix slices through a guy's throat and slams him down onto the floor before attacking another guard.

If I don't stop this, they're going to kill everyone.

"Dad!" I scream.

"Penelope!" he calls for me. "Come to me!"

"I can't!" I yell back. "Call off your men!"

"We're here to save you!" he replies.

I don't know what to do. It's too dangerous to cross the floor. Gunshots fly from every direction, and the people in the side entrance ... I don't recognize any of them.

What the fuck is going on?

Alistair shoves his knife into someone's chest up ahead and throws him to the floor, blood pooling at his feet. But he doesn't stop as he immediately jumps on some dude's back who was about to attack Felix. Felix turns around and slices through his belly like it comes easy to him.

I swallow back the panic and focus on the rain of fire coming from the front door. He has to be there somewhere in the smoke.

"Dad!" I yell across the room.

But the noises of an all-out war between Mafia families drown out my voice.

I don't want them to fight.

Even though these boys have caused me trouble, someone far worse is out there.

Suddenly, a guy from the right-side entrance who doesn't look anything like a guy my father would hire aims his gun right at my face before I even have the chance to pull out my knife.

From the stairs, Felix jumps down right on top of him, elbowing him in the head and crushing his skull. He gets up and turns to me, breathing wildly, his whole body covered in blood.

"Are you okay?"

I nod, but I don't know if I really am.

A guy with a machete charges at him from behind.

My eyes widen, and instinct takes over as I jump at Felix and ram my knife straight into the guy's guts.

He groans, and blood spills from his mouth before I pull out again. The guy falls down in front of us, dead.

Felix's strong arms are on my waist and arm as he glances at the man. "That would've killed me."

I wipe my knife on my pants and tuck it back into my pocket. "I guess we both owe each other a life now."

As I'm about to walk off, he grabs my arm, forcing me to stay put. The look in his eyes is feral. And he leans in, whispering, "I'll protect you with mine."

He presses a kiss right underneath my ear.

I'm too stunned to even respond.

His lips leave a scorching hot mark on my skin.

He marches off, pulling more knives out of his belt before continuing his hunt.

I'm left in a daze, utterly confused and enamored by how hard he fights for me.

Until I see Dylan getting pummeled in the back of the head by a gun while he had his back toward the side entrance.

"Dylan!" Alistair's voice rips through the hallways as he fights off two other guys, unable to assist.

I jump over a dead body and rush to his side, but they drag Dylan's body away through the side entrance.

And a bunch of guys with heavy guns blocks the way.

Fuck.

67

DYLAN

My head fucking hurts when I come to. But my arms ... what the fuck is happening to my arms? They're above my head and painful like hell as though someone's tugging at them.

When my eyes briefly open, smoke and flashes are everywhere.

What's going on?

Weren't we ... fighting?

My eyes burst open.

Penelope's father. His henchmen flooded the building.

My head flicks up to the two guys dragging me across the pavement to the right side of the frat house.

"What the ...?" I murmur, my voice croaky. I flail back and forth to try to shake them off.

"Hold him tighter," one of the guys says, and squeezes my wrists so harshly it feels like my hands might fall off.

They lift me from the ground, and a car door behind me opens up.

Fuck, I need to get out of here, fast.

"Get your fucking hands off me!" I yell, thrashing around as they hoist me into the back seat. My brain is still screwed because of the harsh blunt hit it endured, and I can't even move my legs right. Still, I kick around as best I can. The guys shove both my feet inside and shut the door on me. It instantly locks.

Fuck.

"Stop destroying my car, Dylan."

My eyes widen at the sound of that voice. I freeze halfway through kicking in the window, and I look up.

My father's sitting right there in the front, next to his driver.

He glances at me through the rearview mirror. "You hurt?"

"What?" My jaw drops. "What are you doing here?"

His eyes stay fixated on mine. "Saving your ass."

I frown, confused. "How did you—"

"Her nice friend Crystal told me she saw you boys chasing after Penelope, so I knew you'd take her back here, and she'd inevitably convince you of all those damn lies."

Wait, what?

He suddenly grips my arm. "But don't you worry, son. I took care of it."

My frown turns into a face filled with disgust. "Wait a minute ... Those men out there ..."

"Her father's," he says. "I knew he was coming, so I came to pull you out of there before he torched the place."

I sit up straight even though my head fucking hurts, and I reach into my pocket to find my phone and I press a button. "How did you know he was coming?" In his eyes, I see the truth, and my pupils dilate. "You told him she was there ..."

"You think I had any other choice? After you caught her, I knew she'd fill your head with nonsense. I had to put a stop to it."

My jaw tightens, and I jerk away from his grip. "So you let her father know so he could kill us all?"

"Not you," he barks. "Your fucking friends. They ruined everything for you. And I'm pretty sure they'll fuck up until all of them are dead including her." He pulls back and seethes through gritted teeth, "Good riddance."

Rage slowly boils to the surface.

My father knew she would tell me the truth.

So instead of owning up to his mistake, he went ahead and let his enemies know exactly where we were so all his problems would be taken care of without having to lift a single finger.

"You ... *you* did this..." I mutter. "All because of Eve?"

"Doesn't matter," he retorts.

"So you're not denying it?"

"I've taken care of things. Be happy," he adds.

"Happy?" I parrot, snorting, before my face turns dead serious. "Did you know Eve was pregnant?"

He just looks at me with a stern gaze.

Grinding my teeth, I bark, "Answer me!"

"Yes."

Good God.

Now I understand how Felix must feel all the time.

So much rage.

"All this time, you knew Eve was carrying a baby, maybe even my baby, and you didn't care to tell me."

"She didn't even know which one of your friends she fucked, and then she tried to rope you in to her mistake for life," he barks back. "I did what I had to do. I took care of it. As a father does for his son."

I'm livid. Completely off my rocks enraged. "Penelope was right."

"Forget about her, Dylan," my father says as he focuses on me through the rearview mirror. "Those Ricci girls are dangerous. Twice they almost ruined your life. I protected you."

"No," I say through gritted teeth, making a fist. "You killed Eve and her kid!"

In a fit of rage, I jump at him and stab him with my knife, straight into the shoulder. If I wasn't so dazed from the attack, I would've stabbed him in the neck instead.

My father grunts in pain but still manages to raise the window between the back seat and the front, sealing me in. I slam the window with my fists until my skin cracks and my knuckles turn bloody.

I won't give up.

I won't fucking stop.

Not now ... not ever.

Not until I've chased him to the ends of the earth.

***

FELIX

I throw a knife at a dude punching away at one of my pledges, and it knocks him to the ground.

"Thanks," the pledge mumbles.

"Consider this your hazing," I reply, and he nods with a smirk before he continues fighting off the men who are pouring in from two sides. It's a relentless assault, and it doesn't seem to be coordinated at all. Almost as if someone other than her father is also sending people to attack us.

My eyes land on Penelope, who's fighting off some dudes near the side entrance, thrusting her knives into their throats. Smoke bombs fill the area, clouding everything, and she runs, coughing her lungs out.

More men swarm in from the front, but I still make the choice to rush to Penelope's aid instead, cutting my way through people like they're made of butter.

"Pen!" I grasp her hand and pull her to me.

"Dylan," she says between heavy breaths. "He's gone."

"What do you mean gone?" I ask.

"They smashed his head in," she says. "I looked everywhere, but I can't find him."

Fuck. Did they take him somewhere to kill him in cold blood?

I turn around for a moment to pull one of my knives from the flesh of one of these fuckers, ready to chase after whoever took Dylan. Because I don't leave any of my boys behind.

CLICK!

I pause.

"Don't move."

As my eyes rise to meet the face of the man in the trench coat, his gun is pointed right at me.

His jaw barely unclenches when he speaks. "Give me my fucking daughter."

I push Penelope behind me, despite the fact that he could pull the trigger at any moment. I refuse to move. I don't care who he is. *No one* points a gun at my girl.

BANG!

A shot enters my shoulder, and I grind my teeth together in pain.

"Move," he growls. "Next shot will enter your brain."

Instinct makes me flick my knife open, and I push the tip against his belly.

"Do it then. Cut me if you dare," the guy taunts.

And it takes every fucking ounce of self-control not to because I can feel the bullet moving in my muscles.

But he's her father.

And I've already hurt her enough.

"After all the fucking shit you did to my daughters ... You've got balls, I have to give you that," the guy grits, pushing the metal farther into my forehead. "But your reign of terror over this fucking campus ends today."

Suddenly, Penelope lunges out from behind me and grabs her father's wrist.

BANG!

The gun goes off, a bullet burying itself into the wall behind me. My skin sizzles from the shot grazing past my cheek as I jerk away from the pungent smell of burnt steel. A drop of warm blood rolls down my face, and I pick it up with my index finger.

"Stop," Penelope says, and her voice echoes through the halls.

Her father immediately grabs her arm and tugs at her. "Come."

"Dad, wait," she says, and she jerks free from his grip. "He's not the enemy."

"Like hell he isn't," her father grits. "He's the one responsible for my daughter's death together with that Caruso family." The gun clicks again, ready to fire.

She grabs his arm and forces it to lower. "Eve was pregnant."

His eyes widen and immediately home in on me again. "Yours?"

"We don't know," I reply.

His nostrils flare. "*We?*"

"It's ... complicated."

"Eve was in a relationship with Felix, Dylan, and Alistair," Penelope explains. "They didn't kill her."

"A relationship?" he parrots, looking leery.

"It's true," I say.

"Yet she never once thought of dying until she met you."

My face tightens as I stare into the barrel of his gun, unafraid. "And I take full responsibility."

Penelope clutches her father's face, forcing him to look at her. "Eve jumped because the dean made her choose between leaving campus and keeping the baby."

His fingers twist around the trigger, lips twitching.

"That is the Caruso I was talking about," she says, still holding his gaze. "Not Dylan."

"But this asshole—"

"Is not the person you want to kill," she says.

His jaw clenches, and he looks around for a second before lowering his gun. With two fingers in his mouth, he makes a distinct, unique whistle, and the gunfire and knife throwing suddenly cease.

"Retreat," he calls, and his men stop fighting and walk back to the front entrance.

The frat boys get up on their feet again and brush off their clothes, but they remain vigilant and on edge. No fucking wonder, with these shoot-crazy mobsters coming in to swoop Penelope out of my arms.

Her dad almost killed me for it.

And I would've died if it wasn't for her intervention.

BANG!

Shots are fired from the side entrance, and all three of us duck for cover behind a pillar.

"More buddies of yours?" I ask.

"No, my men listen to my call," her father retorts. "These are rogues."

"That's where Dylan was dragged through." She clutches my shirt. "What if they work for his father?"

Fuck.

"They tried to kill us all, including you," I reply, and I look at the entrance.

"Then that's our enemy now," her father rasps, and he reloads his magazine.

More bullets rain down on us, and I hide again.

"Wait a minute ..." Penelope's eyes widen. "Where's Alistair?"

68

ALISTAIR

I hang on for dear life as the car skids across the road. My fingers curl around the hood of the car, and I hoist myself up with everything I've got. Despite the strong winds, I refuse to let go. We're headed straight for the gates, and if I don't intervene, who the fuck knows where they'll take Dylan.

Through the window in the back, I can see Dylan kicking and punching the screen between him and his father. There's blood all over the inside of the car and lots of shouting. None of them have noticed me yet.

But they will.

I slide across the top of the car, clutching both sides for support as we veer from side to side. With one hand, I grip the window tightly before I fish the gun Felix gave me from my pocket and smash the driver's window.

The guy screams his lungs out as I shoot.

BANG!

The guy instantly drops dead, and the car begins to veer.

"What the fuck?" Dylan's father yelps.

I shove the driver's limp body against him, and I sit down in the driver's seat.

"ALISTAIR!" Dylan exclaims, elated.

"Get the fuck out of my car!" his father screams.

"Fuck no," I reply as I continue driving so we don't crash into the wall.

He tries to intervene, tearing at the steering wheel like he wants to die, and I only just manage to avoid the gates. A piece of the side mirror breaks off against the metal, but we still pass through.

"Jesus fucking Christ, get off—" his father growls as he fights me for control.

"Ali! Push the button!" Dylan yells through the pane, pointing at some kind of button on the dashboard that I quickly press.

The pane between us comes down, and he immediately puts his father into a headlock, choking the life out of him.

Meanwhile, his hands are still trying to take hold of the wheel. We're off the road and into the woods, driving through thick branches that crack the windshield while I try to narrowly avoid the trees of Priory Forest ahead.

"Let go!" Dylan growls at him.

"F-Fuck, get your hands off m-me," his father gargles while his face turns red.

He throws open the door, and without a second thought, he actually jumps out of the vehicle while it's still driving.

I hit the brakes as hard as I can, and we skid across the grass all the way to the Edge.

Breathing wildly, I glance through the rearview mirror at Dylan, who's as surprised as I am that we actually made it through alive.

"You came after me," Dylan says between breaths.

"Of course I did," I reply. "Where you go, I go."

A big smile appears on his cheeks as he leans in to grab my face, and he kisses me full on the lips. "Wouldn't want it any other way," he says when he pulls back again, biting his lip. "All I need now is Pen, and I'm in heaven."

"Heaven? When your dad almost tried to get us killed?" I retort.

He shrugs and makes a face, nodding softly. "I'll just ignore that part." He cringes in pain, grasping his head. "Fuck, that gun really hit me hard."

I get out of the car and open the back door to help him out. "Where are Pen and Felix?"

"Society house," I reply.

Dylan stops moving. "Wait, it's still under attack?"

"I left when her father's guys were blasting the place," I reply. "But I'm sure Felix will take care of it."

Dylan's gaze focuses on the body crawling around in the grass. "Yeah, well, their real target is right here."

***

PENELOPE

"Dylan's father took him!" I yell. "And Alistair probably went after him."

"Dylan? Dylan Caruso?" my father says.

"We have to help him," I say, turning to face Felix.

Felix nods, and he grabs my hand. "We'll take my bike."

"Whoa, hold on there," my father intervenes, grabbing my arm before Felix can take me along with him. "What makes you think I'm gonna let you take my daughter with you?"

Felix's face darkens as he releases me and gazes at my dad. The tension between them could cut a fucking pillar in half. "You can trust me."

My father snorts and scoffs, "Trust you? You literally destroyed my other daughter's life, and you're asking me to trust you?"

I swallow and step in. "Let me do this, Dad." I place my hand on his arm. "You trusted me to find out the truth, and I did. So please ... trust me with Felix."

An arrogant smirk forms on Felix' lips.

"What are you laughing at?" my father asks.

"It seems like your daughter has chosen," Felix replies.

His nostrils flare, and he lifts his gun again. "Watch it, boy."

Every one of his guards behind us is on edge, ready to start attacking again at even the slightest of signals.

"Dad!" I warn, grabbing the gun to point it away from him. "Stop. Please. If you love me, you'll let me do this."

Only after a few seconds does he actually stop. "I don't want to lose another daughter ..." He looks me in the eye. "But I value your love more than anything in this world."

Tears spring into my eyes, and I swiftly hug him, catching him off guard. His arm still snakes its way around my waist.

"I love you too, honey," he says.

Felix just stands there, staring at the men still waiting at the front door. "Will they let me pass without putting a bullet through my head?"

"Perhaps," Dad replies. "Can't guarantee you'll keep all your limbs, though."

I stomp on his foot, and he grunts from the pain. "Dad."

"Fine," he says through gritted teeth as I step off again. He focuses on Felix as though he wants to gouge his eyes out. "As long as you keep your hands off my daughter."

Felix raises his hands like he's committed to keeping a truce.

And I've honestly never seen him this docile before. Normally, he would've sliced a finger or two off already.

My father tucks his gun into his belt and waves his hand around. "Go."

I don't take his permission lightly. "Thanks, Dad."

Felix and I run off toward the exit, passing by my father's men even though some of them still grimace when they make eye contact with him. But I don't care about their judgment. Right now, we need to stop Dylan's father, and I want my fucking revenge.

Felix jumps on his bike outside and says, "Hop on."

He hands me a helmet, and I swiftly put it on, then jump on the rear seat.

"Hold on tight," he says, and he lowers his visor and races off.

My hands wrap tightly around his waist as we drive, turning corners, the tires screeching across the asphalt. I've never gone this fast before, but I don't know if my heart is raging from the speed or from how close I am to his body. I can feel each of his ripped muscles and ragged breaths, and for a second, I wonder if his heart has picked up too.

One part of me wants to put a knife to his throat for letting my sister die. For hurting me after I burned the whole place down.

But they didn't know Eve was pregnant. Or that Dylan's father was responsible for all our misery.

And when they realized their mistake ... all they wanted to do was make things better, despite what an impossible task it truly is.

I sigh and close my eyes, waiting until the storm inside my heart passes, but it's as relentless as the darkness outside. It doesn't take us long to reach the gates of the property, which are still open to allow firefighters and police inside. We slip past a new convoy of cars and drive off the campus.

It's only been a couple of minutes since Dylan was jumped and knocked out with a gun.

They couldn't have gone far, right?

Felix's body tightens against my hands as he looks around at our surroundings, checking to see if there's a car anywhere.

"There!" I scream and point at an abandoned car in the grass just beyond a few trees near where the bonfire was this summer.

Felix immediately hits the throttle, and we take a sharp turn, directly headed toward the car. A body is curled on the grass near it, and two guys are crawling up from the ground.

Dylan and Alistair.

***

DYLAN

I push away from Ali and stand on my own two feet as I barge over to my father, enraged. With a simple flick, I pull out a knife, clutching it tightly as I approach.

"Dylan, are you sure you wanna do this?" Alistair asks as he follows right behind me.

"I have to," I reply. "All the things Penelope accused him of ... it's all true."

I suck in a breath. The baby. The breakup. Eve jumping because she saw no other way out.

All because of him.

I clutch the knife so hard it leaves a painful indent in the palm of my hand.

But no amount of physical pain can ever come close to what's in this decrepit my heart.

The loss, the grief ... the unending rage.

My father is crawling away like a coward. A maggot.

"But he didn't stop there," I growl, hovering over my father's body. "He literally sicced his worst enemy onto you, onto Felix, onto the entire society, just so he could easily get rid of everyone and escape any sort of blame."

"What?" Alistair mutters.

He doesn't know what I heard in that car. What despicable truth came from my father's mouth. "He called Ricci and told him where we were so you guys would die, and he could take me."

"Wait," my father mumbles as I stick a knife under his throat. "I would do anything for you, Dylan, you know that. I'm your father."

"You're not my fucking father anymore!" I scream in his face. "You almost killed the girls I loved twice!"

"Dylan?" Penelope's voice calls to me, and I look up.

I know she heard me. But I don't regret saying that word out loud.

Felix has his arm around her, keeping her from running to me.

She's here. She's safe.

But Eve wasn't.

We should've protected her from him.

I inch closer with the knife, imagining myself slicing through his throat. But with every passing second and every droplet of sweat rolling down my forehead, the idea of actually committing becomes harder and harder.

"You can't do it, can you?"

I push myself off him and lift him from the ground so we're face-to-face. With my knife still pointed at his face, I brace myself for the attack.

"Do it then," he says. "If you want to kill me so badly."

My teeth grind together, but no matter how hard I try, I can't push myself to stab him.

Fuck!

Why can't I fucking do it? He deserves every inch of pain.

Suddenly, Penelope comes rushing out of nowhere and stabs him in the belly.

He cringes, and I step back in shock.

"That's for driving my sister over the edge," Penelope growls.

"Dylan!" Alistair calls out, but I can barely hear him.

My father stumbles backward while I struggle to hold on to the knife I was determined to stab him with.

"Dylan, what are you doing?" Penelope asks, but I can barely hear her. When she grabs my arm, my eyes fixate on her grip and find her eyes after.

What is going on with me?

Suddenly, my father pulls out a gun and points it at Penelope.

I push her out of the way. "No!"

BANG!

The gunshot hits me in the shoulder, and the force knocks me down into the grass.

"Dylan! Look what you made me do." My father's gun is still pointed right at Penelope. "That girl needs to perish."

When I turn to look at her, Felix has already stepped in front of her.

"I'd rather fucking die than watch you kill her in front of me," Felix rasps.

He'd die for her?

I never realized his obsession with her went that deep ... but maybe he didn't either. And I have a feeling none of us knew we were falling for her until it was too late to stop.

I'm momentarily too stunned to move, not just from the pain but from all the bundled-up emotions too.

Until Ali steps between her and the barrel too. "I won't let you kill her."

My father grinds his teeth. With each passing second, his eyes looked increasingly insane, like he couldn't stomach the idea of all of us protecting this one girl.

"That girl is responsible for all of your problems, just like her god-damn sister, and now you're all protecting her?" he growls.

Suddenly, he points the gun away from them ... and aims it at me.

"What are you doing?" I ask, writhing on the ground.

"Get up," he growls.

I do what he says only because of the barrel of the gun and the imminent threat to my life.

"Come here," he says.

Everyone's on edge, including me.

Would he actually shoot me? But all the schemes, all the lies, they were all to protect me, right?

He whips his gun back and forth and says, "Come. Now!"

Any semblance of emotion is gone from his face, something that's never happened before.

At least, not in my presence.

But I guess he kept this side of him hidden from me all this time.

I swallow and approach him.

"Dylan, don't do it!" Penelope says.

"Don't intervene," I reply, terrified she might try something. "Felix, take her," I tell him.

He nods, but Penelope protests, fighting against Felix's strong grip on her shoulder. "No! Fuck no, I'm not going anywhere!" she yells, tears staining her eyes. "I'm not leaving you."

I'm struck by the sincerity in her voice.

Could she possibly ever forgive me for what I did?

My father grabs my bloody arm and pulls me to him, pushing the barrel into my head. "You drove me to do this. I sacrificed *everything* for you, and for what?"

"You did this to yourself," I growl. "I never asked you for a damn thing."

"That girl was going to ruin your life!" he spits back, shoving the gun further into my head.

"So you ruined hers instead," I grit.

He practically spits out his words. "I had no other choice!"

"So you admit it," Penelope rasps from the side, tears rolling down her cheeks.

Watching her cry hurts more than the wound in my shoulder.

Fuck. I wish I could spare her from this pain.

"You admit you killed her," Penelope says.

My father snorts and throws out a stilted laugh. "I didn't force her to run off that ledge. She made that choice."

"But you told her to leave and abort the baby or face the consequences!" Penelope screams.

Everyone is silent for a few seconds, but the air crackles like lightning.

"I did what I had to, to protect my son and—"

"Your reputation," I interject. "Because that's what this is all about, isn't it?"

But instead of replying, he only pushes the gun further into my temple, confirming my suspicions.

"And then you forced Nathan and Kai to torment me to get me to leave too," Penelope says. "They set fire to the Alpha Psi house because you told them to, didn't you?"

"Nathan's a tool," my father spouts. "They were supposed to retrieve the diary and destroy the evidence, but they couldn't even do that correctly."

No wonder those guys didn't want to talk. If they did, he would have them killed.

"This was never about me ..." I mutter, making a fist, despite the pain.

"It was about you and your poisonous need to be a perfect little family."
I brace myself. "But that family has turned to dust because of you."

I spin on my heels and punch him in the face, but he recoils and knocks his forehead against mine. I punch him again, this time in the gut.

BANG!

The gun goes off, a bullet entering through my waist.

"Dylan!" Alistair says, trying to approach us.

"Don't intervene!" I yell back.

"Come on then, boy," my father taunts him. "I'll blow your brains out before you even so much as touch me."

"You mother—"

I grasp his wrist and force him to lower the gun, but he won't let go without a fight. We struggle for power as we backtrack all the way to The Edge.

"Give up," I tell him. "Give it to me."

"And let my life be ruined by your fucked-up antics?" he retorts. "Fuck no."

He jabs me in the stomach so hard I buck and heave.

"You deserve to rot in jail for the rest of your life," I say through gritted teeth, looking up at him.

"I'll kill every last one of these motherfuckers you call friends before I let that happen," he says.

My eyes widen as he aims his gun right at Penelope.

No.

I can't let it happen.

I throw myself at him as hard as I can, knocking him off balance.

BANG!

The gun goes off as he tumbles off The Edge, grasping my ankle just before he goes, pulling me with him.

69

ALISTAIR

"Dylan!"

Without thinking, I run to The Edge, ignoring Dylan's warning, ignoring everything I know would keep me safe.

He's barely holding on with a single hand clutching a bunch of roots from a nearby tree. I throw myself to the ground and slide to him, reaching out my hand.

"Take my hand!"

But Dylan can barely reach for me with the arm that's still bleeding profusely from the wound his own father created. And the man is hanging onto his ankle, pulling him down farther.

The rocks slip, and more dust and dirt fly down into the gaping abyss below.

"Don't let go!" I yell.

"You take me with you, you hear me?" his father growls. "If you let me fall ..." He pulls up the gun and points it right at Dylan. "I'll take him with me."

I gulp.

Fuck. What do I do? I'm not nearly strong enough to pull up both.

Dylan shakes his feet around. "Let go of me!"

Suddenly, Dean Caruso points the gun at me. "Stop moving, or I'll put a bullet in your fucking friend instead."

Has he lost his mind? Or was he always this insane?

"Felix!" I call over my shoulder, but he's already much closer than

I anticipated, and he kneels in front of us, grasping Dylan's wrist too. Penelope runs up to us too, shaking with terror as she peers over the edge.

"He's alive," she says in shock.

"Not for long if you don't pull us both up," his father rasps.

"Fucking die, you son of a bitch!" Dylan shakes his feet some more.

"What?" Penelope gasps, and she leans in to look over The Edge to witness Dylan's father holding on like a fucking parasite.

"I'll kill all of you if you don't pull me up," his father says, pointing the gun at Penelope this time.

She freezes in place at the sight of the barrel pointed at her head.

"Don't you fucking dare," Felix growls at him, keeping a tight hold on Dylan. "If so much as a single drop of blood rolls down her skin, I will rip every one of your fucking limbs off your body."

The dean's eyes widen and narrow in a split second. "I'll fucking kill her in front of you before you even have a chance."

Dylan's fingers slowly unravel from the piece of rock he's holding on to. But it's the look in his eyes that scares me the most. The only time I've ever seen it is the day Eve died.

Remorse and defeat.

Like he's about to give up.

Surrender his life ... to save hers.

"No, don't you dare," I tell him. "Dylan, don't you dare let go, you hear me?"

"I can't let him win," he says.

"Dylan," Penelope mutters, crying her eyes out. "Please, don't do this."

"All of this is because of me and my father," he says. "All of this misery ... it could end so easily."

"Dylan!" she yells, making a fist. "I won't fucking forgive you."

His pupils dilate, and his jaw tenses in response.

All of us are looking up at Penelope.

"You die now, and I will never, ever forgive you."

"Pen—"

"No! You wanted to be forgiven?" She swallows in the face of a loaded gun. "Then fucking earn it."

Dylan swallows, and his resolve suddenly strengthens as he clutches the caving rocks tighter, fighting for the right to stay alive.

In a split second, he flicks open the zipper that holds his pocket together and out slithers Nessie.

Felix frowns. "Nessie?"

She crawls down Dylan's leg all the way to his father, who begins to panic.

"No, no, stay away," he says with a jittery voice. "Get away from me!"

He tries to shoot but misses.

Nessie wriggles her way across his hand and down his arm, her tail still curled firmly around Dylan's leg as if she's adamant to hold on.

"Get off!" the dean shrieks, wriggling to get her to fall, but the more he moves, the more he loses his grip on Dylan's ankle.

And all of us watch in awe as Nessie opens her jaws and bites him right in the face.

"Arghh!" he yells, slamming himself in the face with his gun, which tumbles down into the void.

But Nessie swiftly strikes again, this time in his eye.

"AHHH!" he screams, and in his panic, his hand loses its grip. "No, no, no!"

Too late.

The last thing we hear are his deathly screams as he plunges toward his end.

And all we can do is stare.

***

PENELOPE

What are they all waiting for? There's no time to lose.

I bend my knees and extend a hand to Dylan too. "Grab my hand!"

Felix and Ali are spurred back into action, tugging at his wrist while

Dylan finally reaches for my hand with his bloody arm. Together, we pull him up from the land of the dead and back onto the actual ground. I breathe a sigh of relief as he lands on top of me, groaning in pain.

"Motherfucker ..." Felix grumbles. "Don't you ever pull that shit again."

Dylan laughs but then grunts in pain again, and he rolls off me and onto the grass to catch his breath. "God, I could really use a cig right now."

Ali rolls over and hands him one from his pocket.

"Wow, that was quick," Dylan says.

"I keep this one for a rainy day," he muses.

Dylan snorts as he stuffs it into his mouth. "Oddly appropriate." He lights it, despite the rain almost dousing the flame, but he doesn't care as he takes a long drag and blows out the smoke.

"Here," he says, and he hands it to Ali, who also takes a drag.

"Thanks," Ali says after taking another whiff, and he pushes it through to Felix. "Take it."

Felix doesn't protest and takes a drag too. "Fuck. What a night."

"What about you, Pen?" Ali asks. "Wanna try too?"

But all I can do is look at them smoking out here in the wet grass, soaked and covered in the blood and guts of their enemies, completely unaware of the magnitude of their actions.

A weird laugh escapes my mouth from the absurdity of it all, which slowly turns into a cry that won't end. All the emotions are pouring out of me like a faucet left open. As though everything that's been cooped up in my heart has finally found a way to bleed out and fade.

My sister is finally avenged.

"Are you crying?" Ali asks.

Dylan crawls closer, despite the pain, and says, "No, no, don't cry."

"Aw shit," Felix growls, pushing the bud into the grass.

"You almost died," I say.

"I'm alive," Dylan says, and he rolls over sideways to rub the tears off my cheeks with his thumb. "Thanks to you."

"Hey now, we deserve a little credit too," Ali protests.

"I'm alive thanks to all of you guys, of course," Dylan says with a smile.

Felix gives him a soft slap on his good shoulder. "You really thought about giving up there. Fuck you."

"Knowing you, you would've chased me down into hell itself," Dylan jokes.

"You bet your ass I would," Felix responds.

"Well, lucky we don't have to," Ali says, reaching for the snake curled around Dylan's leg. "Thanks to sweet little Nessie here."

He grabs and pets her while Dylan slowly sits in the grass.

Rain pitter-patters down onto us, and Dylan raises his face toward the sky. Despite the cold, despite the wounds on his shoulder and waist, despite just losing his father, there's still a smile on his face.

"I'm sorry," I say.

"Why?" he asks.

"Even if he was a bastard, he was still your father," I say.

He swallows and closes his eyes as the rain falls down on him. "I thought I'd be angry. Scared. Bitter." There's a pause. "But all I feel is peace."

Felix and Alistair look at him, and Ali reaches for his hand. "You had to make a tough choice."

"I don't regret it," Dylan says. "Not even one second." He turns his head and looks at me. "Because he hurt you and Eve. I'll never be able to forgive him for that." He licks a droplet of water off his top lip. "And instead of rotting in jail ... he can rot in hell."

Suddenly, a bunch of cars pull up and out step a bunch of my father's men, carrying guns like they're about to go to war. But we're just sitting here in the grass trying to catch our breath, and the contrast is huge.

"Where is he?" my father asks as he gets out of the car.

Dylan makes a face and points at The Edge. "He went flying like a meatball. I think you'll find his guts splattered on the ground down below. A fun twist on spaghetti."

My father's face contorts, and he frowns, confused. "What?"

"He jumped," Felix says.

"Jumped?" My father's face darkens. "I highly doubt that. Did you kill him?"

"No," I interject. "He threatened to kill *us*."

"So you threw him overboard."

"He dragged me with him," Dylan says, petting the snake. "And Nessie took care of him."

"Nessie ..." my father repeats like it's all one horrible joke, but it isn't. "The snake?"

Dylan sports a smirk. "Nessie's the real hero here."

My father snorts and shakes his head. "I can't believe this ..."

"It's the truth, though," I say, but I'm not sure he's gonna believe it.

"We took care of the threat. No one asked you to come to Pen's rescue," Felix says.

My father clutches his gun tighter. "Watch your mouth, or I'll put a bullet through those shiny teeth of yours."

"Felix, Dad," I interject as I get up from the ground. I block his view with my body. "Enough blood has been spilled tonight."

My father just stares at me like he's wondering whether or not to go behind my back and kill these boys too for good measure, but I won't let him.

They might deserve it, but I can't live knowing they won't.

I simply couldn't exist.

I take a breath and glance at the boys over my shoulder. These boys who protected me with their lives, who wanted to take a bullet for me, who killed the sole person responsible for my sister's misery, despite the fact that it would cost them everything.

All because they cared so much about my sister they wanted to find out who hurt her just as much as I wanted to know.

I once thought they were bullies. Bad guys. Villains.

But they really are heroes.

Anti-heroes.

And they deserve far more than the hardship they received.

"You realize that Caruso's death is not going to come without cost," my father says. "There's going to—"

"Be a huge shake-up," I muse. "I know."

He gives me a judgmental look for saying that word out loud. "You know we don't—"

"Call ourselves that," I fill in. "Know that too."

Now he's sighing. Out loud.

"But we know the truth now," I say. "Which is exactly what I told you I would do when I came here." A gentle smile forms on my lips. "Aren't you proud of me, Dad?"

His face softens, and he lowers his gun, then opens his arms. "Come here."

I run into his hug, melting away against the safety of his warmth and love.

Something I'll never take for granted, ever again.

"You got revenge for your sister. You took care of the person responsible."

"And she even set the school on fire," Dylan adds with a grin, like he's proud of me or something, and it makes me chuckle.

My father focuses his gaze on me and says, "I'm proud of you."

"Thanks, Dad," I say, and I hug him tight.

"Let's go home," he says, and he tries to tug me along.

"Not yet," I say. "We need to make sure they're taken care of first." I look at the boys, who are all bloodied up from the big fight in the Skull & Serpent Society building, and especially Dylan.

"Right." My father snaps his fingers, and some of his men step forward with a first-aid kit. They immediately go to work on their wounds, fixing up Dylan first since he's the most injured.

"Don't touch me," Felix barks, and he snatches the tape and gauze right out of one guy's hands. However, he's having trouble applying it to his cut. Smiling, I walk toward him and go to my knees to help him out.

I grab the gauze from his hands and he watches me with a leery eye while I put it around his wound. But he doesn't try to stop me.

I know the kind of pain he's been through would make anyone

apprehensive of touch. So to be able to do this for him—that he lets me help him—is a big compliment.

His lips part. "You don't have to—"

"Shut up."

He tilts his head at me and gives me that same daring look I've grown so used to that it brings flutters to my stomach. "After all you've seen me do ... you still think it's wise to provoke me?"

"Yes," I reply, applying the bandage. "Because if I didn't, I wouldn't be the girl you'd give your life for."

His hollowed eyes flash with an obsession so strong it forces me to pause and gaze into the depth of his soul, a chasm I could dive in without ever finding the bottom.

His hand rises to caress my cheek. "I would've taken that bullet for you."

My lips quiver as his thumb brushes them. "I'm glad you didn't have to."

A small but still visible smile forms on his face.

Someone clears their throat. "Are you done? You're grossing me out."

We all look in the same direction. Lana just jumped off her own motorcycle, her helmet still in her hands. I didn't even hear her arrive, that's how preoccupied I was.

"So what happened?" she asks.

"Dean's dead," Ali says. "He ... jumped."

"Jumped?" She narrows her eyes. "Now why do I find that hard to believe?"

Dylan averts his eyes. It's obviously too hard for him to talk about.

"It doesn't matter," I say. "The point is, he's the reason my sister died and why the Alpha Psi house was burned down."

"Wow," she says, making a face. "And then he attacked the Skull & Serpent Society?"

I nod. "Him and ... well, my father's men." I point at them and my dad, and they all wave at her like it's normal.

"Hi," she says, with a casual smile, and she looks at one guy who can't even stand on one of his legs. "I'm that girl who shot your foot."

I guess that's one way to break the tension after a fight like that.

"Let's not start another war," I say.

"The threat has been dealt with," my father says. "My men are only here to protect me and you."

He eyes me down and then throws a stern look at Lana as though he wants to tell her not to try anything or else, and it makes me snort.

"I don't want to rain on your little death parade here," Lana says, flicking her long black hair back, the ends of the red ribbon dangling down.

"I'm surprised you got off without a single scratch," Felix says.

"I know how to shoot," she says, raising a brow. "Unlike you."

"Ooooh." Dylan makes a cringy face. "Harsh."

Alistair slaps his hand in front of his mouth. "Don't. Unless you want to be Felix's next victim."

Felix gets up, fists balled. "Give me one good reason not to chuck you down that fucking ravine so you can join the dean."

She smirks and approaches him. "Because I'm your sister?" She pats him on the shoulder. "Proud of you, bro."

Felix's fists relax again and he rolls his eyes at her.

"You know, I'd love to chat about a dead dean and all, but I've got worse news for you all," she says, folding her arms. "Dad's on campus."

"Dad?" I ask. "You mean yours?"

She nods and Felix's face turns sour. "Fuck."

I help Dylan up from the ground and support him together with Ali while we walk.

"Exactly," she says. "So let's go back before he puts a bullet in our heads himself."

"Don't you need to go to the hospital first?" I ask Dylan.

He coughs. "Nah, I'll be fine. I can handle a little bit of pain. Besides, the school's got an excellent in-house clinic."

"I doubt they've dealt with stab wounds and gunshots," I reply.

A smirk forms on his face. "Wanna bet?"

But as I help him walk away from the cliff, Lana says, "Hey, Pen."

I pause and turn my head. "Yeah?"

"Thanks for protecting my brother back there at the Skull & Serpent Society." She adds a smile. "You're not half as bad for him as I thought you were."

"Is that a compliment?" I muse.

She shrugs. "Maybe."

"Thanks," I reply and when she smiles I do too.

"Are you two bonding over murder?" Dylan muses. "Aww, cute."

She rolls her eyes. "Shut it before I put a bullet in you too."

70

FELIX

We head back to the campus grounds. Me and Dylan on my bike, Ali together with Lana on her bike, while Penelope drives with her father. I don't think he trusted me enough to take her back safely. But I know he'll take care of her, so I didn't fight him on it.

I've had enough pain in a single day.

For now, I just want to fucking rest and see what the damage is at the Skull & Serpent Society house. It's going to be a massive cleanup that I know we'll need all our men for.

Money won't be an issue, considering who owns this whole campus. The board is still alive, despite one member jumping to his death. The others will probably want to put a lid on this as fast as possible to resume business as usual, and I'll definitely use that to my advantage.

I'm just wondering how many of the board members my father brought to the table ... and if I can convince them of our innocence before they decide to throw us out for good.

When we enter campus, the fire seems to have died down already. Plenty of firemen are still on the grounds assessing the damage, but the immediate threat seems to have dissipated, and the building is still intact, though heavily burned.

We all come to a halt near the big building that Penelope set ablaze, and I turn off the engine and wait until Dylan's jumped off before I do too. Lana and Ali also stop in front of the building, which is still being surveilled by lots of officers, including Ali's dad. They're probably still looking for the culprit, and we all look at each other as Ricci's car comes to a stop. Penelope steps out and makes an awkward face.

"What?"

"Nothing," Ali and Dylan say in tandem.

Lana throws her helmet at me. "Stop ogling."

"Ogling?!" I repeat.

"And keep that tongue inside," she says before she waltzes past the police officers, waving around her student card that carries her name.

A name that carries power.

Penelope's father and his men follow her as we all head inside, but the moment he tries to enter, the guards stop him.

"Not you."

His men reach for their pockets.

Oh fuck no.

"What are you doing?" Penelope asks.

"We can't have an all-out shooting right here in the open where all the other students can see," Dylan says.

"If I can't go in, my daughter doesn't either," her father growls.

She steps outside again and places her hand on his chest. "Dad. I'll be okay. Please."

"I'm worried about you," he says, looking up at the policemen. "And these men are obviously not here to protect *you*."

"They're my father's men, actually," Ali says.

"These boys will protect me," she says, cupping his face before glancing at me over her shoulder.

When her father gives me a stern look, I nod. "I'll protect her with my life. You've got my word."

"The word of criminals means very little to me ..." he says through gritted teeth. Still, he flicks his fingers, and his men stand down again. "But I'll allow it. For her."

"Thanks, Dad," she says, and she presses a soft kiss on his cheek before following us into the building she tried to burn down.

The entire ground floor is covered in soot. Bits and pieces of wallpaper and paint are coiled and hang loose. Paintings destroyed. Carpets gone. Even a part of the staircase has been singed.

"Wow ... you did good," Dylan boasts.

Ali immediately throws his elbow into his waist, making him groan.

"Good on the test," Dylan adds with a cough.

"Thanks," Penelope replies with a smile.

"Came down and delivered vengeance," I muse.

"To her grades," Dylan says.

"What else?" I reply, raising a cheeky brow.

A shaken-up student walks by while staring at us, and we stay silent until she's gone again.

Better not say out loud we're responsible for all of this mess.

Alistair and I support Dylan, but he quickly pushes himself off us. "I can walk by myself, thanks."

"You sure?" Ali asks.

"I'm fine," he responds, still bleeding through the bandage that was applied in a hurry. "Don't need to worry about me."

My eyes narrow. "Yeah, you're going to the nurse's office."

"It can wait," he says.

I push my shoulder underneath his and force him to walk in that direction. "I'm not gonna lose another fucking friend."

"You almost sound like you care about me," Dylan muses.

But he knows as well as I do we'd fucking die for each other.

"Okay, enough talking," I say, and I haul him through the hallways to the clinic.

The moment we step inside, the nurse almost loses all the color in her face. "Jesus—what happened to you?"

She quickly preps the beds and we set Dylan down on one of them before sitting down on the others.

"Got into a brawl," I reply. "Can you take care of him first?"

Dylan groans in pain as she grabs his arm and unwraps his bandage, then pours some alcohol on the wound. His face contorts from the pain.

"Oh dear ... that'll definitely need surgery."

"Surgery?!" Dylan gasps. "Fuck."

"What? Scared of knives?" Penelope jests.

"Anesthesia!" he retorts.

Ali snorts. "He has this thing where he confesses all of his past mistakes and starts talking about true love right after he wakes up."

Dylan covers his face. "I really shouldn't have brought you to that dental appointment."

"Oh, I enjoyed it thoroughly," Ali muses.

"Spare me the corny stuff," I say. "How does it look, nurse?"

The nurse smiles. "I was joking about the surgery part." She winks. "I can take out the bullet and stitch it up. No problem."

Dylan narrows his eyes at her and throws her an annoyed look, making us all laugh.

"What about the other bullet wound?" Penelope asks.

"Another one?!" the lady almost screeches.

I shush the lady. "The entire campus doesn't need to know."

The nurse rolls her eyes and says, "Where? Show me."

Dylan lifts his shirt. The wound is still oozing blood and is covered in dirt.

"Yikes," the nurse says, and she immediately grabs her kit and sits down in front of him. "Lie down."

He does what she asks and she immediately pushes his shirt farther up, then inspects the wound. "This is gonna hurt."

When she pours on the alcohol, he hisses. "F-Fuck."

"Told you," the nurse says.

"Jesus," Penelope mutters.

"Told you, she's used to some shit," Dylan replies.

"No talking," the nurse barks, and she shoves some needles up his waist and shoulder, then goes to work on him, digging like she's trying to find some trinkets.

The bullets finally appears and she drops them into a bowl. "There. Now to stitch it up."

She grabs her suturing kit again and finishes the job, cleaning him up.

"Thanks," Dylan mutters, and he sits up again.

"You're welcome. I guess you're not going to tell me who did this to you?" she asks.

"Sorry, confidential," Dylan replies.

She rolls her eyes again. "Always the same bullshit with you kids."

Lana snorts but hide her laughter behind her hand.

The nurse starts cleaning up Ali's wounds, which are only mild scratches and cuts, easily cleaned with alcohol. The bullet that entered my shoulder is easily taken out and the wound is sutured up. One grazed past my cheek, which only needed some glue after the cleaning, but other than that I'm fine.

I take off my jacket which is covered in blood and drenched in rain and throw it into the bin. I'll buy a new one easily.

Ali does the same with his hoodie, chucking it all away until we're both left in simple white shirts.

"What about you?" the nurse asks Lana. "Are you okay? Got any wounds?"

She throws her hair back. "Not a single scratch. No one touches me without my permission." Lana eyes me and the tape on my cheek.

Dylan bursts out into laughter when he sees my face. "God, this alone is worth it."

"Shut up," I growl back.

"Okay, then I'm all done," the nurse says.

"Thanks for taking care of them," Penelope says. "Are they in the clear now, or will they need more help?"

"Re-bandage him every day," she says, pointing at Dylan. "Keep a close eye on the wound. If it gets infected, go to the hospital."

"Okay," Penelope replies as she and Ali help Dylan up.

"Feels much better already," Dylan says as he pushes himself away from them. "I can walk."

"You sure? We'll probably need to go up all the fucking stairs," I say.

He shrugs, but immediately cringes from the pain. "Pain is for pussies."

Ali snorts and shakes his head. "Typical."

A police officer near the door clears his throat. "Are you all done?"

It's Ali's dad.

We nod and follow him outside.

"Your father's up here," he tell us as he leads the way up the stairs, past the bit that got burned. But we keep going up more stairs until we finally reach the highest floor. The one where the dean's office was.

"He's in the dean's old office?" Ali asks, frowning.

"Typical," Lana says. "Take over. Assert dominance."

Dylan coughs wildly.

"In here," Mr. King says, pointing at the third room on the third floor.

"Right," I say, sighing when everyone else looks at me. "I'll go first."

I open the door, while the policeman stations himself outside, guarding the place as we head inside.

My father's standing behind the desk, looking out at the window down below as though he's admiring his newfound rich view of the world.

"Took you long enough," he says, and he gazes at us over his shoulder, the stern look on his face making me sweat.

Our drenched, bloodstained faces don't seem to impress him in the slightest.

Typical.

"Sit," he barks. "All of you."

The door closes on us, and we sit down on the chairs in the back.

"You made quite a show here ..." he mutters.

"Sir, I can explain," Dylan says.

"Damn right you will," my father says, turning around. "Because the second I left this school in Caruso's hands, it burned down to a crisp."

"That's my fault," Penelope says.

"Wow," Lana says. "You're actually admitting it?"

My eyes widen. "What are you doing?" I hiss.

"I wanted to lure Caruso out," she adds, ignoring me.

"Lure him out?" my father rasps.

"He was responsible for my sister's death," she says. "Eve Ricci."

"And the plot thickens ..." Lana muses, crossing her legs.

"Lana," my father warns, and his eyes home in on Penelope. "Ricci ... That's not what you told me your name was."

Penelope gulps. "I know."

"I wouldn't tell a soul either, knowing how our families live," Dylan says. "I don't blame her for giving a fake name."

"You defend her?" my father asks. "After burning down the entire school?"

"Well, it's not entirely burned down," Dylan says, shrugging. "Just the ground floor."

My father pulls off his glasses and rubs his nose and eyes. "Semantics will do you no good."

"Caruso was threatening her," I say, folding my arms.

"All I'm hearing is allegations with no proof. Where is he?"

"Dead," Alistair responds with a weird grin attached. "Down in the ditch below The Edge."

My father's face turns white as snow as he lowers his hand. "What the hell happened?"

"He tried to kill us all," I say. "It was self-defense."

His eyes narrow as he focuses on me. "Are you telling me you killed him?"

Dylan shrugs. "Well, technically, Nessie did, but—"

"Nessie?" my father interjects.

"Our snake," I respond.

Lana snorts. "This is ridiculous."

"It's true," Ali replies.

"Where is your proof?" my father asks. "Unless you can deliver substantial proof, I'm going to have to let Officer King arrest all of you."

"What?!" Lana gasps. "But I didn't even do anything, I wasn't fucking there!"

Dylan swiftly fishes his phone from his pocket and clicks on some things, then turns up the volume. "I taped everything my father said."

When he plays the clip, his father's wretched voice spells out every part of his diabolical plans. A conversation between him and Dylan after he tried to take him in his car. But Dylan's a smart guy. He knew not to trust his dad.

The moment the clip ends I breathe a sigh of relief. Damn, even though I'm glad Dylan made sure to record that convo, I do not like listening to that asshole's voice.

"There's your proof," Dylan says, holding out the phone.

My father takes it and replays the clip again.

"Well, I guess you're not as dumb as you look," Lana muses.

"Wow," Dylan retorts. "I bet you're just angry Felix won't let you jump on this piece of wood." He makes some lewd gestures at his dick.

Which really, really makes it hard for me not to pummel him in the face and balls.

God knows he likes to fucking test our friendship.

"Keep it in your fucking pants," I growl back.

Lana laughs. "No thanks, I don't take other people's trash."

"Wow," Alistair says. "Well, I guess one man's trash is another man's treasure." And he winks at Dylan.

"Lana, enough," my father growls at her, and she immediately shuts her mouth and averts her eyes, but not before rolling them into oblivion, getting me to seethe with rage.

My father blows out a sigh and turns toward the window, gazing at the scene outside.

"So ... turns out Caruso was nothing but a low criminal." He sighs again. "Can't say I'm surprised. Out of all the board members, he was always the most ... difficult one to deal with." He turns around again. "His death was ... unfortunate. But inescapable, it seems."

"Are you going to arrest us?" Dylan asks.

"For the death of your father?" my father replies, and Dylan swallows. "No."

There's almost a collective sigh of relief.

"Considering his actions, the matter will be taken care of privately."

"You mean you'll sweep it under the rug," Lana says.

"However, I will keep you all responsible for the incredible mess at the Skull & Serpent Society house."

"Aw ..." Dylan groans.

"What about the school?" Ali asks.

"It'll require a ton of renovations," my father explains. "Which will not be cheap."

"It's okay. I'm sure we can work something out," Penelope says, folding her arms.

"I'm sure we can, Miss Ricci." He smiles at her. "I know your father. I'm sure he'd be happy to foot the bill to maintain ... order."

Order. Or in other words, to prevent a massive Mafia war from breaking out between all the families.

"What about us. Are we expelled?" I ask bluntly.

My father clears his throat. "No."

There's a collective sigh of relief in the room.

"So who's gonna run the show now that Caruso is dead?" Lana asks nonchalantly.

"I will," her father replies, and she almost falls off her chair.

"What?!"

"Don't act so surprised," he responds. "It's about time someone actually started managing this place properly." He eyes us all down. "Be happy I'm allowing you all to stay and fix your mess after all the shit you caused."

"Will she be allowed to stay too?" Ali asks, looking at Pen.

There's a knock on the door and my father averts his gaze. "Come in."

Two fuckers, one with a gnarly scar covering his eye, and the other with a missing finger, walk inside.

So I do the only thing I can think of and pull out my fucking knife, ready to take the remaining fingers and eye.

71

FELIX

"What the—" Penelope mutters, eyes widened the moment she sees Kai and Nathan in the door opening.

"You two had better get the fuck out fast before I slice off another finger and eye," I growl at them.

I didn't think they would have the balls to show up here, but apparently they're happy to lose those too.

Nathan pulls out his own knife. "What the fuck are you doing here?"

"We could say the same about you guys," Dylan says as he pulls out his own knife too.

"Motherfucker," Kai grits and he homes in on Dylan. "You're the fucker that made me lose an eye."

"You tried to take my girl. An eye for an eye," Dylan retorts.

"Put away those weapons," my father says.

"Fuck that, don't you know who those fuckers are?" I growl. "They threatened Penelope!"

"They lit the Alpha Psi house on fire," Penelope says.

"And don't forget Kai and his buddy tried to take advantage of her," Dylan adds.

"Hey!" Kai growls back. "That wasn't me."

"You helped your buddy Josh," Ali replies.

"You fucking burned him to death," Kai rebukes.

"Boys ..." my father tries to intervene, but all of us have our knives out, ready to start another fight. Until I hear the clicking of a gun right behind me. "Put down your weapons. Now."

I glance over my shoulder to see the barrel of a gun pointed at us.

"Or I swear to God, I will pull this fucking trigger."

"What?" Nathan scoffs. "That's your son, you wouldn't shoot him."

I smirk. "Oh he would."

Kai looks shocked. "What?"

My father turns off the safety. "I killed my own fucking wife."

Kai and Nathan's eyes widen and slowly but surely they lower their knives, so I do too. I still want to gut them of course, but it's not worth my fucking life. And I know my dad would definitely put a bullet in us all just to prove a point.

"Good." My father turns on the safety again and lowers his gun.

I turn to face him. "Why are they here?"

"I invited them here because I'm tired of your feud on this campus," he replies. "You've both done abhorrent things."

Dylan scowls. "Whoa, you can't compare—"

"You set one of theirs on fire," my father says.

Ali's jaw drops. "How do you know that?"

"Because we told him," Kai says.

"No one asked you a damn thing," I say.

"Calm. Down." My father's stern voice booms through the office. "I will not have this fight go on any longer. All of this is a disgraceful stain on this university's reputation to the public."

"It's not like most people already know this university is full of criminal families," Lana muses, rolling her eyes, but father ignores her.

"Mr. Torres and Mr. Reed have confessed to their crimes personally," my father says. "They were forced to do most of it."

"Really..." Dylan raises a brow.

And I have to admit, this all sounds a little to convenient.

"Caruso said he'd have our families killed if we didn't do his bidding," Nathan explains.

"No wonder he wouldn't tell us who," Penelope says.

Nathan lifts his hand to show his four fingers and the stump. "You think I wanted to lose a finger?"

"I'd have taken more if Penelope wasn't so fucking generous," I reply.

His fist balls and he grinds his teeth, but my father's strict gaze keeps him at bay.

"Wait, so you knew Caruso was a bad actor?" Dylan frowns.

"Yes," my father replies. "I just didn't know the extent of it, so I needed you to provide proof, which you have." My father clears his throat. "All of you with the exception of Lana will be doing community service for this school."

"What?" Ali, Dylan, and Penelope say in sync.

"No ifs. No buts," my father says. "You actively harmed this school and the students. This is your only chance to make amends." He looks each one of us in the eye. "So take that opportunity. It won't be handed to you a second time."

"That's why you called them here?" I ask. "To give us all collective punishment?"

"So you stop the fighting," he responds, looking each and every one of us in the eyes. "Now that the person responsible for your ill behavior is dead."

Dylan swallows, while Penelope's gaze connects with Kai and Nathan.

"We did what we had to ... to survive," Nathan grits.

"Even if it meant taking that diary and burning it," Kai adds.

"Well am I glad you didn't get the chance," she retorts, clutching her seat so tightly her fingers turn white.

"The Phantoms and the Skull & Serpents will stop fighting. Is that understood?" my father's voice booms through the room.

Everyone nods.

"I need answers."

"Yes, sir," everyone collectively mutters with a sigh attached.

"Good. There's been enough bloodshed as it is. The focus must shift toward rebuilding this university and trust."

"Trust," I scoff.

My father continues with his speech. "Everyone will report to the groundskeeper Monday morning, seven a.m. sharp."

"Seven?!" Dylan's jaw drops.

"Yes. Or would you prefer not showing up entirely?" My father raises a brow. "That can be arranged."

A laughably hopeful smile forms on Dylan's face. "What as in I don't have to help?"

"As in, permanently," my father says, lowering his gaze, and Dylan immediately looks away.

"Fine ..."

Suddenly the door bursts open and Pen's father steps in. "That's enough interrogating for one day."

"Ricci ... how nice of you to join us," my father says with an obvious sneer as he picks up his glasses again and puts them on. "Kai. Nathan. Leave us."

They exit the room again. Too fucking bad because I was really looking forward to tormenting that fucker about his finger some more.

My father clears his throat. "How did you even get past the officers?"

"Rivera," her father retorts cynically. "They were nice enough to allow me access after my guards persuaded them."

Oh ... he threatened some cops with a bullet. Bold move.

"I think my daughter has given you enough information."

"Tell me, are you the one who put her up to this?" he asks.

The room is filled with the same kind of tension I felt the second before the entire hallway of the Skull & Serpent Society filled with bullets.

"My daughter died on these grounds. You should be happy I don't press charges," he says.

Or that he didn't send his men to slaughter every last one of us.

"Then you'll be happy to know the real culprit is dead," my father replies.

"How do you know?" Ricci sneers. "It could be you behind the scenes."

"I assure you ... Caruso acted alone," my father replies.

Ricci's grip on his gun tightens. "Your word means very little to me."

My father throws Dylan's phone across the room.

"Hey! That's mine," Dylan mutters, but his protest lands on deaf ears.

"There's your proof," my father says. "Listen to the voice recording."

Ricci plays the tape again, and we all cringe at the sound of Dylan's father admitting to pushing Eve until she saw no other way out.

Ricci grumbles.

"So ... will that settle it for you?" my father asks.

"Perhaps," Ricci replies.

"There is no more that can be done. The perpetrator is already dead. And this institution will live by good and honest rules now that I'm here to take care of things."

"Will you now ..." her father replies. "I doubt it will be any better."

"I can assure you, punishments will be swift and cruel."

There's a sparkle behind his eyes that I recognize all too well.

"C'mon, Penelope," her father says, grasping her hand. "We've done all we needed to do here."

Penelope reluctantly goes with him, but her eyes still fixate on mine, almost as if she's wondering if I'll intervene. If I'll stand up for what's mine.

I scoot my chair back and her father stops in his tracks. "Wait."

Everyone's looking at me.

I know our fathers could probably kill each other. But that doesn't mean I have to suddenly give up everything I ever wanted.

And the only thing I'll ever truly want is standing in that fucking door right now, ready to leave.

"She can stay."

Her father snorts and scoffs, "Can she now? I don't think I ever asked for your advice—"

Penelope shakes her hand free from his grip. "I can take care of myself, Dad."

"You're not staying in this wretched place," he replies.

"You don't decide that for me. Let him talk," Penelope says, pulling out of her father's grasp.

"Felix, what are you doing?" my father asks.

"What I should've done a long time ago, when I could've stopped someone from making a mistake but chose not to because she made me think it's what was best for her," I reply, stepping closer to Pen. "I won't make that same mistake again."

She swallows as she moves away from her father and closer to me.

My hand instinctively rises to cup her face, and I tuck a loose strand of that purple hair behind her ear. I used to hate her with every fiber of my being, but I never understood why. Until now.

She makes me feel things I thought I'd buried along with Eve.

"I can't let you leave, Pen," I say, caressing her. Her face leans into the palm of my hand. "Not until you've forgiven me."

Her lips part and she shivers in place, and I want nothing more than to kiss her right here in front of all of these fuckers, because I don't give a shit what they think, or how much her father and mine hate each other.

Because I don't.

I don't fucking hate her.

Even when I punished her, I didn't hate her. I hated what she made me do, how she forced me to slice open my own heart and cut it with a thousand knives.

But if I was in her shoes, if Lana was bullied and pushed over The Edge, I would've made the same choice.

I'm not a person to beg.

But for her, I will.

And if she wants her freedom back, if she wants all of this to end between us three, all she needs to say is the magic fucking word.

Yes.

72

PENELOPE

"Will you?" Felix asks. "Forgive me?"

I shake my head, tears welling up in my eyes.

I never willingly cried for him. But when he asks me point blank in front of all these people, knowing how much his pride means to him, how could I not?

"You ... I always thought I could never fall for anyone ever again after Eve. Until you came along and consumed my world. And you're so much more than she ever was to me. I've taken a bullet for you. I've killed for you. And I would kill a million more men if it means you'll absolve me of the pain I've caused you."

He licks his lips, his thumb brushing across my skin to pick up the single tear rolling down.

"But if you don't ..." he says, looking deep into my eyes. "I won't stop. I won't stop fighting for you."

I shake my head. "Then fight."

A crazy smirk slowly forms on his lips. "You really don't like the easy way out, do you?"

I laugh through my tears. "Fuck that. Fuck it if it's wrong. I don't care. Fuck whatever anyone else thinks. No, I won't forgive you."

He grabs my face with both hands and whispers, "Last chance to walk away now, Pen. Or our new deal will last until the end of your life."

"New deal? There was an old deal?" Lana mutters, but we both ignore her.

It takes me not even a second to say the word, "Deal."

Even if they hate me for burning down the school, even if I hate them for hurting me ...

The hate couldn't possibly be as strong as the need deep inside in my heart to be close to them. To belong to these sick boys.

Suddenly he smashes his lips on mine, taking away any and all doubt I had in my mind. Because this kiss ... God this is a kiss I couldn't possibly live without.

"Whooo!" Dylan cheers, and my lips unlatch to gaze across Felix's shoulder.

His dad seems pissed as hell. "Care to explain yourself?"

"She stays. Or I go," Felix growls, leering at his father over his shoulder. "End of story."

Felix's father grinds his teeth. "This ... this is what you choose after all this mess?"

He nods without a single sliver of shame showing on his face. "She's worth it."

And that comment ... God, I didn't think anything could make me blush this hard.

"Penelope ..." my father mutters. "After everything that happened. To your sister. To you ... why would you want to stay here?"

I look at Felix and at Dylan and Alistair who sit in their chairs, gazing at me with pure and utter devotion, and I realize I've fallen too deeply, too fast to let go.

I sigh. "Because I belong to them."

The relief that shows on their faces makes me feel better about my decision, despite the fact that I know I'm disappointing my parents. They hate this place with every fiber of their being, and for good reasons. But they don't know these boys like I do.

"I want to stay."

They would destroy the world to save me.

"Are you sure?" my father asks. "This place hasn't been kind to our family."

"I know," I reply, and I look his way. "But we've taken care of the person responsible. And this university paid a heavy price for it. I made sure of that."

My father swallows and puts his hand on my shoulder. "I don't trust these people," he says. "But I trust you."

"Thanks Dad," I say, covering his hand with mine.

He ogles the boys from the corner of his eyes. "But if I have to come back here even once..."

"Don't worry, sir. She'll be in good hands," Alistair replies.

"Expert hands," Dylan adds, running his tongue along his teeth.

My father might not know what that means, but I certainly do.

"I doubt that," Lana mutters. "But I guess it's already been decided."

"It's not up for debate," Felix says. "So what's it gonna be, Dad? Her or me?"

His father sighs, rubbing his face. "Fine," he says after a while.

A smile erupts on my face.

"But." His father waits until everyone looks at him. "No more killing."

Felix grumbles but doesn't respond.

"And no more fires either," his father adds, glaring at both Dylan and me.

"Awww," Dylan mopes, and Ali swats him. "No one said nothing about a barbecue."

"Not on school grounds," Rivera says.

Dylan sighs out loud. "Whatever."

"In Felix's words ... it's not up for debate," Rivera replies, and he grabs a pen and some paper. "Now, since you all decided to destroy the school, you will also help rebuild it."

"Wow, wow, wait a sec," Dylan mutters. "My dad might've been rich, but I don't have that kind of money."

"I will take care of the school," Rivera says. "Someone will need to chip in on the restoration of the Skull & Serpent Society building." He lowers his glasses. "And as I've heard it got damaged quite severely from a certain shoot-out."

"I will take care of that," my father suddenly fills in.

All eyes are on him.

"Since my daughter is to stay on these grounds, I want her to be safe and taken care of."

"How kind of you," Rivera sneers. "Since your men were also kind enough to sieve it through with bullets."

"I will have the damages fixed," my father retorts. "To settle that score."

He's trying to avoid another war. Smart.

"And to have a piece of the pie in management, I suppose," Rivera muses.

"I wouldn't decline such an offer," my father replies, an arrogant smirk on his face.

Wait, is this Rivera's way to call a truce?

"I guess that's settled then," Rivera says, penning some things down.

"What about ..." Dylan mutters.

"Your father?" Rivera looks up at him.

Dylan swallows.

"He had an unfortunate ... accident." Rivera adds a smug smile. "A deadly one. It happens."

"So, we're off the hook?" Alistair asks.

"Good one," Lana jests.

"Caruso was a loose end," his father replies. "That has been taken care of."

"By us," Dylan says.

Chief King raises a brow. "And as a thank-you, I won't have you arrested."

Alistair makes a face.

"So I guess we all have something to be grateful for," he adds with a stern gaze before smiling like the crazy person he is.

Just as his entire family.

I guess we're not that much different after all.

"Okay, are we all done now?" Lana asks. "Because I'd like to go back home."

"Same," Alistair chimes in.

Felix suddenly places a hand on my shoulder, pulling me away from my dad. "C'mon. Let's go."

I nod and let him tug me away, despite my dad's unwillingness to let me go. "I'll text you every day, okay?"

As we pass him, my father growls at Felix, "If anything, and I mean anything happens to her ... I will personally put a bullet through your skull."

A smirk forms on Felix's lips. "The only thing that will be happening to her ... is us."

"Us?" He frowns as Dylan and Alistair pass by us swiftly to avoid more punishment.

Felix squeezes my shoulder tightly and whispers, "It's our little secret."

Dylan walks past us and stares out the window at the bottom of the stairs as he picks up his phone.

"What's he doing?" I ask.

Alistair sighs as he walks past us. "Probably calling his mom."

My heart suddenly feels too heavy for my body to carry.

"Hey ... can we talk?" Dylan mutters as he paces back and forth. "It's about Dad."

"Oh God." Alistair walks to him and snatches Dylan's phone from his hand. "Not on the phone."

Dylan looks enraged. "What?"

"Do it in person," Ali says, looking at him intently.

It takes awhile for the anger to settle. "How? What am I supposed to say to her? Sorry, Mom, I killed Dad?"

Alistair shushes him. "Not so loud."

Dylan gulps. "Give me back my phone."

Alistair brings it to his ear. "Sorry, Mrs. Caruso. Dylan would like to speak with you in person today." And he turns off the conversation before Dylan can say anything else.

Dylan shakes his head. "Don't make me go over there." Tears well up in his eyes. "Don't make me face her like this."

I almost want to run over to him, but Felix's strong grip keeps me here. "Alistair can handle it."

"But he needs me. He needs us," I say, gazing up into Felix's eyes.

"It's already hard enough to tell his mom this. Don't need us seeing the show," Felix says, his fingers digging into my skin. "We don't need to see his heart bleed."

I hate to admit it, but Felix is right. My emotions will only get in the way. It'd be selfish to ask him to let me come along. As much as I'd like to help him right now, I know I wouldn't be able to do anything else that Alistair isn't already doing. Even though I know Dylan is suffering because he has to tell his mom the worst news she'll ever hear. Not just that but he's going to have to choose to tell the truth or lie about it ... to protect himself from his mother's wrath.

And me being there will not make it better for him. Alistair knows him much better than I do, and it's already hard enough to do this. He doesn't need us there too.

"Alistair," I call out. "Don't let him do it alone."

He nods at me.

"I can't do this," Dylan mutters.

"Yes, you can," Alistair says, squeezing Dylan's shoulder. "I know you can."

"And my little brother—"

"They *have* to know. In person. Face-to-face." Alistair lowers his face. "She needs her son now, more than ever."

Dylan quietly nods a few times.

"I'll be there with you, every step of the way." Alistair throws his arm over Dylan's shoulders, and says, "C'mon, I'll drive."

73

PENELOPE

Hours later

Felix and I have been helping with the cleanup in the main school area, but the moment I spot their car, I drop everything I'm doing and run outside.

"How is he?" I ask as Alistair jumps out.

"Could be better," he replies.

Dylan gets out and shuts the car door. I've never seen his eyes as red as they are now.

I immediately run to him and give him a big hug. "I'm sorry."

"Don't feel sorry," he replies, placing his hand on my back. He cringes. "Ahh."

I lean back and realize I've been pressing on his wounds. "Sorry, I forgot."

He cups my face and leans his forehead against mine. "I'm okay. Stop worrying about me."

"How did they take the news?" I ask.

He rubs his lips together. "Not good."

I gulp. "Did you tell them—"

"That he jumped off the ledge? Yeah. That he tried to kill my friends and me? No."

Some of the tension in my body immediately dissipates.

"I didn't want to make the pain any worse," he adds. "So I just told her ... we watched him jump." He adds a loud sigh. "Mom will be okay. It'll take her a while to get over him, but ... I know her. She can do it."

He caresses my face and smiles gently. "You make everything better."

"Hey," Alistair grumbles.

"And you too," Dylan says, and he extends a hand. "Come here."

Alistair joins in on the hug, and Dylan adds, "Thanks for being there for me."

He kisses Alistair first, and watching them makes my heart flutter. But then he turns to me and kisses me full on the lips too, and that just made my pussy flutter as well.

"Well, aren't you three getting cozy," a familiar voice calls out.

My lips unlatch to smile at Lana as she playfully slaps her brother on the arm. "Don't you need to join in on the action?" She winks at him. "You know, the more the merrier?"

"I don't do men," Felix retorts with a stoic face.

"You don't?" she jests, curling the red ribbon that's in her hair around her finger. "Aw ... but you'd make such a good boyfriend."

She presses her fingers to her lips and throws Felix a kiss right before she sidesteps to avoid his rage.

"Hope you trained your glutes," Felix growls at her.

"Oh boy," Dylan mutters.

"Why? What's he talking about?" I ask Dylan, who begins to grin wickedly when he looks at them.

Lana's eyes glimmer.

"Because when I fucking catch up with you," Felix starts, and Lana bolts off, "your ass is gonna be mine to whoop!"

They run off, and Alistair and Dylan laugh.

"That's gonna hurt," Alistair says.

"Him falling to the ground, yeah," Dylan replies. "She's much faster than him."

"Really?" I ask.

"Oh yeah," Dylan says. "They do this a lot, and he rarely wins. But it keeps him humble."

"Felix Rivera? Humble?" I snort.

"She matches his energy," Alistair says as we follow them back to the Skull & Serpent Society house.

Their chase ends at the steps she beats him to, and she throws him a wicked look before she heads inside.

"Bitch," Felix grumbles.

Alistair laughs behind his hand.

"You love her, though," Dylan says.

Felix glances at him over his shoulder, butt hurt he can't catch up with her in time. "Shut up."

I laugh. "You two are funny to watch."

Felix rolls his eyes and tucks his hands into his pocket, pretending not to care. "Whatever."

We head into the building, where some of the guys have already started fixing up the shattered windows with cardboard and tape.

"Nice job, guys," Dylan says, patting one of his friends on the back. "Let's get to work."

The cardboard isn't permanent, but it's a good temporary fix while we get ahold of a glazier. I'm glad my father's willing to help out. The place looks beaten up, with chips and pieces of the walls coming off and broken-down furniture scattered all around.

"Well, this is gonna be one hell of a cleanup," Dylan says, folding his arms.

"Yeah, good luck with that," Lana says as she marches up the stairs. "I'm gonna go find Jason."

"Lana," Felix warns, but all she does is stick a middle finger up at him.

And it makes me laugh. Good for her.

"I'm gonna go put Nessie in her spare cage. Be right back," Dylan says, and he retreats into the kitchen.

"Grab a broom," Alistair says to Felix. "Let's clean up the place."

"Fuck no," Felix says as he grabs my hand and drags me up the stairs. "We've got some unfinished business."

"What are you talking about?" Ali asks as he follows us upstairs.

"Hey!" Dylan calls from downstairs, carrying Nessie around. "Where are you going?"

But I can't even respond as I'm being dragged around.

Dylan quickly follows suit.

Felix heads into his bedroom and locks the door when everyone's inside. The floor is still covered in shards of glass, and he grabs a broom and stuffs it into Ali's hand. "Wanna sweep? Have at it."

Okay, I guess we're gonna do this right now.

Ali swiftly brushes most of the glass to a single corner while I grab some of the filling that's burst out of the expensive seat and stuff it back inside.

"What are you doing?" Felix asks me with a raspy voice.

"Helping," I reply.

"No," he says, the look in his eyes deadly. "Don't help. Don't do anything at all. Just sit."

What, why?

I frown but still sit down anyway. "Oh...kay."

Felix meticulously starts to clean up his room until most of the debris is gone, and Dylan finally starts to help him too, even though I can tell he's really not feeling it. When they're done, it's almost as if a giant weight rolls off Felix's shoulders.

He sighs out loud. "It's not enough."

"What isn't?" I ask.

"This. Labor. Work. Sweat." His nostrils flare. "I need more."

"You can clean up downstairs too if you want," I reply. "I can help."

"No. You've done more than enough." He clutches the broom in his hands so tightly I'm afraid it might snap. "But I ... I haven't done enough to fix the damage I caused."

"It wasn't your guys who did this. It was my father's men—"

The broom drops to the floor. "Shut up and fucking use me."

My eyes widen. "What?"

"You heard me." The look on his face is dead serious. "Use me like I used you."

I'm too stunned to even say a word, let alone breathe.

But goddamn ... is that proposition hard to refuse.

"Oh ... this sounds interesting," Alistair says as he gets up from the floor to throw the last bit of glass into the trash.

"Use you ... how?" I ask, tilting my head.

Felix's jaw tightens. "You know exactly how."

"Wow, I am here for this," Dylan murmurs as he sits down backward on a chair, pointing it in my direction like he's gonna watch a show and doesn't want to look away.

"Anything I want?" I ask, raising a brow.

"*Everything* you need," he replies.

The look in his eyes is lethal as though he could snap a neck at my beck and call, and it makes me feel powerful. The kind of power no one can take but is only given. And right now he's handing it to me on a silver platter.

"You think you could take that?" I ask as I close in on him.

His eyes sparkle with greed. "Give me your worst. Everything you've wanted to call me. All the pain you wanted to dish out. Give it to me."

I'm right in front of him, and I can't resist.

Slap!

An imprint of my hand is left on his cheek, glowing red.

I've wanted to do that for ages—ever since I learned the truth. And fuck, does it feel good to get it out of my system finally.

"Again ..." he says.

But instead of slapping him, I point at the cross they hung me from. "Stand there."

His brows draw together, but he still does what I say. I follow him and stand right in front of him, taunting him with a devious look. Then I grab his wrist, pin it to the cross just as he did with me, and I tie the leather strap around it, and then do the same to the other wrist, tying him in place.

Now he knows how it feels.

But I'm not there yet. Not even close.

I grab his face and lean in, rubbing my lips across his, but not close enough to actually kiss. "I want to see how much you can take."

"Oh fuck ..." Dylan groans. "This is gonna get me hard."

I pull away right as he leans in for a kiss, and I love to leave him hanging for more. I head to his cabinet and check out the drawers. It's filled with kinky toys that I don't even know the name of, but some of it sure looks interesting, and definitely something I'd love to use. But for now, this set of handcuffs will do.

"Hard you said?" I glance at Dylan over my shoulder. "Turn around in your chair, then."

With a filthy smirk on his face, he spins the chair around with ease and sits back down. "Too late. I'm already there." And he points at his dick protruding through the fabric of his pants.

But I ignore it and grab his hands, pinning them to the back of the chair until he yelps, "Ow. God, this could almost make me forget about being gunned down."

"Good." And I lock them in place, putting the key that's on a chain around my neck.

"Wow, is this some sort of revenge for what we did?" he asks as I step back and admire both of them hanging there, helplessly.

"Maybe," I say.

I admit it does feel good to have them in the same position they kept me. But this time, I'm the one in charge ... and boy, does it feel good.

"Ali, close the curtains," I say, even though there are holes in them, but at least it'll provide some sort of privacy for all the filthy stuff I have in mind.

He immediately springs into action and does what I ask. "Good boy."

He turns to throw me a surprised look and then side-glances at Dylan.

I know that's what Dylan called him.

But now it's my turn.

And I'm going to have a lot of fun torturing these boys.

I sit on the edge of the oversized couch that I filled up again and part my legs.

Felix's lips part, and a hampered breath leaves his mouth the second I start touching myself through the fabric of the pants I borrowed from him.

"You denied me over and over again, pushing me to the edge without relief," I say, playing with myself right in front of them. "So let me return the fucking favor."

I slide my hands up and down until the wetness begins to soak my pants.

There aren't enough mops in the world to swivel up the drooling faces in this room.

"Oh fuck ..." Dylan groans, squirming in his chair like he's already having trouble staying put.

"Enjoy what you can't have," I say, bringing my fingers to my lips so I can lick them, right before diving in.

Felix swallows, trying so hard to keep himself from grumbling, but his hard-on is already massive. I can see it poke out through his pants, begging to be released.

"Penelope ..." he rasps. "This is—"

"Cruel?" I interject.

Touching myself like this has never felt like heaven until I saw three boys clambering to get a taste.

"Hot," he says, his Adam's apple bobbing in his throat.

A smirk forms on my face. Well, I'm glad he finally admits it.

I look at Ali, who's been watching me from the windowsill, grasping at his bulge like he wants to stroke it.

"You," I tell him. "Crawl to me."

And within seconds, he's on his knees. Listening comes naturally to him.

So of course I'm going to reward him first.

"Fuck ..." Dylan rasps as he watches Ali kneel and crawl across the floor to me.

I stop Ali with my shoe, pushing him away right before he's at my feet. "Take off my pants."

He eagerly goes to work, sliding it off my thighs with care as though he doesn't want to damage the expensive goods. Like I'm priceless.

And that ... that's power.

Alistair tugs down my pants and throws them away, then pecks my calves like he wants to worship me.

And finally I hear Felix's first groan.

"Is this your way of punishing me?" he asks. "Letting my friends have what I can't?"

"Oh no ..." I mutter, pushing Ali down on the floor with my foot again so he's out of reach. "No one gets to touch this until I say so. And until then ... moan and beg."

"I would beg for this pussy every single day of my life," Ali mutters while kneeled in front of me, and he spreads his legs to touch himself.

"Show me then ... show me how badly you want it," I say, and I open my legs and start rubbing myself right in front of him.

"Fuck, you're getting me so hot," Dylan moans, biting his lip.

"You all called me your slut ..." I say, tilting my head as they writhe in their binds. "But now I've turned you all into mine."

74

DYLAN

Hours later

Good God. I don't think I've ever been hornier than I am now.

Is this what it felt like to her?

No wonder she wants us to suffer just as badly.

"Yes," Ali groans, rubbing himself through the fabric of his pants. "I'm your slut just like you are mine."

He's only ever begged like that to me. But I guess Pen holds us all in a vise grip. And I am more than willing to submit to anything she wants.

Penelope slides her fingers through her slit, and I can almost feel my own fingers touch her, feel her wetness, dive into that pussy like I wanna drown in it.

"God, you're torturing me," I mutter.

"Good," she responds with a wicked grin. "Don't even think of looking away."

She gyrates against her own hand, and her fingers dive into her pussy, sloshing wetness all around. She licks her lips, and my lips part in response, dying to get a kiss.

I'm breathing wildly at the sight of her plunging her fingers inside. My pants are tented, bursting at the seams with a cock so hard I could kill with it.

God, I could kill for this.

I really could.

***

ALISTAIR

"You want it?" she asks, gazing into my eyes.

I immediately nod.

"Beg."

Her stern voice gets me off. God, I've never been so turned on in my life.

"Please," I moan, my cock leaving a stain of pre-cum in my pants.

"Take out your cock."

I immediately zip down and pull out my throbbing length, coating it with the pre-cum.

"Show me how much," she says.

I start rubbing myself in front of her, still on my knees, and I can't fucking look away. She looks like a goddess, even in her oversized shirt she borrowed from Felix. To me she's never been anything other than something I desire. Something I crave so badly I would sacrifice my life for.

And maybe that makes me a bastard, but I don't give a fuck. For her, I'd happily fall to my knees.

My breathing becomes ragged as she begins to flick her clit, and I swallow away the lump in my throat. My hips instinctively thrust into my hand as I begin to whimper.

"Don't come," she murmurs. "Or I won't ever let you touch me."

"Fuck." I can barely hold it.

"You can do it. You want to please me, right?" she muses, dipping her fingers inside.

"Yes, please," I mutter.

She circles her sensitive bits faster and faster, alternating it with pussy thrusts, and the sight is mouthwatering.

"Fuck, I'm gonna come, and you're gonna watch," she says.

Within seconds, she moans so loudly the whole house might hear.

But none of us care.

All I can do is whimper as I watch her fall apart from her own fingers, wishing she was riding mine instead.

"Please," I murmur.

"You want it so badly?" she replies, leaning over to tip my chin up.

"Yes, please," I say.

Being like this comes naturally to me. It's what I've always loved, what Dylan has always done to me, but now that she does it ... Fuck, I might be addicted.

"Then come all over yourself like a good slut," she replies.

And it's all I need to start thrusting into my own hand like a maniac, hips popping as the cum jets out right onto my white shirt. It's so much, and it's everywhere; I'm completely soaked.

"F-Fuck ..." Dylan groans behind me.

"Having a hard time?" she muses as she gets up from the couch. "Then let me help you."

***

DYLAN

Penelope waltzes over to me, and I jerk my wrists in an effort to free them, but to no avail. Of course not. I know these fucking cuffs. I've used them a million times, yet I never once thought of the possibility that a purple-haired girl would someday use them on me.

And that I'd actually fucking love it.

She approaches the chair, and I shift in place, trying to keep my bulge from tearing a hole through my pants. When she leans over, exposing her tits right in my face, I literally lean in to try to bite them.

"Ah, ah," she muses, leaning back again. "That's only for good boys. And you all have been so fucking bad ..."

I groan in dismay, but then she grips my chair. "You want to be good for me, don't you?"

"Yes. God yes," I reply, gazing up at her.

"Then be a slut for me and eat this pussy." She sets her foot down on my lap, grips my face, and lowers it right against her mound.

My tongue immediately dips out, desperate for a taste. And fuck me, her clit is still throbbing with desire.

I moan as she pushes herself against me, burying her slit in my face.

"That's it. Use your tongue," she says, grasping the back of my head to shove me farther in.

I swivel my tongue back and forth as she starts rubbing herself against me.

I can barely breathe, and you know what? I actually wouldn't mind if I choked on this pussy because it's worth it.

"Fuck, yes, smother me," I murmur between licks.

"You're whimpering for me, aren't you?" she murmurs with a fistful of my white hair in her hands. "Make that sound again."

It's almost as if it comes naturally to me as I writhe on this chair, moaning against her.

"Your cock wants it so desperately, doesn't it?" she asks.

I nod against her slit. "I want it ... God, I want to bury my tongue inside you."

"Do it then. Make me come, and maybe I'll let you too," she says, driving me insane with lust.

I roll my tongue up and down her wetness, sucking on her clit like my life depends on it. When I stick out my tongue, she gyrates on top of it, getting herself off on my face.

"Fuck, I'm gonna come again," she moans.

"Penelope ..." Felix rasps, and even though I ignore him, she can't.

Her eyes home in on him as I flick her clit as fast as I can, and it's almost as if her pleasure is taken from me. Like this is her ultimate revenge ... refusing to even look at me as she uses my face, and I fucking hate to love it.

Her moans grow louder and louder, her eyes still fixated on his like she wants to punish him with orgasms we give her. Suddenly, she explodes all over my face, and I lick it up with glee. It's so fucking hot, too hot. And as I whimper, I explode inside my pants, filthying myself with my cum.

But I don't even care.

It's that hot.

She lifts herself off me, only to smile when she sees the stain visible on the outside. "Aw ... got a little too turned on, slut?" she muses, like she enjoys this.

I don't mind. Felix asked for this. And I'm just a happy participant, deserving as much punishment for my part.

"See? You could do it too," Ali says.

Pen's fingers briefly slide along my dick, which thumps in my pants, still pumping.

"A ruined orgasm," she murmurs. "Exactly what you deserve."

"Fuck, Penelope, I want it too," Felix groans, clearly struggling.

She turns to face him. "Do you now?" She struts toward him, staying just out of reach, despite the fact that he's almost ready to rip through the straps to get her. "And what are you willing to do?"

***

FELIX

I swallow away the lump in my throat as she kicks off her shoes in front of me and then takes off her shirt. Completely nude, puckered lips, prim ass, ready for the taking. Fuck, she knows how to get me riled up.

"I won't beg like those two miserable assholes." My cock is already fully erect, and I know I'm fucking lying, but fuck ... I've never had anything like this done to me before.

Do I deserve it? Yes.

Do I hate it? I should.

But the closer she gets, the more my cock throbs, and the truth becomes too fucking hard to deny.

She has me on a leash.

Her brow playfully rises. "Won't you?" Her fingers dive into my pants, and she slides in so deep I can feel her fingers at the tip of my length. I suck in a breath. "Because I'd love nothing more than to hear it."

When she rubs me, I groan, unable to keep the sounds at bay.

I've been brimming with desire the second she started touching herself, and it's been so fucking hard to watch and not be able to touch and lick and suck and fuck her soul out of her body.

She pulls out her hand, and my shaft still throbs.

"But let's see how long you keep that up," she murmurs, and she zips me down, then lowers my pants and boxer shorts until my dick bursts out, bobbing up and down, jewelry covered in pre-cum.

She touches the tip with her finger, spreading it around like it's lube, before she gently starts to tug at me. And fuck me, I can feel it in my entire body. Raging arousal.

She jerks me off to the point where my breath picks up and sweat drops roll down my forehead ... and then she stops.

My length bobs up and down again, desperate to jet its seed, but I can't fucking do it. I'm all tied up and can't even reach, let alone will it to come.

Fuck.

Is this what she wants? To keep me on edge like I forced her to be when I tied her to this cross?

A smile forms on my lips, and I lower my head.

"Why are you smiling?"

"You're cruel," I reply, looking up into her eyes from underneath my lashes. "Just like me."

"Hmm." A smile forms on her lips, and she begins to touch me again, all the way from the beginning, slow and torturous. "And don't you fucking love it?"

God, I can barely take it. Her fingers coil around my shaft, dipping low, before coming back up to my jewelry again, and fuck me, I could almost shoot my load right here right now.

She suddenly pulls away again, leaving me in agony.

"Fuck..." I grit.

"She's enjoying this," Dylan muses from his seat.

"No shit," I retort.

"I am too," Alistair says, still on his knees near the couch.

Penelope laughs. "A punishment fit for the crime of toying with my body because someone else told you to."

A lopsided grin forms on my face. "Oh, I'd toy with you regardless of what anyone said."

"I guess that's not up to you to decide now, is it?" she says, rubbing my dick again until my entire body tenses and all my muscles begin to twitch.

Fuck. I didn't think anything could make me snap.

But this ... this kind of torture definitely could.

She leans away, leaving my cock bobbing up and down as she lies down on the bed and parts her legs, showing off her wet slit, and fuck me, I've never wanted anything more in my life.

My wrists jerk against the straps, but no matter what I do, they won't loosen.

"You know that won't work," she says. "I tried, believe me." She keeps circling her clit, like she's trying to taunt me. "You keep watching. Eyes open."

She tilts her head back, hair rolling over her back, body arched as she starts rubbing faster and faster. And I'm sweating from every pore in my body, struggling to fucking breathe. My fucking dick pulses with greed.

Her moans grow louder and louder, moans I wish I was giving her, but instead, I'm tied up here, forced to endure with a throbbing shaft.

"Fuck," I groan.

She circles around and dips inside, moaning so hard the entire house can hear, and I just know she fucking came. The sound and view flips a switch inside my head.

A stifled moan leaves my throat as I jet some cum right on top of the bed.

Fuck.

I actually came without so much as a touch.

But it's a ruined orgasm, and I'm not nearly satisfied.

"Oh ... you liked that, huh?" she murmurs as she crawls across the bed and lies down, spread-eagle. "Come and get it, then."

I jerk the straps, but they won't release. "Untie me."

"Untie yourself," she says.

"What?" Dylan gasps. "We can't do that."

"Then try harder," she muses.

When Ali gets up, she raises a finger. "Don't help. Sit on the bed and wait for them while you stroke yourself mad."

He does what she says, kneeling on the bed, still thrusting into his own hand like a maniac. And fuck me, I want to rail her face-down into the pillow until she chokes on her own saliva.

My muscles harden, and I jerk the straps again. I can hear them crack, but not far enough.

However, I do know one thing ... when I'm out of these chains, I'm going to fuck her brains out. And we'll both fucking love it.

75

PENELOPE

"Go on then ..." I muse, looking at Dylan. "Show me how badly you want it."

Dylan's scooting his chair closer and closer. "I can't."

"Yes, you can."

He needs to learn what I had to learn.

Satisfaction comes at the hefty price of insanity.

"How?"

I tilt my head, narrowing my eyes. "You know how."

He swallows. "Please ..."

"Please what?"

"Please untie me," he begs.

God, I love hearing him grovel.

"Why?" I ask, my hand slipping between my legs again. "Give me a good reason."

"I want you," he says like a hussy drunk on lust.

"More," I say.

"I want to kiss you, lick you, fuck you, drive you mad," he says. "Please."

That's it. That's what I'm looking for.

I slide off the bed, slowly approaching him. He gulps, saliva rolling down his mouth as he looks up at me. And I zip him open, pulling out his already hard cock.

"You want it?"

He nods vehemently. "God, yes, please."

I straddle him and lower myself onto his length.

"Penelope," Felix growls, "don't you go fucking them without me."

"I'll do whatever I want," I murmur, glancing at him over my shoulder. "Who's going to stop me?"

The rage on his face is magnificent as I begin to gyrate on Dylan's lap. His eyes almost roll into the back of his head as I go to town, lifting myself before dropping down again, getting him all worked up.

"Oh fuck, yes." His wrists jerk against the cuffs, hip muscles pushing up to meet my body with frenzied desire.

This is the kind of love I want. Uninhibited debauchery. No more lies. No more denial. All the fucking submission they could ever wish for.

I roll around on his lap, enjoying myself thoroughly, head thrown back, moaning like a kinky fucker. And Dylan leans in, his tongue dipping out to catch even the slightest bit of nipple as my breasts bounce up and down against him.

"You gonna come deep inside me?" I say. "Fill me up?"

"No," Felix growls. "That pussy belongs to me."

But Dylan doesn't even hear him as he whimpers, "Yes, God yes, I'm gonna come so hard."

"Then give it to me," I whisper into his ear, smothering his face with my breasts.

A muffled groan leaves his lips, and I can feel his length pulse inside me.

"Penelope ..." Felix grunts as I slowly move off Dylan's lap.

I approach him as the cum drips out onto the floor. "What do you want, Felix?"

"You," he says through gritted teeth after a while.

My brow rises. "How much?"

"More than anything ..." he says between ragged breaths.

I place my hands on his cheeks, leaning in to whisper against his mouth, "You know what I want to hear."

After a few seconds filled with more groans, he finally grits, "Please."

A smile forms on my lips as my hand moves up to his strap, releasing one hand. "Just one. Because I want to hear you say that word again."

But the moment the strap comes undone, his hand snaps around my throat, squeezing tight. I suck in the air, but it won't go past his tightening fingers latching around the base of my neck.

"What did you want to hear?" he grits. Leaning in, he whispers in my ear, "Penelope ... please?"

I whimper from the sound of his low voice humming in my ear.

"You want me to be your fucking slut?" he asks, and I can feel him smile against the rim of my ear.

RIP!

The other strap came loose just from his incredible muscle strength.

"Wrong. Now you become *mine*."

He forcefully shoves me onto the bed, his hand still locked around my throat as he spreads my legs wide and plows in without asking, without begging, without even so much as a single word.

And fuck me, is it everything I wished for.

With his hand clasped around my throat, he thrusts in wildly, pouring all his anger into me.

"You drive me fucking wild," he says, his hoarse voice filled with desire. "Now take my cock like a fucking good slut."

I can barely breathe, and I don't even care.

Felix buries himself to the hilt, and I groan, stunned.

RIP!

With ease, he tears the chain off my neck and throws the key to Ali. "Free him."

"What?" Ali mutters. "But she said—"

"I don't care. That game's over now. It's about time we had our fucking way." His grip on my neck loosens a little to allow me a breath. "Because that's what you wanted all along, didn't you? Fuck me up until I break." His fingers slide down my skin like he's savoring all of it before he devours me. "Well, don't worry, Pen, I know how to give it to you."

He pulls out only to thrust in full force, and my eyes roll to the back of my head. Even though I had so much fun giving them what they deserve, this is so much better as the icing on the cake.

"Fucking finally," Dylan groans as he jumps onto the bed and immediately grips my nipple, twisting and pinching it until I squeal. "I never realized how addicted I am to touching you, Pen."

Ali crawls on too, watching us while he's still stroking himself.

But Felix doesn't relent, thrusting back in to the hilt. "You like to be owned."

"Fuck," I mutter when he touches my G-spot.

He lowers himself on top of me, grinding away. "Because you were always fucking mine, weren't you? Even without that fucking deal we had."

I nod, unable to even form the words.

"I don't do temporary, Pen. Once you belong to me, you're mine forever. Understand?"

I nod, not giving a shit whether I have to sacrifice my soul to the devil to be fucked by him because I'd gladly sign away my life right here, right now.

He grips my hands and pins them above my head.

"Say it. Say the words," he says, pounding into me.

"I'm yours," I say. "Forever."

He leans in and licks my skin from my ear all the way down to my neck, and he whispers, "Good girl. Now tell me what you want."

"I want you to fuck me," I say.

He slaps my vulva and says, "No. Tell me what you really want. Not your fucking pussy. Your head."

"I want this to last forever," I murmur. "I want the world to know. And I don't ever want to share." I look at Ali and Dylan. "None of you. I want to be the only one."

A smirk forms on his lips. "You want us all to yourself?" He brushes his fingers along my slit, circling my sensitive bits. "All three of us, together? Greedy whore."

"Yes," I moan when he slowly pushes in again.

"Then you'll be fucking ours, and we'll be fucking yours," he groans, pounding into me again so hard my whole body shakes. "Until your last"—*thrust*—"dying"—*thrust*—"breath."

"Yes," I moan, delirious with desire.

And he bends over and whispers, "If that's what you really want, then I'll make that fucking wish a reality." And he laces his fingers through mine. "Because I fucking love every inch of your fucked-up soul."

My eyes burst open but before I can respond, he thrusts in so deep my toes curl, and he covers my lips with his. The kiss is intoxicating, out of this world mind-blowing.

My body explodes from the orgasm rolling through me, taking my soul into the nether.

He spins me around on the bed and immediately buries himself into my ass, making it impossible for me to even react to what he just said.

Ali suddenly perches himself near my mouth. "Open wide, Pen."

And he pushes in his big cock, the girth barely fitting down my throat.

Felix pounds into me from behind, shoving me farther and farther onto Ali's cock, and it makes my eyes water. But every tear that rolls down my cheek makes me that much needier.

I truly have become their whore, and I wouldn't have it any other way.

"Fuck yes, ride that dick," Felix groans, and he slaps my ass. I can feel every piece of jewelry, every inch of him as he fills me up.

Dylan's jerking himself off, fondling my breasts as they bounce around, and the more I choke on Ali's length, the harder Dylan tugs at my nipples.

"That's it, Pen, take him deep. Show me what you've got," Dylan rasps.

Ali's hand rests underneath my chin, gently tipping me up as I find it hard to swallow him.

"You're so good for me," he murmurs. "But I'll always want more. Think you can handle it?"

I nod, taking him even deeper, despite the gag. "Good girl."

That's what I do it for.

The praise after complete degradation.

Dylan's whole body tenses up against me. "Oh God, I can't hold it."

And he covers me with even more jizz, coating my back. The sight sets Ali off.

"Fuck, I'm gonna come again." Ali buries himself to the hilt in my mouth until my nose is buried in his cum-covered shirt. "Take it deep. Swallow all of it."

His length throbs inside me as he gives me everything he's got, and it's so much that I struggle to take it all down.

Felix thrusts so hard into me I can barely even think straight.

"Fuck, I'm gonna fill up this ass," Felix groans, plowing away so fast he forces me to keep Ali in my mouth. "You wanted to drive me mad? You got it. I'll fucking destroy this ass."

He's so harsh on me that it makes my eyes sting, but I fucking love it. I never realized how much of a sucker I was for being used like this until I met these guys.

These sick boys who've captured my heart and refuse to let it go.

One. Two. Three. He roars out loud and finishes inside me.

Ali finally pulls out, and I cough wildly, licking up the remains off my lips. But as Felix releases me from his grip, my knees collapse onto the bed under my own weight.

Panting heavily, Felix grabs my body and curls up against me, spooning me from the back, while my head rests on Dylan's lap. Ali lies down beside him, curling his arm across us both.

A perfect quartet of madness.

"God ... that was amazing," Dylan rasps.

Ali laughs. "It was, though."

"I know we're supposed to clean up, but fuck, I needed that first," Dylan adds.

"I still haven't forgiven you guys, though," I mutter between ragged breaths.

"I know," Felix mutters into the nape of my neck. "But we'll have a lifetime to make up for it."

"Hmm ... only if I'm the only girl."

His eyes narrow. "Who else would there be?"

"Well, you were dancing with one at your father's club."

His mouth quirks up into a lopsided smile. "You're jealous."

I playfully slap him in the stomach. "You were trying to make me jealous."

"Maybe," Dylan jests.

"No," Felix interjects.

"Felix was trying to pretend he didn't have any feelings for you," Ali says.

I frown. "Wait ... I thought that was—"

"A lie?" Ali raises his brow, and he gazes at Felix. If looks could kill, Ali would be dead by now.

"Don't be a wuss and deny it," Dylan says.

"Who are you calling a wuss?" Felix barks, and he leans up on his elbow, ready to start a fight.

"Did you boys fight like this over Eve too?" I ask them.

"What?" Dylan frowns.

"No," Felix replies, and he waits until I spin around and face him before he continues. He slides aside my hair. "You mean far more to me than Eve ever did."

I smirk, and Dylan snorts and looks down at me. "What are you smiling at?"

"So you meant what you said?"

"Who?" Dylan points at Felix and then himself. "Him or me?"

"Both of you."

"Well, I ..." Dylan mutters, and I gaze up at him.

"Are you blushing?" I ask.

He rolls his eyes and laughs it off, then slaps himself. "No, of course not."

"Just tell her you love her," Felix grumbles. "Stop fucking lying to yourself and admit it."

Why am I suddenly all warm and fuzzy inside?

Fuck. I'm not normally like this at all, but with them ...

I'm protected. Needed. Desired.

"I love you too," I say with a soft voice. "All of you."

Even if I hated them for what they did to me, I still couldn't deny that I needed them.

Ali looks at me with an admiring gaze. "Even when you got under my skin, I've never not loved you."

I smile at him, and he leans in to give me a sweet kiss on the lips.

"But love's a funny thing for guys like us," he adds. "It's more like—"

"Obsession," Felix fills in.

"I know," I reply, content.

Dylan caresses my hair. "If you wanna know the answer to your question, it's yes."

He leans in and grabs my chin to press a possessive but tender kiss on my lips. "And I'm glad you love me too."

"And me," Felix growls, making me laugh, but the laugh is immediately interrupted by a crazy-obsessive kiss.

Always the jealous one, even when he has nothing to be jealous of, because the fighting is over.

I am theirs, and they are mine.

Epilogue

֍

PENELOPE

Days later

I brush up the last bit of dirt from the floor and throw it into the trash.

"There. All done. Looks much better now," I muse as I gaze around the university hallway. So many things still need to be done, but the painters have done a fabulous job of fixing the walls at least. The floors and the staircase are still being renovated, but it all looks so much better than it did before, after the inferno that took place.

I must say, being the one to burn it down and then having to clean all my shit up has been cathartic to say the least. And it's nice to see the boys doing something that isn't completely destructive. Watching them toil around with a shovel and a paintbrush is actually rather ... sexy.

"What are you looking at, Pen?" Dylan muses, rolling the paintbrush around the walls where the painters haven't been yet.

"Enjoying the view?" Ali adds as he throws a piece of broken furniture in the trash. "I know I am."

"Pervs," Felix says as he gets up from cleaning the floor by hand.

"Damn right I am," I retort. "And proud of it."

I mean, I don't care if they caught me lurking.

They know I like watching them.

Ali high-fives me, and Dylan pulls up his white button-down, then slides the brush across his abs, avoiding the bullet wound. "Yeah, you like this?"

"FML." Felix sighs out loud and grabs his cigarettes. But the second he tries to light one, his father suddenly comes up behind him and snatches it from his hands.

"No smoking inside."

Felix grumbles, "You're all going to be the end of me."

"I'm sure you'll be glad to hear you're done for today," his father replies.

"What? All of us?" Dylan asks, pausing with his brush midair.

When his father nods, Ali immediately drops the broom he was holding. "Sweet."

"But I expect you all back tomorrow morning, same time sharp," he says.

"Aw ..." Dylan groans.

"We're almost finished," I muse.

"Only got the whole of the Skull & Serpent house left."

"We've got Penelope's father to help there," Ali says. "I'm sure he doesn't need a bunch of lazy students to clean that shit."

Dylan folds his arms. "Besides, we weren't the ones who destroyed that place."

"Technically, you were, since all of this fuckery points back to the four of you," his father says, and he places a hand on Ali's and Dylan's shoulders. "So be glad cleaning in your vacation week is the only thing I'm asking you to do."

He pats them on the back. "Now get out of here and enjoy the rest of your day."

***

In the cafeteria, Kayla, Crystal, Jeremy, and Calvin are already waiting on us at a table.

Felix grumbles with a tray that carries only a single cup of coffee. "Do we have to?"

Dylan shoves his elbow into his waist. "Be nice."

"I am being fucking nice," he seethes back.

"We can do this for her," Ali says, taking a bite from his apple. "Besides, her friends aren't bad."

"Hey, girl," Jeremy says as we approach, patting the seat next to him. "Plenty of room here."

"Got space for these boys too?" I ask.

Kayla makes a face and takes a big breath, but Crystal's soft nudge gets her over her reservations quickly. "Yeah, yeah." She scoots up to allow for more room. "There are more chairs over there." She points at another table. "No one's sitting there so you can grab 'em."

"Sorry we're late," I say as I sit down.

"Still helping with the big clean, eh?" Calvin asks. "Trying to score extra points?"

I smile. "Sort of."

Dylan whispers into my ear, "They don't know?"

I shake my head. "Better keep it that way."

"Better keep what?" Kayla asks.

"Oh, nothing," Dylan replies. "Just some sex talk."

Her eyes widen, and she makes a weird face.

God, why does he always embarrass me?

"So y'all are still together?" Kayla asks.

A blush forms on my cheeks, but Ali swings his arm around me, pulling me close. "Yup."

"Wait ... as in all three of you?" Calvin asks. "Wow, way to go, Pen. Triple dicking."

Now I'm blushing even harder.

"How's the Alpha Psi doing?" I ask to change the subject.

"Oh, the girls are fine," Kayla replies, smiling. "The renovation of your sister's room is well on its way. It wasn't cheap, but it had to be done."

"That's good to hear," I say.

"But I just wanna know ... is it all over now?" Crystal asks.

"What is?" Felix says.

"The one who threatened her, who set that fire in the Alpha Psi house, and maybe even the school ... Did they catch him?"

Ali, Dylan, and Felix all look at each other, and then at me, like they're waiting for me to tell my friends the truth. But I'm not sure I'll ever tell the full story of what happened. Of Dylan's father, the shootout, my sister, all of it.

"Yes, they're gone," I say, swallowing. "For good."

Dylan breathes a sigh of relief.

"But you know who did it, then?" Jeremy asks.

Felix frowns. "Is it important?"

"Well ..." Jeremy shifts in his seat, intimidated by Felix's taunting gaze. "I don't know, I just figured after all the damage he did."

"It's done. Over. It won't happen again," Felix says, and he takes a gulp of his coffee.

Crystal sighs and nods. "I'm glad. I don't need to know who it was. I just want to know that it's over. It's about time this school became boring again."

Everyone laughs, and the tension breaks.

Felix's phone buzzes, and he picks it up. "Pen ... Time."

"Time?" I mutter. I didn't think it'd slip by this fast.

"Our appointment," he adds.

"Right," I say as I get up.

"Oh, got somewhere important to be already?" Calvin asks.

"Hope it isn't one of those sex-talk things you mentioned," Jeremy muses.

Kayla grumbles, "Cringe. I don't want to hear it."

I laugh. "No, we're going to RINGO's."

"Wait ... that tattoo parlor down in Crescent Vale City?" Kayla asks.

"You're getting a tattoo?" Crystal mutters, like she couldn't fathom me getting one.

"Yeah, I already got one long ago with my sis," I reply.

"Awesome! Can I see it?" Crystal pleads, putting up some big, cute eyes.

"Ah, I—"

"We're out of time, ladies," Dylan muses as he gets up and tugs me along with him. "Let's go, Pen."

"We've got somewhere to be," Ali adds. "See ya all later."

"I'll show my tats to you next time," I tell everyone, and I add a wink.

***

My skin stings, but it's nothing I can't handle. I've gotten a tattoo before. I just forgot what it felt like.

"All done," the tattoo artist says as he slides away in his chair to grab a mirror.

I lift my shirt a little farther up, revealing my under boob, and I check out my tattoo right underneath. An elongated set of words strewn across my chest in beautiful calligraphy.

Felix. Dylan. Alistair.

A smirk forms on my lips as I turn to them. "What do you think?"

"Perfect," Dylan replies.

Alistair nods too. "I like it."

I turn to Felix, who just studies it, and his tongue slowly runs across his teeth. "Exactly how it should be."

"Well, I'm glad you're happy," the tattoo artist says as he moves to the cash register. "Cash or credit?"

Felix slaps down his credit card. "Credit."

My alarm clock goes off, and I check the time. "Shit, we're late." I grab Dylan's and Ali's hands and race out the door.

"Hey, wait on me," Felix says, and he follows suit.

"C'mon, it's just down the road," I say, and I drag them all the way to Fi's Cups And Cakes.

"It's only been a minute. Relax," Dylan says.

We cross the street, and I check my phone several times to hurry us up. "Here it is."

The second we all step inside, my mother's eyes homing in on us almost make me drop my bag.

It's the first time she's seeing me with the boys.

The same boys who hung out with my sister.

The same boys who carry some of the blame.

I wave awkwardly and approach the table she's sitting at with a steaming cup of tea in her hands. There are just enough chairs for us all, and when I sit down, she picks up her tea.

"Hi," I say.

She takes a sip before responding.

"Pen," she says. "I'm glad you're okay." She eyes the boys next to me with mistrust. "But them ..."

The air is uncomfortable.

The server comes and takes the boys' orders, but when they say nothing, I fill in for them, "Four coffees, please. Black."

The server leaves again, but the whole café still feels too small for all of us sitting at this table.

"Mom," I mutter.

"Is he dead?"

I nod, and she sucks in a hampered breath.

"I'm sorry," I say, and I reach for her hand.

"I almost lost a second daughter," she mutters, tears welling up in her eyes. "My only one left."

I can't let her cry like that. I jump up from my seat and circle around the table, and I hug her tight. We cry and smile and hug so tightly I never want to let go.

"After your father told me what happened, I thought I almost lost you," she murmurs.

"I'm not going anywhere. Not anytime soon. I love you, Mom." I pull back and look her in the eyes, crying too. "I avenged her."

She smiles through her tears. "I'm proud of you." When I pull away, her eyes are already fixated on the guys. "What about them?"

I sit back down on my seat again.

"Why are they with you now?" she asks.

"They helped me kill the man responsible," I explain.

Felix and Ali nod. Dylan swallows. "He was my father."

Her face contorts. "Then you know that rot grows deep."

I grasp Dylan's hand, settling him. I know it's hard for him. He lost a father that night, no matter how evil.

"I know what my father did was unforgivable. But I am not my father," Dylan says. "And I will spend every day of the rest of my life proving that to your daughter." He leans in. "And I promise to you, I will take good care of her."

Her lips grow thinner. "I know what you did with Eve ..."

"I loved her," Dylan says, and I squeeze his hand. "Just like I love Penelope."

"And the others?" she asks.

Felix grabs my thigh.

"She's ours as much as we are hers," Felix says.

"Yes," Alistair adds. "We'd take a bullet for her."

"And you think you can claim my daughter after being responsible for the death of the other?" she seethes.

"Mom," I mutter. "I love them."

She stares at me for a moment with her jaw dropped. And I don't think I've ever seen her this amazed.

"You ... *love* them?"

"Yes," I say.

The server returns with our cups of coffee, but the silence is brutal and feels like it lasts an eternity until she finally leaves again.

"So you love those boys..." my mother murmurs.

"And I don't intend to stop," I say. "Ever."

Ali's and Felix's grips on my arm strengthen.

My mother sighs, defeat showing on her face. "I just pray you made the right decision."

"I'll protect her with my life," Ali says.

"And I'll kill anyone who dares to hurt her," Felix adds.

"Even yourself?" my mother retorts.

A soft smile spreads on my lips. "I'll kill them myself if it ever comes to that."

Dylan looks at me, sporting a smirk.

I know he likes it when I get violent.

My mother snorts. "Well, sounds like you've found yourself some boys that fit you."

"What can I say?" I muse. "Like mother, like daughter."

She smiles, and it brings warmth to my heart. "I guess I may have told you a bit too much about my life and how I met your dad."

"Nope. It gave me all the inspiration I needed," I retort, and I wink.

"She's a real firecracker, this one," Dylan says, licking his lips. "And I wouldn't have it any other way."

"As long as you protect her," Mom says.

"Until we die," Ali replies.

"How do I know for sure?" she asks.

All the boys raise their shirts in unison, showing off their new tattoos across their torsos.

My name.

She gasps.

"She belongs to us," Felix says, lowering his shirt. He grabs my face and makes me look at him, the affection in his dark eyes impossible to ignore. "And we belong to her."

Thank you for reading!

Thank you so much for reading Sick Boys. Please leave a review if you enjoyed!

You can stay up to date of new books via my website: www.clarissawild.com

I'd love to talk to you! You can find me on Instagram: https://www.instagram.com/clarissa.wild, make sure to follow me!

You can also join the Fan Club: www.facebook.com/groups/FanClubClarissaWild and talk with other readers.

Enjoyed this book? You could really help out by leaving a review on Amazon and Goodreads. Thank you!

ALSO BY CLARISSA WILD

Dark Romance
Beast & Beauty Duet
Debts & Vengeance Series
Dellucci Mafia Duet
The Debt Duet
Savage Men Series
Delirious Series
Indecent Games Series
The Company Series
FATHER
New Adult Romance
Fierce Series
Blissful Series
Ruin
Rowdy Boy & Cruel Boy
Erotic Romance
The Billionaire's Bet Series
Enflamed Series
Unprofessional Bad Boys Series
Visit Clarissa Wild's website for current titles.
www.clarissawild.com

ABOUT THE AUTHOR

Clarissa Wild is a New York Times & USA Today Bestselling author of Dark Romance and Contemporary Romance novels. She is an avid reader and writer of swoony stories about dangerous men and feisty women. Her other loves include her hilarious husband, her cutie pie son, her two crazy but cute dogs, and her adorable kitties. In her free time, she enjoys watching all sorts of movies, playing video games, reading tons of books, and cooking her favorite meals.

Want to be informed of new releases and special offers? Sign up for Clarissa Wild's newsletter on her website www.clarissawild.com.

Visit Clarissa Wild on Amazon for current titles.